A Heart Worth Stealing

A Heart Worth Stealing

PROPER ROMANCE

JOANNA BARKER

SHADOW
MOUNTAIN
PUBLISHING

Library of Congress Cataloging-in-Publication Data

Names: Barker, Joanna, author.
Title: A heart worth stealing / Joanna Barker.
Other titles: Proper romance.
Description: Salt Lake City: Shadow Mountain, [2023] | Series: Proper romance | Summary: "When Miss Genevieve Wilde hires the thief-taker Jack Travers to find her late father's stolen pocket watch—and possibly unravel the mysterious circumstances of his death—she doesn't expect to also have her heart stolen by the flirtatious rogue"— Provided by publisher.
Identifiers: LCCN 2022047899 | ISBN 9781639931040 (trade paperback)
Subjects: BISAC: FICTION / Romance / Historical / Regency | FICTION / Romance / Clean & Wholesome | LCGFT: Historical fiction. | Romance fiction.
Classification: LCC PS3603. O54728 H43 2023 | DDC 813/.6—dc23/eng/20221107
LC record available at https://lccn.loc.gov/2022047899

Printed in the United States of America
Lake Book Manufacturing, Inc., Melrose Park, IL

10 9 8 7 6 5 4 3 2 1

For Audrey,
Always be you, my fierce girl. I love you forever.

CHAPTER 1

My study had been overrun by men.

I sat on the high-back chair near the fireplace, hands gripping the scrolled armrests. Normally this room was a place of quiet refuge, with its dark paneled walls, wide and inviting windows, and high ceiling. Now, however, my study contained not only myself but three men—which was three too many.

Mr. Northcott examined the desk, moving aside an inkwell with care. His pale blue eyes squinted, long features arranged in careful concentration. The magistrate was hardly an expert on investigating home thefts, better suited as he was to judicial hearings, but he was the first—and only   person I'd thought to call upon. He'd arrived at Wimborne within an hour of my sending him a plea for help. Now he picked up a red leather-bound book and flipped through the pages.

"What is this?" he asked.

I shot to my feet. "You needn't worry about that," I said, hurrying to my desk and taking the book from his hands.

"My apologies." His eyes lingered on my journal. I could only imagine his face if he read what I'd written about him inside.

A cough drew my gaze to Mr. Crouth, a parish constable. He halfheartedly inspected the area around the window, his rounded, red face and rough spun clothes reflecting in the surface. I'd never liked him when he worked with Father, and I liked him even less now as he rubbed a dirty boot on my rug.

Marchant, my butler, stood inside the open door and watched Mr. Crouth with a narrowed gaze, as if he thought the constable might break something. Marchant was no stranger to my study, of course. He'd served at Wimborne for more than a decade. But he had the tendency to hover over me, as if to ensure I was doing things properly, and that always made his presence feel a bit . . . much.

He would never have hovered over Father.

I took a steadying breath and turned back to Mr. Northcott.

"No matter," I said, tucking my journal against my chest. "Have you discovered anything suspicious?"

"No, unfortunately not." Mr. Northcott frowned and settled his walking stick beneath both hands. He always had it with him, though he hardly needed it. He was a perfectly healthy man of three and thirty years, with a full head of pomaded sandy hair that was never out of place. But I daresay he liked the feel of the cane, the authority of it. He'd adopted the affectation when he'd become the magistrate six months ago. Six long months ago.

"You are sure this is where you left the watch?" he asked, gesturing at my desk.

"Yes," I said. "I always have it beside me as I attend to business."

"And now it is gone." Skepticism did a horrible job of hiding in his eyes.

"Yes." I struggled to keep my voice even. "I arrived this morning to begin work for the day and noticed the watch missing. Marchant recommended we search the servants' quarters and question the staff, but we found nothing." I'd done this most reluctantly—my servants had never given me a reason to mistrust them. But I had to search out every avenue.

He offered a smile, which was meant to be kind but instead made me feel like a child. "Miss Wilde, is it possible you simply misplaced it?"

My back was already ramrod straight—*lazy posture is a sign of weak character, Genevieve*, my half sister Catherine often insisted—but I squared my shoulders as I fixed Mr. Northcott with a determined gaze.

"No," I insisted. "It is not possible. I distinctly remember placing the watch beside that ledger before I went to dress for dinner." I'd hosted a small dinner party last night, my first since ending my mourning for Father. Beatrice had attended, of course, with her parents, as well as the vicar and his wife. Mr. Northcott had come too. Though he was a decade older than my twenty-three years, he'd been Father's friend—and mine, I'd thought. Our interactions *had* been strained in recent weeks, but surely he wouldn't let our personal relationship interfere with what was clearly a criminal matter. Would he?

"I did not reenter the room until this morning," I went on, "which means it must have been stolen during the night."

Mr. Northcott lowered his voice. "Are you suggesting someone from the dinner party might have taken it?"

"Of course not." As if Beatrice or the vicar was a thief. "I simply wished to give you a span of time during which the theft was committed. I imagine the thief entered through the window."

"The window," Mr. Northcott repeated doubtfully. Mr. Crouth gave a snort, a sad effort at suppressing laughter. My jaw tightened.

"Yes," I said. "The window was open when I arrived this morning. A catch must have been left undone by mistake, allowing the thief inside."

Mr. Northcott eyed the gold candlesticks near the door. "And he took *only* the watch?"

Heat bloomed on my cheeks—a horrible combination of embarrassment and frustration. It did sound absurd when I said it aloud. What thief took a simple pocket watch but left so many valuables untouched? Yet I knew for a fact I had not misplaced Father's watch. The logical conclusion was that someone had taken it.

Mr. Northcott's narrow jaw softened as he regarded me. "Can you think of any reason why someone would steal the watch and nothing else?"

My thoughts flashed to the past few weeks—the missing sheep, the flooded irrigation channels. But those were just unfortunate events. They had nothing to do with Father's watch, and if I told Mr.

Northcott about my recent string of bad luck, it would cement in his mind that I was unable to run Wimborne, that I was incapable of protecting my house and land. He would pity me.

He would probably propose again.

"No," I said. "I cannot." And that was the crux of the matter. *Why* would someone take Father's watch? It wasn't elegant or valuable—at least, to anyone else. To me, its worth was incalculable. Just touching its smooth brass casing brought me a steadying peace, and since discovering it missing this morning, I'd felt uneven. Incomplete. Like I was missing one shoe or I'd forgotten my name—but only if either of those also made me feel like my chest had been torn into ribbons, reviving and inflaming my grief yet again.

A memory tugged at the edge of my mind—Father pressing his watch into my hands, his face pale, fingers trembling, eyes painted in a strange desperation.

I looked down, blinking to clear my vision. "Please, Mr. Northcott," I said, my voice fragile. "I need to find it."

He sighed, leaning forward onto his walking stick. "Of course. Of course I shall help. If there wasn't this business with the highwaymen, I would make it my sole occupation."

I bit my lip. Highwaymen had plagued the roads around Little Sowerby for years, but they'd grown bolder in recent months, their robberies becoming more frequent—and more violent. My missing watch paled in comparison.

"But I shall have my constables make inquiries," Mr. Northcott went on. "I will do what I can. I promise."

I'd thought his help would reassure me, but the heaviness in my heart did not abate. When Father had been magistrate, he had often grumbled about the relative uselessness of his constables. These men were private citizens serving as part of their civic duty, or often paid replacements for men who could afford such a thing. Their responsibilities lay in keeping the streets clear of vagrants and controlling crowds, not in investigation and detection.

"Perhaps we will be lucky and your watch will turn up," Mr. Northcott said.

Turn up. As if my family heirloom had simply gone for a walk and lost track of the time.

I moved to the door. "Thank you for sparing me a few minutes, Mr. Northcott. I know you are much occupied."

He raised an eyebrow at my sudden dismissal. "Perhaps you might consider taking an advertisement in the paper," he suggested. "Offer a reward for the watch."

He was trying to make peace between us, but I didn't feel particularly peaceful.

"Perhaps," I said, clasping my hands. "Good day, sir."

"Good day, Miss Wilde." Mr. Northcott offered a bow. Mr. Crouth abandoned his pretense of an investigation and made for the door, giving me the slightest tip of his balding head. I tried not to frown at the odious man and only just succeeded.

Marchant saw the men out, giving me a sympathetic look as he closed the door behind him. I sighed and went to my desk. Mr. Northcott had left everything askew, and it would irk me if I did not set it right. I laid down my journal, straightened a stack of letters, and adjusted my inkwell. My fingers rested on the empty spot where Father's watch ought to be, the polished wood of my desk gleaming in the morning light.

There was only one man who belonged in this study—not Mr. Northcott or the constable or Marchant. How easily I could picture Father here in his great leather chair by the fire, the dark, woody smell of his pipe filling the air. I'd so often come to him, crying over a scraped knee when I was younger, or wishing for his advice as I grew older. And always, always, he had his watch.

"This watch is my god," he'd often joked, which earned him censuring looks if one did not know his favorite book was *Gulliver's Travels*. Like Gulliver, Father rarely did anything without consulting his watch. It was a part of him. If ever a soul could be seen in an object, that watch was Father. Steady, sturdy, practical. Loved.

I swallowed hard. What if I never found the watch?

I'd expected something from Mr. Northcott's visit, the discovery of a helpful clue or an insight into local thieves. Yet it was clear Mr. Northcott did not entirely believe me. It did not matter that *I* was certain I'd been robbed. My word—a woman's word—was not evidence enough.

But someone *had* broken into my house. Someone had violated the place I felt safest and taken the item I loved most. My shock grew thin, fear greedily eating away at me. Though I had control of my own estate, I was just a single woman. How was I to keep my home safe? I had no one left to guide me. No mother since the day I was born. No sister since Catherine had decided I was a thorn in her side.

No father.

Tears burned in my eyes. I fought them back. I needed solutions, not a headache.

What would you do, Father? I'd asked myself that question countless times over the last few months. It had sometimes brought me comfort, clarity, but now the words simply sharpened the ache in my chest. Father could not answer me, and he never would.

I inhaled a stiff breath and set my jaw. As I saw it, I had two problems. One being the security of my home and all those who lived here, the other being the matter of my father's watch. While the first required a bit more thinking, I needed to act now if I ever wanted to see the watch again. Mr. Northcott had proven less than helpful, and so I would take matters into my own hands.

CHAPTER 2

Beatrice waited for me outside the milliner's an hour later, her blonde curls dancing in the April breeze, her bold yellow pelisse striking against the browns of the bustling crowd. My mouth tugged upwards in spite of myself. Only Beatrice Lacey could wear such a color and think nothing of it. I straightened my own skirts, a mourning gray. I would need to have new dresses made soon, though I kept putting it off. These days, my red hair provided the only spot of color when I caught my reflection in a mirror.

Holloway—my lady's maid—made a sound of amusement upon seeing Beatrice. "Easy to spot in a crowd, isn't she?"

"Thankfully."

Beatrice caught sight of Holloway and me descending from the coach and hurried to meet us, her own maid, Mariah, following in her wake.

"Genevieve Wilde," she scolded, amusement hiding in her voice. "There you are. I thought the highwaymen had gotten you."

"I know, I know, I'm terribly late." In truth, I nearly hadn't come. After Mr. Northcott had left, I'd wanted nothing more than to retreat to my room and ensconce myself with a tray of tea and pastries—with my door firmly locked. But Beatrice and I had arranged last night at the dinner party to meet, and I did not want to leave her waiting. Besides that, I knew she would make me feel better.

She planted one hand on her hip, her netted reticule swinging from her wrist. "What happened? It must have been something dreadful. You'd be early for your own funeral if you could manage it."

"I like to be punctual," I said with a laugh. "It's polite."

"Haven't you heard?" She grinned. "Politeness is no longer the thing. Men now want unpredictable, messy-mannered, free-thinking women."

"Then you will make some fellow perfectly unhappy one day." I smiled at the petite girl standing beside Beatrice. "Good morning, Mariah."

She bobbed a curtsy, her eyes twinkling. "Morning, Miss Wilde." As the housemaid assigned to keep Beatrice out of trouble, Mariah spent a great deal of time sharing in my exasperation over the things my friend said.

Beatrice waved a hand. "Never mind all that. What happened this morning?"

I sighed. "It is not what happened this morning but, rather, last night."

I told her everything that had occurred since my dinner party, her face sobering with every word I spoke. When I finished, she simply stared at me. The morning crowd moved around us as we remained quite rudely in the middle of the walkway, but Beatrice paid them no mind. She took my hand. "Oh, Ginny, I am so sorry. I know what that watch meant to you."

I squeezed her hand. Beatrice had been my closest friend as long as I could remember, and she knew better than anyone how much the last six months had cost me.

"In any case," I said, swallowing against the lump in my throat, "since Mr. Northcott is no help at all, I am determined to do what I can on my own. Would you mind if we stopped at the printer's before doing our shopping?"

"Of course not," she said. "But what for?"

"Mr. Northcott suggested I place an advertisement in the paper," I said. "He only said it to placate me, but perhaps he had the right idea of it. If the thief sells the watch, then a reward might tempt the buyer to return it to me." Though that result was improbable—and naively optimistic.

"Or," Beatrice said with narrowed eyes, "the thief might see your advertisement and return the watch himself for the reward."

I did not much like that thought, coming face-to-face, even unknowingly, with the thief who had entered my home while I lay sleeping. But I raised my chin. "It is possible. Still, I should be glad to have my watch back, whatever the means."

We walked to the print shop, where a few passersby had gathered before the broad windows, reading the latest caricatures and cartoons the owner posted in hopes of luring more readers to purchase the weekly paper, *The Little Sowerby Review*. It wasn't much in terms of literature—political articles poached from the London papers, a bit of local gossip, weather reports. But it would do for my needs.

I was reaching for the door when Beatrice grasped my arm.

"Ugh," she said. "It's Catty."

"What?" My head snapped up. She was right. My half sister was marching down the walkway, her eyes already locked on me. Drat and drat.

"Best of luck to you," Beatrice whispered with a laugh, then slipped away to hide behind those gathered at the windows. Mariah shot me a look of apology as she followed after her mistress.

"Beatrice!" I hissed, but she was gone. Holloway still stood beside me, but my lady's maid would be little help in escaping.

"Good morning, Genevieve," came Catherine's voice from behind me.

I squared my shoulders and faced Catherine Davenport. She wore a beautiful, red wool pelisse and a silk bonnet with white feathers, her dark hair curled about her face in tight ringlets. I hardly noticed any of that, too focused on the look of intent curiosity in her sharp blue eyes.

"Good morning, Catherine," I managed. She was technically my half sister, her mother being Father's first wife, but we'd never had anything resembling a sisterly relationship. One might think it was the fifteen-year age difference between us, but that was nonsense. She had simply always disliked me.

Of course, it did not help that Father had left Wimborne to me and not her. Her envy was absurd—she was married and settled in a house of her own, after all. She hardly needed Wimborne too. Just one of the many reasons Beatrice had dubbed her "Catty."

"Have you business in the print shop?" Catherine arched one brow.

I forced a smile. It would be my luck if she discovered why I was here. "No, no. Simply looking at the prints in the windows."

Since Father's death, it seemed all of Little Sowerby—and Catherine in particular—had watched me closely, certain I would be unequal to the task of running Wimborne. I'd done well so far, aside from a few minor problems, but it wouldn't do to have her learn about the theft that had taken place right under my nose.

"I see." She craned her neck around me. "Was that Miss Lacey I saw with you?"

"Yes, it was," I said.

"Hmm," she said disapprovingly.

Even though I was vexed at Beatrice for abandoning me, I still felt that familiar protectiveness rise inside my chest. Beatrice wasn't well liked by the women in town—she was too forthright, too brash—and there was the matter of her scandalous Season in London last year. But careful as I was with my reputation, I would never give up Beatrice. She'd visited me every day after Father died, forced me to eat and take walks. She held me when I cried. She was the truest friend I had, current abandonment notwithstanding.

"Do not let me keep you, Catherine," I said. "I'm sure you've things to do. Good day."

She opened her mouth, no doubt to provide another criticism, but I waved and tugged Holloway with me. We joined Beatrice and Mariah at the window.

"Has she gone?" I whispered, not daring to look over my shoulder.

Holloway looked for me. "You are safe, miss. She's crossed the street."

I shook my head. "You are a wretch, Beatrice Lacey."

I expected a laugh and a jest. When she didn't respond, I turned to face her. She was staring intently at a page of advertisements posted in the shop's window.

"Beatrice?"

She tapped one finger on the glass. "This is what you need, Ginny. Right here."

I stepped to her side and read the block of tiny black print:

For hire
A man of certain talents being recently employed as a princi-
pal officer of Bow Street. List of services: recovery of lost property,
investigation and detection, pursuit and capture of criminal per-
sons, etc. Fee varies. Inquiries made to Mr. J. Travers.

"A man of certain talents?" Mariah said. "What does that mean?"

I crossed my arms. Beatrice could not be serious. "It *means* Beatrice would have me hire a thief-taker."

"What is so wrong about that?" Beatrice asked. "That is their oc- cupation, is it not? To recover stolen items? Capture the criminal?"

"They cannot be trusted, that is why." I'd heard far too many sad tales from my father about thief-takers taking advantage of desperate folk. These were men who worked with criminals, who used whatever means necessary to gain their rewards.

"But look." She jabbed her finger at the advertisement again. "He was a Bow Street Runner, not some footpad from Seven Dials."

She had a point. It was no small thing to be associated with London's Bow Street Runners, an organization of magistrates and offi- cers responsible for policing the city. When I was perhaps seven years of age, Father had worked with a Bow Street Runner, a Mr. Townsend, while he pursued a murderer supposed to be hiding in Little Sowerby. Father had invited the man to stay at Wimborne during the case, and

I still remembered the fine cut of his clothes and his elegant voice. He was nothing like the rough constables I was used to. He was respectable, well-spoken, and efficient. Might this Mr. Travers be the same?

Then again . . .

"'Recently employed,'" I read again. "Why would he leave a reputable position at Bow Street? Does that not make you suspicious?"

"A man could have many reasons to change employment," she said. "Besides, even if he is a scoundrel, if he can find your watch, does his character really matter? All he wants is to be paid."

I considered that. I hadn't any idea what "fees" this Mr. Travers might charge, but even if he demanded a hundred pounds, it would be worth the price to have Father's watch back in my hands.

"Miss Wilde." Mariah stepped forward. "If I may."

"Of course."

"Last year, my uncle was the unfortunate target of a pickpocket," she said. "He lost some money, but besides that, he lost a snuff box, a wedding gift from his wife. My uncle decided to employ a thief-taker, who managed to track down the pickpocket and negotiate the return of the snuff box."

"How did he accomplish that?" Beatrice asked, her voice colored with interest. Leave it to Bea to be fascinated by the workings of a thief-taker.

Mariah shook her head. "I haven't any idea. But my uncle did indeed get the snuff box back, though he had to pay the thief-taker a hefty reward."

I bit my lip. Hiring a thief-taker? It sounded so risky, so impossible, so . . . unlike me. If only I had Father to advise me. I looked at Holloway, who gave the smallest shrug of her shoulder. She'd been my lady's maid since I came of age, and though she was as sweet as could be, she did not know what I should do any better than I did. It was my choice alone.

I raised my chin. I was perfectly capable of making decisions, as I'd proven time and again over the last few months. This theft had only rattled me, left me unsure, and—frankly—rather frightened. Mr.

Northcott's lukewarm response had not helped anything, either. I read the advertisement again, trying to picture the sort of man who would answer my call for help. Would he simply make my troubles worse?

"What will it hurt to write to him?" Beatrice asked. "See, his direction is in London. Write to him but also place your advertisement as you intended. Better to have more than one plan, don't you think? I'd wager this Mr. Travers could be here in less than two days if there are no issues with the post."

London was but a half day's journey from Little Sowerby. Father had always said the first days after a crime were the most vital. Beyond that, the trail grew cold and evidence was corrupted. Speed was of the essence if I ever wanted to see my pocket watch again.

Which I desperately, desperately did.

And I admitted, if only to myself, I should like to see the look on Mr. Northcott's face when I told him I'd recovered the watch without his help.

"Very well." I gave a firm nod as if that would help settle my nerves. "I'll write to him."

"Excellent." Beatrice's eyes gleamed. Part of me wondered if she'd only suggested this course of action because of how exciting it sounded—employing a thief-taker to recover my family heirloom. But I pushed that aside. Even if she did think that, it did not mean that this was the wrong decision. A thief-taker would have connections I lacked, experiences and knowledge that not even Mr. Northcott possessed. This Mr. Travers was likely my best chance at ever seeing Father's watch again. Even if he was a scoundrel of the worst sort, it would all be worth it.

I hoped.

CHAPTER 3

Over the next two days, I kept myself occupied for every minute of every hour, so that when night came, I would fall into bed already asleep. At least, that was the theory. I did indeed fall into bed every night exhausted from the day: meeting with a locksmith to discuss improvements to the security of Wimborne, working with my housekeeper to plan menus and approve purchases, and riding out with my steward to oversee repairs on a tenant house. I also wrote long, expansive entries in my journal in the evenings, hoping to tire my eyes.

But that exhaustion was never enough. I lay awake each night, watching the shadows steal across my ceiling, wondering if the creak I heard was the tree outside my window or the quiet step of an intruder in the corridor.

I hated feeling so vulnerable in my own home. Hated that I wished I had taken Marchant's offer to station a footman at my door.

Finally, on the second night, when the clock struck two in the morning, I slipped from my room, crept down to the kitchen, and took a large knife. I placed it in the drawer of the bedside table, within easy reach, and then fell fast asleep.

I was shaken by gentle hands, the bright sun of morning slipping through my eyelids. "Miss Wilde."

I threw a hand over my eyes to block the light. "A few more minutes, Holloway, please."

"I would let you sleep all day, miss," Holloway said, "but you've a visitor."

I pried one eyelid open and squinted at the clock on the mantel. "It's not yet eight o'clock. Who is here so early?"

"A Mr. Travers, miss."

"Who?" I shook my head, foggy with sleep.

She lowered her voice. "The thief-taker."

I sat up abruptly. "He's here? Now?"

"In the parlor."

I clutched my blankets to my chest, as if the man might burst into my room at that very second. That was foolish. Of course he wouldn't. But how could he be here so soon? I certainly hadn't expected him to land on my doorstep so unceremoniously. But he had, and now I had to manage. I relaxed my grip and threw off my covers. "Let us hurry."

Ten minutes later, hastily dressed and my red tresses in a passable state, I approached the parlor. My heart thrummed inside me, as if damselflies had taken up residence in my chest. After I'd sent the letter to Mr. Travers, I'd regretted it almost instantly. How could I trust anyone who made his living as he did? This was what came from making such a spontaneous decision. I'd secretly hoped many times over the last two days that this thief-taker would not come. That the letter would go astray, or that he simply did not care about one woman's lost watch when there were greater prizes to be had.

But he *had* come, and I needed to prepare myself. I would not be taken advantage of, no matter that I was a woman and young and admittedly a bit inexperienced. I *was* smart and resourceful and more knowledgeable than most, what with having a magistrate for a father.

I stopped at the parlor door and adjusted my fichu, my hands shaking slightly. Then I squared my shoulders. This was my home, and Mr. Travers was just a man. I opened the door and strode inside.

And came to an immediate stop. The parlor—decorated in pale blues and pinks, with delicate rosewood furniture and ormolu-framed paintings—was empty.

I spun in a full circle. Had Holloway said the parlor? I was quite certain she had. But where had Mr. Travers gone?

I hurried back into the corridor, intent on finding Marchant, who had surely answered the front door. But as I passed my study—door slightly ajar—I heard something. A rustling, then quiet footsteps. Who was it? I stepped closer and peeked inside. Through the sliver of open door, I saw a dark-haired man near the desk. A flame of fear licked up my spine. It was not anyone from my staff, which left only one option. The thief-taker.

He was . . . he was *robbing* me.

A sudden, ferocious anger gripped me. How dare he? How dare he enter my house under false pretenses and then rob me blind?

I did not stop to think. I was done cowering in my room, afraid of every shadow. I picked up a slender vase from a nearby table, marched to the door, and threw it open. "Stop at once!" I ordered, raising my vase like a cricket bat.

The man jerked upright from where he'd stooped over Father's— my—desk. "What the bl—"

"Don't touch anything." I raised my vase higher. "Marchant!" I cried, hoping my butler was within shouting distance.

The man stared at me, as if *I* was the dangerous criminal breaking into *his* home. Then a look of understanding crossed his face. "I'm not stealing anything, miss," he said in an amused voice. "Though your weapon of choice would certainly make me think twice."

Of course he would *say* he wasn't robbing me. "Marchant!" I called again, never taking my eyes from the man. He stepped out from behind the desk, and I shrank back. He stopped.

"My name is Jack Travers," he said slowly, like I was a frightened horse on the edge of a cliff. "I was summoned here by a Mrs. Wilde to locate a stolen pocket watch. Would that be your mother?"

I barely heard his words, so loudly did my pulse echo in my ears. "Why are you in here? You were left in the parlor."

"Yes," he said, "but as it has been nearly a half hour since I was deposited there, and I really am rather a busy man, I decided to begin without my hostess. My letter from Mrs. Wilde said the theft took place in the study, and so I made an educated guess that this was it."

My letter *had* mentioned the study. I glanced at the desk—books and papers and ink and pens. Nothing was missing or even out of place. I lowered the vase slightly. "*Miss* Wilde," I corrected.

"Pardon?" His brow furrowed.

"The letter. It was from Miss Wilde."

Something flashed in his eyes—which were a brilliant blue, I noticed now that I did not believe myself in immediate peril. Before he could speak, footsteps pounded in the corridor and Marchant burst through the open door. He came to a stop as he took me in, still holding my vase, and then stared at Mr. Travers.

"Miss Wilde?" Marchant's chest heaved.

I lowered my vase, feeling every bit an enormous fool. "I'm sorry, Marchant. Everything is fine. Mr. Travers only startled me."

"*You* wrote to me?" Mr. Travers asked, eyebrow raised. "You can't be eighteen."

"I am three and twenty, thank you very much." I'd never looked my age and had always been told I would be grateful for it one day. Today was *not* that day.

I turned to Marchant, heat creeping up my neck. "I apologize for the alarm, but you can leave us."

"You are certain?" Marchant eyed Mr. Travers, who held out his hands as if to show he was not hiding a weapon. "I can stay, miss."

I hesitated. I should keep Marchant in the room, if only to calm my still-pounding heart. But I did not want to show any weakness in front of the thief-taker. "Yes, I'm certain. Thank you, Marchant."

Marchant looked unconvinced. He pointedly pushed the door wide open and gave Mr. Travers one last look of warning as he left. "I'll be down the corridor."

I faced Mr. Travers. He crossed his arms, one corner of his lips pulled up in clear amusement. His clothes were rumpled and dusty, but well made—quality I'd expect from a gentleman rather than a thief-taker, especially one so unexpectedly young. He had a crop of ink-black hair, wild curls looking as if he had just run his hands through them, and a sharp jaw with the dark stubble of a man who had yet to shave. Thick brows perched above those blue eyes, balanced with a strong nose. He might have been handsome if not for that irritating, lopsided grin.

And he was absolutely *not* what I had pictured a thief-taker would look like.

My embarrassment faded, annoyance quickly taking its place. What sort of man went wandering about a house he'd only arrived at? Especially when he wasn't a guest but a potential employee. He watched me, calculating, probably already counting the money he'd profit off my naivety. He assumed he had the upper hand here, that I was some silly girl out of her depth.

"Perhaps we might try starting out on a different foot?" Mr. Travers asked. "Since clearly *that* was the wrong one."

"I . . ." I had half a mind to send him on his way, to pretend I no longer needed him. Everything about our meeting set me on edge. Dangerously on edge.

He bowed, a jaunty bend of his neck. "Jack Travers, at your service. I am sorry, truly. I tend to make terrible first impressions. I'm much better on the second go round."

I blinked. I could not take this man's measure. He dressed like a gentleman—albeit one in need of freshening up—yet snooped about my house and made quips as if he hadn't a care in the world.

"And you are Miss Wilde?" he prompted.

"Miss Genevieve Wilde." I did not curtsy. I did not think I owed him that after the way he'd behaved.

"It is a pleasure to make your acquaintance, Miss Wilde." He smiled then, a wide, disarming smile that only made me more wary. I would *not* be disarmed.

"Mr. Travers," I said stiffly. "I shall be perfectly frank. Now that I have met you, I am not certain you are the right man for the job. I had expected someone with a bit more. . . ."

"Girth?" He patted his narrow stomach. "I assure you I am as good in a fight as anyone."

That was easy to believe. Though Mr. Travers did not have the thick shoulders of Marchant or the towering height of Mr. Northcott, he carried himself with confidence, his movements full of bridled energy. It was clear to see he was in excellent form, evidenced by the pull of his jacket over his arms and chest.

I tore my eyes from examining his figure. "No, I was going to say experience."

Mr. Travers couldn't have been older than thirty, and likely a year or two younger. He didn't seem offended in the slightest as he clasped his hands behind his back. "Ah, so *you* are allowed to criticize *me* for my age. I can assure you I am perfectly capable."

I ignored his slight. "Yes, I did want to discuss your qualifications." I still held the vase. I gathered what little dignity I had left and placed it on the edge of the desk. "You were a Bow Street Runner?"

"Yes, though I've never cared for the term," he said offhandedly. "Runner is rather demeaning, don't you think? Makes one think of a messenger boy."

I raised an eyebrow. "Might I inquire as to the reason you are no longer employed there?"

"Simply a difference of opinions," he said. "Nothing so interesting as whatever story you've imagined, I can assure you."

"And I can assure *you*," I said, "that I've not had time to imagine anything, which is why I asked. I am curious why a man placed at Bow Street would then turn thief-taker."

He grimaced. "I'm afraid I don't much care for that term either. Some uncomfortable connotations there."

I fought to keep my voice level. "Then what, pray tell, would you call yourself, if not a runner or a thief-taker?"

"I am quite partial to 'special investigator,' if you please."

I did *not* please. Was I truly thinking of hiring this man? I wasn't stupid—he'd clearly avoided my question about why he'd become a thief-taker.

Mr. Travers had begun a slow circle about the study as we talked, but now he stopped in front of my father's portrait, examining it.

"Robert Wilde," he read from the inscription. "Your father?"

"Yes," I said. "And the former magistrate." I traced the edge of the desk with my finger. "He died six months ago."

Mr. Travers inspected the portrait a moment longer, then his gaze flicked to me. "You have his eyes."

I cleared my throat. I liked my green eyes for that very reason. But who was this man to make such an intimate observation within five minutes of meeting me?

"My father sometimes worked with officers from Bow Street," I said, more to change the subject than anything. "I remember a Mr. Townsend in particular."

Mr. Travers brightened. "Ah, Townsend. I haven't seen him in an age."

"You know him?"

"Most people in London do," he said. "He's more popular than Prinny himself. He was a mentor of sorts when I started at Bow Street. We used to drink at the Brown Bear across the street to celebrate a conviction, though we haven't done that since. . . ."

He rubbed his neck as his voice drifted off, lost in a memory, I assumed. He came back to himself a moment later.

"Any more questions about my qualifications?" he asked, rubbing his hands together, as if we were discussing a book we had both read recently. As if I should blindly accept every nonanswer he'd given me and trot along to handing over my money.

I had more questions. Of course I did. But I swallowed them. What was the use? I needed him, as much as I wished I didn't. And besides, he'd worked with Mr. Townsend, who I knew to be honorable and skilled. Father had followed the man's career after he'd left Little Sowerby, often reading to me from the papers about his cases. If Mr. Travers was anywhere as competent as his mentor, then perhaps my cause was not so lost as I thought.

"No, I am ready to discuss details." I sat behind my desk and gestured for him to take a seat. I felt better, more secure, with the large desk separating us.

"I suppose I might begin," he said as he sat, "by asking if you simply wish to recover the watch, or if you also want to apprehend the thief. Your letter was unclear."

That was because I hadn't yet decided when I'd written to him. Did I want to be dragged into an expensive prosecution? The matter would no longer be private then, but gossiped about in every parlor in Little Sowerby. Yet, in the last few days since the theft, with my inability to sleep, my determination had increased. Rotten reprobates like this thief should not be allowed to roam freely.

"First and foremost, I desire the return of my watch," I said. "If you should catch the thief as well, I would be perfectly satisfied."

"And your reward would be adjusted accordingly?"

I nodded. "Ten pounds for the watch, and ten more if the thief is convicted."

"Twenty pounds?" Mr. Travers raised an eyebrow.

I flushed. Was it too high a number? Too low? "Is that agreeable?"

"It will do, I suppose," he said. "Of course, there may be other expenses, if I need to travel or loosen someone's tongue with a . . . consideration."

"You mean a bribe."

"Oh yes, it's very common. Expected, really, among those I associate with." There was a gleam in his eye. Was he teasing me? Or trying to frighten me?

I would not let him. I leaned forward and rested my forearms on the desk, lacing my fingers. "What is your rate?"

"A guinea a day, plus living expenses for room and board in town."

I considered that. I had the money—Wimborne was as profitable as it had ever been. But I did not like to give in so easily.

"I will agree to that rate," I said, "but *you* will give my case your full attention. No distractions. I'll not be paying you to work for another's reward."

He sat back, tipping his head to one side. "Agreed," he said finally. "Now, tell me about this watch."

I exhaled. The difficult part was done. "It was my father's. It's been in the family for four generations."

He nodded, listening closely. That blasted grin had thankfully disappeared.

"The case is made of brass, with a white enamel face," I went on. "It has an inscription on the back, a favorite of my great-grandfather's. *Esse quam videri.*"

"'To be, rather than to seem,'" Mr. Travers murmured.

I raised an eyebrow. "Is translating Latin one of your 'certain talents,' then, Mr. Travers?"

"Hardly. It is simply an unfortunate side effect of my upbringing." He leaned forward, eyes intent. "What else can you tell me about the watch?"

"I can show you, if you like." I shuffled through a stack of paper. "I have a drawing of it."

Beatrice had sketched it for me, since my own artistic talent could fit in a thimble. I slid the paper to him, a detailed drawing of Father's watch as well as the watch chain and key. How easily I remembered Father winding his watch with that key at the same time every day. A familiar lump rose in my throat.

"What is this here?" Mr. Travers pointed at the watch chain.

"I made that watch chain for my father as a child. Red plaited silk." It had gotten ragged as of late, but I'd wanted the drawing to be as accurate as possible. "I daresay it will help in identifying the watch, assuming the thief does not remove it."

"Indeed." He examined the drawing another moment, then folded it and tucked it inside his jacket. "What can you tell me about the night it disappeared?"

"Nothing more than I described in my letter, unfortunately," I said. "It's really rather baffling."

His eyes moved to look behind me. "You said the thief must have come through the window?"

"Yes, this one here," I said, gesturing at the window to my right, "though there were no signs of intrusion."

"Hmm," he said, standing and coming around the side of the desk to examine the window, standing too close beside me. I leaned away in my seat, though not before I caught the scent of his light cologne. I happened to like cedarwood, but here in my inner sanctum, anything different felt intrusive. I tried not to breathe overmuch as he inspected the casement with his hands.

"Certainly seems possible," he said, returning to his seat. "The opening is large enough."

It had been a rather cursory inspection. Likely he didn't want me looking over his shoulder during his entire investigation.

"I've placed an advertisement in the local paper," I said. "Asking for any information regarding the watch. I do hope—"

He sat up. "You did what?"

I pulled my chin back. "Placed an advertisement."

He scrubbed a hand over his face. "Of course you did."

"And what is so wrong about that? I was advised by the magistrate to do so."

Mr. Travers leaned an elbow on my desk, and I sat back, drawing my hands into my lap. "You've just announced to everyone who reads that paper that your home is a target."

"I am in the process of adding additional locks and safeguards to the house," I protested.

"Soon?"

"The locksmith said a week or two."

"Not soon enough," he said. "Not to mention the unsavory types that such rewards tend to bring out. I've no doubt you'll be inundated by thief-takers soon enough."

I narrowed my eyes. Clearly, he did not consider himself an unsavory type. "If you're as good an investigator as you profess to be, you needn't fear competition."

"I don't." He spoke so flatly that I believed him. "But having too many in pursuit can muddy the waters."

I pursed my lips. He had a point.

Mr. Travers sighed. "What's done is done. I recommend you cancel the advertisement immediately and hope no one worrisome takes notice."

I hesitated, loath to take him at his word. But logic won out in the end. I pulled a sheet of paper toward me, my already overwhelming list of things to do. My eyes wandered up the list, to where I'd written *visit clockmaker*. For weeks, my pocket watch had been sounding odd, and, though I'd wound it daily, the time was off ever so slightly. I'd thought to have it inspected. At least I would have one less thing to do now.

I shook off that thought and dipped my pen in the inkwell. *Rescind advertisement*, I wrote in my precise hand.

Mr. Travers bent over my desk. "I would suggest moving it to the top of your list. Perhaps there, above *dress fitting*."

I moved my hand to block the rest of my writing, glaring at him. "I will thank you not to tell me what tasks should be prioritized, Mr. Travers." There was no need to tell him that *dress fitting* had been constantly pushed back by more pressing matters.

I straightened my papers, eager to turn the attention back to him. "What will be your first step, Mr. Travers? I should like to be kept aware of your actions on my behalf."

He sat back in his chair, resting his arms comfortably on the sides. He looked too at ease for my taste, as if he'd sat there all his life.

"I'll start by interviewing your staff," he said. "Anyone who was here the night of the theft is suspect, including your dinner guests."

"Are you sure that ought to be the priority?"

"Why should it not?" He propped an ankle on his knee. "Have you a suspect in mind?"

"No, but I have already questioned my staff, as well as searched their rooms. Besides, the watch isn't worth enough to jeopardize their employment."

"It is not always about the money, Miss Wilde."

I ignored him. "My guests consisted of my closest friend, the vicar and his wife, and the magistrate. I can assure you that none of them had any reason to steal the watch either. It must have been an outsider."

Mr. Travers sighed. "When you hear hoofbeats, look for horses, not a zebra."

I blinked. "Pardon?"

He ran a hand through his dark curls, throwing them into casual disarray. "It is something I've learned after years of pursuing criminals. Reason dictates that it is generally the easiest, most obvious answer that holds the truth. Yet you insist it was a housebreaker in the middle of the night, taking nothing but a brass watch?" He shook his head. "I am sorry, but that is nonsensical."

I gripped my pen so tightly I thought it would snap. Nonsensical, was I? He sounded like Mr. Northcott.

His face softened. "It is difficult to face the prospect that someone close to you is lying. But I assure you that the best path forward is to interview all possible suspects, compare stories and details, gather alibis. Only then can I begin to form a picture of what happened here that night."

I exhaled through my nose. What he said made sense. I simply hadn't expected someone like him to be quite so methodical.

"Very well, Mr. Travers. We will do this your way. For now. But know that I expect results." I almost winced at how harsh my words sounded. I'd never spoken so in my life. But I had to be careful, firm, so this man did not take advantage of me. I stood, balancing my fingertips on my desk. "I want my watch back."

He stood as well, his gaze direct and confident. "You shall have it." He held out a hand to me.

That was quite the promise to make. I hesitated, then surprised myself by taking his hand. His grip was strong and warm, and heat rose in my chest. Had I ever held a grown man's hand like this, save for Father? And here I was shaking hands with a stranger.

I'd hired this man, for good or for ill. If the churning in my stomach was any clue, it seemed to be a mix of the two.

CHAPTER 4

I decided to settle Mr. Travers in the library for his interviews, tucked away where hopefully he would cause less trouble.

"We must keep a close eye on him," I said to Marchant in a low voice. We watched from the doorway as Mr. Travers walked up and down the length of the library, examining his new surroundings. For what, I hadn't the faintest idea. "I shouldn't like him to harass any of the servants."

"I'm not the harassing type, fortunately," Mr. Travers called from where he stood at the window. "But you may wish to warn the maids about my charming smile."

Marchant looked affronted, his hands clenched into fists. "An eagle eye, miss, you can be certain," he said loud enough for Mr. Travers to hear.

"Thank you, Marchant." I made to leave.

"Will you not be sitting in on the interviews, Miss Wilde?" Mr. Travers asked from behind me.

I turned back. He stood with his hands in his pockets, watching me with a nonchalant expression.

"I will join you shortly," I said. "I've several tasks of vast importance I must complete this morning."

I was lying, of course. Although I had a mountain of paperwork and correspondence to catch up on, and I really did need to see about hiring a new maid, it wasn't anything that would suffer from a slight delay. But Mr. Travers was wearing on me. I wanted to hide from him and shore up my defenses.

"Surely it can wait," he said. "I do not know these people as you do. You might notice something and perhaps help them talk more."

"Talk? Or confess?" I couldn't say why I was so particularly offended that he thought of my servants as suspects.

"While an admission of guilt would be most convenient, that is not all I am looking for."

"What then?"

"Anything useful," he said. "Perhaps the kitchen maid left a door unlocked, or the gardener saw a suspicious figure lurking behind the hedge. Any clue that might hint at the thief's identity. But I will be much more likely to learn these things if you stay and assist me."

He sounded sincere, but I was sure he could make himself sound any way he liked.

"Very well," I relented. "Though I do hope it won't take long."

"That I cannot promise you," Mr. Travers said with a quirked smile. "I am quite thorough in *everything* I do."

I only narrowed my eyes. It seemed Mr. Travers took a certain enjoyment in making others feel uncomfortable, and I would not allow him any satisfaction from me.

<hr/>

We spent the next hour together in the library interviewing the principal members of my household—Marchant, Holloway, and my housekeeper, Mrs. Betts. I watched Mr. Travers curiously throughout the interviews. He had a way of changing his manner and questions so they were specifically suited for each person we spoke to. With Marchant, he was clear and concise, no nonsense. With Mrs. Betts, he was softer, taking longer pauses, which allowed her to gather her thoughts. With Holloway, who unsurprisingly seemed utterly taken with him, he flashed a broad smile every other minute. Apparently, setting people at ease was one of Mr. Travers's *special talents*.

Unfortunately, even with his skilled questioning, our interviews proved unproductive: no one had seen or heard anything unusual during the night of the theft. Mr. Travers wrote notes in a small black book as his questions were answered. He was clearly trying to find details that did not match up to another's story, but to no avail. Now I was glad to be present for the interviews. It bolstered my belief that my staff was innocent of wrongdoing.

After Holloway left the library, I shot Mr. Travers an appraising glance and turned to him. "I cannot help but think this a waste of time."

"A morning spent with a beautiful lady is never a waste," Mr. Travers said as he perused his notes.

If he meant to charm me, he was going about it the wrong way. "Flattery will not help us find my watch," I said, my voice sharper than the kitchen knife I'd hidden beside my bed.

He looked up at me. "Three and twenty, you say? Never married?" A muscle twitched in his cheek, betraying his desire to grin. "How utterly perplexing."

"I don't believe ruminating over my marriage prospects is listed as one of your services."

"Don't you worry," he said. "We are making excellent progress. You'll be on your way to your dress fitting in no time."

Oh, this man. Thinking he knew everything about me. I fought to keep my anger at bay as I locked my fingers together. "Mr. Travers," I said, "I contacted you with heavy misgivings, and I am regretting that decision with nearly every word out of your mouth. You might rein in your tongue if you wish to continue in my employ."

If I thought he might balk at my reprimand, I was sadly mistaken. Instead, he leaned back, a strange fire lit in his eyes. "Interesting."

"What is interesting?"

"Nothing." He waved me off. "Only, do allow me to explain something, Miss Wilde. I decided to take your case not because I was desperate, but because I found it intriguing. If you dislike my manners and methods, then by all means, dismiss me. I've plenty of work."

"I see," I said stiffly. "You are doing me a favor, and I ought to be grateful rather than complain about your lack of decorum."

"Believe me, you'll be glad for my bluntness. Better to know up front who you are dealing with. I've long since given up trying to change myself to appease the sensibilities of others."

I stared at him, completely taken aback. His words touched a nerve inside me, a vulnerability that had plagued me since birth. I'd long endured society's whispers and judgments. That was what happened when one's father married a lowly governess only months after the death of his first wife. I had no choice—I was what the world demanded of me. Proper, careful, demure. What would it be like to be a man, to act however one wished?

Thankfully, the stablemaster, Mr. Hewson, stepped into the library and saved me from having to respond. I wasn't entirely certain what I might've said.

Mr. Travers began questioning Mr. Hewson as if nothing had just passed between us, asking the stablemaster about the events of that night—the arrival of the guests, the hours he spent with the coachmen who waited with their equipages outside, and the time he went to bed. Mr. Hewson answered every question in his slow and steady voice, never hesitating.

"Did you see anything suspicious that day?" Mr. Travers's fingers tapped restlessly on the table. An irritating sound, like the constant drip of a leaky roof.

"No, sir."

"Nor that week?"

Mr. Hewson paused. "That week?"

A knock at the door, and Marchant stepped inside. "Pardon me, miss, but Miss Lacey is here."

Thank heavens. I could feel a headache coming on, and there was no faster fix for it than to escape from Mr. Travers and tell Beatrice everything.

I stood quickly. "Thank you, Marchant. I'm sure Mr. Travers can handle things for a few minutes." Before he could protest, I hurried from the room.

Beatrice was waiting in the parlor, her cheeks pink and her eyes bright from the walk over.

"You, my dear Beatrice, have excellent timing," I announced as I entered.

"Why is that?" She greeted me with a kiss on my cheek. "Does it have to do with Marchant looking like he stepped in something foul?"

"Most assuredly." I sat on the settee. "You'll never believe who turned up this morning."

"Who?" She sat beside me.

"The thief-taker, Mr. Travers."

Her eyes widened. "He came?"

"He did indeed. He arrived practically before the sun and has spent the entire morning irritating me to no end."

Beatrice leaned toward me, grasping the back of the cushion. "Tell me everything. Is he frightful looking? Does he have a great beard and smell terrible?"

"He's a thief-taker, not a hermit, Beatrice." She read far too many novels.

"So, what does he look like, then?"

"He is—" I paused. "Well, he's not what I expected. He is rather young, and . . . well . . ."

A slow grin spread across Beatrice's face. "Genevieve Wilde, you think he's handsome."

"Hush." That was the last thing I needed—Mr. Travers overhearing such a comment. "I do not. And it wouldn't matter anyway, since his manners are atrocious."

"So are mine," she said. "Yet you like me just fine."

"That's different. *You're* inescapable. I don't have a choice."

She laughed. "Mama says if I would simply apply that particular talent towards men, I'd be married in a fortnight. But what's the fun in that?"

I quite agreed. When Beatrice's mother had planned her first

Season in London four years ago, Bea had begged me to come with her. I went mostly out of curiosity. What would the infamous "Marriage Mart" prove to be like? A disappointment, as it turned out. A few gentlemen paid me small attentions, but I was the daughter of a country magistrate. They soon moved on to more tempting prey, and I returned home more content than ever with my lot in life. I had Father, after all, and I would have Wimborne as my inheritance. But if I married, my husband would assume control of me and my property, and I would lose the freedom I loved. I was in no hurry to do that.

"In any case," I said, "I am still not sure he is right for the job. I made it quite clear I believe the thief came from outside my household, but he is just as certain the thief was a servant or a guest."

"Is he now?" Beatrice looked fascinated. "Do you know, I read the most egregious story in the *Times* the other day. There was a woman with only one eye—"

But I never learned what happened to the one-eyed woman. Sudden footsteps sounded in the corridor and Mr. Travers marched through the open parlor door, a scowl marring his face. Mr. Hewson trailed behind, not meeting my eyes.

"Miss Wilde," Mr. Travers growled, "did you not think it would be helpful to inform me that your estate has been the target of malicious misdoings?" He crossed his arms, eyes piercing.

"Malicious misdoings?" I stood, disliking how he towered over me. "What do you mean?"

He gestured at Mr. Hewson. "Tell Miss Wilde what you told me."

Mr. Hewson looked as if he would rather face the gallows. "I didn't mean any trouble."

I took a steadying breath and forced a smile at Mr. Hewson. "Please, tell me what happened."

"Well," he said hesitantly, "three days afore the dinner party, one of the stable stalls was left open and a carriage horse escaped. We found 'im eventually, but it took the better part of a day."

I furrowed my brow. "An inconvenience to be sure, but what is suspicious about it?"

"Because I check all the stalls myself, miss, every night afore I re-tire. I swear nothin' was amiss when I left, but come mornin' the stall was empty, door swingin' wide."

Heavens, not again. Why was it that horrible things tended to happen all at once?

"You ought to have told me this when it happened," I said, trying to hide the frustration in my voice. "I need to know everything that occurs on my property, Mr. Hewson."

"Sorry, Miss Wilde." He looked properly apologetic. "I didn't want to worry you none, considering all the rest."

"Yes, the *rest*," Mr. Travers said, flipping open his little book. "Mr. Hewson informed me of several other incidents in recent weeks. A broken fence, missing sheep, a flood after an irrigation ditch was blocked—"

"It's nothing more than a string of bad luck." My shoulders tight-ened. "I have everything well in hand."

"Save for a missing watch," he said dryly.

"Unrelated, I am certain." I glanced at my stablemaster. I did not wish to argue in front of him. "Thank you, Mr. Hewson. You may go."

Mr. Travers continued impatiently as the man left. "Miss Wilde, far be it from me to tell you how to—"

Beatrice gave a cough as she stood from the settee. Mr. Travers straightened. Had he not seen her when he'd come in?

I sighed. "Mr. Travers, may I introduce my friend, Miss Beatrice Lacey? She is keen to meet you, for reasons I cannot comprehend."

"Good day, Mr. Travers," she said, ignoring me as she bobbed a curtsy. "An absolute pleasure."

Mr. Travers bowed. "The pleasure is mine, I'm sure." Though he'd been frowning at me only moments before, he managed to flash a charming smile at Beatrice.

Beatrice shot me a sly glance, which I interpreted with ease after a lifetime of practice. *He* is *handsome*, her eyes were saying. "Please don't let me be a bother," she said aloud. "Do go on. What were you about to tell Ginny?"

"Ginny?" Mr. Travers repeated, turning back to me. I disliked the familiar sound of my name from his mouth. "A nickname I'd not imagined for someone so . . ."

I narrowed my eyes, daring him to continue.

"Straitlaced," he said.

"Just because I do not wish for strangers to wander my house un-supervised does not make me *straitlaced*."

That gleam of amusement slipped back into his eyes. "I did not mean it as an insult, Miss Wilde."

"Your intentions hardly matter if I still feel insulted."

Beatrice watched with such delight one would think she was ob-serving a performance at Covent Garden rather than an argument be-tween two near-strangers in my parlor.

Mr. Travers shook his head. "This is all beside the point."

"Which is?"

"That the situation here at Wimborne is more serious than I'd thought."

I shifted my weight. "You cannot mean to say these incidents are connected to the disappearance of my watch."

"In my experience, such things are never coincidence." He rubbed his chin. "Do you know of anyone who might have a reason to harm your estate?"

"No," I said firmly. "I haven't a quarrel with anyone." Present company excluded.

"What about Catty Davenport?" Beatrice piped in.

I sent her a look of exasperation, but Mr. Travers fixated on her words. "Who is that?"

"No one," I insisted. My family history was not something I wished to discuss with this man. "Just a relation."

"Not just a relation," Beatrice countered. "A half sister who makes no secret of her distaste for you."

I blew out a breath. "You are not truly saying that Catherine is going about freeing carriage horses and breaking fences."

"No, but perhaps she hired someone." Beatrice arched one

eyebrow. "You know she'd love nothing more than to see you fail spec-
tacularly at running Wimborne."

"Perhaps she took the watch too?" Mr. Travers suggested. "Did
she have any attachment to it?"

That gave me pause. *Had* Catherine been attached to the watch?
Father had left Catherine a tidy sum of money, but he'd left everything
else to me, Catherine being married and well provided for. I hadn't
ever considered whether she might have liked to have some of his
things. I could hardly tell Mr. Travers that, though. He'd surely chase
that lead and cause all sorts of trouble.

"If she did, I never knew of it." That much truth I could give.
Every interaction I'd ever had with Catherine was cool and detached.

"What about your father?" Mr. Travers pressed. "As magistrate,
surely he made enemies over the years."

"Undoubtedly. But he's been gone half a year now. Who would go
to such lengths to pester *me*?"

"You might be surprised how far a person would go for revenge,"
Mr. Travers said darkly.

A shiver skittered down my spine. *Revenge?*

"Let me take this on," he said, stepping forward. "You are clearly
out of your depth here."

"Out of my—" I made a noise of disbelief. He'd been here all of
one morning and had decided, like every other man in my life, that
he knew better than I did. I stepped forward to meet him, determined
not to back away.

"I hired you to find my watch, Mr. Travers. Not to protect my
estate from imagined dangers." I did not mince my words. For all I
knew, he did this with every client—created false but alarming claims
and pressed for more money. "You do your job and I shall do mine."

We stood nose to nose, and his eyes drilled into mine. For a
breath, neither of us moved. Then he stepped away, his body taut with
repressed energy. "As you wish, Miss Wilde."

I nodded, gracious in my victory.

"Is there anything else I should know about?" he asked, his voice thorny. "Any other unfortunate incidents or strained family relation-ships?"

"Nothing," I said, chin high. "But I think we are finished with interviews for today."

He watched me a moment longer, which somehow made me feel like I had not actually won our argument. Then his eyes released mine and he moved to the door. "Very well. I will go to town and work my contacts, perhaps visit local pawnbrokers in the area."

Finally, something that could prove worthwhile.

"I will return with any news," he said. "If you should need me, I'm staying at The Bull's Head."

"Oh, they have excellent lamb and potato pies," Beatrice said, as if he and I had not just been involved in a verbal tussle.

He looked at her with a strange expression before a smile climbed his lips. "Then I shall certainly try them." He gave a short bow. "Good day, ladies."

Beatrice rounded on me as the door closed behind him. "Well, I must say I am disappointed in your description of him. Not what you expected? Try roguishly attractive."

"More like irritatingly overbearing." I flopped back onto the settee.

"Well, I like him," she declared. "He knows his business."

"Does he? It seemed to me he was only trying to fish for more money, when I am quite sure I am already overpaying him."

Beatrice's expression turned thoughtful. "He seemed truly worried about all those things that have happened to Wimborne. Are you sure . . ." She trailed off.

"I'm sure," I said firmly. "It is only a few minor problems. Nothing I cannot handle."

She nodded. "Of course. You know Wimborne better than any-one."

I shook off any lingering doubts. I should not let Mr. Travers af-fect me so. I had to be careful around him or I would find myself paying him to protect me from shadows and ghosts.

CHAPTER 5

I did not hear from Mr. Travers for the rest of that day, nor all of the next. Though part of me was relieved not to have to match wits with him, I did not like the idea of him running around Little Sowerby causing mischief. I trusted he would be discreet, considering his reaction to my posting the advertisement, but his silence ruffled me. Hadn't I told him I wished to know what steps he would take?

I tried to use his absence to complete my list of things to do, but somehow it only grew longer the more I worked.

"I don't know why you take so much upon yourself," Holloway said as she brushed my hair that night. "You've plenty of help."

I sighed, tired of our old argument. "I refuse to be a disinterested landowner, Holloway. I refuse to be wasteful and ignorant."

"Yes, but even thrifty and knowledgeable landowners allow themselves to breathe every now and again." She smiled at me in the dressing table mirror. "Your father wouldn't like to see you work yourself to the bone."

I looked away. She squeezed my shoulder before bidding me goodnight. She knew my father was the very reason I did it, why I kept myself so busy I did not have time to think.

But her words stayed with me, and when I rose in the morning, I determined to do something about it. After breakfasting, I pulled on my gloves, slipped into my sage green pelisse, and tied on my bonnet.

Then I went for a walk.

It was as rare an occasion as anything. I wasn't one for nature, which I knew was a terrible thing to admit in proper company. After all, nature was beautiful and romantic and inspiring, as the poets liked to remind us, and one ought to be constantly humbled by the magnificence around them. But I'd always preferred the indoors, where there were significantly less bees and mud and wind that blew my hair into my eyes. Beatrice was always urging me to spend more time out of doors with her. "It is good for your health," she insisted.

Well, then I would do it for my health and my sanity.

I went west, wandering the path beside the stream. I'd played here for hours as a girl, pretending to find pirate treasure or fight in the Crusades. It had all seemed very exciting and grand when I was seven. But now I found the stream small, the shrubbery sparse, and the April air too cold even with my pelisse.

I looked back at the house. Wimborne was not the most impressive of estates. It was a tidy red brick—three levels with orderly windows marching across its face, framed by enormous oaks. The wooden shutters had recently been given a fresh coat of white paint and the wandering ivy cut back, but somehow the gray clouds made the house look sad. Wanting.

I had no one to fool but myself. I closed my eyes against the hot press of tears. It wasn't the gray clouds that made the house look that way—it was the absence of the man who had built Wimborne from the ground up, the man who had watched over Little Sowerby as best he could.

The man who had cared for me day and night for twenty-three years, with every beat of his heart and tick of his watch.

"You must wind it each day," he'd told me once as I sat on his knee, watching him slip the key into the hole on the brass case. He'd carefully guided my hands as he showed me how to wind it. "It would not do to have your watch run down. If you care for the things you love, if you protect them and cherish them, then they will shine."

It wasn't until years later that I realized he wasn't just talking about the watch. That was Father's way, though—a life lesson disguised as an everyday task. But he also lived the way he taught, and I had never felt more loved or cherished than when he smiled at me with pride in his eyes.

"Miss Wilde?"

I started, clutching my bonnet ribbons. For a moment, I thought it was Mr. Travers, finally come to deliver some news. But no, it was not the thief-taker's head of dark curls coming my way but Mr. Northcott's gray silk topper.

"I am sorry," he said, drawing closer. "I did not mean to startle you. I called at the house and your maid said you'd gone for a walk."

If the sight of me outdoors was unusual to him, he did not betray his surprise. He only smiled, planting his walking stick in the dirt as he stopped beside me.

"No trouble." I blinked a few times, hoping my eyes were not red. "What brings you to Wimborne this morning?"

"Something not particularly pleasant, at least for me." He tipped his head to one side. "I have been thinking on our conversation from a few days ago and I believe I owe you an apology."

I raised an eyebrow. "Might I ask what in particular you feel apologetic for?"

He frowned. "A great deal. To start, I was dismissive and overbearing. But mostly I regret doubting your word. If you said the watch was stolen, I should have believed you."

I appreciated his words. He had made a mistake, and he was making amends. But was he truly sorry, or did he think he'd ruined any chance to secure my hand? After two refusals from me, one might think he would grow less determined. I was certain he'd only proposed at all because of some ill-conceived notion that my father wanted him to look after me. Both Mr. Northcott and I knew we did not love each other, after all. "A marriage of companionship and understanding," he'd said during his first proposal, only weeks after Father's death. Which it could have been, no doubt. Mr. Northcott was a good man, if a bit high-minded at times. His attempts to court me had been sweet: flowers, carriage rides, small gifts of books and pens. But he was only Mr. Northcott to me, a kind friend, a constant in my life. Not a husband. Besides, I had no desire for marriage. Perhaps in the future, after things had settled down. Only when—or if—I found love.

"My only excuse for such behavior," he went on, "is the stress I am under from magisterial duties, which I do think you of all people would understand. But that is not reason enough for my disrespect, and I am sorry for it."

I sighed. No matter his motivation, he was making an honest effort. "You are quite forgiven, Mr. Northcott. I admit the tale was hard to believe." I dipped my head toward the path as an invitation. "And I daresay you *have* been busy of late."

"Quite," he said as we started down the path. "I should have liked to come see you sooner, but we had two more robberies in the last three days alone."

"The highwaymen?"

He narrowed his eyes. "Yes. It is maddening. I post watches along every main road, but to no avail. It's almost as if the highwaymen *know* where my men are."

My stomach twisted. I'd been so distanced the last few months, brought low by grief and distracted by my new duties, that I hadn't given much thought to Mr. Northcott's troubles.

He stabbed his walking stick into the path. "I hate that my first year as magistrate will be marked by my failure."

"Of course it won't," I reassured him. "You've done a remarkable job, considering."

Considering the highwaymen had been a bane even to Father, especially during the years just before his death. Mr. Northcott knew this well, having been at Father's side during many of those years, learning from him as Father prepared him to one day take his place as magistrate. This resurgence was hardly Mr. Northcott's fault.

"The thieves cannot elude you forever," I said. "You'll have a bit of luck one of these days."

"I do hope so." He glanced sideways at me. "Speaking of luck, have you any new leads on your watch?"

"None so far, I am afraid."

"I am sorry," he said. "I will reapply myself to my efforts to find it. I had Crouth make some inquiries in town, but I will personally set aside time to pursue any leads."

"Oh." I cleared my throat. "I do wish for your help, Mr. Northcott. But you are so busy, and—well—"

He furrowed his brow. "What is it, Miss Wilde?"

I adjusted my gloves. "I—I hired someone to find it."

"You hired someone?" Mr. Northcott stopped. "Not a thief-taker."

"No, of course not," I assured him. "That is, not really. He calls himself a special investigator. He worked at Bow Street, you see—"

"Worked? As in, no longer?"

I flapped my hand about. "That hardly matters. He seems competent enough, even if I don't necessarily agree with his methods."

"Miss Wilde," Mr. Northcott said shortly. "I cannot believe you would do such a foolish thing."

I blinked. "*Pardon?*"

He did not seem to notice my consternation. "Your father was a magistrate. Surely you know what a despicable creature this thief-taker is—"

"Special investigator," I cut in, my eyes narrowing.

"—and I cannot imagine what you were thinking to involve yourself with one."

I straightened my back. "I involved myself with one, *sir*, because after our meeting, I was convinced that you did not actually believe I'd been robbed." He opened his mouth to speak, but I went on. "I own Wimborne and I will do everything in my power to protect it and the people it provides for. If I cannot feel confident in the local authorities, then I will certainly make my own decisions regarding my home and property."

"Miss Wilde—"

"Good day, Mr. Northcott." I turned on my heel and strode away as quickly as I could while still looking dignified. He did not follow, likely because he hadn't any defense. I kicked a loose pebble in the path, my stomach a simmering stew of irritation. Why was it that every single man in England believed he knew better than I did? Mr. Travers, Mr. Northcott—heavens, even my butler thought I was mad for hiring a thief-taker.

It made me miss Father more than ever. He'd had a way of guiding me, helping me find my way in the world, without ever making me feel foolish or incapable. These men could certainly take a page out of Father's book—or take the *whole* book, really. Not that I needed or wanted their guidance.

I trudged back up to the house. This was why one shouldn't take walks.

But as I approached Wimborne, ready to shut myself in my study and bury myself in work, I was surprised to see Mrs. Betts, my housekeeper, hurrying toward me across the lawn with a worried expression. I groaned. Why was it no one ever hurried to deliver good news?

"What's happened now?" I asked, already resigned.

"It's the conservatory, Miss Wilde," she said. "You had better come and see."

I followed her through the back door, trying to soothe the knot that had overtaken my chest. But it was worse than I'd imagined.

The conservatory had been built along Wimborne's eastern wall, its glass-paned walls enclosing a variety of exotic flowers and citrus trees. It had been my mother's domain during her short life here at Wimborne, before she'd died giving birth to me. She'd been quite the accomplished artist and had spent many happy hours in the conservatory capturing the slant of light through the glass, the curves and shadows of flowers. Wimborne was filled with her paintings.

As a girl I'd often brought my pencils and sketchbooks, drawing for hours on end as I tried to find some connection to my long-gone mother. However, I had no natural talent, and though Father encouraged me, I'd never improved even after lessons and practice. But I still found some satisfaction in the attempt. These days I didn't have much time for artistic pursuits, but a week ago in a sudden enthusiasm, I had set up my paper and watercolor paints to capture the blooming orchids.

Now those paints were scattered across the stone floor, my easel and paper collapsed together in a jumble of wood and scraps of color. A cool wind wrapped around me, strange and wrong in a place that should have been warm and humid. I swallowed and forced my eyes across the room.

A jagged hole pierced one of the wide panes, cracks radiating outward. Shards of glass littered the stone floor. The bright blue sky and wavering trees beyond the hole seemed too vivid as I focused on them, trying to come to terms with what I was seeing.

Mrs. Betts cleared her throat. "The gardener came this morning and found it like this."

I stepped forward and my foot caught on something. A rough, gray rock twice the size of my fist lay on the floor, some fifteen feet from the hole in the glass wall. It must have been thrown hard to have broken the glass, overturned my easel, and landed all the way over here.

"What should I do?" Mrs. Betts asked anxiously.

I shook my head, my pulse like a warning bell in my ears. This was *not* a broken fence or a loose horse. This was not a missing watch. This was an attack on my home. Someone had taken it upon themselves to shatter any remaining illusion of safety I had left, making it clear that walls and glass were not enough to stop them.

Worse still, whoever had done it had also destroyed my painting. Not that I had any particular fondness for that painting. No, it was more than that. It was seeing something I'd made—a beauty I'd tried to create with my own hands—dashed against the floor. It felt like a message, a whisper in the dark. *You are seen*, it said. *I know you.*

"Miss Wilde?"

I cleared my throat, trying to focus. "We'll need to patch that hole until it can be repaired, or else the plants will suffer. But do not clean up the glass yet."

"Of course." She rubbed her hands together, not meeting my

eyes. "I know it's not for me to ask, miss, but do you know who . . ." Her voice drifted off.

"I don't know," I said, my voice tight. "It could have been anyone."

But as she curtsied and left, I knew my words were not true. It hadn't been just anyone. Whoever had thrown this rock, whoever had taken my watch and done every other horrible thing in the past few weeks, they had a reason.

I sat down heavily on a stone bench. My hands trembled, and I clasped them together in my lap. I could not deny the facts any longer—someone was threatening my home. It all *had* to be connected. Mr. Travers had been right. I rubbed my eyes with the palms of my hands. He'd been right, and I had been foolishly stubborn.

It occurred to me that I could run to the front of the house, stop Mr. Northcott before his carriage left. I could ask him for help.

But my teeth ground together, my body resisting the idea before my brain had fully developed it. I had just scolded Mr. Northcott and insisted I could take care of myself. Going to him now would be a special kind of torture, certainly worse than admitting to Mr. Travers that I'd been wrong. No, I had to deal with this alone. Well, not alone. Mr. Travers had offered to help me. I disliked the thought of trusting even more in the thief-taker, but what else could I do?

Where *was* Mr. Travers, anyway? It had been two days since I'd seen him. Had he taken the advance on his daily fee and run off, cackling with glee? Somehow, I doubted it. Why go through the pretense of interviewing my servants if he simply planned to run? But he should have contacted me by now.

I stood abruptly, taking one last look at the broken glass—slivers of sunlight dashed across the stone floor. Then I hurried for the front door, calling for my coach. It was time Mr. Travers earned his wage.

CHAPTER 6

Little Sowerby bustled as always, completely unchanged, though my world had tipped on its axis. I watched the passersby even as I kept an eye on the door of the Bull's Head Inn. Were one of them responsible for the horrible things happening at Wimborne? Was he an enemy of Father's, as Mr. Travers had posited? Or was Beatrice right that Catherine Davenport's envy had descended into madness?

Finally, Holloway stepped out from the inn's door, squinting in the sunlight as she made her way back to the coach.

"Did you find him?" I asked after she climbed inside.

"No," she said. "The innkeeper said he's been out since dawn. I left word that Mr. Travers is to come see you immediately."

I pursed my lips. Drat. I hadn't thought the man would be quite so industrious. But then, if Mr. Travers *had* been sitting about at the inn, I would've pegged him as lazy.

"We'll wait back at Wimborne," I said with a sigh.

I crossed my arms. How long until Mr. Travers came? My house needed security. Now. I could hire men to patrol my estate, but that would take time. And how could I know whom to trust?

I stared out the window, lost in thought, when a face flashed between flowered poke bonnets and men's tailored jackets. I sat up, peering. For a moment, I'd seen dark, curly hair and bright-blue eyes.

I hesitated, then knocked on the roof. The coach came to a stop.

"Miss?" Holloway asked.

"I thought I saw . . ." I opened the door. "Wait here. I'll return in a moment."

"Do you want me to—"

But I was already stepping down onto the cobblestones, closing the door behind me. I wanted to talk to Mr. Travers alone. I did not need my servants knowing how precarious Wimborne's situation was, and though Holloway was sweet, she had a tendency to gossip.

I rose on my toes to peer over the crowd. There. The man I'd seen walked a few paces ahead of me, and as I watched, he looked to the side, his eyes wary. It *was* Mr. Travers.

I hurried to catch him. "Mr. Travers!"

He jumped, staring at me without recognition. Then he blinked. "Ah. Miss Wilde." He glanced around. "What are you doing here?"

"Looking for you, sir." I clasped my gloved hands. "I need to speak with you immediately, about—"

"Right now?" he asked.

I raised an eyebrow. "Yes, right now. If you recall, I am the one currently paying your expenses, and—"

"All right." To my surprise, he took my elbow and moved us along down the street. "Let's talk."

He walked quickly, and I was hard-pressed to keep up. Why was he in such a hurry?

I took a quick breath. "Mr. Travers, as much as it pains me to admit, recent events have led me to believe that you were, in fact, correct about the circumstances surrounding the theft of my watch. I now believe that someone is indeed trying to undermine my stewardship of my estate and—I say, are you even listening?"

Mr. Travers was glancing behind us every few seconds, his expression tight. "No, miss, I'm afraid I am not."

"Mr. Travers." Anger crept into my voice. His indifference was enough to make me rethink my entire plan. Was I really going to put Wimborne's safety into the hands of such a man? "I am trying to speak to you about something important."

Without warning, he pulled sharply on my arm, yanking me into the shadows of an alleyway, cobblestones strewn with—well, I hardly wanted to know exactly what had been dumped here.

"What are you—"

He covered my mouth with his rough hand, pressing me against the brick wall. My eyes widened. He was so close I could see the smallest white flecks in his otherwise blue eyes, feel his warm breath on my nose and cheeks.

His grip was strong. Too strong. My heart tried to wriggle its way out of my chest, panic boiling me inside out. I could hardly breathe. I made a sound, a short-lived whimper smothered by his hand.

"Quiet," he hissed. "They'll hear."

Who would hear? Anyone who might help me? My throat closed over and my mind jumped, erratic and confused. What was he—he couldn't be—was he? But why else would he corner me so?

A clatter came from the mouth of the alley and Mr. Travers whipped his head around, his broad jaw now filling my entire vision. He was distracted. I had a choice. I could cower and hope for rescue. Or I could save myself.

I chose the latter.

I raised my knee and stomped my heel onto the top of his foot. He yelped and jumped away, but not far enough. I strode forward and, drawing back my fist, drove it directly into his fleshy cheek.

Or, at least, I wished it had been fleshy. In truth, Mr. Travers had a jaw built like an iron door. But he staggered back, cursing, from which I took great satisfaction even as I shook out my hand, pain ringing through it.

"Heaven and hell," he sputtered. "What was that for?"

I fell back against the wall, as far as I could get from him. "For assaulting me in broad daylight!" How could I escape him? The other end of the alley was solid brick. Mr. Travers blocked my only route.

He gawped at me. "Assaulting you? Blast it, woman, I'm protecting you."

"From what?" I tried to edge around him, intent on escaping back to the main road while he still felt the effects of my fist. Should I scream? No, I had to get away without damaging my repu—

"Jack Travers," a gravelly voice spoke from the mouth of the alley.

I froze. A man leaned against the brick wall, his frame small and spindly, his angled features set off by red cheeks and a flash of amusement in his eyes.

"I can't say how delighted I am to find you in such a predicament," he said.

Mr. Travers stared at the man, rubbing his already red jaw. He let out a laugh. "Wily? Is that you?"

"Most of me," the man—Wily, I assumed—said with a chuckle. He wore a jacket of vivid green with striped breeches, both items patched a dozen times over. A limp cap that must have once been yellow perched atop his head, held together by sheer stubbornness.

To my utter surprise, Mr. Travers strode forward and the two men clasped hands, slapping each other on the shoulders like they'd just won a bet at Newmarket.

"I thought you were a carrier, or worse," Mr. Travers said with a broad smile as he pulled back.

"Nah, just wanted to be sure it was you." Wily spread his lips, displaying a missing tooth.

My mind was spinning, a Maypole caught in a violent wind. What was going on? How did Mr. Travers know this man, this down-on-his-luck dandy? I used my hands to feel along the rough wall behind me, moving slowly, never taking my eyes off the two men.

Wily's intense eyes focused on me. "Who's the rum doxy?"

I stiffened. "I beg your pardon?"

Mr. Travers held out a hand to me as if I might bolt—which was certainly my intention if I did not like what I heard.

"This is my client," he told Wily, "so I expect a bit of decorum."

"Decorum?" Wily huffed, pulling out the edges of his absurd green jacket. Had he stolen his clothes from a court jester? "I am the picture of gentility, Jack, you know that."

"Aye," Mr. Travers said, a smile in his eyes. A smile that soon faded as he looked at me again.

"What," I asked far more calmly than I felt, "is happening here?"

He nodded at Wily. "An acquaintance of mine, Will Greaves."

"Wily, if you please." The man offered such an elaborate bow that I nearly looked behind me for someone of royal birth. Did people truly call him by such a ridiculous name?

"This is Miss Genevieve Wilde," Mr. Travers said. "I do apologize, Miss Wilde. I thought I saw someone following me."

Wily laughed. "I never was much of a tail."

Mr. Travers shook his head, facing me. "I wasn't sure who it was and I was trying to keep you out of danger. It's more common than you'd think in my line of work."

"From your little disagreement," Wily said, smirking, "I'd wager the miss thought you were trying a bit more than keeping her safe."

My face burned, worse even than when I'd spent the day at the seashore as a girl and earned myself a bright red sunburn. "What precisely was I supposed to think, being handled so?"

"Believe me," Mr. Travers said, lips curving upwards, "if I was trying to kiss you, you'd know it."

I shook my head, cheeks aflame. "You are a scoundrel."

"I've never claimed otherwise."

Wily slung his hands in his pockets, eyeing me curiously. "Where'd you learn to plant a facer like that, miss? Takes a lot to bring down ol' Jack here, and you're a wisp of a thing."

"She did not bring me down," Mr. Travers insisted.

Though my knuckles still protested as I bent them, I had to fight a smile. Maybe this Wily fellow wasn't all bad.

"I didn't *learn*," I said. "I simply acted as any woman would."

"Most would have panicked." Wily tapped his head. "Good instincts is what it is."

Mr. Travers was looking between the two of us, his expression not particularly pleased. He crossed his arms. "What're you doing in these parts, Wily?"

"Laying low," the man said easily. "A job went bad in London so I came north. Been here a couple months. I was in my cups over at the Bald Faced Stag when I heard talk of you here in Little Sowerby. Thought I'd see if you had any work for me."

"What sort of work do you do, Mr. Greaves?" As soon as the words left my mouth, I regretted them. I had asked to be polite, as if this were a normal conversation and a normal new acquaintance. But clearly he hadn't any respectable position, or he wouldn't have a need to lie low.

"Call me Wily, miss," he said. "The last time someone called me Mr. Greaves, I was on trial at the Old Bailey."

I balked. "On trial?"

He smirked. "Grand larceny. Never you fear, I was fully acquitted."

"That time," Mr. Travers said.

"In answer to your question, miss," Wily said, ignoring him, "I'm a receiver."

"A receiver," I said flatly.

"Yes, I help—"

"I know what a receiver is." I frowned. "Otherwise known as a fence. You help sellers find buyers for particular goods. Usually stolen goods."

Father had arrested his fair share of fences, though they were difficult to convict considering they simply claimed they had no idea the items they were negotiating for were stolen. Slippery, the lot of them. It was a pity. I'd almost begun to like Mr. Greaves, but his sort were not to be trusted.

Wily looked utterly delighted at my response. "Where did you find this lovely creature, Jack?"

"Never mind that." Mr. Travers gave his friend a pointed look. "Miss Wilde had something she needed to tell me."

"Yes." I straightened, my purpose once again fresh in my mind. "I should like to speak to you *alone*."

Mr. Travers raised an eyebrow. "Is this about the vandalism on your estate?"

What was he thinking, spouting out my secrets in front of a man like Wily? "I had hoped to keep that between us."

"Vandalism?" Wily questioned. "What sort of job is this, Jack?"

I turned suspicious eyes on him. "Nothing you need concern yourself with."

"Actually," Mr. Travers said thoughtfully, "perhaps Wily might be of use to us. He'll have more connections in the area than I do."

I pressed my lips together, unable to stop myself from giving Wily another once over. He grinned, as if that might make him appear more trustworthy.

"He could help us find the watch," Mr. Travers said. "It's his specialty, really, these sort of dealings."

I rubbed my forehead, debating. Wily had a strange charm about him, and yet I could not pretend he was anything but a criminal. How could I trust him? No honor among thieves, as they said.

Then again, Mr. Travers had already given away my secret. Plus, it was becoming clearer and clearer that I needed help. Even though I could not at all approve of the sort of man this Wily appeared to be, perhaps he was the answer to my predicament. My father, like many men of the law, had had informants in all walks of life, and it had proven useful on more than one occasion. If Wily was a fence, then perhaps he did have a better chance of locating my watch than either I or Mr. Travers.

"Very well," I said resignedly. "He can stay."

Wily offered a mock salute, and I nearly changed my mind. I took a deep breath. "As I was saying before you accosted me—"

"Protected you."

"—there was an incident this morning that has made me question my previous belief that the events that have occurred on my property in the last weeks were only coincidental accidents."

Mr. Travers tipped his head to the side, one brow arched upwards. "Are you saying that I was right?"

I raised my chin. "Yes. You were right."

He opened his mouth, no doubt to gloat, but I held up a hand.

"Of course, you must admit that I was *also* right. The watch was clearly not taken by my staff or dinner guests."

He paused, considering that. "That may be true," he conceded, "but I am not ready to rule anything out. Now, tell me what happened this morning."

I explained about the rock and the broken glass and my ruined painting. "So, you see, this feels very much more personal than anything that has happened thus far, leading me to conclude that the perpetrator has a specific ill intent."

"You talk like a barrister," Wily said curiously. "How is that?"

"My father was the magistrate for nearly ten years." I could not help the hint of pride in my voice.

Wily blinked. "A magistrate?" He cut a glance at Mr. Travers. "I don't want to be mixed up in any magistrate's business."

"Her father died months ago," Mr. Travers reassured him.

It was a statement, a fact, and yet his words stabbed a fresh wound in my heart. I swallowed hard. My emotions were too close to the surface with all that had happened today. But I could not let these men see me cry.

"Yes," I said, my voice like a creaky door. I cleared my throat. "I hired Mr. Travers to recover my stolen watch, but it seems I need his help with much more than that."

I looked at him now, mouth dry. I did not know what I would do if he refused. Swallow my pride and go back to Mr. Northcott?

He watched me, arms still crossed. "Very well, Miss Wilde," he said finally. "I'll do it. But I intend to do things my own way."

"So long as it's *legal*," I said, disliking that I even had to make that distinction. Was I truly making a deal with a thief-taker and a fence? Father would've had a great deal to say about my decisions as of late, I had no doubt. But my options were limited. I had to act.

Mr. Travers looked slightly offended. "Of course it will be legal." He turned to Wily. "I should like your help, if you're willing."

Wily's brows drew into a skeptical V. "Honest work?"

It unnerved me that I could not tell if he thought honesty was a benefit or a deterrent.

He exhaled. "All right, Jack, you've got me. This had better pay well."

"I've no doubt Miss Wilde will make it worth your while."

Kind of him to make promises on my behalf. "Assuming the culprits are caught," I said, "then yes, you have no need to worry in that respect."

Wily nodded. "I'll fetch my things and join you at the Bull's Head, Jack. You can fill me in on the rest then." He dipped his head to me. "A real pleasure, Miss Wilde. I look forward to our continued acquaintance."

"As do I." I blatantly lied, of course. But if this man could help me secure Wimborne and get my watch back, then I would spout any number of falsehoods.

With a wave, Wily trotted off down the alley and vanished around the corner, leaving an awkward silence in his wake.

"You have . . . interesting friends," I observed.

Mr. Travers waved that off. "Wily is harmless. He's a good man, even if his choices are sometimes questionable."

I smoothed my skirts. "I had better return to my coach. My maid will be beside herself."

"Little does she know her mistress can deliver a trimming with the best of them."

"More insincere flattery, Mr. Travers?"

He laughed, rubbing his jaw. "I wish very much that it was. Might have saved my face."

I bit my lip. "I am sorry for that. I hope it won't bruise."

"I've seen far worse, I assure you." He gestured down the alleyway and then fell in beside me. "I did want to tell you that I've made progress in the search for your watch. I've visited every pawnshop within ten miles and showed every ferret that drawing you did. They know I can pay a pretty penny for it if it comes their way. And now that I have Wily, we can use his connections with other fences, see if the watch has made its way onto the market."

"Oh." I tried to hide how very impressed I was. He *was* thorough. "It sounds as though you have that well in hand."

He frowned as we stepped onto the bustling street. "Yes, but it appears this case just grew more complicated. I will need to see the conservatory and examine the sites of the other incidents."

"Of course," I said. "The conservatory is untouched, but I cannot vouch for the others."

He nodded. "I'll see Wily settled at the inn and have him start working through his contacts, then I'll come meet you. This afternoon, if you are agreeable."

"I am."

He looked at me, then smiled. "I do believe, Miss Wilde, that we just had our first civil conversation."

I raised an eyebrow. "We are not including that very, *very* rough start?"

He laughed. I pressed my lips together to keep from joining him.

"No," he said, still chuckling. "I should like to forget it happened, but I doubt Wily will ever let me."

"With good reason."

Mr. Travers tipped his hat. "I'll be to Wimborne in an hour or two. We'll do as much as we can before sundown."

I took a deep breath. I couldn't say why, since I hardly knew Mr. Travers, but he made my anxiety soften. He had a plan, and that was reassuring in a way I hadn't expected from a man like him.

"Thank you, Mr. Travers," I said, toying with the sleeve of my spencer. "I . . . well—" I cleared my throat. "Thank you."

His eyes traveled over my face, curious and far too intense. "You are welcome, Miss Wilde."

I nodded and hurried to where my coach waited for me, Holloway's bonneted head sticking out from the window. My step had a bounce to it. For the first time in nearly a week, I had hope.

CHAPTER 7

As promised, Mr. Travers arrived at Wimborne before two hours had passed. I showed him the conservatory, where he spent a quarter hour inspecting every angle of the broken glass, the rock, even the ground outside. He made a few notes in that little book of his, and I tried to withhold my many questions, not wanting to distract him.

He finally made his way over to my painting, the bent paper like a bird with a broken wing. He crouched beside it and carefully laid it flat on the ground. I bit my lip as he examined it. I never showed my paintings to anyone—not out of false modesty, but because they were really quite terrible. I had none of my mother's talent, and now Mr. Travers was inspecting my work in a manner that felt far too intimate.

"It is a very pretty . . ." Mr. Travers paused. "Boat?"

"It is an orchid." It wasn't a da Vinci, but it was *clearly* a flower.

He looked up at me, grinning. "I am only jesting, Miss Wilde. I can see it's an orchid."

"Oh." Every time I thought I'd begun to understand this man, he said or did something new to confuse me. "Have you learned anything?"

He rose, brushing off his breeches. "Based on the impressions I found in the grass and the height of the hole in the glass, I think we are looking for a man of some height. I'd like to search the perimeter of the house, try to spot where he found the rock. That might help us see which direction he came from."

I was impressed once again. "Of course."

I ordered my horse readied, along with a groom for propriety's sake, and we accompanied Mr. Travers and his mount as he circled the house in ever widening arcs. We soon reached the stream and the small wooden footbridge.

Mr. Travers dismounted and strode to the stream bed. He picked up a rock and tossed it between his hands.

"Was his taken from the stream, do you think?" I called.

He frowned. "It's of a similar size and color. But that's not particularly helpful."

"Why is that?"

He nodded to the west. "The main road is that way, as is town. Anyone might have come from that direction." He dropped the rock back into the stream and mounted again, his movements fluid. "We've still some time before dark. Shall we make use of it?"

We spent the next two hours traveling the estate, from the blocked irrigation channel that had flooded to the broken—and now mended—fences that had led to several sheep going missing. Unsurprisingly, we found no additional clues, considering the incidents had taken place over the course of several weeks.

I found it rather fascinating to watch Mr. Travers work. He inspected everything with a critical eye and noticed things I never would have. Based on our first few interactions, I hadn't expected such thoroughness, and it was gratifying to see his expertise. I could endure a few flirtations from him if it ensured his continued interest in my case.

Though we learned nothing new, I still felt a sense of accomplishment as we started back toward Wimborne, the lowering sun peeking through the trees. There was someone besides myself trying to solve this problem, someone who clearly had more experience than I did.

Mr. Travers was pensive as we rode together, my groom just behind. I hesitated to interrupt his thoughts but eventually my curiosity won out.

"Have you reached any conclusions?" I asked him, one hand on my lower back as I stretched. The sidesaddle beneath me was as comfortable as could be expected, but it had been years since I'd ridden for so long. "Does our criminal have fair hair and crooked teeth? Perhaps he owns a dog or works as a baker?"

Mr. Travers blinked as if I'd pulled him from a trance. "A baker?"

"You seemed so certain about the man's height, I thought you may have deduced other facts about him."

He exhaled a laugh. "No, I'm afraid I've nothing so useful as all that. But I would hazard a guess that he is a sturdy type, used to hard labor. Blocking an irrigation ditch is no easy task."

I sighed. "I thought it was the storm we had a few weeks ago, that the frightful wind had blown the debris into the ditch." I looked out over the landscape, not truly seeing it. "Now it seems a foolish assumption."

"Not foolish," he said, surprising me. "When one has the advantage of time and knowledge, it is easy to look back with new understanding. Perspective is almost impossible when you are in the thick of it."

I cast him a sideways glance. "How shockingly insightful you are, Mr. Travers."

He grinned. "I cannot be dashing and witty all of the time. One must be well-rounded."

I shook my head, though I fought a smile.

"Miss Wilde," he said, shifting on his saddle. "Might I ask you a question?"

I eyed him. "Will it be terribly prying?"

The corner of his lip lifted. "Indeed, or I would not ask for permission."

"Very well." I had no reason to say no. I'd hired him to ask questions, after all.

He paused before speaking. "How was it your father died?"

My hands tightened around my reins. "That *is* prying." I spoke lightly, trying to hide the sudden catch in my voice.

"I am sorry for it," he said. "But I need to be informed. You never know what will prove valuable in a case."

I paused, gathering my thoughts. I usually did everything in my power to avoid dwelling on that day. I made lists. I kept to a routine. I painted dozens of terrible watercolors. But now I could not stop the press of memory. The grooms carrying Father inside, his head bloody and his eyes dazed. He was disoriented, slipping in and out of consciousness. They laid him on his bed, and I held a bandage to his head, shouting at Mrs. Betts to send for the doctor. But he'd lost so much blood. I'd known even then that it was too late.

Near the end, Father regained some lucidity. His green eyes cleared. He fumbled for the pocket watch inside his coat, taking my shaking hand in his and pushing the watch to my palm. He tapped the glass front, eyes wide and intent.

"Here," he croaked. "Here."

I'd shaken my head. Why was he so insistent? But I held the watch as he took his last breath, my hands stained with his blood. The sun of my world gone forever.

I turned away from Mr. Travers to hide the sheen of tears in my eyes. "It was apoplexy," I said in a raspy voice. "He'd suffered a previous bout the year before, but this time he was riding when it happened. He fell, and . . ."

He did not speak, kindly allowing me to collect myself. "I am sorry," he said finally, "that you had to endure such a thing."

I swiped away a lone tear. "That is the way of life, is it not?"

Mr. Travers tipped his head. "Do you have other family nearby? Save for your half sister of ill repute?"

"None." I gratefully followed him to our new topic. "My mother had one sister, but she lives in Northumberland. I know nothing about her side of my family, really. And my father was an only child."

"Hmm," he murmured, facing forward on his saddle again. The fading light illuminated the ridges of his jaw and nose. He had a striking silhouette, bold and strong.

"What does *hmm* mean?"

He shrugged. "It is no easy feat to hold an estate together, and you an unmarried woman. I find it fascinating."

Fascinating. Not a word often used to describe me. "It is my life's work. My father wanted me to care for Wimborne, and so I will. And it isn't as if I am alone. I've a wonderful steward and loyal servants."

"And friends, I hope."

"Yes, of course. Miss Lacey is my dearest, and I quite depend on her mother as well. And Mr. Northcott, of course."

Mr. Travers squinted at me. "The magistrate?"

"Yes," I said. "His father and mine were friends, and so naturally we spent a great deal of time together. In recent years, he also aided my father in his duties." I did not mention how attentive Mr. Northcott had been since Father's death—offering to help me with estate business and visiting often to ensure I was well. I also did not mention Mr. Northcott's two proposals. Some things a woman kept to herself.

I cleared my throat. "So yes, I consider him a friend. Though he is one who will not appreciate you poking around, even if it is to help me. He despises thief-takers."

"Fortunately, *I* am a special investigator." He raised his thick brows at me, and I could not help a laugh.

"Yes, be sure to tell him exactly that," I said. "It will put his mind at ease."

We reached the main road where we would part—he to town and I to Wimborne. I sobered as we pulled our horses to a stop.

"Might I ask what our next step should be?" I fidgeted with my reins. "When it was just a missing watch, everything felt much more manageable. Now I am rather lost."

His brow furrowed as he adjusted his seat. "As I see it, we have no substantial leads. The barest description of a man's physique is not enough to go on."

I nodded, discouragement tugging in my chest.

"But," he said, "the evidence has led me to believe our miscreant is someone known to you. Why would a stranger target your painting?

Your watch? No, this man knows you, and we should proceed under that assumption."

His words only confirmed what I already knew. How odd to find myself in agreement with him after all our arguing.

"It is clear someone wishes to intimidate you," he said. "But what we need to learn is why. I am still of a mind that it could be one of your father's enemies." He rubbed his chin. Fortunately for him, the redness from my fist had faded and left no bruise. "Is there any way to see the magisterial records from when your father was justice of the peace?"

"No *easy* way," I said. "Mr. Northcott has them and would likely suffer a conniption if you asked to read them. Not to mention that I should like to keep my . . . problem a secret, if possible."

"Why is that?" Mr. Travers asked. "Would you not want help from the authorities?"

I let out a short laugh. "Everyone already doubts my ability to run Wimborne. If this were to become public knowledge, it would only prove that my father's trust in me was misplaced. My reputation, and his, are at stake."

"While understandable, that does make things more difficult," he said. "Especially with precious few leads."

I thought a moment. "Perhaps I might help. I could make a list of Father's rulings in the last few years, and people who felt wronged by him. It would be far from complete, but it would give you a starting point."

He looked at me strangely. "You have that information?"

I lifted one shoulder. "Father always told me about his work, and I have written daily in a journal since I was eight. I am certain I wrote about the most important cases."

He shook his head in disbelief. "Would that all my clients were so thorough." He straightened in his saddle. "If you could provide such a list, it would be incredibly helpful. Wily and I can work through it and eliminate suspects. We can also surveil the estate, watch for suspicious activity, and try to catch the man in the act. But neither of those options will be quick or easy."

"They could take weeks." My throat tightened.

"Possibly," he said. "Which is why we might consider a third option."

"Which is?"

"A trap," he said, eyes glinting with a hint of danger. "We create an opportunity for the thief that he cannot refuse."

"Heavens. That sounds . . ." I swallowed. "Effective."

"I promised results. But we will have to think on what sort of trap might lure him in."

I chewed on my lip. There was another problem I wanted to voice—the fear that overcame me at night, the chill that whipped through my chest when I thought about the broken window in the conservatory. How was I to keep my home safe? My staff was not prepared for such a threat, and neither did I expect them to be, whereas Mr. Travers clearly faced trouble like this on the daily.

"Mr. Travers," I began, "what if this man comes again while you are not here? Tonight, even? Would you ever consider . . ." I paused, not entirely sure how to phrase my request.

He raised an eyebrow. "Are you asking me to spend the night, Miss Wilde?"

My cheeks flushed. Why must he always turn my words into something so terribly off color? "Not anymore," I said hotly, turning my horse toward Wimborne.

"Come, I was only teasing." He brought his horse in front of mine, stopping me. "I had thought of it, but we would risk your reputation should I be found out."

He was right, of course. If Society discovered I let a thief-taker sleep in my home, even in pursuit of a criminal, my reputation would be shredded. But what could be done? I was ragged from lack of sleep as it was.

We both heard the creak of the carriage at the same time and our heads turned in unison. A team of horses headed our direction—a well-matched pair of black, high-stepping mares. I groaned.

"You know them?" Mr. Travers asked, following me as I urged my mount to the side of the road.

"Unfortunately. It is the half sister of ill repute we were discussing a few minutes ago." I tried to prepare myself. Two interactions with Catherine Davenport in the space of a few days? Normally I could manage to avoid her for weeks at a time. My stomach twisted. How would I explain Mr. Travers's presence without revealing Wimborne's terrible predicament to the one person who would relish it the most?

The carriage slowed to a stop. "Why, Genevieve," Catherine said. "How wonderful to see you again so soon."

She almost made it sound believable.

"Good afternoon, Catherine." I spoke slowly, as if that might give my mind time to come up with an adequate excuse for why I was riding about the estate with a strange man, my groom's presence notwithstanding. "I hope you are well."

She waved a hand. "Perfectly well, thank you." She was, clearly. Catherine was always the epitome of perfection—stylish dresses, thick dark curls, pretty eyes, and a ready smile. For everyone but me, that was.

Now she turned that smile on Mr. Travers, though it had a curious tilt to it. "Who is this? A new acquaintance?"

I might have laughed if I weren't short of breath. Catherine Davenport wanted an introduction to a thief-taker. "Y-yes," I said, choking a bit on the word. "Mr. Travers, this is Mrs. Catherine Davenport."

"A pleasure, madam," Mr. Travers said, tipping his hat.

She offered a lazy nod in return. "What brings you to Wimborne, Mr. Travers?"

I blew out a breath. I had no choice but to tell the truth and hope for the best. She hated me already, so how much worse could it be? "Mr. Travers is a—"

"A cousin," he cut in quickly. "Visiting from Northumberland."

I stared at him. What on earth was he thinking?

"Cousin?" Catherine's eyes narrowed. "I wasn't aware you had any contact with your mother's family, Ginny."

"I . . ."

"Oh, it's a recent connection," he said smoothly. "My mother wrote to Genevieve a few months ago, wishing to know more about her niece. They've since kept up a lively correspondence. When Ginny heard I would be traveling to London, she extended an invitation to stay with her for a short while."

I was gaping. How did he manage to make the lie sound so real? I shut my mouth hard, my teeth rattling. He offered only the slightest wink.

"Yes," I said, trying my best not to glare, since that would give me away faster than anything. "Yes, I invited him. It does get lonely in that big, empty house."

Catherine sniffed, disliking the reminder that Wimborne was mine, not hers. "How interesting. A cousin, after all these years."

I could not breathe normally. I knew how to read between Catherine's words. She knew something was not quite right here.

Mr. Travers let loose that wide, contagious grin. "I am sure I will enjoy my stay very much if all my cousin's neighbors are so welcoming."

Catherine surprised me by smiling in return—though her smile was more like a cat about to claw one's eyes out. "I can see why you've kept him all to yourself, Ginny."

"Indeed," I said dryly. "I would hate to share such a specimen of manners and sophistication."

Catherine sat back in her seat, still eyeing Mr. Travers in a way that made unease curl inside me. "I'm afraid I must be off, but I look forward to furthering our acquaintance, Mr. Travers." She signaled for the driver to go on. "Good day."

Her carriage jolted forward and she departed with a dismissive wave, leaving behind the scent of her jasmine perfume. As soon as she was out of sight, I turned murderous eyes on Mr. Travers.

"What," I hissed, "was *that*?"

"That," he said, plucking a stray thread from his jacket sleeve, "was our way in."

"Forgive me, but our way into *where*?"

My obvious irritation did not seem to bother him at all. "Into Society. As your cousin, I can attend events while investigating our suspects, which, if your friend Miss Lacey is to be believed, includes Catherine Davenport. It is the perfect cover."

"No," I replied hotly. "The perfect cover would be if you actually *were* my cousin."

"And," he went on as if I hadn't spoken, "as your cousin, I can stay at Wimborne without suspicion. Two birds, one stone, as they say."

I hadn't thought of that. It *was* a good idea. Albeit a good idea with a very real problem. "Someone will discover us sooner or later."

"But by then, we will have found our perpetrator."

"You cannot guarantee that."

"I *can* guarantee that we have a better chance of stopping more vandalism through this plan than with any other."

"Even if you are right, of which I am not at all convinced, you might have asked my opinion before taking me by surprise like that."

"Yes, that would not have been suspicious." He held up a finger as if playacting. "Ah, Mrs. Davenport, wait a moment before we are introduced. Your sister and I need to have a heated argument about *if* or *how* we are related."

I pinched the bridge of my nose. It sometimes seemed he said such outlandish things just to provoke a reaction, as if he was testing me. It was absolutely infuriating. But this went beyond teasing me. How could he take such a risk? Hadn't he mentioned his concern for my reputation?

But I could not deny the simplicity of the solution. As my cousin, he could stay at Wimborne. Regardless of my personal feelings for him, the safety of my home was my foremost priority. As for Catherine . . . well, it no longer seemed so terribly ridiculous that she might be behind Wimborne's misfortunes. The calculating way she'd spoken to Mr. Travers. Her sly eyes. Was it possible that she was involved? I sighed. If she *was*, then I needed Mr. Travers to help me hold her accountable.

I exhaled and lowered my hand. "I suppose I haven't got a choice," I said. "What's done is done. But are you certain you can play the part of a gentleman?"

A strange shadow crossed his eyes. He looked away. "Yes, I can play the part," he said. "You needn't worry on that account."

I furrowed my brow. What had caused that shadow?

When he turned back, it was gone. "I will go to town and fetch my things and explain the change in plan to Wily."

"Oh." Inviting Mr. Travers to Wimborne was one thing. Inviting his less-than-honorable cohort was another entirely. "I . . . I had not intended—"

He smirked. "I would not expect you to take Wily too. A woman can only endure so many criminal types in her home at once."

"The fact that you consider yourself a criminal type does not reassure me."

He dismissed that with a wave of his hand. "I'll need Wily in town to pursue leads and contacts. He would hate being cooped up in a house all day."

"It's a very nice house," I said, though why I cared what a fence might think of my home was beyond me.

He raised an eyebrow, the twitch of his lips giving him away.

I cleared my throat. "I'll have a room readied for you. We are fortunate you met only a few of my staff, who can be trusted to be discreet."

He turned his horse toward town. "Good. I'll return shortly."

"Perhaps armed?" I hinted. I did not keep a weapon in the house.

He flipped back his jacket, revealing a pistol strapped to his side. "I always am, Miss Wilde."

He urged his horse into a canter and disappeared into the twilight.

CHAPTER 8

"The thief-taker will be staying here?" Mrs. Betts stared at me, eyes wide. Marchant and Holloway stood beside my housekeeper, and if their expressions were anything to judge by, they shared her disbelief.

"Yes," I said, crossing my arms on my desk in what I hoped was a confident manner. "He will need a room for the duration of his stay, the length of which is uncertain at this time. Prepare a dinner tray for him tonight as well."

Marchant cleared his throat. "I assume, Miss Wilde, that you have considered the possible repercussions for inviting such a man to stay."

"Thoroughly." I raised my chin. Even after half a year as Wimborne's mistress, I still often felt the child many of my staff saw me as. "We will claim that Mr. Travers is my cousin, come to visit a few weeks. He will use the opportunity to not only ensure Wimborne's safety but to discover who our unwelcome trespasser is."

My housekeeper and butler shared a glance. They thought me foolish. I wanted to explain that Mr. Travers had not left me a choice, that even I thought the idea ridiculous and fraught with impossibilities. But then they would only distrust Mr. Travers more. I simply had to make the best of it.

"But what of your personal safety, miss?" Marchant pressed. "Your reputation?"

"We will do all we can," I said. "I shall trust you to watch Mr.

Travers while he is in the house, and I intend to have Holloway sleep in my room to further protect my reputation."

Holloway nodded immediately, though her teeth worried her lip.

"Of course, I do not entirely trust the man," I assured them. "But I do think he is our best chance at ending all this nonsense. To that end, the servants will need to believe he is truly my cousin, or this will all be for naught. Only we and Mr. Hewson in the stables know his true identity, and my reputation depends on us keeping that secret. Can I count on your help?"

Mrs. Betts's expression softened. "Yes, of course, Miss Wilde. It is a difficult situation, to be sure. We will do our part."

I nodded, grateful for her acquiescence.

Marchant still looked unconvinced. "Are you sure this is the best course of action, miss? Should we not try again to involve Mr. Northcott?"

"Mr. Northcott refuses to take me seriously," I pointed out, "and as such, I will act as I see fit."

Marchant pressed his lips together. I exhaled. "I need your help," I said softly, trying another method to appeal to him. "It is not the path I would have chosen, but it is the one I have been forced to travel. Will you help me, Marchant?"

He nodded. "I will, miss. You may count on me."

After they left my study, I sank back into my chair and inhaled deeply. In the weeks after Father's death, the leather chair had smelled of his pomade and pipe smoke. Comforting. Familiar. Haunting. But those scents had long faded, lost to the distant reaches of my memories.

I kicked off my shoes and curled my feet up beneath me, turning on my chair to face out the wide window, chin in my hand. What a mess I had gotten myself into. If Father was watching me from heaven, he was surely shaking his head with an indulgent smile.

"I am trying," I told him. "I am."

But I wished that so much of my plan did not depend on a man I hardly knew. Doubt began to creep back into my mind. Mr. Travers

would be staying *in my home*, a man as flirtatious as he was impetu-
ous. It was a sign of my desperation, depending on a near stranger.

Esse quam videri. To be, rather than to seem. At that moment, all
I wanted was to see everyone around me for who they truly were. My
path forward would be much clearer if I knew who was trying to harm
me and who stood as my friend.

Perhaps if I wished desperately enough, all my problems would
disappear and Father would again be alive. At the very least, I wished
that I had Father's watch back. The tumult of the last few days had
overshadowed that longing, but I felt it keenly now. I hated to think
of it in the grubby hands of some nibbler, hidden away in one of those
horrible flash houses or being sold for ale money.

I leaned my head against the back of my chair. The sun had disappeared beyond the trees and night came on swiftly now, the sky a
deepening blue and purple. It was beautiful—the shadows clinging
to the trees, the stars beginning to peek from the black folds of the
heavens. No doubt it was something my mother could have painted
beautifully.

I released my hold around my knees and sat up. Such skills were
beyond me, even if something inside me still wished to try. But I did
not have time for painting; I was frightfully behind on my paperwork.

Not to mention that the image of my easel and painting in a heap
was still scorched into my mind.

I took one more look out the window, which now reflected my
face, pale in the candlelight. I could see nothing beyond but a dark
void. I shivered, then stood and closed the curtains.

⚬⟨✕⟩⚬

After working a short while and then eating a quick evening
meal, I retired to the drawing room to wait for Mr. Travers. I took the
chance to write in my journal, detailing all that had happened since
my entry last night, as well as my feelings toward Mr. Travers.

Beatrice says he is handsome, I wrote. *As an impartial observer, I can admit she is right. A younger, more fanciful version of myself would have been quite taken with Mr. Travers and his dark features. It seems unfair for someone to be so intelligent and attractive. But I know better than to fall for his tricks. No doubt he is accustomed to using his good looks to manipulate and coerce.*

I paused, not sure I believed my own words. Despite his impulsive actions with Catherine, I'd seen another side of Mr. Travers today, both in town and during our ride. Still . . .

I must be on my guard, I wrote to end my entry.

Writing had always helped me examine my emotions and sort out my problems. When I was eight years old, Father and I had first read *Gulliver's Travels* together. I'd been swept up in the tale and had insisted I needed to write an account of my own life, which would surely be as interesting as Gulliver's. Father bought me a beautiful leather-bound book, and I'd filled it with observations and awful poems and silly stories. As I grew older, I grew more thoughtful in my writing, and eventually my journal became a refuge, one that I'd needed more and more in recent days.

As I set down my pen, I heard horse hooves on the drive, then the murmur of voices as Mr. Travers was taken to his room. I bit at one of my nails. He was here. A strange man in my home.

To protect *my home,* I told myself. I thought of the way he'd grabbed me in the alleyway that morning, putting himself between me and the danger he thought was coming. If nothing else, I did believe he'd had only good intentions. He *had* been trying to protect me.

If only he didn't say such ridiculous things all the time, he would be much easier to trust.

Mrs. Betts appeared in the open doorway. "Mr. Travers will be down after eating," she said. "I told him you wished to see him."

"Thank you, Mrs. Betts."

I paced for a quarter hour before I heard slow, careful steps on the stairs, as if Mr. Travers was inspecting every inch of my home. I straightened when he stepped into the drawing room, his gaze sweeping across the room to find me.

"Good evening," I said briskly. "Have you settled in? Is the room to your liking?"

He swept a hand through his dark curls, taking in the room around me. "I shall miss my lumpy straw mattress and the raucous singing at The Bull's Head, but I suppose it'll do."

I allowed that a smile. I was adjusting to his quick humor, which oddly reminded me of Beatrice. "That would be a yes, then?"

"Quite," he said. "Your home is charming, truly."

I hadn't expected that. "Thank you, Mr. Travers."

"Mr. Travers? That will not do," he said. "If we are to be cousins, you must call me Jack."

I laughed. "You might be staying in my home, but I shall not dispense with all rules of propriety, *Mr. Travers*."

He waved a hand. "We'll work on that." He moved around the edges of the room. "Now for some logistics. I will keep my patrols to between the hours of eleven and five, so your staff does not wonder why your cousin wanders the house with his pistols at the ready."

"Eleven to five?" I furrowed my brow. "When will you sleep?"

He shrugged, apparently unconcerned. "If there is anything my time in His Majesty's army taught me, it is to sleep in whatever circumstances I can find. You needn't worry about that."

"The army?" I moved to my armchair. "I thought you were a Bow Street man."

"I was both." He stuck his hands in his pockets. "I bought a commission in the army at the behest of my father. But I never took to soldiering. After a few years, I left and followed a friend of mine to Bow Street, which was a much better match of my talents."

"I see." That was a lie, because nothing this man did made any sense to me. A career in the army seemed a superior option, especially as an officer. And who might Mr. Travers's father be to afford a commission? I traced my finger along the edge of my chair. "And your father, does he live in London as well?"

Mr. Travers raised an eyebrow. "Perhaps you ought to take up detection, Miss Wilde, with such a subtle question as that."

"I do not mean to pry—"

He shook his head. "No, if there is anything I understand, it is curiosity. I daresay you might trust me more if you know a little about me." He looked down, examining the rug beneath his feet. "My father is the right honorable Earl of Westincott."

"An earl?" I blurted out. I could not have stopped my tongue for a thousand pounds. I'd been matching wits with a member of the peerage? I'd *struck* a member of the peerage?

"Before you go feeling too intimidated," he said dryly, "be assured that my father would never acknowledge our relation in public. I was born on the wrong side of the blanket, if you take my meaning."

I blinked. "Oh." I tried to hide my reaction, though I surely did a poor job of it. Was he in earnest? Or did he only mean to shock me, as he was wont to do? But no, his expression was perfectly staid, no hint of jest. I cleared my throat. What would a woman who was unaffected by such news say? "I am sorry?"

He grinned. "I am not. I admit that the money would be a boon, but I'd sooner cross the river Styx than suffer the responsibilities of such a title."

My mind spun with questions. He was an illegitimate son of an earl. Who, then, was his mother? I stopped myself. That line of questioning brought forth far too much awkwardness, and I did not want to offend the man who was currently responsible for my safety.

"No, my life suits me fine," he went on. "I have all the advantages of the expensive education paid for by my father, but I live as I wish."

"*That* is how you knew Latin," I said, eager for a new subject. "I did wonder."

He laughed. "It has been useful a surprising number of times."

"Is the cant of thieves rooted in Latin, then?"

"Oh, yes," he said. "It is positively academic in those circles."

I realized I was smiling. I pressed my lips together and looked away.

"I am not what you expected in a thief-taker," Mr. Travers observed. "Am I?"

"Not in the least," I said. "Though I thought you preferred 'special investigator.'"

He stopped before the fire and leaned an elbow on the mantel, shooting me a mischievous smile. "In truth, I don't care what you call me. I only said that because it seemed to irk you."

"Yes, offending potential clients is always a good way to expand business."

He laughed again, the sound both full and bounding. The laugh of a man who held nothing of himself back.

"Forgive me," he said. "I know I come across as brash. But I spent too many years being proper and polite and dreadfully dull, and I've since learned there is no surer path to unhappiness than by pretending to be something I am not. As a result, I tend to let my mouth run more than I should, if only to prove to myself that I can."

I tipped my head. "Why would you need to pretend?"

He paused, eyeing me. "Being the baseborn son of an earl gives one a peculiar life," he said finally. "I had the upbringing of a gentleman, and yet I will never be accepted as one. For so long I fought against that fact, determined to prove to my father that I was worthy of his attention. I've since realized I do not want that. I simply want to live my own life, beholden to no man."

I tried not to stare at him but I could not help it. Here was a man who knew precisely who he was, while I was still trying to discover who *I* was. A small tendril of envy wound through me. If I had even a hundredth of the confidence this man possessed, how different might my life be?

"Now," he said, pushing himself off the mantel. "I've given you a secret of mine. I think you ought to offer me one in exchange."

I allowed one side of my mouth to curl upward. "Why would I do that?"

"Mutual trust?"

"I hardly care if you trust *me*."

He narrowed his eyes in mock concern. "How do I know you will not rob me in my sleep?"

"I daresay that is simply a risk of your trade, Mr. Travers."

He grinned again, and I wanted nothing more than to smile back. He had a face that drew me in, made me forget my hesitancies and apprehension. My heart ticked a beat faster.

I checked myself. I couldn't be too friendly with Mr. Travers. This was a business arrangement, nothing more. There was too much at stake already without blurring the lines between employer and employee.

I stood. "I will bid you goodnight. You may send for Mrs. Betts or Marchant if you need anything."

He bent his head. "Of course. Good night."

On instinct, I bobbed a curtsy. He *was* the son of an earl, after all. But he looked so amused that I immediately flushed and retreated to the door.

Even in my embarrassment I paused, hand resting on the door handle. This was my home. Everything I valued most in the world was within these walls. I glanced back at him and saw that he watched me.

I cleared my throat but couldn't find the words I needed. He found them for me.

"You *can* trust me, Miss Wilde," he said gently, his blue eyes intent. A curious tingle uncurled inside my chest. "I promise I will do my best to keep you and your home safe."

His words wrapped around me. I'd known this man only a few days, and in that time he'd nearly driven me mad with his flirting and flippancy. And yet somehow I believed him.

Somehow, I *did* trust him.

"Thank you, Mr. Travers," I whispered, then slipped from the room.

CHAPTER 9

If I thought having an armed man in my house ready to defend me against any and all attackers would help me fall into a blissful sleep, I was sadly mistaken. Even though I'd decided to trust him, knowing that Mr. Travers was walking the corridors of my house set me on edge. I kept squinting at the faint line of moonlight shining beneath my door, as if I might see his shadow cross it, but I never did.

Holloway slept on a trundle on the floor, and while in theory her presence also should have helped me sleep, it only added to my difficulty. Her breathing, the shifting of her body, and the creaks of her bed continually pulled me from crossing over into blessed oblivion.

Still, even with all my tossing and turning, my listening to every tick of the mantel clock, I managed to snatch a few hours of rest. At least my crippling fear was tempered. Perhaps I might even return the knife from my bedside table to the kitchen.

After Holloway helped me dress and arrange my hair, I dismissed her and turned back to the dressing table, leaning forward to inspect my reflection. I looked tired, my skin pale, with gray smudges beneath my eyes. I had never paid much attention to my toilette—who had time for intricate hairstyles when a simple chignon did the trick? But today I lingered, turning my head back and forth, running my fingers over my cheekbones and down my jaw. Then I straightened. I dabbed some rouge on my cheeks and lips, then rifled through a drawer for my small silver comb, embellished with seed pearls. I tucked it into my hair.

I paused when I spotted the little flask of perfume in the drawer. Father had given me the scent for my twenty-third birthday, orange flower and amber. The memory raced back to me, strong as the gusting wind outside my window. Father's dancing eyes and content smile when I opened his gift, the weight of his arms around me as I'd embraced him.

When Father had given it to me, I'd been determined to save it for special occasions. But three days after my birthday, Father had died, and no occasions were special after that.

I closed the drawer.

I took one last look at myself. It was only a slight improvement, but it was more for my state of mind than anything. Perhaps Holloway had been right the other day, that I needed to take more time for myself. Constant work and fretting could not be good for one's health.

But I *would* draw the line at going for a walk.

I headed downstairs, leaning over the railing as I peered toward the breakfast room. The door was ajar, so I approached quietly. Mr. Travers sat at the table, his back to me, reading a newspaper folded beside his heaping plate of honey cakes, toast, and eggs. I took a moment to observe him, since he would think far too much of it if he caught me staring any other time. He wore a navy blue jacket, fitted well over his shoulders, and his dark curls were arranged into some semblance of order. His left hand drummed on the paper as he read, unable to be still even a moment. He sipped his tea slowly, as if he had all the time in the world.

"Never fear, Miss Wilde," he said. "I left some eggs for you."

Blast. He'd still caught me staring.

I raised my chin and swept into the room. "I do not like eggs, but thank you."

"Don't like eggs? Why did you have them made?"

I busied myself with a plate at the sideboard. "Father was fond of eggs. I imagined you might be as well."

Mr. Travers was quiet behind me, an unusual event. When I joined him at the table with my plate of honey cakes and a steaming cup of chocolate, he eyed me over his raised teacup. But I wanted none of his sympathy, so I flicked my napkin over my lap and addressed him immediately. "I assume you had no trouble last night?"

"None. Quiet as the grave."

I sighed. "Of course nothing would happen when you are here."

He raised an eyebrow.

"Not that I wish for another incident," I hurried to say. "I only want this nightmare over and done with."

"Believe me, I want that as well." He set down his tea. "I am going to meet with Wily today, and hopefully he will have some news regarding your watch. If you have the time, I would appreciate that list you mentioned yesterday, of your father's cases."

"Yes, I'll start on that this morning, though it might take some time. My journals are rather . . ." I paused. "Well, let us just say I was quite verbose as a young girl."

Mr. Travers adjusted the newspaper beside him. "Should I pretend surprise?"

"You think me loose-lipped?" I asked, truly curious. I'd always thought of myself as quiet, although perhaps that was simply in comparison to Beatrice.

"Well, not so loose as many," he said. "But you always have *something* to say."

I decided to ignore that and gestured at his broadsheets. "What paper is that? Not *The Little Sowerby Review*, I imagine."

He held it up for me to see—the *Hue and Cry*. I made a face. "You must have a strong appetite to read such things over a meal."

Father had also often read the *Hue and Cry*, a paper published by the Home Office that detailed recent crimes in London, missing property, wanted persons, and punishments carried out.

"One must stay apprised of the news in my profession," he said easily. "Even at the cost of eating toast over a necktie party."

"A what?"

He glanced up at me again. "A hanging, Miss Wilde."

I grimaced. "How crass."

"Remind me not to let Wily near you again."

"A good idea, regardless," I said. "We could never keep up the ruse of you being my cousin with him around."

"You do not think he could play my faithful valet?" He sat back in his chair. "Wily would be utterly offended."

"I *should* like to see him dress you after his own fashion," I said, smirking at the thought of Mr. Travers in Wily's flamboyant outfit from yesterday.

"You would like to see him dress me?"

I raised my fork at him, my cheeks pinking. "None of that, sir." How odd it was to be sitting here with Mr. Travers, discussing matters both serious and silly. I'd breakfasted alone since Father had died, and this felt . . . well, it almost felt nice.

He laughed and pushed back from the table. "I'll be a few hours in town. When I return, I'll keep watch around the estate. Perhaps we might paint your cousin as an avid horseman? In any case, I'll watch until dark, and then we can go over your list together."

The image came to me, the two of us sitting close to the fire, he looking over my shoulder at the list I held. I coughed and took a sip of tea. I was being ridiculous. "Sounds perfectly reasonable," I managed.

He tipped me a bow. "Until tonight, Miss Wilde."

I tried very hard *not* to let my eyes linger on his form as he left.

※

After relocating my stack of leather-bound journals from the shelves in my room to the study downstairs, I pulled the curtains open wide. It was a dreary day, with thick clouds and a blustery wind, so I lit a lamp for extra light before I sat at my desk. I pulled out paper,

pen, and ink, and opened the first journal, from the year Father had
been appointed magistrate. In the careful but unsophisticated hand
of my thirteen-year-old self, I'd written on the first page the dates this
journal covered—only spanning six months. Verbose was perhaps an
understatement. I would have to do a great deal of skimming.

I began reading. The first few entries were sparse, short recollec-
tions of childhood. A story of my governess despairing over teaching
me French, which I found utterly amusing. The time Beatrice and I
sailed boats made of newspaper down the stream. A quick note de-
scribing Father's birthday celebration with a few friends.

As I read, the entries grew longer and more detailed. By the time
I finished the second volume, my page of notes had been filled and
I reached for another. I discovered bits and pieces of Father's cases,
trickling through my own words. A poacher caught red-handed. A
highwayman shot by a constable. A maid accused of theft. I wrote
down everything—names, dates, details—anything that might be
useful.

If it had not been cloudy, the shadows would have moved across
my study, marking the passage of time. So, when my stomach growled
ferociously, I looked at the clock in some confusion. It was nearly
five o'clock and I hadn't eaten since breakfast. I would need to dress
for dinner soon—Mr. Travers would likely return any minute. I had
been so caught up in my own past that the hours had flown by. The
characters of my childhood danced across the pages, brought to life by
my memories of them. I wrote of Father most of all, the constant and
happy pillar that my life was built around.

I stretched my back, shaking out my writing hand. My desk was a
mess of pen shavings and ink blots, several of my journals lying open
as I consulted them. My notes had grown exponentially, and I hoped
Mr. Travers would be pleased. I wasn't finished—the journal before
me was from my nineteenth year—but I'd made excellent progress.

I marked my spot in one journal and moved to close it, but I
paused as I read the first lines of the next entry.

Father and I attended church today. Mr. Brixton's sermon was moving, and something in it seemed to touch Father in particular. When we left the church, we stopped at Mother's grave as we often do. I'd brought a sprig of foxglove to lay on her headstone.

This time was different. Father took my hand, squeezed it tight. I asked him what was wrong, concerned he was ill.

He shook his head. "Nothing is wrong, my dove. I am only so very happy. So very happy I have you."

Even now, hours after, I can still see his face in my mind's eye, tearful and joyful all at once. I do not know what thoughts brought on his words, but I hugged him for a long while. He is never appreciated as he should be, for the countless hours he sacrifices as magistrate. But I see him every day in his struggles, and I know the truth. I am the most fortunate of daughters to have such a man as my father.

Tears fell from my cheeks and splashed onto the page. I shoved the journal away, pressing the palms of my hands into my eyes as if that might stop the tears. But they came and they came and I could not stop them.

When Father died, I had wept and raged. *It isn't fair,* I'd shouted at the heavens. There were so many horrible people on the earth, people who hurt and stole. Why should God take a man who was doing his best to right life's many, many wrongs?

Six months had passed, and I still had no answer. I'd thrown myself into the running of Wimborne, surely far more than my steward or staff wished me to. I craved distraction. I did not let myself slow. But I couldn't hold it back any longer. What was missing inside me echoed like a hymn in an empty church. It tumbled and broke and bled. I tried to stifle my sobs, but they escaped in short, gasping breaths.

"Miss Wilde?"

I jerked my head up. A blurry figure stood in the doorway. Mr. Travers.

"Oh," I croaked. I stood too quickly, sending my pen clattering to the floor.

He hurried behind me, bending to pick up the pen. I wiped at my eyes and cheeks, which was pointless. My entire face was likely splotchy and swollen—I did not cry prettily.

"What's happened?" Mr. Travers asked, hand on the back of my chair.

I shook my head, refusing to meet his eyes as I fished around in a drawer for a handkerchief. My throat ached and I could not speak.

Mr. Travers said nothing as I turned away from him and tried to regain some control over myself. My handkerchief was soon wet through, but after a minute I could breathe again even if my eyes remained watery.

"Can I do anything to help?" His voice was gentle behind me.

I shook my head. "I—" My voice cracked. I cleared my throat. "I am sorry for that."

"You needn't apologize for being human, Miss Wilde."

I looked at him over my shoulder. "No, but it is hardly in your job description to console crying women."

He smiled. It was different from his usual arrogant grin. Kinder. "I promise I won't bill you for it."

I let out a slow, long breath, dabbing my nose once more. Then I nodded at the journals open on my desk. "I'm afraid I came across a difficult memory I was not expecting."

"May I?" he asked, stepping forward.

My emotions swam dangerously close to the surface, but it felt good to speak to someone. It distracted me from the abyss I'd just plunged into. I nodded.

Mr. Travers picked up the journal. "'Today Rupert Howard told me my red hair was unnatural and that I must be a witch. I told him to be careful during the next full moon and he paled so quickly I thought he might faint away.'"

He looked up at me, perplexed. I stared back at him. Then I laughed. I laughed so hard I had to sit and brace myself on my desk.

"You think," I said in between bouts of laughter, "that I was crying—crying over *that*?" I rubbed my forehead. "Heavens, Mr. Travers, do you think so little of me?"

"Quite the contrary," he insisted, chuckling. "Surely you can see why I was confused."

"No, I was not crying because a silly boy teased me as a girl," I said. "I actually find that memory rather amusing." I nodded at the other open journal, closer to me on the desk. "You simply picked up the wrong journal."

The room quieted as he read the short entry about Father. When he finished, he closed the journal and handed it to me. Our fingers brushed, the slightest of connections. I'd shaken this man's hand on our first meeting, but somehow this felt like . . . *more*. My face warmed.

"He sounds like a good man," he said as he stepped back.

"He was." I held the journal against my chest. "It caught me by surprise, is all. I haven't read most of these in years, and none since he died."

He sat across the desk. "You were right, you know. What you wrote there. You were very lucky to have such a father."

I hardly knew what to say to that, considering what he'd told me last night about *his* father.

"But," he went on, "that does not make your grief any easier to bear, I imagine."

"No," I said softly. "I daresay it makes it harder."

Silence fell between us, but it was a hushed tether that drew us together rather than pushed us apart. I could feel him looking at me, but I did not take my eyes from the desk before me. I had not expected Mr. Travers to be so thoughtful or understanding.

"If it would help," he said, "I would be happy to give this Rupert Howard a good trouncing."

I laughed again, though it made my throat hurt. "Actually, I do think it would make me feel better."

"It is settled, then." He grinned. "One trouncing, free of charge for the lady."

"Quite the bargain I am getting."

"You are an excellent negotiator."

I took a few deep breaths, then straightened and looked him in the eye. "Did you learn anything from Wily about my watch?"

He let me change the subject. "No, but it's only been a day. He'll need more time. His work is very subtle, you see. If someone hears him asking around about your watch, they'll know he wants it and the price will double. Or the thief might decide to skip town. Either way, it is better to be cautious."

"I understand," I said, folding my arms on my desk. "I am anxious to have it back, but I will try for patience."

"We both will be tested in patience, I think." He rubbed the back of his neck. "I spent the better part of the day patrolling the estate and saw nothing suspicious. Surveillance is a long game, unfortunately."

I nodded. "Perhaps your idea of setting a trap has merit."

"A compliment?"

I raised a playful eyebrow. "I said *perhaps*."

He leaned forward. "Well, if you—"

He stopped, his eyes caught by something over my shoulder. Then he rose, leaning on my desk and peering around me.

I turned on my chair. "What is it?"

"I thought I saw . . ." He came around to the window, pulling back the curtain more. The setting sun had broken through the heavy clouds, leaving orange streaks across the landscape.

"Saw what?" I joined him at the window, looking in the same direction. What was he searching for?

I saw it the same moment Mr. Travers stiffened. A flash, bright and winking, came from the tree line, and then a dark form dropped from a branch and darted away.

"Someone is out there!" I exclaimed.

But I spoke to an empty room. Mr. Travers was already gone.

CHAPTER 10

I dashed after him, skidding around the corner and pushing off the opposite wall as Mr. Travers sprinted to the entry. He must have heard my footsteps, because he turned back as he yanked open the front door. His eyes burned, his pistol in one hand.

"Stay in the house, Miss Wilde," he ordered, then disappeared into the howling wind.

Indignation kindled inside me. Had he forgotten this was *my* home? Who was he to shout orders like a general in the heat of battle? I wanted nothing more than to charge after him, to prove myself brave and capable.

But I stopped myself, bracing my arms in the open doorway, breathing hard. I'd *hired* Mr. Travers to protect my home. I would be a fool to put myself in jeopardy to prove a point.

And that look in his eyes—that glint of danger—made me realize how very little I knew about the man.

I watched from the doorway, the wind whipping my hair around my face and into my eyes. Mr. Travers was halfway to the tree line now, the branches and leaves dancing in the wind. I peered into the distance, looking for any sign of that dark form. What had that flash been? Not a lantern or torch. More like the reflection of a mirror.

Mr. Travers stopped beneath the enormous elm tree, pistol at the ready, peering in every direction. He crouched, inspecting the ground. Then he strode into the trees without looking back.

Now what was I to do? I couldn't let him go all alone. Should I rally my manservants to his aid? But Mr. Travers knew what he was doing. If I sent anyone after him, they might get in his way or, worse, be harmed somehow.

I was still debating when he appeared again a minute later. He was far enough from me that I could not hear him, but I was fairly certain he was using words I wouldn't appreciate. He started back toward the house, and when it was clear I was in no immediate danger, I hurried across the grass to meet him. It had rained earlier, and my slippers were soon soaked through, the hem of my skirt clinging to my legs.

When he looked up and saw me, he scowled.

"I told you to stay in the house," he said crossly.

I ignored him. "What happened?"

He shook his head, a sharp jerk. "He's gone. From the look of the tracks, he had a horse hidden in the wood." He paused. "I found this."

He held out a small brass spyglass. I stared at it.

"Do you mean to say . . ." I swallowed. "Someone was watching us?"

His jaw tightened. "Someone was watching *you*."

The hot energy that had engulfed me since spotting the intruder vanished. I suddenly wanted to sit down, right there on the sodden grass, exhausted and afraid. I was being watched by a stranger. I braced my hands on my waist and stared into the trees, breathing harder now than I had after running the length of Wimborne.

Mr. Travers took my arm, his touch gentle. "I think we ought to get you some tea," he said quietly. "And something to eat."

"I am perfectly all right," I managed, though I allowed him to steer me back the way we'd come.

"Of course you are." Though his voice held a trace of amusement, it did not feel patronizing. "But tea will help all the same."

He guided me into the house, past a bewildered footman who was no doubt wondering why we'd gone for a walk in such blustery weather, and back into the study. He sat me down by the fire, yanked closed the curtains, and rang for tea.

I tried to compose myself. I could not afford to collapse into tears for the second time in a half hour. I steadied my breathing, staring into the fire and grasping the arms of my chair.

After a maid brought the tray of tea, Mr. Travers poured a cup, adding cream and sugar and handing it to me. Then he placed a chair across from me and sat. He looked pointedly at my tea. I took a sip, the heat plunging down my throat and warming my stomach.

"Miss Wilde, did you recognize that man?" he asked, leaning on his elbows.

The memory played in my head, the figure wrapped in shadows dropping from the tree. I shook my head. "No."

"Did you notice anything about him that could help identify him?"

"He *was* tall," I offered. "But that only confirms what you already deduced, which does not help."

He exhaled. "No, it does not. Although the fact that he had a horse was telling. It is no small thing to afford a mount, so either he is relatively well off, or he hired it. It does narrow the field a bit."

Our talking was helping me focus. I straightened, resting my tea on my lap. "Perhaps he stole it. You might look into recent horse thefts."

He gave a half smile. "I'll make a regular investigator of you yet."

"A female thief-taker?"

"It's not unheard of," he said with a wink.

I tried to smile back but failed miserably. Mr. Travers sobered and clasped his hands between his knees.

"I know that was startling," he said. "But in truth, it was good what happened."

"Yes, I often wish for Peeping Toms to terrorize my estate."

He raised an eyebrow. "Drink more tea," he ordered. "You are feistier than usual."

I narrowed my eyes but obeyed.

"I meant it was good we *caught* him at it," he said. "My guess is that he used his spyglass to ascertain when and where he could approach the house undeterred."

Thoughts clicked in my head. "And perhaps to learn what might hurt me most. My watch. My painting."

He nodded. "But now we know his strategy, and now *he* knows the house is protected. He will think twice about returning."

"You think he might give up?"

"It is possible. Thieves are not known for their courage. The slightest opposition is enough to frighten off most ne'er-do-wells."

That was an encouraging thought. And yet— "But we do not believe him to be a common thief, do we?"

Mr. Travers sat back in his chair. "No. From the evidence, I would wager this intruder has malice in his heart."

But who? And why? Determination stirred inside me. Whoever it was, I would not let them strike again. I would protect my home.

"Well," I said briskly. "Let us not waste any more time." I set down my tea and went to my desk, gathering the notes I'd taken and handing them to Mr. Travers. "It is not complete, but I hope it will be a good start."

He flicked through the papers, reading quickly.

"There are a few more promising than others. Like that one there." I bent and pointed at the top of the second paper. "Hammon Palmer."

"Caught housebreaking and sentenced with transportation," Mr. Travers read. "Hardly a threat if he is an ocean away in New Holland."

"Not Hammon himself," I said. "But his father. The man was beside himself with rage and threatened my father."

Mr. Travers looked up at me. "How do you know this?"

I lifted one shoulder. "Mr. Palmer came to Wimborne, drunk and shouting. I heard everything."

It had been terrifying as a girl, hearing threats against my father. It was the first time I had realized that not everyone loved him as I did. My journal had consoled me that night.

Mr. Travers nodded, though his eyes were still intent on me. I pointed at another name. "This one also stood out to me. Matthew Rockwell, a coiner and horse thief. He was sentenced to hang two years ago but escaped before it was carried out."

I took him through the notes, pointing out cases of particular interest. Mr. Travers was oddly quiet, interrupting only a few times to ask a furthering question.

"It seems you have done all my work for me," he said when I finished, straightening the papers. "Are you sure you are committed to Wimborne? I could use an assistant like you."

"Just the life every girl dreams of," I said dryly.

"I am in the habit of making dreams come true," he said with a rakish grin.

I shook my head, though the corners of my lips turned up. It seemed strange how comfortable I felt with Mr. Travers. I ought to be racked with shame and guilt, sitting here alone with an unmarried man, and a thief-taker, no less. But somehow in the last two days, Mr. Travers had begun to feel less like a hired man and more like a friend.

I straightened. That was an alarming thought to have. I could not be friends with a thief-taker, no matter how charming. It was already risky enough, allowing him to stay at Wimborne. I could allow nothing but professionalism between us.

I stood, smoothing my skirts. "I'm going to bed." The room had grown dark around us while we'd talked, lit only by the flickering of the fire.

Mr. Travers focused his attention back on my notes. "Yes, get some rest. I'll need that brilliant brain of yours again tomorrow."

I stared at him. He hadn't said it in that teasing, flirtatious way of his but rather matter-of-factly. I could not remember the last time I'd been complimented on anything besides my appearance or performance at the pianoforte. My chest warmed, a pool of sunlight in summer.

I cleared my throat. "You are aware tomorrow is Sunday?"

He looked up again, bewildered. "Is it? Blast. That does put a damper on my plans. I'd hoped to start working through the list, interview and assess our possible suspects."

"I will attend services in the morning," I said, "but perhaps after—"

His eyes lit up. "Excellent. I will join you."

"You wish to come to church?"

He tapped his temple. "It is the perfect time to use my cover as your cousin. Mrs. Davenport will be there, I assume?"

"Unfortunately." Catherine had a way of making every other woman in attendance look wan and colorless in comparison.

"Then I will use this as an opportunity to further charm her."

I frowned. After our fright that evening, it seemed ridiculous to think Catherine was involved. Would she really hire someone to harass me? But then an image of her face came to mind, from when Father's solicitor had read the will and announced that I would be inheriting Wimborne and everything in it. Everything that was Father's. Catherine's glare had been so piercing I'd truly worried that looks *could* kill.

I sighed and moved to the door. "Are you not overwhelmed by the enormity of our task? How many possible culprits there are? I am exhausted just thinking of it."

"Better to have too many suspects than none," he said.

"I hadn't pegged you as an optimist."

"And I hadn't pegged you as a woman who gives up easily."

I looked back at him. He watched me, his features bathed in the warm glow of the fire. At some point, he'd loosened his cravat and thrown his jacket over the back of his chair. I hadn't even noticed, so involved in our conversation I had been. His hair was tousled, his eyes alight.

He looked utterly indecent.

I thought I'd prepared myself for the ramifications of allowing Mr. Travers to stay here at Wimborne. But I hadn't fully accounted for the fact that he was handsomer than any man I'd ever seen.

What had I gotten myself into?

I swallowed so hard I nearly choked. "Good night, Mr. Travers," I managed.

Then I fled.

CHAPTER 11

I'd never found it particularly difficult to focus on the vicar's sermons before. Mr. Brixton was a lively speaker, full of spiritual knowledge and the unique ability to make ancient scripture come alive with modern parallels. Though I missed Father, I relished the chance every Sunday to sit in the echoing beauty of the Little Sowerby chapel, with its stained-glass windows and towering belfry. I *enjoyed* listening in church.

That was before I sat through a service with Mr. Travers.

"Is anyone here on your list?" he whispered as he leaned close. His breath stirred the hair near my ear, tickling me. I rubbed my ear, irritated.

"No," I managed. "Though I cannot get a good look at the gallery."

"Who is that?" He gave a pointed nod. "The man ahead."

"Mr. Cardale." I barely moved my lips. "He owns the print shop."

Mr. Travers did not miss a beat. "What about the woman behind him? She keeps looking at us."

"*Everyone* is looking at us." Even with our story of him being my cousin, I could not like the attention. It meant more people to convince of the ruse.

"You can hardly blame them." He grinned as he straightened his cravat. He was no better dressed than any other man in attendance in his dark green jacket and tan breeches, but his was not the figure of a leisurely country gentleman. Far too many ladies had tracked him as we'd come down the aisle earlier, and he was clearly well aware of that fact.

I gripped my prayer book, wishing I could use it to smack him upside the head. Would it be considered sacrilege if I only did it in order to hear the sermon?

"If you will please refrain from speaking," I said through my teeth, "I will answer your questions to your heart's content after the service."

"And what if my heart is only content when your face turns as red as your hair?"

I shook my head, using every last drop of willpower I had to stop myself from blushing. He really would say anything to gain a reaction from me, wouldn't he? "I no longer wonder why Bow Street didn't want you."

If I thought an insult would do the trick, I was mistaken. He only chuckled, the sound reverberating in his chest. "Well played, Miss Wilde."

But he did quiet, crossing his legs and tapping his hat against his knee. The man could not sit still for even a moment.

Beatrice caught my eye from across the aisle, her eyebrow raised as high as the soaring chapel beams above us. I had wanted to find her before the service started, to ensure she did not say anything about who Mr. Travers really was, but she had arrived late with her family.

Now I sent her a pleading look, begging her to keep quiet until I had a chance to speak with her. She nodded, though her eyes danced with laughter. Of course she would find this amusing.

I tried again to focus on Mr. Brixton's sermon, but his words felt elusive, flighty. They refused to settle in my mind. Other thoughts—dark, frightening thoughts—pressed in around them. Even with Mr. Travers again patrolling the house last night, I had not slept well. Would I ever again?

I let my gaze run over the congregation, inspecting my fellow parishioners. I'd told Mr. Travers the truth—I didn't recognize anyone from my list. But then, I'd never met most of them, and the ones I did have memories of I was recalling through the haze of childhood. That same hopelessness from last night crept through my chest. What if we never caught the culprit? Would I have to live with this dread forever? I doubted Mr. Travers wanted to play the role of bodyguard for the rest of my life.

I spotted Mr. Northcott looking back at me from a few rows ahead. I studiously avoided his gaze, trying not to imagine what he thought of me sitting here beside a strange man.

When the last prayer was said and the soaring notes sung by the parish choir had faded, I breathed a sigh of relief. Which was incredibly foolish considering who I sat beside. Mr. Travers was on his feet in a flash, his eyes roving over the slow-moving crowd.

"Ah," he said. "There is Mrs. Davenport. Perhaps if I am particularly charming, we'll receive an invitation to a dinner party or musicale."

He held up his hand in greeting, beaming profusely. Catherine gave the barest nod in return, her expression indifferent. I cast my eyes heavenward. He looked like a witless milksop.

He noticed my look, of course. "You doubt my abilities."

"I am doubting everything about you right now."

His eyes narrowed. "A wager, then. Five crowns says I can procure an invitation."

Five crowns? He was mad. "You must have me confused for someone with loose purse strings, Mr. Travers."

"So, you think I'll succeed and you're unwilling to pay?"

"On the contrary. Catherine does not take well to strangers." Or to half sisters. Or to anyone, really.

"If you are so confident I will fail," he said, leaning close, "then I do not see the issue."

The challenge in his eyes was too much for me to refuse. Besides, I knew what he did not—Catherine did not just dislike me. She *hated* me. And if she hated me, then she would certainly hate any cousin of mine. Mr. Travers had a better chance of successfully swimming the Channel to France than he did of garnering an invitation from Catherine Davenport.

"Very well," I said. "On Friday, Catherine is hosting a ball. It is the talk of the town." I, of course, had not been invited. "If you somehow manage to obtain an invitation . . ."

"Five crowns?" he asked.

"Five crowns," I agreed. "And I'll try not to laugh too hard when she sends you running."

He placed his hat on his head at a jaunty angle. "So little faith, Miss Wilde. So little faith."

We moved to the door, and although the vicar was undoubtedly curious about my never-before-mentioned cousin, he greeted us briefly, for which I was grateful. Coming down the steps, Mr. Travers straightened his jacket.

"Observe carefully," he said. "You might learn something."

Before I could offer a laugh of derision, he was striding across the church yard to where Catherine held court with her friends. I moved closer to watch. If nothing else, it would be entertaining to see Mr. Travers's unrelenting confidence take a beating.

"Ginny!" Beatrice pulled me beneath the shadow of the belfry, her eyes wide. "Why on earth was the thief-taker sitting in your pew box? I had to pretend ignorance when Mama asked who he was."

"Hush," I whispered. "Someone will hear you."

"Then you had better explain fast."

I quickly summarized the incident at the conservatory and our run-in with Catherine on the road and Mr. Travers's careless lie about being my relation.

"So you see," I concluded. "It is preposterous and yet I must play along or Catherine will know everything."

Beatrice stared. Then she let out a disbelieving laugh. "Your cousin? Ginny, I do think this is the funniest thing I have ever heard."

"Yes, it is hilarious," I said dryly, "when it is not *your* reputation at stake."

She waved that off. "Oh, do not worry. It is so absurd no one will ever believe it." She craned her head around me. "What is he doing now?"

"He has delusions that he will obtain invitations to Catherine's ball."

Beatrice dropped her voice. "Is Catty a suspect then?"

"Everyone is, apparently."

She nodded behind me. "Including Mr. Davenport?"

I peered over my shoulder. To my surprise, Mr. Travers was not standing beside Catherine. Instead, he was engaged in earnest conversation with her husband, Mr. Davenport. Mr. Travers gestured wildly, telling some story, and Mr. Davenport listened with an expression crossed between amusement and delight. Catherine watched from where she stood with her friends, eyes narrowed.

I shook my head. "Nothing that man does makes any sense to me."

Movement from the church caught my attention—Mr. Northcott paused at the top of the stairs, looking over the lingering crowd. His eyes met mine and I pointedly looked away. I had not yet forgiven him for either of our recent conversations.

But he started toward me anyway. I grimaced. "I must go. Mr. Northcott has a determined look in his eye."

Beatrice saluted. "I shall protect your retreat."

I smiled and kissed her on the cheek. "Thank you. I'll visit soon. Heaven knows I'll need to escape from Mr. Travers too."

Beatrice gave a short laugh. "Must be difficult, having a handsome, charming gentleman in such close quarters."

I cut her a glare but had no time to offer a retort as I hurried across the yard toward where Mr. Travers and Mr. Davenport spoke. How to interrupt without looking rude?

Mr. Travers solved my dilemma for me. "Ah, Ginny!" he said upon spotting me.

My stomach flipped. Only my friends called me Ginny. Well, my friends or Catherine when she wished to be particularly condescending. I did not know how to feel hearing Mr. Travers throw my name about so casually.

He waved me closer. "Join us. Mr. Davenport and I were just becoming better acquainted."

Catherine's glare warned me off, and yet what could I do? My face heated as I stepped forward. "Good day, Mr. Davenport."

"Good day, Genevieve," he said with a pleasant smile. I'd always liked him, even if he was generally happy to stay beneath Catherine's thumb. He at least had a kind disposition. I'd never quite understood what drove him to marry my half sister.

"Your brother-in-law was just telling me about the fishing on his estate," Mr. Travers said. "I am only passable at the sport, but I do enjoy it every now and again."

I forced a tight smile. Could he be any more conspicuous?

But Mr. Davenport seemed oblivious to Mr. Travers's motivation. "You must join me sometime. I shall ask Catherine. She has our lives scheduled rather tight." He leaned toward us. "She cannot resist a party."

Catherine stiffened at her husband's openness, and I caught my breath. Mr. Davenport spoke as if his wife simply liked to socialize. I knew better. Catherine and I were similar in only one way—we hid from our sorrows and fears by keeping occupied. She'd never spoken before about the absence of any children in her life, but Father had often whispered to me in broken tones about her grief. It was something I reminded myself of when she was needlessly cruel. We all fought our own battles, some more personal than others.

"Oh, I love a party," Mr. Travers said quickly. "Balls, in particular. There is nothing like the energy and excitement of a dance."

The utter ridiculousness. And yet Mr. Davenport did not turn suspicious, as Catherine would have. Instead, he brightened even more.

"We are hosting a ball at Harpford House on Friday," he exclaimed. "You must attend."

I whipped my head to stare at Catherine, who was gaping at her husband. Mr. Davenport seemed to realize at the same moment what he'd done. He stood stock-still, smile pressed onto his lips.

But it was too late.

"Nothing would delight me more!" Mr. Travers clapped his hands. "Ginny, are you not thrilled at our good luck?"

I swallowed. "I . . . I do believe we are otherwise engaged that day—"

"Nonsense," Mr. Travers said. "Surely we can postpone anything for our dear Davenports."

Our dear Davenports looked half aghast and half murderous. Mr. Davenport glanced at his wife before pulling back his shoulders. "Yes," he said firmly. "You must come. Both of you."

I tried to keep my mouth from dropping. Mr. Davenport never did anything to upset the delicate balance of his marriage, knowing it was simply not worth a fight with Catherine. This was outright rebellion for him.

Despite the warning in my mind, my heart softened at the sincerity of Mr. Davenport's gaze. How could I refuse now?

I sighed. "We should be glad to attend. Thank you for the invitation."

Mr. Travers bowed. "Indeed! How kind you are, Mr. Davenport, to include me."

He was making an utter fool of himself. I forced a smile and offered a curtsy to Mr. Davenport before taking Mr. Travers's arm and yanking him away.

"What is your hurry?" he said. "You've already lost the five crowns."

"You cheated," I protested. "You were meant to receive the invitation from Catherine."

"I do not believe that was specified."

"It was *assumed.*"

"Then it is a hard lesson you've learned," he said as we reached my coach. "Never assume when money is on the line."

He held out a hand to help me inside. I wanted to refuse him, but there were more than just Catherine's eyes watching us. I had no choice but to take his hand, large and foreign around my own. He stepped closer to help me inside, bringing with him that whispered scent of cedar. I tried to ignore the strength I felt in his hand, the warmth between us, and I did not let myself look at him as he joined me inside. He had the uncanny ability to read my mind at the most inopportune moments.

Instead, I peered back the way we'd come. Catherine had marched to her husband's side and now whispered into his ear. Mr. Davenport's expression was difficult to read, but I doubted he was enjoying whatever lecture his wife was delivering. Still, it was difficult not to feel some satisfaction in seeing Catherine on the defensive. It happened so rarely.

Further on, I could see Beatrice talking animatedly with Mr. Northcott, who listened with polite disinterest. I owed her an enormous favor.

"In any case," Mr. Travers went on, "this will allow me to investigate your sister more closely. One can learn a great deal by simple observation."

"*Careful* observation," I corrected, straightening my skirts. "Catherine Davenport is no fool, and we should not take her for one."

I tapped on the roof, and the coach started forward, bumping along the cobblestone road. Mr. Travers shook his head, leaning back against the seat cushions. Gone was the foppish dandy from the church yard. He looked thoughtful, calculating.

"I never underestimate an opponent," he said. "We will be careful."

I sighed and nodded. I had little choice, after all.

"*After* you pay me my five crowns," he added with a saucy grin.

I threw my prayer book at him.

CHAPTER 12

The next few days passed quickly. I rarely saw Mr. Travers during daylight hours, as we were both caught up in our individual pursuits. He spent his time riding the estate or investigating the names on the list I'd given him. Meanwhile, I stayed safely tucked away in my study. Well, I *hoped* I was safe. I'd sharpened my letter opener and kept it within easy reach. Apparently, my anxiety was only eased by having a variety of pointy objects at my disposal.

I threw myself back into the running of Wimborne. This was the work I loved, knowing that what I did made a difference for those who depended on the estate. In between meetings about menus and counseling with my steward about a tenant behind in rent, I continued to read through my journals and make notes.

In the evenings, we dined together, as anything else would make my servants suspicious. We spoke of banal topics while the footmen served, then retreated to the privacy of the drawing room. Mr. Travers would give me a review of his work in town. He and Wily had seen no sign of my watch, and many of the names on my list had been crossed off without difficulty. Some no longer lived in Little Sowerby, others were serving prison sentences, and still others were long dead.

"This one here," Mr. Travers said, holding the list up to the light of the fire. "A Mr. Williams. Transported to New Holland. His family relocated to Kent after his trial, and from what I gather, they are

intent on putting the whole affair behind them. So I doubt they are
coming up to harass you."

I nodded my agreement as he went on.

"This next one," he said. "John Garvey. A poacher. Sentenced to
transportation but chose to join the army instead."

I remembered this one well, a case from a year previous, when
summer was high and hot. Father had been battling a ring of professional poachers who trapped in the country and sold their bounty to
the London market, desperate for game. It all came to a head when
the gang scuffled with a gamekeeper who defended his master's land.
The gamekeeper died from his injuries, and Father and his constables
had arrested the poacher responsible.

"Have you tracked him down?" I asked.

"My contact reports that he died on the continent last year," he
said, referring to his paper. "No sign of family in the area that I can see."

I sighed. It was all good news, really, that we were striking suspects from our list. Each elimination narrowed the field and made our
search more pointed. But it was taking so long. Any day, the vandal
could return and find some new way to frighten me.

Mr. Travers noticed my sigh. "It is simply a matter of time," he
said, folding the list and tucking it inside his jacket. "Something will
turn up."

"Let us hope so."

Mr. Travers was quiet a long moment, then sat forward in his
chair. "I did have something I wanted to tell you. This afternoon, one
of my peachers—"

"Your what?"

"Peacher. Informant." He waved a hand. "I have men all over who
come to me with bits of information, some useful, some not. For a
price, of course."

"Of course." I tried not to think too hard on what sort of men
these were.

"This man who came to me," he said, "had information about
your father."

My fingers had been toying with the fringe on my shawl, but now they stilled.

He leaned his elbows on his knees and interlocked his fingers. "He claimed," he said, voice hushed, "that your father had a mole among his men."

"A mole?" I repeated. "How do you mean?"

"He insisted that someone close to your father, someone aware of his actions and the movements of his constables, was selling that information."

My blood cooled. "What exactly would that achieve?"

"A great deal," he said. "If the magistrate—your father—sent out for an arrest, this inside man could warn off the offender. Or in the case of the highwaymen who have plagued Little Sowerby, he could reveal to them where the constables would patrol. From what I can tell, the local highwaymen have had a lucky run of it, haven't they?"

My mind flew back to my conversation with Mr. Northcott last week. Hadn't he said something along the same line?

"There might be something to this," I said. "Mr. Northcott himself told me he thought it odd that the highwaymen always evaded his patrols."

"Did he now?" Mr. Travers's eyes flashed curiously. "What of your father? Did he ever mention such a thing to you?"

"No. If he was worried, he kept it to himself." But even as I spoke the words, my memory turned back to the weeks before Father's death. He'd been quieter, tense, but whenever I asked him what was wrong, he always made excuses. After his death, I'd attributed it to ill health. But had it been something more?

I turned my gaze to the fire, suddenly too warm in the seriousness of our exchange. "Who might the mole be?" I asked, voice shaking. "A constable? I've never liked Mr. Crouth."

He shook his head. "We do not have proof that there *was* a mole. It is only hearsay, from one source, and it may not be connected to your current situation. I wanted you to be aware, but we would do better to direct our focus towards the main problem—the vandal."

My shoulders slumped. "Why is it always one step forward and two back?"

"There are ways to hasten the process," he said. "I've been careful until now, trying for subtlety rather than efficacy. But the underworld is not terribly loyal. A few bribes placed in the right hands . . ."

"The right hands," I repeated slowly, turning to face him. "Criminals, you mean."

"Naturally."

My pulse ticked faster. He could not be serious. Did he truly mean to bribe highwaymen? Coiners? Thieves? A new vision came to mind: Mr. Travers meeting with a faceless shadow in a dark alleyway, a whisper, the glint of a knife—

"That is far too dangerous," I blurted.

His brow furrowed. "Is that not the reason you hired me?"

"I . . ." I cleared my throat. "Well, yes, of course, but surely there must be another way."

Mr. Travers leaned forward, the flickering light from the fire catching the sloped angles of his nose and cheekbones—and the upward turn of his lips. "Are you *worried* for me, Miss Wilde?"

I raised my chin. "For my investment in you, perhaps."

But his grin persisted. "Never fear, my lady. I assure you I have bested my fair share of riffraff. I am not worried in the slightest."

"Good," I said briskly. "Then that makes two of us."

I excused myself soon after as I had done every night, though it was only nine o'clock. I was far from tired, and yet I had to. I could not make a habit of spending unnecessary time with Mr. Travers. He never said a word of argument when I left so early, and tonight was no different.

Besides, I needed to think. Mr. Travers's revelation had spun me around, the possibility that someone had been working against Father. We didn't know for certain, of course, but I could not stop myself from examining every person Father had worked with, from his constables to his clerks to the town watchmen. Could one of them have betrayed Father?

Hearsay, I reminded myself. It was hearsay. But I had to be prepared for the truth.

I would settle for nothing less.

❧❊❧

I awoke with a start, heart pounding as I sat up in bed.

I'd heard . . . something. I'd just drifted off after my usual tossing and turning—which had been particularly bad tonight, my thoughts full of Father—when a noise had jerked me from the haze of sleep.

Holloway's soft snores still drifted up from the floor beside me, so it must not have been as loud as I'd thought. I peered about my bedchamber, skin hot, trying to see into every shadow. Ball gowns hung around me like specters—Holloway and I had been attempting to choose what I would wear to the Davenports' ball tomorrow night. Or was it tonight? A quick glance at the clock told me it was nearing one o'clock in the morning.

I sat still, listening. Had it been my imagination, or perhaps a servant? Had Mr. Travers dropped something?

Or was he in trouble?

Blast. There was no sense in lying about imagining the different possibilities. I already knew it would take me ages to fall asleep again, so I might as well find some answers.

I slipped from my bed and shrugged into my dressing gown, knotting it about my waist as I toed on my slippers. Holloway slept as I crept past her and into the corridor, closing my door softly. I strained my ears but heard nothing more.

I padded down the stairs, trying to spot whatever had made that noise. I saw nothing out of the ordinary, just the glittering moonlight and the dancing leaves outside.

It wasn't until I reached the back corridor that I noticed something odd—a gust of cool air. I followed it, footsteps silent on the carpeted floor. Had someone left a window cracked? I would have a word with Marchant tomorrow about being more careful when we locked up at night.

But it was not a window. I froze as my eyes fell on a warped rectangle of moonlight spilled across the floor. The garden door stood ajar.

I clutched my dressing gown. Where on earth was Mr. Travers? The cold from the open door crept around me, slipping over every inch of exposed skin and raising bumps.

"Mr. Travers?" I whispered. If he heard me, he did not answer.

My heart bounded, leaping to conclusions I knew were far-fetched, and yet, in that moment, felt entirely too possible. The vandal had returned. He'd picked the lock on the garden door, hit Mr. Travers over the head, and was even now pillaging every room on the ground floor.

Common sense took hold and forced me to move to the door, though my legs shook. I peered out into the moonlit garden, all shadows and bushes and fountains.

One shadow moved, separating itself from the garden bench to my left. I jerked back. But the shadow only meandered along the path, staring up into the clear night sky, the wind ruffling his mass of dark curls.

I let out my breath. It was only Mr. Travers. I squinted at him. He had something in his hands, a small brass item that gleamed in the moonlight as he spun it between his fingers. But what was he doing out here?

It hardly mattered. Everything was well—no thief had violated the safety of my home. I could retreat now, before Mr. Travers saw me.

But as I backed away from the door, the wood floor creaked beneath my feet. Even from this distance, Mr. Travers's form stiffened. He spun, his eyes finding me in the shadow of the doorway.

"Oh," he said, breathing hard. "Miss Wilde."

My eyes flicked to the object in his hand. I could see it clearly now—a dark wooden baton about six inches in length, topped with a gilt crown of brass. I recognized it immediately. A Bow Street stave.

Mr. Townsend, Father's acquaintance, had shown me his once when I'd asked him about it. All Bow Street officers had such a baton, he'd explained. It was both a weapon of defense and a symbol to identify himself as an officer.

"I am sorry," I said as I stepped onto the pebbled path of the garden. "I did not mean to startle you."

He shook out his arms, as if brushing off a rush of energy. "I do not recommend sneaking up on a fellow then."

"I hardly expected to come across you in the garden in the middle of the night." I glanced again at that baton in his hand. "What have you there?"

A thousand emotions played across his face. He cleared his throat, rolling the baton between his hands. "Nothing."

"Nothing?" I raised an eyebrow. "If I'm not mistaken, that looks terribly like the staves issued to Bow Street Runners."

He blinked, then gave a short laugh.

"Remind me not to employ myself with magistrates' daughters in the future," he muttered, though in good humor. He tucked the stave inside his jacket, clearly not wishing to speak more of it. I wanted to press him. The familiar way he held it, the forlorn look in his eyes—it told me more than anything he'd said about his past before tonight. Whatever had caused him to leave Bow Street brought him great pain.

But I stopped myself from asking the question on the tip of my tongue. If he did not wish to tell me, that was his business.

Mr. Travers brushed his hands on his breeches and focused on me. "Why are you about at this hour?"

"I heard a noise and wanted to check."

He rubbed his neck. "I apologize. That was likely me. The door was a bit jammed."

I nodded. The garden door often stuck when the weather warmed.

It was only then that I remembered how out of sorts I looked. One hand rose to touch my hair, my curling papers disheveled after a few hours of sleep. Why hadn't I taken a moment to find a cap or scarf for my hair?

His eyes tracked my movement, and one corner of his lips turned up. "You needn't worry. You look charming in curling papers. Much better than my sister does, anyway."

I blessed the darkness as my face heated. But my mind immediately snatched up this new bit of information about him. Mr. Travers had a sister.

"You needn't have come down," he said. "I will alert you if anything happens."

"And how will you alert me if something happens to *you*?"

He paused. "An excellent question." He leaned forward conspiratorially. "What if I promise to make a great deal of noise should I meet a foe beyond my capabilities? Shout and yell and curse. Perhaps knock over a vase—or better yet, use it as a weapon."

My lips twitched without my permission. "I hear they are rather good for deterring thieves."

"I *know* they are. Personal experience, you see."

A laugh escaped me. The sound was soft, whisked away by the wind, and yet it startled me. How odd that the sound of my own laughter—my real, unguarded laughter—should feel so utterly foreign.

Mr. Travers tipped his head to one side. "You ought to laugh more, Miss Wilde."

My smile slipped. "Why do you say that?"

He furrowed his brow. "I only meant that I like your laugh and wish I heard it more."

"Oh." I wrapped my arms about myself, feeling every pebble beneath the thin soles of my slippers. "I . . . I used to laugh a great deal. Father said it was his favorite sound in the world." What was I going on about? I cleared my throat. "There hasn't been much to smile about lately. One does not laugh while in mourning."

"Yes, but you are finished with your mourning period, are you not?"

"One does not finish mourning, Mr. Travers."

"Jack," he said. "Call me Jack."

I said nothing.

"Believe you me," he said softly. "I am fully aware that grief is a never-ending trial, lasting far beyond the bounds of official mourning. But I daresay your father would be glad to see you laugh, no matter how recent his death."

My eyes pricked, a now familiar sensation. I turned so Mr. Travers would not see the emotion in my face. "It is not for my father that I take such care."

"For whom, then?"

I waved a hand. "I've always been an object of—shall we say—*curiosity* in Little Sowerby. Especially since inheriting Wimborne. I've had to take great care in my actions, even while in mourning. I cannot laugh too loudly or dress in the wrong colors or keep company with anyone deemed unsuitable."

"Such as a thief-taker?"

"Precisely." I smiled sadly. "If I misstep, it only gives fodder to the gossips."

"Ah," he said. "You and I are more similar than I first thought."

I hadn't ever thought of it that way. But he was right. If I was clinging to the edges of society, so was he, the illegitimate son of a peer.

It was then that I realized precisely where I was and what I was doing—standing in the garden in the dead of night, discussing myself in such an intimate way. Merciful heavens, why could I not seem to keep my mouth firmly shut? It was something about the whispering trees, the intense gleam in his eyes as he watched me. Secrets seemed to have no hold here.

"My mouth has run away with me," I said hastily, backing away a step. "I am sorry. I can see now that all is well. I shall go in—"

"Don't be silly," he said, following so that the distance between us lessened rather than grew. "We are finally getting somewhere."

"Getting somewhere?" I exhaled a laugh. "And where precisely are we going?"

"To the root of what makes you *you*, Genevieve Wilde. Your secrets and desires."

My cheeks flushed at the word *desires*. "I haven't got any secrets."

"Everyone has secrets," he said. "Just as everyone has desires."

"And why should you care what mine are?"

I'd meant to say it disarmingly, flippantly. But instead my words came out breathless. As if I cared far too much what his answer would be.

He stopped, his expression difficult to read in the moonlight. "I cannot truly say," he said finally. "You're a puzzle, a difficult one. A lady through and through, but so much more. Reserved, yet passionate. Logical, yet stubborn. You are as much a mystery to me as our unwelcome vandal, and I find myself quite keen to figure you out."

"Figure me out," I repeated, crossing my arms. "As if I were a mathematical equation?"

He laughed. "In a manner of speaking. If your life experience and memories and relationships were numbers, and your very being the sum."

"People are not that simple."

"No," he said. "I don't mean to say they are. I've met a great variety of folk in my time, and I am convinced that it is impossible to ever truly *know* someone."

"And why is that?" I asked in spite of myself. In spite of the voice telling me I ought to leave, that I should not be out here in the moonlit garden, the night air wrapped around us. The space between us seemed to dwindle.

"Because people constantly change," he said. "Every day, we make new decisions, ones that shape our future selves. The Genevieve Wilde of last week, you see, is quite different from the one standing before me. How can I possibly imagine to know every version of a person?"

"Why, then, are you so intent on trying?"

"Because it is part of the job," he said, "and I am very good at it. Prying back layers and learning what makes a person tick. Discovering a person's past, their likes and dislikes, their motivations and goals. Everything I learn brings new light to a case, to the people I'm investigating."

Prying back layers. I narrowed my eyes. "And how do you pry back layers? With flirting and teasing and outrageous statements?"

He grinned, clasping his hands behind his neck. "You've found me out. Sometimes, yes, that is a very effective method. I like to catch people off guard, surprise them, make them uncomfortable. I can learn a great deal about a person based on how they react to such things."

I thought back over our interactions, recalling every ridiculous thing he'd said, which apparently he'd only said in order to provoke a reaction, to gauge and learn and record. I shook my head in amusement. "Is the knowledge you gain worth the contention it causes?"

"Usually," he said. "Save when a woman is somehow resistant to my charms." He tipped his head pointedly at me.

"Quite thankfully, considering what I've just learned."

"I am what I am, Ginny." He spread his hands out wide before him. "Admit it, you've grown fond of my outspokenness."

"That is one word for it."

He held my gaze, raising one eyebrow. I sighed.

"*Esse quam videri,*" I said. "To be, rather than to seem. If there is nothing else I can say of you, Mr. Travers, at least I can say that you are exactly as you seem."

"I shall take that for a compliment and never give it up."

I could not help my smile then. I nearly always felt this way when we talked, as if the tangled webs of my mind had been cleared away. It was the same feeling I got after writing in my journal every night. Somehow, Mr. Travers—Jack—made everything simpler. Easier to understand. Easier to handle. I found I no longer wanted to retreat to my bedroom, to the bed that had grown cold. Because this energy, this heat, between the two of us . . . it was far more than enough to warm every inch of me.

"You know why I came down," I said, "but why is it *you* are out here?" I had assumed he remained in the house all night, watching the main floor.

He shrugged. "I slip out for a few minutes every night. As lovely as your house is, I far prefer to be out of doors."

"We certainly do not have that in common."

"I'd noticed." He quirked his head. "Surely you can appreciate nature in small doses."

"One has to, if one ever wants to go anywhere."

He chuckled, then a strange light grew in his eyes. He stepped forward. "Close your eyes," he said.

I drew back my chin. "Pardon?"

"I want to try something. Close your eyes and take my hand."

I narrowed my eyes. "Has this been your goal all along? Convince me to trust you and then lead me from the house to do away with me?"

"Do you always immediately think the worst?" he said with a laugh.

"If life has taught you that you cannot truly know someone," I said, "then life has taught *me* to expect the worst."

His face softened at that. "I am not going to murder you in the woods, Ginny. Now close your eyes and take my hand."

I hesitated. The way he said my name. Like he knew a part of me no one had seen before, and that knowledge was woven into the very sounds he spoke. It was unnerving. Besides, conversing with him in the garden was one thing. I had a reason for being there and I could leave at any moment. But going off with him to a location unknown? That was much riskier.

And somehow much more tempting.

In the end, it was simple curiosity that made me give in. What would his hand feel like, without the barrier of gloves? The answer made my heart pound quite alarmingly in my chest. His hand, large and entirely masculine, made mine look like a child's. Long fingers wrapped beneath my palm, holding my hand in a gentle embrace. Warmth radiated from our connection. Was it only me who felt it?

I looked up at him, but he was staring at our joined hands. He cleared his throat and pulled me forward. "Close your eyes," he ordered once more.

I sighed but acquiesced. He tugged me forward and I cautiously moved after him.

"I hope we are not going far," I said. "I am not dressed for a walk."

"You're not dressed at all."

I opened my eyes with a laugh. "Mr. Travers!"

"Jack," he said again. "And close your eyes. It's not far."

I obeyed, reassured at least by the fact that it was dark and late and surely no one would see us. Or if they did, we would be nothing more than shadowy figures.

He led me to what I knew was the edge of the garden, where the pebbles gave way to the soft dewiness of grass. I said nothing even as my slippers soaked through. I was determined to see what he meant to show me.

I heard his breathing ahead of me, his hand still leading mine. I could not help myself—I peeked at him through the narrowest gap in my eyelids. A glimpse of his dark hair curling around his high collar, the lean edge of his shoulder as he glanced upward.

"All right," he said, coming to a stop and releasing my hand. "Open your eyes."

I did so, pretending I had not been watching him. We stood in the middle of the lawn, the footbridge spanning the stream to our right and trees just beyond. Wimborne stood like a huddled mountain behind us, dark and silent.

"I do not walk often," I said, "but forgive me if I am not entirely impressed by the sight of my own estate."

"Quiet now." He stepped closer. My pulse leaped—only inches separated us now. I felt his hand come under my chin, his touch far softer than I'd ever imagined. He tilted my head upwards, fingertips whispering against my skin, sending delightful tendrils of heat along my jaw and neck.

"Look again," he said, pulling away.

Stars filled my vision, an expanse of flickering pinpricks against the ink black of the sky. The night was clear, not a cloud to be seen. The moon hovered above the nearby hills, glowing with strange fervor.

"This is why I come out at night," he said. "As much as I love

London, it has far too much light and smog to see the stars properly. Here, they shine like diamonds."

I swallowed. I could not seem to find anything to say. It was not the stars or the moon that held me captivated—I'd seen them before. It was everything. The cool night air laced with rose and dew, fresh and silky against my skin. The ground firm beneath me, yet tilting as if I were perilously close to falling over an edge. The man close beside me, his presence so full and heart-poundingly real.

"It is . . ." My voice caught. "It is lovely."

He shot me an exasperated look. "Lovely? That is the best you can do?"

I gazed back up into the night sky, into the endless abyss that felt both all-encompassing and terribly intimate. "Stunning," I said quietly. "It is stunning."

"That is better," he said, and I could hear the satisfaction in his voice. "This is not so bad, is it?"

We stood there for a few minutes, not speaking. It was not a delicate silence, waiting to be broken, but rather a voiceless agreement to simply *be*. I closed my eyes again and filled my nose with the scent of damp earth, the chill air sinking into my lungs and coming out warm and alive. Perhaps I might need to rethink my position on taking walks. At least, during the night.

I heard a click and looked over as Jack slipped his pocket watch back inside his jacket. No, not Jack. *Mr. Travers*. Drat him for continually correcting me.

"Expecting someone?" I asked.

His eyes jumped to mine. "What? No. Not at all. But I should get you back to the house."

He was right—if anyone were to catch us out here, it would be difficult to explain. But that was the least of my worries, compared to the strange stirring in my chest. I should not have come out with him. I should not have let down my walls. What good could come from it? There could be nothing between us.

We began walking back, and even consumed by my thoughts, I

watched him from the corner of my eye. Was he looking around more than usual? He seemed a bit jumpy.

"Are you—" I began, but a rustling in the trees to my left made me stop. "What is that?"

"Just the wind," he said, urging me forward. "Or a deer."

"We haven't any deer at Wimborne," I said suspiciously.

"Which is unfortunate," came a voice from the trees. "I wouldn't mind some venison every now and then."

I jumped as a narrow shape emerged from the shadows, smirking, hands in his pockets. If the smirk hadn't given him away, his spotted waistcoat would have done the trick.

Jack blew out a breath. "Blast it, Wily."

"Mr. Greaves!" I held a hand to my stomach, trying to calm myself. "What on earth are you doing skulking around here?"

"Skulking?" He held a hand to his chest, the picture of offense. "I'm only helping Jack."

I shot Jack a look. "Helping him with *what*?"

"Surveillance, of course," Wily said. "I've been here every night from the start. You didn't think Jack was doing it all on his own, did you?"

Jack ran a hand through his hair. "You know very well that's what she thought." He turned his eyes to me. "I am sorry I did not tell you. I thought it might make you anxious. But it has been useful having a second set of eyes."

"Yes," Wily said. "For example, when I see two mysterious figures in various stages of undress, I can take a second look."

I crossed my arms, as if I could hide myself entirely. "I heard a noise and came to investigate."

"Certainly, you did," Wily said easily. Too easily.

My mouth dropped. What exactly was he insinuating?

Jack rescued me. "Have you any word about the watch, Wily?"

"No, I haven't." He pulled his green topper from his head, gave it a thump to straighten out a dent, then placed it back on his head. "And I find it very odd indeed."

"Why is it odd?" I asked.

He shrugged. "If the thief stole it to sell, we would've seen it by now, in a shop or through a fence. Or if he wanted a reward, he would have tried to negotiate with you through a thief-taker like our Jack here."

"Special investigator," Jack and I said together.

Wily grinned. "As you say. But I find it strange not to have heard one whiff of this watch. If you ask me, which you should since I am quite knowledgeable, then I would say the thief wanted the watch for himself."

"Or *herself*," Jack said meaningfully.

I met Jack's eyes. "Catherine," I said. "She is the only one who knows what that watch means to me. And I daresay she would want it herself."

He set his lips in a grim line. "It would appear so."

Wily gave a long whistle that floated out into the night. "What intrigue. Two well-bred ladies coming to blows over a pocket watch."

I exhaled a breath that was half laugh, half exasperation. "We will not come to blows."

"Disappointing." Wily stuck his hands in his pockets. "I also should tell you I looked into those two names you gave me, Jack. Nothing to be had from them, unfortunately. One died two years ago, and the other is in jail as we speak."

I chewed on my lip. With every name crossed off our list, Catherine was looking more and more suspicious.

Jack caught my eye. "If she has it," he said, "we will get it back."

"*If*," I said. "We must be careful. We cannot accuse her without proof."

"Right you are," Jack said, a new twist to his lips. "Proof."

Wily clapped his hands together. "Well, it seems you've got it all figured out. Now if you'll excuse me, Miss Wilde, I'll get on with my rounds."

A fortnight ago, the thought of a man like Wily watching the grounds at night would have driven my anxiety to unseen levels. But now it did not even occur to me to protest his presence. Discovering one is being stalked by a dangerous criminal has that effect on a woman.

"I'll let you two get on with"—Wily trailed off, his eyebrows waggling suggestively—"whatever it was you were doing."

My cheeks burned, embarrassment climbing into my chest. Normally I might brush off such a comment, but considering what I'd been thinking about Jack only minutes ago, I found my tongue quite tied.

"Actually, I need to speak to you, Wily, if you'll wait a moment," Jack said. He turned to me. "I'll walk you back first."

With Wily's comments and suggestive eyebrows still forefront in my mind, I took a step back. "No need," I said. "It's not far."

He furrowed his brow. "If you're sure."

"Quite," I said. "Good night, Mr. Greaves."

Wily offered a lazy wave.

"Good night, Ja—" I stopped, my eyes flashing to his. A smile danced at the edge of his mouth. "That is, good night, Mr. Travers."

"Good night, Genevieve."

I felt his eyes on me the entire walk back to the house. When I finally reached the safety of my room, Holloway still sleeping, I crept to the curtains and parted them, a beam of moonlight playing across my arm. The grounds were still. I saw no sign of Jack or Wily, but I supposed that was the point.

Tucked back beneath my covers, I curled one hand under my chin. My mind dashed about, recalling bits and pieces of our conversation. I could not seem to calm my heart, which pounded away in foolish determination.

Mr. Travers. Jack. I could still feel his fingers beneath my chin, hear his soft breaths so close to mine. I'd never spoken to a man the way I'd spoken to him tonight.

I'd never felt the way I'd felt tonight.

Everyone has secrets, he'd said. *Just as everyone has desires.*

Heaven help me.

CHAPTER 13

I dressed with care for the ball that night, selecting a sky-blue gown with ruffled sleeves and an embroidered hemline. Heavens, it felt good to wear anything besides black and gray. It was an old dress, but it felt new again after such a long time in my wardrobe. I let Holloway toy with my hair, adding a few intricate braids and twists that did look rather lovely with my red curls. She seemed pleased, at least, and I gave her a kiss as she left.

Tucking a handkerchief and comb into my reticule, I paused as I spotted the perfume Father had gifted me in the drawer of my dressing table. I picked up the delicate filigree flask, opening it to take a sniff. The scent was as lovely as I remembered, amber and orange flower. When Father had died, I'd shut so much of myself away, as if that would help heal the aching inside of me. But right now, I wanted to feel a little bit of that aching, if only to help me remember how much Father had loved me.

I opened the flask and dabbed a few drops of the perfume on my neck and wrists. I looked in the mirror and smiled past the heaviness in my chest. One dragon slayed, albeit a small one.

Then I coughed. The perfume was a bit stronger than I'd thought. Perhaps I'd applied a bit too much. No matter, my gloves would dull the scent. I slipped them on and picked up my ivory shawl.

Jack was waiting at the foot of the stairs, one elbow resting on the banister as his free hand tapped a rhythm against his tan breeches. He stared absently away, not hearing my footsteps as I began descending. I observed him closely. If I'd doubted before that he could look the part of a society gentleman, I certainly did not now. His dark curls were carefully tamed, his jaw clean-shaven and cravat tied elegantly. He had no valet, so I could only imagine how he'd managed to keep his clothing free of wrinkles, but his black jacket and cream waistcoat were spotless.

He finally heard my approach and looked up. He blinked, lips parting, then his gaze ran over the length of me, from my hair to my slippers. My stomach flipped like an acrobat. I'd forgotten what it felt like to be admired—if that's what this was. His eyes met mine, a thread of energy strung between us, warm and sweet.

"Well, my dear Genevieve," he said with that dratted grin. "I am surprised."

I raised an eyebrow. "Surprised that I can look presentable?"

"No," he said. "Surprised that no man has made it his mission to sweep you off your feet."

I paused two steps above him. A man of certain talents, indeed. How did he manage to compliment me and insult me at the same time? "That is quite an assumption to make."

"I make assumptions for a living." He crossed his arms, watching me. *Assuming* things about me.

"Well, you are wrong in this case," I said. "I have suitors." One suitor, anyway.

I descended the last two stairs and brushed past him. He coughed, covering his mouth with a fist. "Heavens above."

I stopped, turning back. "What is it?"

His expression twisted into something I could only identify as disgust. He looked around, searching for something. Then his eyes settled on me and widened in . . . realization? "Oh," he said with another cough. "Is that—is that a new perfume?"

I stared at him. Why was he acting so strangely? "Yes. I quite like it."

"Clearly."

"What is that supposed to mean?"

"Only that you seem to have used the entire bottle."

I gaped at him. His eyes were watering. *Watering*! The sweet, rich scent of my perfume seemed to fill my nose, suddenly overwhelming and cloying. My body turned hot.

I turned and marched to the front door, rubbing hard on one gloved wrist as if that would eradicate the smell. He hurried after me.

"I did not mean that," he said, though laughter hid in his voice. "I'm sorry. Your perfume is just a touch strong."

"Then you are welcome to stay far, far away," I shot back.

The poor footman holding open the front door watched with wide eyes as I stalked past him. The coach was waiting and I hurried across the pebbled drive. But Jack took two long strides and rounded on me, taking my arm and stopping me short.

"Pardon me," I said stiffly. "We have a ball to attend."

But he did not move aside. In fact, he stepped closer, ducking his head to meet my eyes. His face had sobered, his eyes sincere. "I am sorry," he said. "Clearly I am trying my hardest to prove I am anything but a gentleman."

I exhaled, my chest tight.

"I will be on my best behavior the rest of the night," he said. "I promise, Ginny."

I did not know if it was the gentle tone in which he spoke my name, or the warm touch of his hand on my arm, but I found myself clearing my throat and staring down at my feet. "My father gave me this perfume," I said. "I've never worn it before tonight."

His hand tightened slightly, as if he might pull me toward him. Instead, he released me and stepped back. "I see," he said. "Now I am more ashamed than before."

I sniffed one of my wrists and made a face. What had I been thinking when I applied the perfume? He was right—I smelled as if I'd doused myself in the entire flask.

"Allow me," he said. He took a handkerchief from his jacket and strode to the fountain of water that ran beside the front steps. He wetted his handkerchief and returned, gesturing to the coach. I eyed him but accepted his help inside. Once he was seated across from me and the coach had started off, he leaned forward and took my gloved hand. I opened my mouth to protest—he should not act so familiarly with me—but then he began to pull at the fingers of my glove, one at a time until the silk slipped from my skin.

My breath caught in my throat, and any protest died inside me. He began rubbing lightly at my wrist with the damp handkerchief. I could only watch in stupefied silence as he worked, one wrist and then the other. There was none of the confident, arrogant thief-taker in this man before me. Only contrition and kindness. I swallowed hard, my heart beating a stilted rhythm. The featherlight brushes of his fingers against the delicate skin at my wrist made it difficult to think of *any-thing* else.

When he finished, he offered the handkerchief to me and I took it, wiping my neck beneath my jaw. His eyes followed my movements for the briefest moment, bright pools reflecting the setting sun, then he astutely looked away. The powerful scent slowly began to fade, leaving just a touch of the warm, lightly spiced amber. When I finished, I folded the cloth into a neat square and handed it back to him.

"Thank you," I managed.

He nodded. In the dying light, his features were shadowed and intensified.

I busied myself with pulling on my gloves, my breathing unsteady. "What is your plan for tonight?" I asked. "How will you charm Catherine into revealing all her secrets?"

He leaned back in his seat. "Charm only goes so far in detective work."

"What do you mean?"

He grinned. "I cannot tell you all my methods, or I will be out of a job."

"I know when you are using flattery to avoid a question."

"A quick learner, you are." He adjusted the sleeve of his jacket.

"I was thinking," he said a moment later. "If you *do* have a horde of suitors, I ought to know about them. As your cousin."

"And why is that?"

"So I might defend your honor, if necessary."

"It will *not* be necessary."

"Because there are no suitors?"

I blew out a puff of air. "Because you are not actually my cousin."

He furrowed his brow in an exaggerated manner. "How very odd that no one has pursued your hand. Have you a penchant for gambling? A terrible family secret? An irritable disposition ill-suited to teasing?"

How could he make me want to both burst out laughing and kick his leg? "I'll have you know, I've had two proposals in recent months."

His eyes sharpened. "Ah. There it is. Mr. Northcott?"

I gaped. "How did you . . . ?"

He laughed. "I didn't know. Not until now."

"Blast you and your wicked assumptions," I muttered.

"Wicked or not, they are usually right," he said. "Which is why I am here tonight. If I am to play your cousin well enough to avoid suspicion, then I need to know these things."

I rubbed my forehead. Could he ever be wrong, just once? I would delight in that beyond reason. "Very well," I said finally. "Yes, Mr. Northcott proposed twice. I refused twice. We have generally remained on friendly terms, our latest interactions notwithstanding."

"Why did you refuse him?" Jack asked, genuine curiosity in his eyes. "Far be it from me to *assume*, but he seems a logical match at a glance."

I looked down, running a finger over the seam in one of my gloves. "Logic has little to do with marriage, Mr. Travers, at least where I am concerned."

He remained silent a long while, long enough that I finally glanced up at him. He watched me, those shadowed eyes seeming to pierce straight through me. The air in the coach grew thin, as if we stood atop a mountain, and I forced myself to look away, to breathe.

Quiet fell upon us, for which I was grateful. I tried to prepare myself for the evening ahead. Beatrice would be there, at least. And there would be dancing. I did like to dance, and it had been far too long since my last ball. But I would have to endure Catherine's veiled slights and the side-eye glances from the rest of Little Sowerby's society. I grimaced.

"Are you nervous?" Jack asked.

I straightened. "No, of course not."

"Then why do you look as if you've eaten spoiled meat?"

My lips twitched. "This is simply how I look when I go to balls."

He laughed, and I took perhaps too much enjoyment in that.

"Perhaps my assumption is wrong here, then," he said. "Since I assume you hate her enough to dread attending her ball."

"Catherine?" I tipped my head. "I don't hate her."

He looked at me in disbelief. "How can you not? I've seen how she treats you."

I lifted one shoulder. "I understand it, that's all."

He leaned closer. "Tell me."

A week ago I would have easily refused, but now I looked into his eyes and found myself talking.

"Catherine's mother was Father's first wife." My voice was barely audible over the creaking of the coach. "It was an arranged marriage, and not a very happy one. When Catherine was thirteen, her mother died, and Father hired *my* mother as Catherine's governess. He promptly fell in love with her, truly and deeply." I shook my head. "In Catherine's mind, Father ought to have remained a widower for the rest of his days. Instead, he horrified her by marrying only a few months after her mother's death."

Jack was quiet, listening closely.

"I came along a year later," I went on, "and Catherine has despised me ever since. She never forgave Father for what she saw as betrayal."

"Even now?"

I offered a sad smile. "Unfortunately. When Father was alive, she still cared for his opinion and wanted his respect."

His eyes softened. "It was the younger sister who bore the brunt."

I looked away, my throat raw. "Like I said, I understand how difficult it must have been for her. And she's never had children of her own, which undoubtedly made it worse, watching me grow up in the same home she did." I paused. "Despite my grief over Father's death, parts of these last months have been a relief. No more pretense between Catherine and me. We can live separate lives, no longer bound by a relationship she never wanted."

"Did *you* want it?"

"When I was young," I admitted. "When I thought she was beautiful and grand and everything a girl should aspire to. I've since learned."

"And your father?" he asked. "What did he think of it all?"

I sighed. "He hated that we did not get along. He was always trying to mend things between us." I paused. "He loved her and made certain she knew it."

Jack watched me with an unreadable expression.

"There you have it," I said, my voice light. "You were right. Everyone does have secrets, and you've managed to discover mine. Another one of your methods at work, no doubt."

"No," he said, quite seriously. "Not at all. It is an honor to keep your secrets, Genevieve."

His words were like slipping into buttery sunshine, still and warm and alive. I could not look at him, not without knowing what I might find in his eyes.

The coach came to a stop, and I blessed the driver for his most excellent timing. Jack descended from the coach and offered me his hand. As I stepped down, I noticed the brass tip of his Bow Street baton inside his jacket. A needed reminder. Jack had his secrets as well.

After helping me down, he stared up at Harpford House. "It is always lovely to visit a small, quiet estate, is it not?"

I snorted, unable to help myself. Harpford was enormous, with countless rows of gleaming windows, six pillars surrounding the front door, and a massive hedge maze. Light and laughter spilled from the open door, where a footman waited to greet us. Why Catherine even cared that I had Wimborne, I could never guess. Why envy the apple when you owned the orchard?

Jack offered me his arm and we started up the stairs leading to the towering front door. After handing our things to a footman, we moved down the corridor. The open doors of the ballroom were ahead, bouncing figures laughing and clapping as they danced a reel. My mood lifted. Perhaps I might enjoy myself after all.

We joined the short line waiting to greet Catherine and Mr. Davenport. When it was our turn and Catherine's gaze moved to meet mine, I straightened my back. Her eyes narrowed, though she kept a polite smile on her face.

"Genevieve," she said, dipping her head. "Mr. Travers. How glad I am that you could come."

I gave a slight curtsy, but Jack bent into a full bow. "We are absolutely delighted to have been invited," he said.

Mr. Davenport smiled cheerfully. "So pleased to see you. I assume you've been enjoying your visit, Mr. Travers?"

"Yes, we've been getting along splendidly," Jack said. "Ginny is a dear, is she not?"

A dear? I should have reminded him to restrain his ridiculousness.

A flash of disbelief crossed Catherine's face before she again mastered her expression. My doubts from before came rearing back. She might not know what was really happening between Jack and me, but we clearly hadn't convinced her completely.

"Thank you for the invitation," I said, taking a step toward the ballroom. We needed to move along before Jack said anything else foolish.

"Of course," Mr. Davenport said, with a discreet glance at his wife.

Catherine managed a taut smile. "Enjoy the evening."

I tugged Jack into the ballroom. "You must be more careful," I told him as we took up a position near a window, pretending to watch the dancers. "Catherine is clearly suspicious."

"Suspicious?" He chuckled. "Hardly. She thinks I'm an idiot, which is what I want her to think."

"You're not having to try very hard."

He snorted.

"I am in earnest," I said. "You ought to avoid her for the rest of the night."

"Not a difficult task," he said. "Considering my plan involves her not—"

"Miss Wilde."

I spun to see Mr. Northcott standing behind me. Had he heard anything? His face was neutral as ever, though his eyes flicked toward Jack.

"I had hoped to see you tonight," Mr. Northcott said. "I admit I have been rather eager to meet your cousin here, since I was unable to speak to you after church."

I cleared my throat. He knew I was avoiding him. "Mr. Northcott, may I present Mr. Jack Travers?"

Jack offered a bow. "At your service. I've heard *so* much about you, Mr. Northcott."

I clenched my hands into fists behind my back. Mr. Northcott was even more perceptive than Catherine. Surely, he would see through our ruse in a second.

The magistrate dipped his head in greeting. "A pleasure, sir. I hear you come from Northumberland?"

"Indeed," Jack said. "Rothbury, to be precise."

When had we decided that?

"Rothbury?" Mr. Northcott repeated. "I've friends in that area."

My heart skipped a beat. Would he press Jack for more? But Mr. Northcott turned to me in the next instant, all but dismissing Jack. "Miss Wilde, I wondered if I might speak to you? Briefly, of course, so you might enjoy the dancing."

I softened, looking at his hopeful face. He knew very well I liked dancing, and it was sweet of him to mention it. Besides, I hated to be at odds with him. His proposals notwithstanding, I liked Mr.

Northcott. He was intelligent and witty, and far better company than most of the other guests crowded into the ballroom. It was time to mend our friendship.

But Jack took my elbow. "Genevieve and I planned to dance the next set," he said, a bright smile on his face. "Perhaps you might find her later on."

He steered me away, and all I could do was cast an apologetic glance back at Mr. Northcott, who stood stock-still, blinking.

"What," I whispered as Jack guided me to the edge of the dance floor, "are you doing?"

Jack raised an eyebrow. "Rescuing you."

"Rescuing me? From a friend who wished to speak to me? When I gave no indication that I wanted you to interfere?"

He frowned. "I assumed—"

"Yes, that is the problem, isn't it?" I rubbed my temple. Why did he always have to rush into things without thinking of the consequences?

The music stopped, the dancers applauding with gusto before moving to find their next partners. I had no choice but to follow Jack as he led me to our position, facing each other in the line of dancers.

When the music began, I offered a curtsy, he a bow. We stepped to meet each other, our gloved hands gliding together before separating again. I refused to meet his eyes, though I knew he watched me intently. This man was somehow both the cause and solution to all my problems, and I was beginning to dislike that fact very much.

"You are angry with me," he said as I circled around him, following the other women up and down the line.

I sighed. "It feels like I am always angry at you, so that should hardly be a surprise."

I returned to my spot and we watched as the opposite couple came together.

"Always angry?" he asked. "That seems an exaggeration. Surely there must have been some moments where you tolerated me."

"I cannot think of one."

His lips quirked up. "Not even when I chased an intruder from your estate?"

"Yes, well, if you had caught him, perhaps we'd be having a different conversation."

He laughed. He had such an easy manner, his laugh as natural to him as breathing. I could not help the small smile that climbed my lips.

It was our turn again, and he took my hand to lead me up the aisle of dancers. We rose and fell to the rhythm of the music, and despite everything, my heart lifted. I loved to dance. To feel the euphoria of executing the steps perfectly, my breaths coming faster, my cheeks flushing.

To my surprise, Jack matched my enthusiasm with unexpected energy. His steps echoed mine, his hand always at the perfect position for me to take. After a few minutes, I stopped fighting my inhibitions and allowed myself to smile, to laugh. Come what may, I *would* enjoy this dance.

It helped that Jack had an irresistible smile, bright eyes, and a talent for making me laugh when I least wanted to.

Our two dances seemed to flash by. He teased me when I made small mistakes, and I shook my head at his antics. When the music ended, we applauded, both breathless. How wonderful it felt to move and be seen, even just by a man pretending to be my cousin. Six months had been too long to go without dancing.

"You dance as well as you paint," Jack said, escorting me from the dance floor.

"Considering our conversation about orchids and boats, I hesitate to blush, Mr. Travers."

He stopped us amidst the milling crowd, gentlemen searching for new partners, ladies laughing behind fans. "Well, that just won't do," he said, raising my gloved hand between us. "Every lady should blush at a ball."

I thought he would press a kiss to my glove, but instead he turned my hand, presenting my wrist. My protest caught in my throat. He brought my wrist to his nose and inhaled a breath, then he winked at me. "I do believe that scent is growing on me, Miss Wilde."

I swallowed—hard. "You are not acting like my cousin." My voice sounded too high.

"That is your fault, I'm afraid," he said. "You make it so easy to forget."

He should not be allowed to look at me this way, as if I were a rich dessert, or a bouquet of rare flowers, or . . . my mind was so muddled I could not think of another comparison.

"I . . ." I tugged my hand from his grip. "I have to speak to Beatrice." I hurried away, desperate to put any amount of distance between us. I swore I heard him laughing behind me.

Peering above the crush, I spotted Beatrice beside a potted plant, looking deathly bored. She fanned herself as she watched the dancing. When she saw me coming toward her, she snapped her fan closed, a smile leaping to her lips.

"There you are," she declared. "I was afraid you'd changed your mind and would not show."

"It crossed my mind a few dozen times today," I said. "But Mr. Travers insisted."

"Where is that thief-taker of yours?" She turned back to the dance floor. "Ah, I see him. Is that Miss Rupert he is talking with?"

I followed her gaze. "Yes. It looks as though Mr. Davenport is introducing them."

As I watched, Jack led Miss Rupert out onto the dance floor, giving her that broad smile that had such a dizzying effect on me. She laughed, light and delicate. My stomach turned, and I forced my eyes away.

"Good," Beatrice said. "Finally, we have a chance to talk."

"Not if your mother has any say in it." I nodded at Mrs. Lacey across the ballroom. She spoke to Mr. Dupins, a widower nearly forty years of age, gesturing at Beatrice all the while.

Beatrice groaned. "Oh, that woman!"

I laughed. "You ought to open your eyes to the possibility. Mr. Dupins has three thousand a year and a London townhome."

She snorted. "Bite your tongue. He also has five children and an obsession with rocks."

"He is passionate about geology, that is all," I teased.

She pointed her fan at me. "I will turn him on to you if you don't stop that."

I held up my hands in surrender, though I still grinned.

"Now tell me," she said, "have you had any other incidents at Wimborne since I saw you last?"

"None," I said. "It has been a week. I cannot help but be hopeful."

"I shall also hope, for your sake." She slipped her arm through mine, pulling me close. "You have done so marvelously well with everything, Ginny. I know your father would be proud."

A lump formed in my throat. "Thank you, Bea," I said, my voice cracking.

She squeezed my arm. "Shall I prove my worth even more by once again deflecting our good magistrate?"

I followed her eyes. Mr. Northcott stood nearby, beside the arched doorway that led to the dining area. He brooded, likely still irritated by Jack's behavior earlier.

"No," I said. "In fact, I need to speak to him."

Beatrice elbowed me. "You and all your men. What a flirt you are, Genevieve Wilde."

"Quiet, you." I rapped her on her arm as I left, and she laughed.

I approached Mr. Northcott, stopping with a curtsy. "Mr. Northcott."

"Miss Wilde." His mouth pulled down.

I sighed, knowing precisely what I'd done to earn it. "I am terribly sorry for my—my cousin's rudeness. He can be rather oblivious where manners are concerned." At least I wasn't lying about that.

Mr. Northcott's expression softened. "An apology is not necessary, Miss Wilde. You did not commit the offense."

"No, but I am sorry all the same."

Mr. Northcott directed his gaze to the dance floor, landing on Jack. "He is . . . not what I expected from a relation of yours."

He did not look suspicious, or particularly offended, just baffled. The unease inside me settled somewhat, but I still did not want Mr. Northcott focusing too much of his attention on my "cousin." I changed the subject. "You had something you wished to speak to me about?"

"Oh. Yes." He cleared his throat. "Perhaps over here?"

He guided me toward a pillared alcove, where the music and laughter dulled slightly. I was straightening my gloves when I caught the eye of a passing footman in livery. I froze. Then I stared.

It was *Wily*. Ruddy cheeks, thin, bony frame, and alert eyes. He grinned at me, held a finger to his lips, and slipped away into the crowd.

"Here we are," Mr. Northcott said, clasping his hands behind his back as he faced me.

I snapped my eyes to his, though they begged to follow Wily's carefully combed head through the crowd. What was he doing here?

Mr. Northcott sighed. "There is no easy way to say this, so I'll be out with it."

"Say what?" I tried to focus.

He fixed me with his steady gaze. "I know everything."

I blinked. "Everything?"

"I know your estate is in trouble," he said. "I know Wimborne has suffered an alarming number of unfortunate events, and I am here to offer my help as I should have done when you first came to me about the watch."

The watch. Wimborne. I breathed again. He did not know about Jack.

"How . . ." I swallowed. "How did you find out?"

He waved a hand. "You know how servants talk. I daresay one of your maids is related to my gardener or some such thing, and word spread. My valet was the one who told me as I was dressing tonight." He stepped closer. "Now, I know why you did not tell me, considering how our last few conversations have gone. And I know you've already hired a"—his eye twitched—"a thief-taker to find the watch."

I knew he was only referring to our last conversation, but I had to force myself not to look at Jack. "Yes," I said, clearing my throat. "Yes, I have."

It was clear he wanted to say more about that, but he restrained himself. "Still, I hope you will allow me to provide you aid. At least a constable to patrol Wimborne and follow any leads. I would be glad to investigate myself, though it is not my particular area of expertise. I can also support a prosecution to the best of my abilities once we catch the culprit."

He moved even closer, his shoes too near mine. I forced myself not to step away.

"You have my full support," Mr. Northcott said, "whatever you may need."

His eyes were full of kindness. Concern. There was so much I admired about this man. How he'd taken his father's failing estate and turned it profitable within a few short years. How he'd helped my father with his magisterial duties without need for praise. He was ambitious and intelligent and loyal. I knew him well. Not for the first time, I wished I felt something for him other than friendship.

He would make any woman a good husband. I was just fool enough to want more.

"Thank you, Mr. Northcott," I said softly. "You cannot know what that means to me."

"Perhaps I might call on you in the next few days?" he asked. "You can inform me of all that's happened and we can discuss arrangements."

Arrangements. I'd already *made* arrangements to solve Wimborne's problems. And if Mr. Northcott thought badly of me hiring a thief-taker to locate my father's watch, I could only imagine his reaction when he learned I'd allowed the man to stay in my home and masquerade as my cousin.

Mr. Northcott looked at me expectantly, and I scrambled for

words. "Actually, I am hopeful the incidents have come to an end. But I shall certainly call upon you if anything else should occur."

At the very least, I would have a bit more time to find a way to tell him the truth.

"If you are sure." He smiled. "I'm glad we had this chance to talk. I hope you will come to me in the future with any worries."

For a moment, I debated telling him what I'd learned last night from Mr. Travers, that Father might have had a mole among his constables. If anyone would know more, it would be Mr. Northcott. But if I mentioned it, I would also have to tell him where I had gotten my information, and that would open a line of questioning I was not at all keen on.

"I will," I said. "Of course."

"Now, let us speak no more of it," Mr. Northcott said. "Shall we dance?"

I was reaching for his outstretched hand when an earth-shattering crash echoed through the ballroom. I jumped, the sound reverberating around me, then peered over heads to see what had caused the commotion.

A footman stood beside the overturned table where the lemonade had been. Now it was a watery puddle seeping across the chalked floor of the ballroom. Catherine stalked across the room, murder in her eyes. That poor footman.

He looked up as she approached, appropriately chagrined. I caught a glimpse of clever eyes. *Wily*. Of course it was him. But why . . .

I turned just in time to see a head of black curls slip from the ballroom. Everything connected in my head at once. Jack insisting he had a plan. Wily's unexpected appearance. The spectacle of the spilled lemonade.

Wily had been a distraction for Jack to sneak out.

To sneak out and do what, I hadn't any idea. But I would not allow my thief-taker to wander about Harpford House unattended, not with my entire reputation at stake.

"I'm so sorry," I said quickly to Mr. Northcott, my words tumbling over each other. "Do excuse me a moment."

He took a step after me. "Our dance?"

"I'll return shortly," I called over my shoulder, inwardly cursing Jack. Now I'd been rude to Mr. Northcott twice tonight, neither time being my fault.

I hurried through the crowd, still watching as servants cleared away the mess Wily had made. He was nowhere to be seen, off being reprimanded, no doubt. How had he managed it? Catherine had surely hired extra staff to help with the ball, but it took only one look at Wily to know he was up to no good.

I reached the door Jack had gone through and stepped into the corridor. Empty. Candles lit the way, though shadows stretched between them. Where had he gone? I would have to make my best guess. I started toward the west wing, toward the billiards room and the library, peering into deserted rooms with no success.

I reached the stairs leading to the family's private rooms. I knew that well enough from my visits over the years. I swallowed. Had Jack lost his mind? He was going to land *both* of us in a world of trouble.

Glancing behind me, I wished desperately that I could return to the ballroom and dance with Mr. Northcott. But instead, I took a steadying breath and began climbing the stairs. The corridor was darker here, with no candles and little moonlight. I moved slowly, my steps muffled by the carpet beneath my feet.

"I thought I had a tail."

I leapt a foot in the air. Jack emerged from a shadowed corner ahead, one eyebrow raised.

"Go back to the ball, Ginny," he said. "Let me do my work."

"Your work?" I was hissing like a snake, but I did not care. "You work for me, and I do not recall asking you to snoop about Harpford House."

"I am trying," he said slowly, as if I were dreadfully dimwitted, "to find evidence that your half sister is the one behind your misfortunes. If you haven't the stomach for—"

"For housebreaking? Thievery?"

"I'm not planning on *stealing* anything."

A sound skittered up the hallway. Footsteps. Jack hooked an arm around my waist and yanked me to him, both of us stumbling back into the shadows. My hands were forced to his chest—his impossibly firm chest—and my pulse took off like a kite in the wind.

The footsteps grew closer. Purposeful. Quick. A servant's, no doubt. I held my breath, which wasn't difficult seeing as I wasn't breathing at all. Jack pulled me nearer, his hands still at my waist, fingertips pressed into the small of my back. I was far too focused on the movement of Jack's chest beneath my hands. Was it more labored than usual? I dared not meet his eyes. I stared at his throat instead, at the corded muscle pulled taut as he also tried not to breathe. No, I should not look there. I directed my gaze at his ear, around which curled several locks of his dark hair. Not any better.

Heavens, was there any part of this man that did not make my skin heat? I closed my eyes.

We both stood desperately still, listening. The footsteps sounded in the next corridor. Then they moved off, quieter, just as suddenly as they'd come.

We did not move, neither of us willing to risk detection. At least, that had to be why. It was certainly *not* because I enjoyed being in Jack's arms. In fact, I reminded myself, I was *angry* with him. I detested his strong arms around me, his heady warmth, that subtle scent that continually toyed with my senses.

"I think they are gone," he said in my ear, in a husky voice that sent a tingle down my spine.

Angry, I said again to myself. *I am* angry.

I pushed away from him, hard, though he did not move in the least, perfectly steady.

"This is absurd, Mr. Travers," I whispered, drawing myself up to my full height, which was sadly not very impressive. "You are going to get caught. I insist you return with me to the ballroom."

His eyes narrowed. "Insist all you want. I intend to get results."

He turned on his heel and strode down the corridor. I stared, wanting once again to throw something at him. Then I let out a groan and darted after him.

He seemed to be looking for a certain room, opening doors and peeking inside before moving on to the next.

"I'm certain she keeps her instruments of torture in the dungeon." My voice was a hard whisper as I caught up to him.

"Ha," he said. "Unfortunately, I'm searching for something more subtle than chains and racks." He opened another door. "Here we are."

I followed him inside, immediately closing the door behind me. "Where is *here*?"

"Catherine Davenport's private parlor," Jack said, hands at his waist as he took stock of his surroundings. "Rumor has it, if she has any secrets to find, they would be here."

The room was dark, lit only by the barest stretches of moonlight from the bank of windows. I'd never been here before, relegated as I'd been to the rooms Catherine could tolerate me in. In the center stood a sofa and divan, upholstered in pink. Intricate floral wallpaper climbed to the ceiling. Flowing curtains surrounded the windows, fluttering at our entrance. Everything was pale and cold—rather like Catherine.

"How do you know about this room?" I stayed by the door, listening for approaching footsteps, though my heart pounded so loud in my ears I wouldn't hear them anyways.

"I asked the right people."

"You *paid* the right people."

Jack strode to the writing desk in the corner, rifling through a drawer. I still did not move. What if Catherine noticed us missing from the ballroom? What if Mr. Northcott came after me?

"We shouldn't be here," I insisted. "This is not the right way to go about this." I tried not to imagine what Father would think of our actions. I could only hope he was otherwise occupied in heaven at the moment.

Jack ignored that. "This would go faster if you helped."

"I don't *want* to help. Besides, I haven't the faintest clue what you are looking for."

He held up a paper to the moonlight. "Anything, really. Perhaps a letter linking Catherine to someone on your list." He paused. "Or your watch."

I bit my lip. Was it possible that Father's watch was in this room? I was just standing here. I might as well be useful, and then I could convince my idiot thief-taker to return to the ball.

"This is madness," I muttered, reluctantly moving to the bureau beneath a wide gilded mirror. Jack said nothing, which was wise. I had great aim and easy access to a variety of ceramic figurines atop the bureau.

Opening the top drawer, I sorted through a few curios: an empty snuff box, a scrap of paper, a few hairpins. I looked through the other drawers, which were empty. Each time I took hold of a knob, I felt a surge of nerves. Would I see the familiar glint of my watch?

"Nothing here," I said. "May we go now?"

"A few more minutes." He flicked through the pages of a book. A journal? A ledger of some sort?

I blew out a breath and moved to the low table beside the couch. I was bending to pick up the book resting on top when I heard a click. A simple sound, and yet the worst that could reach my ears at this moment. I jerked upright as the door swung open.

Catherine stepped into the doorway, eyes gleaming like a cat's.

CHAPTER 14

I stood frozen, unable to move, speak. Catherine looked from me to Jack, her expression unreadable.

"What is this?" she said softly. But soft for Catherine was dangerous, and I was well aware.

"I . . ." I gulped, my throat dry. Jack slowly set down the book he'd been reading. "We were only—"

She raised her hand. "Before you offer some preposterous explanation, let me make one thing clear: there is nothing you can say to convince me that this man is your cousin."

My knees felt weak. I was going to be sick. Every fleeting and impossible excuse that darted through my head used *that* lie as its basis. If she did not believe Jack to be my cousin, then it was over. Every care I'd taken in the last decade to guard my reputation was wasted.

All because of Jack.

Jack strode forward. "Mrs. Davenport—"

I held up a hand, and he came to a halt, blinking.

"No," I said, an edge to my voice that I'd never heard before. Neither had I ever felt this rush of emotion so strongly, a stomach-churning mix of embarrassment and anger. "You've done enough. I will talk now."

He met my eyes, and I saw the fight within those blue depths. But he set his jaw and nodded.

I turned back to Catherine. I was tired of the pretense. I wanted to know, once and for all, if Catherine was to blame for Wimborne's troubles. "You are right," I said. "He is not my cousin."

The slight widening of her eyes was the only indication she'd still doubted her own theory. She quickly recovered, her shoulders straightening. "Why?" she asked. "Why such a lie?"

I took a deep breath. "Father's watch was stolen," I said. "Taken from Wimborne's study right under my nose."

She did not react, her posture rigid as a stone column.

"I hired Mr. Travers to find the watch," I went on. "However, it soon became clear someone was targeting Wimborne, and so I also hired him to safeguard the estate and investigate these incidents. He has experience with this sort of thing."

"You hired a thief-taker."

"Yes."

"And allowed him into your home, masquerading as your cousin."

"Yes."

Catherine gave a harsh laugh. "I always thought you rather dim, Genevieve, but even I did not think you could be this foolish."

I forced back my hot surge of anger. I had to remain in control of my emotions, or I would have no chance of diffusing this situation.

"I had no choice," I said, clasping my hands tightly before me. "I needed assistance, and the local authorities refused to help."

"You mean Mr. Northcott." Catherine paced a few steps toward the window, her eyes never leaving mine. "You cannot expect me to believe that man refused you anything."

"Believe what you will. But I had no other option than to protect Wimborne however I could."

Something in the hard angles of her face shifted at my words. It was gone in the next instant as she turned her glare to Jack.

"Why the lie about being related?" She dared him to speak.

He looked at me, his eyes cool and calculating, no doubt concocting another lie. But I was done with our dishonesty.

"We lied so Mr. Travers could investigate," I said. "So that he could move freely through society."

Catherine whipped back to me. Even in the bare light, I could see twin spots of red spread across her cheeks.

"That is what you were doing here," she said, her voice thin. "Investigating *me*?"

My stomach twisted, a physical wrench. She stepped toward me, raising one finger at my face. "You think *I* stole my father's watch? That *I* am behind the mess that you've made of Wimborne?"

I raised my chin. "You've made it no secret you despise me." But my voice wavered, doubt creeping in.

She laughed again, but this time the sound had a touch of madness to it. "Of course I do. You are the upstart daughter of a governess *my* father married on a whim, and yet I am to treat you as my equal."

I swallowed. "Then it stands to reason that you might be involved."

"Reason took a quick step off a high cliff the moment you thought I was capable of something so beneath me."

Her indignation was so strong, it was like a slap to the face. I did not speak, unable to find the unraveling thread of my argument. How could I have believed Catherine was involved? She was a gentlewoman of status and wealth, born for a life of prestige. The thought of her hiring shifty men to harass me now seemed ridiculous. Besides, Wimborne had been her home for twenty years before she'd married, and while she hated me, she loved the estate more than anything. She would never hurt Wimborne. It was perfectly obvious to me now that she was as innocent as she was furious. And she was *livid*.

In wake of my silence, Jack stirred. *Please do not speak*, I begged. He would only make things worse.

But Catherine spoke next, her teeth clenched. "Leave my house."

Jack shook his head. "Mrs. Davenport, allow me to ex—"

"I'll hear nothing from you," she seethed. "I knew you were trouble the moment I laid eyes on you, and I will bear your presence in my home not one minute longer."

It would do nothing to say more, but I could not help it. "I am sorry," I whispered, a flood of emotions pulling me along in its current. But guilt pulled the strongest. I'd accused *my sister*. If Father had been here . . .

Catherine barely breathed, her eyes ripping me to shreds. I turned and fled.

I made it all the way downstairs before Jack caught me, grabbing my elbow and pulling me to a stop. "Ginny—"

The look I shot him must've been pure poison, because he released me with a jolt. I stalked out the doors, hurriedly opened by a footman, and descended the stairs. I found my coach down the line of vehicles and climbed inside, ignoring the protests of my coachman. I shut the door and buried my face in my hands.

I was a fool. A dimwit. A ninny. A dolt. Every horrible thing I could think of, I called myself.

Voices outside the coach. Jack. The door opened, my seat shifting as he sat across from me and tapped on the roof. The carriage jolted forward. I refused to look up, my palms pressing into my eyelids.

"I brought your shawl," he said quietly.

Did he expect me to thank him?

"Ginny, I'm sorry that—"

I finally looked up. "It is Miss *Wilde*."

He swallowed, the bob of his throat illuminated by the coach lantern. "Miss Wilde. I'm sorry that I dragged you into this. You must know it was never my intention to cause you pain."

"No, simply to embarrass me and ruin my reputation and destroy what small bit of civility I had with my sister."

His jaw tightened. "I had everything well in hand before you interfered. I have no doubt that Mrs. Davenport only discovered us because *you* led her to me."

"If you will recall," I said roughly, "you work for me. And when I told you to return to the ballroom, *you* refused."

He said nothing to that, the rattling of the coach filling the space between us.

"You should have listened to me." My voice was raw, filled with every broken thing that tumbled around inside me. "I haven't years of experience in the army or at Bow Street, but I know my town. I know my estate, my friends, and I know Catherine. Yet you blazed ahead with no regard for how your actions might affect me."

His eyes met mine then, filled with remorse and . . . pain? Silence filled the space between us for a long moment before he spoke.

"You are right," he said. "Of course, you are right. But surely, we can fix this."

I exhaled a disbelieving laugh. "You cannot fix this, Mr. Travers. In fact, I am of the opinion that you simply make everything worse. So no, I do not want your help."

As soon as I finished speaking, I regretted my words. They were too harsh. But I was angry and hurt. He deserved to hurt as well.

I turned away, grasping my elbows as I glared out the window. He followed my lead and did not say another word. I spent the drive reliving every agonizing moment of Catherine's confrontation. How shocked she'd been that we considered her a suspect, her spiteful words about my mother, the way her eyes had regarded me with such hate. I'd given her no choice *but* to hate me.

What would she do with the knowledge she'd gained tonight? She'd not only learned that Wimborne was in trouble, but that I'd allowed a thief-taker to impersonate my cousin and live under my roof. Surely in spite of her indignation, she was giddy. I'd proven her right. I'd acted in a way completely unbefitting of my station and privilege, and now she had every tool at her disposal to ruin me entirely.

Perhaps I could remove to Brighton. I'd heard it was lovely.

But my stubbornness took hold, rooting through my body until I took a determined breath. No. This was my home. It would take more than a damaged reputation to see me abandon it. And I still had friends. At least, I hoped I did. I knew I could depend on Beatrice, but Mr. Northcott might be the one angry with *me* after I'd deserted him on the dance floor.

I shot a glance at Jack. He sat with his jaw in hand, staring out the opposite window. What was I to do? Much as I hated to admit it, despite his arrogance and misguided actions, I'd come to regard him as a friend. More than a friend—I'd trusted him and he'd broken that trust. Besides, I now had Mr. Northcott's promise of help. I did not truly need Jack any longer.

The coach rumbled to a stop. I reached for the door, but Jack was there first. He descended and held out his hand to me, expression inscrutable. Not wishing to fall on my face amid the other insults I'd endured tonight, I took his hand and stepped down. But when I tried to pull away, he kept hold of my hand.

"I am sorry," he said. "Truly and sincerely."

I wavered. The look in his eyes, the set of his jaw—I knew he meant what he said. But the very fact that I hesitated spoke to a problem I was only just starting to recognize.

I was beginning to *feel* something for Jack. Something deeper than friendship or mere attraction. A low burn in my stomach when he looked at me. The urge to laugh when he teased. Yet it simply could not be. Not now, with my life coming unseamed. Not ever.

I pulled my hand free and took a deep breath. "I think it would be best if we ended our arrangement, Mr. Travers."

He took a step back. I kept my gaze focused on the carriage over his shoulder. I could not look in his eyes.

"I will pay you, of course," I went on, my voice catching, "for services rendered on my behalf. But I will not need your assistance after tonight."

He looked as if he might argue. As if he wanted to take me by the shoulders and give me a good shake. But after a few moments, he bowed his head. "As you say, Miss Wilde," he said, his voice thick. "I will be gone by sun up."

I nodded. "Thank you." I turned to go inside but paused as he held out my ivory shawl, shining like a pool of moonlight. He said nothing as I took it, my hands trembling, and I hurried up the front stairs without looking back.

CHAPTER 15

I awoke feeling ill the next morning. I knew I wasn't sick, what with the absence of a fever or any serious symptoms, but my stomach turned nonetheless. It was early, the rosy light of dawn just beginning to slip through my curtains. *Sun up.*

I went to the window and drew the curtains. It was useless, considering the front drive was hidden by unrelenting brick walls. I sat on the window seat and tucked my knees under my chin.

I'd made the right choice, hadn't I? I could not keep Jack on, not after what had happened last night.

What about Father's watch? A small voice inside me persisted. I shook that thought away. The watch no longer seemed as important, with so many more pressing problems. If I hadn't found it by now, it seemed unlikely that I ever would, much as I hated to admit it. I leaned my head against the cool glass, glistening with morning dew. My eyes dragged closed once again, exhausted from my sleepless night.

Holloway found me an hour later, head resting against the glass, fast asleep.

"We work hard to ensure you have a comfortable bed," she scolded me as she guided me to my dressing table. "The least you can do is sleep in it."

I rubbed my eyes, forcing a smile at her teasing. "I promise to sleep until noon tomorrow." In truth, I wanted nothing more than to bury my head back in my heap of pillows, but I had work to do today. Hiding in my room would not help anything.

Holloway tsked and then began undoing my braids and brushing out my red locks. I fiddled with the sleeve of my dressing gown, then summoned my courage. "Has Mr. Travers gone?"

Her hands paused. "Yes. That's what Marchant said." She gave a few strokes with the brush. "Has he finished his business here, then?"

"Yes," I said firmly. "He has, quite thankfully. I daresay Wimborne is at the end of its troubles."

I was not being the least bit truthful. I was not thankful Jack was gone. In fact, all I wanted was to go downstairs and see those alert blue eyes peering at me over his tea. But that was why this separation was necessary. Unavoidable. Better now than later, when my heart might have been truly at risk.

Holloway sighed. "It was good for you to have company, even his. You seemed happier than you've been in a long time."

Since Father died is what she meant. And while happy did not seem exactly the right word, I understood what she meant. Jack brought life and energy wherever he was. Even angry at him as I was, I could admit that. The house felt dimmer already.

I spent the morning in earnest efforts to alleviate the fiasco at the ball. First, I replied to Beatrice's worried note that had arrived before breakfast, wondering where I had disappeared to last night. I assured her I would visit her later to explain everything. Next, I wrote to Mr. Northcott and apologized profusely, citing a sudden illness that had forced me home. Then I spent nearly an hour debating the merits of writing to Catherine. I wanted to apologize—I *needed* to apologize. I had been so very clearly in the wrong. But neither did I want her to think me insincere, writing only to stay her hand of social execution.

I wrote several horrible drafts of a letter, tossing each into the fire with increasing frustration. There was no way to put into words how I felt, and Catherine would only scoff over any attempt.

"Tell me everything," Beatrice said when I arrived later that afternoon. Her mother must have been feeling poorly again, tucked away in her room where she spent many of her days. I sometimes felt sorry for Mrs. Lacey. All she wanted was to see Beatrice happy and settled. And while I thought Beatrice the happiest person of my acquaintance, *settled* was certainly not how I would ever describe her.

I sat heavily in an armchair. "It was awful, Beatrice. Whatever you are imagining, it was multitudes *worse*."

She raised an eyebrow. "Well, since I am imagining that Mr. Travers kissed you—"

I bolted upright. "What? Of course he didn't kiss me!"

"How disappointing." She tugged on a loose curl. "I was looking forward to teasing you."

"*No*," I reiterated. "Believe me, even a kiss from him would've been vastly preferable to the truth."

"Vastly?" she echoed.

"Please stop," I begged. "I cannot bear any teasing now."

Her smile faded and she moved to the edge of her chair. "I am sorry," she said. "Tell me, please."

The events of last night somehow sounded worse when I recounted them. My mouth ran dry as I spoke, the words fighting to stay within me.

"Oh, Ginny." Beatrice was pale. "Was Catherine terribly angry?"

I rubbed my throat. "I've never seen her like this, not even when I inherited Wimborne. There is no telling what she might do."

Beatrice bit her lip, her eyes never leaving my face. "What of Mr. Travers? What does he say about all this?"

"His opinion no longer matters," I said. "He left this morning."

"He *left*? After putting you in such a mess?"

Her indignation on my behalf was somehow calming. "I asked him to leave," I said. "I will not have someone in my employ whom I cannot trust."

She mulled that over, leaning back in her seat. "I do not doubt your decision, Ginny," she said finally. "You have every right to feel betrayed. My only worry is for Wimborne."

"Mine as well," I admitted. "But it has been over a week without any new incidents, and I am tempted to believe my tormentor is gone. Perhaps Mr. Travers *did* frighten him off. Besides, Mr. Northcott has pledged his aid, and I intend to hold him to it."

"Even knowing he might expect an engagement in return?"

The housekeeper brought tea, and while Beatrice poured, I considered her words. Did Mr. Northcott intend to use his help as a way to further his courtship? And was it truly so terrible a thing if he did? Fear was a powerful motivator. I was already dreading tonight, when my home would once again be vulnerable, my protector gone. A marriage of convenience to Mr. Northcott would certainly be a simple solution to many of my problems.

If only my heart did not falter at the very thought.

"What will you do now?" Beatrice blew on her tea in a fashion that would make her mother wince. "About Catherine, I mean?"

I stirred my steaming tea, watching the cream swirl about. "I do not know," I confessed. "I do not wish to make anything worse, and yet sitting here doing nothing feels foolish when she could already be telling everyone from here to London about Mr. Travers."

"You know I have a bit of experience with rumors." Her voice was light, though it held a slight edge.

I looked up at her. "Oh, Bea, I didn't mean to remind you."

Beatrice's Season in London last year had been marred with horrible gossip, so much so that she had been forced to leave Town and retreat to Little Sowerby. She hadn't minded too much, or at least that is what she told me. I knew better.

She waved me off. "Never mind that. I only mentioned it because of some advice I received from a friend in the midst of that debacle."

I crinkled my forehead. "Who?"

She laughed. "It was *you*, Ginny. Do you not remember?"

"Me?" I searched my memories. "I do hope I said something terribly wise."

Her smile turned wistful. "You did indeed. You told me to hold my head high and not let anyone's words keep me from being the person I knew I was. That actions and character are more important than idle gossip, and that those who truly loved me would stand by my side."

I let out a breath, my lungs pinching inside me. I remembered now. I remembered because those were words Father had often told me. Though he never knew the whole of Catherine's feelings for me, he knew enough. His admonitions had kept me from falling into the trap of anger and spite for so long, knowing he at least had a good opinion of me. That had always been my guiding light, my north star. It was as if his voice had come alive again in Beatrice's words—a reminder that I had endured much already, and could endure more.

"That *was* very wise of me." I forced a smile. "Well, who needs a great deal of friends anyway? I already have the only one who matters."

Beatrice came to sit on the arm of my chair and wrapped her arms around me. I closed my eyes, tears welling as I embraced her in return.

"You will always have me, Ginny," she whispered. "Whenever and wherever you need me."

⊰❋⊱

When I returned to Wimborne, an unfamiliar horse waited outside. I eyed it curiously. I did not receive many visitors.

Marchant met me inside. "Mr. Crouth is here to see you."

I nearly dropped my gloves. The constable? My heart pounded, thudding along in my chest as I handed Marchant my things. Had Catherine involved the law, furious after our intrusion last night?

I hurried to the parlor. Mr. Crouth waited there, picking his teeth in a mirror. I grimaced. Awful man.

As I was about to step inside, I paused, remembering what Jack had said about Father having a mole on his staff. What if it had been Crouth? What if he was still informing, but on Mr. Northcott now? I shook my head. I was as bad as Jack, leaping to ridiculous conclusions. Just because I did not like the man did not mean he was a traitor. Besides, I could not trust Jack's information. Whispers among criminals did not hold much weight with me.

I squared my shoulders and stepped into the room. "Mr. Crouth."

He faced me, his mouth dropping into a frown. "Miss Wilde."

"How might I help you today?"

He crossed his arms. "The magistrate sent me. Said I was to keep an eye on Wimborne."

I released a long breath. Catherine hadn't sent him, then. But still, this was unexpected. Hadn't I told Mr. Northcott that I would inform him when I needed help? "Oh," I said. "That is very kind of him. But I really don't think—"

"Mr. Northcott ordered me to patrol the estate and inform you if I see anything," Mr. Crouth said shortly. "That is what I aim to do."

I could not decide what I should feel. I was grateful that Mr. Northcott had taken some initiative and yet also somewhat annoyed that he had done so without confirming with me.

"I see," I said. There was nothing for it. At the least, having an armed constable on patrol would frighten off anyone thinking of further mischief. "Thank you for your help, sir. I am in your debt."

He grunted as a farewell, touching his hat as he left. Well, he certainly wasn't a charmer. Not like—

But I gritted my teeth and refused to think about *who* Mr. Crouth was not at all like.

Night fell a few hours later, and Mr. Crouth returned to inform me he'd seen nothing suspicious. I thanked him again and sent him on his way with a bundle of Cook's meat pies. I watched from the parlor window as he rode off, my anxiety mounting. I did not much like Mr. Crouth, but I would have given a great deal for him to stay at Wimborne through the night.

I dropped to my chair and kneaded my forehead. Constables were meant to keep the peace, not provide security to my household. I could hardly expect anything more—Mr. Northcott could only do so much. Now, if he were my *husband* . . .

I sighed and fell back against the cushion. No, I mustn't entertain the thought. I would not marry because of fear. I would not.

It was a reassuring thought by the light of my roaring fire, surrounded by servants. But late that night, when all was quiet and dark, I doubted myself again and again. I missed the nights when I'd known Jack was awake and alert, my home his priority, my safety his only concern. Had I been too hasty in his dismissal? My mind would circle back to our confrontation with Catherine and I would tell myself I'd made the right choice.

Apparently, I was quite good at lying to myself, if not to others.

Morning dawned and I faced the day with grim determination. Thankfully, I had the distraction of seeing new locks installed on every door. At least I had taken what steps I could to protect my home.

I was with the locksmith in my study as he explained why these new Bramah locks were impossible to pick—something about cylindrical keyholes and multiple slides—when Marchant approached.

"Miss Wilde, you've a visitor," he said. "Mrs. Davenport."

I stared. *"Catherine* Davenport?" As if there were any other.

"Yes, ma'am," he said, doing his best to restrain his curiosity. But he knew better than anyone that Catherine hadn't come to Wimborne since Father had died.

I left the locksmith and followed Marchant to the sitting room. I paused in the doorway. Catherine stood at the window dressed in a deep green pelisse and cream bonnet. I smoothed my skirts, bracing myself for what would surely be an unpleasant conversation. Then I stepped inside the room and closed the door behind me. No need for everyone else in the house to hear what Catherine had come to say.

She turned, eyeing me in that disconcerting way of hers.

"Catherine," I greeted her and offered a curtsy. She did not offer one in return, which did not bode well.

"You are installing new locks," she said without a word of pleasantries.

I clasped my hands before me. "I ordered them as soon as Father's watch went missing."

She did not speak but instead circled the room, inspecting everything as if she might find a flaw. I was sure she would. She had been mistress of this house for years before she'd married, and she alone knew it as well as I did.

The silence grew too intense. I decided it was better to have this over and done with. "Might I inquire as to the reason for this visit?"

"I am not here to gloat, if that is what you are wondering," she said evenly.

It had certainly crossed my mind. "Blackmail then?"

"Tempting," she said. "But no, I am afraid not."

I sighed. "Then *why?*"

She picked up a small ceramic figurine, a shepherdess Father had been fond of. "I had a very interesting visitor yesterday," she said. "Quite early in the morning."

I shook my head. "What has that to do with—"

"It was your Mr. Travers," she interrupted.

My mouth dropped. "Mr. Travers?"

"Yes," she said matter-of-factly. "He came knocking on my door at such an ungodly hour I thought some horrible accident must have occurred. But no, he simply wished to *talk.*"

My knees felt unsteady and I lowered myself to the chair beside the door. Jack had gone to Catherine? "What did he say?"

"Oh, a great deal." She cast her eyes to the ceiling. "That man has quite a mouth, hasn't he? Ever so frustrating."

"On that we can agree," I said, though my mind was spinning.

Catherine set down the figurine. "He told me it had been his idea to claim to be your cousin, that you had no choice but to go along with the charade. It was hard to disagree with that, since I'd seen your face on the road when he first spouted off that nonsense."

I said nothing. I knew Catherine well enough to realize when she wanted to speak uninterrupted.

"He also insisted," she went on, "that he was entirely to blame for breaching my privacy at the ball. That you tried to stop him and he ignored your orders. Is that true?"

I nodded, my voice hidden somewhere deep in my chest.

Catherine's eyes narrowed. "Why did you not say so that night?"

I took a moment to think, to form my answer. "There was no point," I finally said. "You would not have believed me, and I can hardly blame you. But more importantly, he was in my employ, and so I am responsible for his actions."

Her gaze burned into me, and I met it steadily. I would face whatever punishment she decided to mete out.

Her next words caught me by surprise. "Is Wimborne really under such a threat as to install new locks and hire a thief-taker?"

"Yes," I said. "It is."

"Tell me everything," she insisted.

This new interest was odd, but I would not refuse her. "We've had a dozen small incidents—broken windows, a suspicious flood, missing sheep, and the stolen watch, of course. Then Saturday last, Mr. Travers spotted and pursued a man who had been watching the estate through a spyglass. He was unable to catch the culprit, but it proved our suspicions correct, that someone was targeting Wimborne."

She listened, fingers tapping against her crossed arms. "Mr. Travers told me he was returning to London."

I cleared my throat. "Yes. I thought it best to end our ridiculous charade, now that . . ."

"Now that you know I am not stealing sheep and watches?"

My cheeks grew hot. "I am sorry for that. But please allow me some honesty. You cannot be truly surprised that I suspected you. You have made no secret of your feelings toward me."

Catherine turned away, but not before I caught a strange look in her eyes, one I'd never seen there before. *Confusion.*

"I will be blunt as well," she said, facing the window. "I do not like you, and I do not think I ever will."

Her words hit me like a sheet of cold, blinding rain. Some small part of me still held out hope, even after all these years, that we might have something of a relationship. She was all the family I had left. I inhaled a ragged breath, glad she wasn't looking at me.

"That being said," she went on, "I have no interest in making what happened between you and Mr. Travers public knowledge."

It took me a moment to realize what she'd said. "What?"

She let out a short laugh. "You believe me so blinded by my feelings for you? No, I have thought this through carefully. Any stain on your reputation is a stain on Wimborne's—on my father's—and I will not see his memory besmirched so."

Catherine looked at me over her shoulder, and it seemed—for the briefest of moments—that her face softened. "And," she said, "after speaking with Mr. Travers, I have come to admit that your choices were perhaps not so flighty and reckless as I first thought."

"A compliment?" I released a puff of air. "You are all surprises today, Catherine."

Any softness in her expression vanished, and she set her mouth in a firm line. "It was an observation," she said briskly. "Now, Marchant said the constable was here yesterday. Has Mr. Northcott come to his senses and provided you some aid?"

I sighed. "Of a sort. Mr. Crouth patrolled a few hours."

She snorted. "Crouth is worthless. He could not catch a real criminal if a highwayman knocked down his front door. No, that won't do. The best thing to do is fetch Mr. Travers back right away."

"What?" I repeated yet again. Was she mad?

"Wimborne must be protected," she said. "Mr. Travers is clearly the man for the job."

I stared at her. "Even after what he did, you would advise this?"

Catherine raised her chin, and for the first time in my life, I saw myself in her. We did not look alike in any way, but the stubbornness in her jaw was all too familiar. "His character may be wanting, but he produces results. You cannot afford to be picky at a time like this."

This was too strange to be true. Catherine, advocating for Jack?

"You really are not going to tell anyone that he is not my cousin?" I asked, my voice soft as a morning mist.

"No."

I took a steadying breath. "Thank you," I said. "I know you are not doing it for me, but I will thank you all the same. And I *am* sorry, for what it is worth. I should never have let our deception go so far."

She nodded, as much of an acceptance as I could hope to receive. For a moment, it seemed like she might say something more, her mouth parting. But she set her jaw and strode to the door. "Do try not to muck everything up again, Ginny."

I went to the window and watched as she stepped into her barouche, far grander than my own little coach. I shook my head, unable to comprehend what had happened. Catherine Davenport would not be ruining my life. She held the most damaging tidbit of truth in the palm of her hand and she was keeping it to herself. I had no doubt she would lord this over me for the rest of my life. But she had chosen not to hurt me, even when I had hurt her.

A tiny seedling of hope bloomed inside me even as I tried to smother it. I could not let myself go down that path again. Catherine wanted nothing to do with me and I had to resign myself to that fact.

I leaned against the window as her coach rolled away, so well sprung it hardly bounced. Despite the questions flying about my head, a flicker of heat sparked inside me. Jack had gone to Catherine. He had explained his actions, defended me, tried to fix his mistakes. I winced, thinking of the words I'd cast at him. *You cannot fix this, Mr. Travers. In fact, I am of the opinion that you simply make everything worse.*

I'd been so wrong. Even if he hadn't found my watch or caught the criminal, he *had* succeeded in other things. Convincing Catherine to rethink her options. Helping me feel safe once again in my home.

Making me laugh. Looking at me in a way that made me feel like I might burst into flames.

Drat it all, I missed the arrogant cad.

But the fact remained that Wimborne had seen no new threats since before he'd left. There was no point in bringing him back. No point at all.

I knew my reasoning was sound, but my heart did not care for reason.

CHAPTER 16

The days passed in a slow haze. I tried very hard not to think of Mr. Travers and failed very badly. In the short time he'd been at Wimborne, he'd impressed himself into the memory of the house, and it was difficult to forget him.

But I must, I scolded myself. What was my heart longing for anyway? A flirtatious, maddening, sometimes sincere thief-taker? That would never do. I could never *marry* such a man, and so any paths leading that direction were impossible.

Early in the morning three days after Catherine's visit, I was reading a letter from my solicitor. Well, *re*-reading, since my thoughts wandered constantly toward dark curly hair and vivid blue eyes. So, when Marchant knocked on my open study door, I was more than happy to set down my letter.

"Today's mail, miss." He set a small stack of letters on my desk.

"Thank you." I reached for them as he left. Perhaps there was something more interesting than the investments my solicitor was droning on about. I flipped through the letters and one caught my eye. It had my name written across the front in an unfamiliar hand, but no direction. I frowned as I unfolded the paper.

My heart stopped.

Do not sleep too soundly, Miss Wilde. The worst is yet to come.

My fingers curled around the letter. The words leapt at me,

jumping off the page and burrowing into my mind. *The worst is yet to come.*

It was from him—my tormentor. It had to be. I tried to breathe as I read it again. I could not feel the warmth from my fire, my senses withdrawing as I tried to process what lay before me.

But how? How had he managed to get this letter to me?

"Marchant!" I jumped to my feet and hurried to the door. Marchant was halfway down the corridor and turned at my shout.

"Miss Wilde?" he said.

I brandished the paper. "This letter. Where did it come from?"

He looked bewildered. "Same as always. John fetched it from the post office."

But that was impossible. It did not have my direction. "I need to speak with him immediately."

My poor footman seemed no less confused when Marchant brought him to my study and I showed him the letter.

"Did this come from the post office?" I asked.

"That?" John squinted, stepping forward. "Yes, I believe so." Then he paused. "Although, after I left the post office, a boy came after me. Said I'd dropped a letter and handed me that very one. I even gave him a penny for his troubles."

"Did you know this boy?" My voice rose in pitch.

He shook his head. "Sorry, miss, I can't say I did. I was in a hurry, see. I doubt I'd even recognize him if I saw him again."

My hopes deflated. There would be no tracing this letter. I swallowed. "Thank you," I said. "You may go."

John left with one last curious glance, but Marchant remained, moving closer with a furrowed brow.

"That letter," he said. "What does it say, Miss Wilde?"

I passed it to him without a word. He read it in an instant.

"What can the blackguard mean by sending this?" he asked, anger darkening his eyes.

"To frighten me," I said. He'd succeeded. Fear clenched inside me, unrelenting. Would this never end? Would I never be free from terror?

"'The worst is yet to come,'" he repeated. "A bluff? Or a warning?"

I shook my head. It did not truly matter. The effect was the same. This man, this shadow figure from my nightmares, would not give up. He would torment me so long as I allowed him to.

I stood and braced my hands on my desk. Marchant watched, unspeaking. I had to act. I had to protect my home, my servants. Myself. This had gone on long enough.

I took the letter from Marchant and folded it carefully. It was evidence, and I would keep it safe. But I needed more than circumstantial evidence. I needed to catch the fiend responsible. I needed help.

I should have gone straight to Mr. Northcott, told him everything. But there was only one man who could deal with such a threat, only one man who had kept me safe.

I needed Jack Travers.

⊱✦⊰

Holloway packed my small trunk with enough clothing for two days while I gave instructions to my butler and housekeeper.

"Keep the doors and windows locked whenever you can," I said. "I don't want anyone wandering about by themselves, especially the maids. Be vigilant. I'll return soon."

Marchant coughed. "Will Mr. Travers come, do you think?"

Though he tried to hide it, I heard the hope in his voice, and it almost made me smile. Even if my butler did not approve of Jack's manners, he seemed to recognize his value.

"I do not know," I said honestly. "We did not part on good terms. But I will do whatever it takes."

We left within the hour, a footman above with my coachman. London was but an afternoon's journey on good roads, so we would arrive before dark.

"You don't think highwaymen will stop us, do you?" Holloway asked nervously as we passed out of town and onto country roads.

"I would dearly love to see them try." My normally quiet temper was near to boiling, the words of that threatening letter emblazoned on my mind. Let the highwaymen come. Let them underestimate me just long enough to plant my fist right between their eyes.

I formed a plan as we traveled—I would go in the direction I'd found in Jack's newspaper advertisement and convince him to return with me. It was simple and straightforward. Save for the fact that he might refuse, considering how I'd treated him the night of the ball. Or perhaps he was already occupied with another case. It *had* been five days since he'd left Wimborne.

But I could not think of that now. *He will be there*, I told myself. He had to be.

We entered the maze of London's twisting streets as the sun began to set behind the rooftops above us. Despite how close I lived to London, I'd visited only a handful of times, including my less-than-wonderful Season. Father preferred the country, and I generally agreed. I was far better suited to a slower pace of life. But the bustling city now filled me with energy. I could ignore the haze and horrid smell for a day or two.

I'd given my driver the direction, and we entered the neighborhood near Covent Garden, filled with shops, trades, and narrow townhomes. It seemed a reasonable place for a successful thief-taker to take rooms, especially considering how near to Bow Street it was. The coach came to a stop, and when the footman handed me down, I looked up at my destination, ready to face any obstacle. Instead, I could only stare at what lay before me.

It was an open-air butcher's shop. If the sign above the door wasn't clear—*Wilson's Fine Meats*—then the enormous sides of beef hanging from the low rafters were firm clues.

"Is this the right place?" I asked Mr. Rigby.

"Aye," my coachman said, eyeing the shop. "Unless the direction was wrong?"

"No, it wasn't." If the direction was wrong, my letter would never have made it to Jack in the first place. Perhaps he lived above the shop? I would only find out by inquiring.

Holloway followed me, raising a handkerchief to her nose as we approached. The area behind the low counter was empty, and we had to duck beneath the prominently displayed meat. A door led back into the building, from which great chopping noises escaped.

"Pardon me?" I called.

I heard footsteps, and a great hulk of a man appeared in the doorway, nearly bald but with great black side whiskers. He wore an apron covered in . . .

I forced myself to meet his eyes, even as my stomach turned. "Good day, sir. I am hoping you can help me."

He grinned, his gaze running down my figure. "Certain I can."

Was he flirting with me? Perhaps this was some relation of Jack's and suggestive comments simply ran in the family.

I raised my chin. "I am looking for a Mr. Jack Travers. Is he a tenant of the rooms above?"

The butcher had been wiping his hands on his apron, but he paused. "Who be asking?" he said apprehensively.

"A former client," I said. No need to go into detail. "I am looking to hire him again."

He leaned on the counter with his thick forearms, and I forced myself not to step back. Holloway gave a little whimper behind me.

"I don't know where Jack be livin'," he said. "I'm just here to collect his mail and frighten off anyone who sniffs after his trail."

It did make sense. Surely Jack had a great deal of enemies in his line of work. He could hardly advertise his home direction in newspapers all over London Town. "Please, I need to speak with him. I do not mean him any harm."

He narrowed his eyes. "Ye be a might too fine and pretty to run with a bad crowd, I'm thinkin'. But it's not up to me, miss. If ye leave a letter, I'll see he gets it."

"I do not have time for a letter," I said sharply. Too sharply. The man straightened, muscles flexing as he crossed his arms. Some tact might be better. "I have a most urgent matter and it cannot wait."

"I'll see he gets the note quick," was his only reply, his dark eyes warning me not to press him.

I had no choice but to give in. He provided me with a scrap of paper and a pencil, and I scrawled a quick note. I could provide Jack only the barest of details—that I needed to speak to him right away and that I would be staying at the Golden Lion in Cheapside. So many words hovered at the tip of my pencil, all I wanted to say to him. But this was all I could do for now.

"Thank you kindly," I managed as I handed the man my folded note. Perhaps a bit of civility would convince him to pass on my letter sooner rather than later.

But he only mumbled and waved me away as he placed the note beneath the counter. Holloway and I left, my heart heavy as the coach started off through the crowded streets.

This was a dreadful turn of events. I'd hoped to see Jack tonight—depended on it, really. Instead, I had to wait until the butcher delivered my note. But when and how would he do it? He'd said he didn't know where Jack lived, and I'd believed him. *I'm just here to collect his mail.*

I gazed out into the streets, the late afternoon light reflecting in every window. Then I sat up straight, the butcher's words once again rolling through my mind. *I'll see he gets the note quick.* If he couldn't deliver the mail, that meant someone would have to retrieve it.

And perhaps that someone was coming tonight.

I opened the window. "Mr. Rigby?"

"Yes, miss?" said my coachman.

"Turn back to the butcher's," I ordered. "Stop down the road so we can see the shop but not draw attention."

If he thought my instructions odd, he refrained from saying so. "Yes, Miss Wilde." The coach turned and my hope came back in a sweeping rush.

"What plan have you got into your head now?" Holloway asked with a sigh.

I smiled. "Hopefully one absurd enough to work."

CHAPTER 17

We watched the butcher's shop for close to two hours, the city growing darker around us as evening approached. A few shoppers came and went, but none took anything from the butcher except meat wrapped in paper, and neither did the man react to any customer in a way I thought suspicious.

And none had a head of dark curly hair or a wicked grin.

Holloway had fallen asleep across the coach, which was for the best. I knew she meant well, but her fretting was rather tiresome.

I leaned my head against the cool window, my eyes tired from constant vigilance, but I was determined to miss nothing. The lamplighters would be going around soon, the gas lamps brightening the London haze. Perhaps I'd been wrong. Perhaps no one was coming.

A figure caught my eye, a woman in a blue pelisse moving past my window as she crossed the road, dodging behind the wheels of a slow-moving cart. I couldn't say why I watched her—I could only see the back of her red hat, set at a saucy angle. But there was something about her, something about how she moved . . .

I peered after her as she went to the butcher shop. The butcher immediately waved the woman over, reaching beneath the counter to retrieve a small bundle. My heart pounded. It had to be the mail he collected for Jack. Including my note.

The woman took the bundle and slipped it into her basket,

offering the man a wave over her shoulder. She started in the opposite direction, a bounce to her step. Who was she?

I opened the window again. "Mr. Rigby, do you see that woman there, across the street?"

He jolted when I spoke—he'd likely fallen asleep too. He cleared his throat. "Yes. Yes, Miss Wilde."

"Follow her," I said. "Carefully. I wish to see where she goes."

The coach jerked forward, awakening Holloway. I told her what had happened even as I craned my head to see down the street.

"So, we are following a strange woman to an unknown location in London just as night is falling?" she asked, her eyes dim with sleep.

"Precisely," I said, not looking away from the road for fear of losing our lead.

She exhaled. "I do miss the quiet days."

Part of me agreed with her, wanting nothing more than the safety of my fireplace, my home secure around me. And yet another part of me, small but bright, had sparked to life in the last few hours. Taking action, taking charge of my life—it was invigorating. This was something I could *do*, rather than sit and hope for the best.

We followed the woman for nearly a quarter hour. She looked back once or twice, but our nondescript coach was clearly not interesting enough to alarm her. Mr. Rigby did an excellent job of stopping every now and again to keep our distance. When she finally went up the steps to a small and tidy townhome, with warm brown stone and diamond-paned windows, we came to a stop once again. As she entered the home, a light inside lit up her silhouette. She removed her hat, revealing an unruly mass of dark curls as the door closed behind her.

I blinked. Had I imagined it?

"What do we do now?" Holloway asked nervously.

I reached for the door handle. "Now we find Mr. Travers."

I did not wait for the footman's help in descending the steps to the street. "Wait here," I instructed Mr. Rigby. Then with Holloway looking distinctly nervous at my side, and my pulse thumping in my ears, I climbed the steps to the door and knocked.

It opened almost immediately by the woman we had followed. I froze. I'd expected a servant.

"Good evening," she said, eyeing me with no small amount of curiosity. "Might I help you?" Along with her dark curls, nearly black in this light, she had a heart-shaped face, pink cheeks and lips, and limitless blue eyes. This must be Jack's sister. That, or I had terrible skills of observation.

I cleared my throat. "Is this the residence of Mr. Travers?"

Her eyes narrowed and she stepped into the gap of the open door, blocking my view of the house. "And you are?"

"Miss Genevieve Wilde," I said. "I recently employed Mr. Travers, and—"

"Oh!" she said, staring at me. "You are *her*."

I was who?

"Do come inside, Miss Wilde." She opened the door wide. Holloway gave me a look of warning as I entered without hesitation. I could not say why, but I knew I was in no danger here.

A maid scurried toward us, taking my spencer, bonnet, and gloves. I glanced surreptitiously at what I assumed was Jack's home. A slender set of stairs lined the wall to the right, parallel to a corridor leading to the back of the house. Simple, elegant artwork adorned the walls, everything clean and placed with care. *Not* what I'd imagined for a bachelor's rooms in the city.

"Do forgive me coming without an invitation," I said, feeling suddenly awkward. Meeting Jack alone was one thing. Meeting his family was an entirely different matter.

The woman with Jack's eyes laughed. "Oh, we do not stand on ceremony here. Jack's profession has made that impossible." She helped the maid manage our things, her movements quick but graceful. I realized why she had caught my eye on the street. She moved like Jack—always in constant motion.

"I am Verity Travers," she said. "Jack is my brother, though you might already know that."

"I made a guess," I admitted. "He did not tell me much about his family." Well, besides his father. But broaching Jack's illegitimacy was not a bright idea, especially since Verity looked just like him. I could only assume her . . . situation was the same.

Verity grinned. "We are terribly embarrassing. Can't have anyone finding out about us."

I did not know whether to laugh or protest, and she went on before I could decide. "Are you hungry? Your maid can go down with Pritchett to the kitchens and eat. You are welcome to join us for dinner when Jack arrives."

I was taken aback. I barely knew this young lady, and she was inviting me to dinner. "I . . . I really only need to speak to Ja—Mr. Travers. I did not intend to disrupt your evening."

She waved that off. "Oh, you've done nothing of the sort. Now, come and meet Grandmother and Mama."

Would I meet every member of Jack's family tonight? Holloway shot me an amused glance as she followed after the maid. I gave a helpless shrug. The evening had taken a very unexpected turn.

Verity led me to the sitting room off the entryway. I glanced around, unconsciously seeking any sign of Jack. A copy of the *Hue and Cry* on the arm of the sofa. The familiar little black book, the one Jack was always writing in, on the writing desk. A pair of brown gloves on the table beside the door, surely too large to be a woman's. I tried to calm my racing heart, but it was impossible. I was *here*, in Jack's home, intruding upon his privacy and meeting his family uninvited. What on earth had I been thinking?

An older woman sat by the fire, embroidering by the flickering light. She looked up at our entrance, spectacles balanced on her nose. She was nearing seventy years of age, guessing by her lined face and thoroughly white hair beneath her cap. Her body was rounded and soft, like I imagined a grandmother's should be. She looked every inch the gentle matriarch.

"I thought I heard voices," she said, her voice sharp. "Who is this?"

My smile faltered. So much for gentle.

"Grandmother, this is Miss Wilde," Verity said. "One of Jack's clients."

"Miss Wilde." The woman said my name slowly, as if trying to recall where she had heard it before. "Miss Wilde . . . Oh. The wench with the watch."

I blinked. Verity looked close to bursting out in laughter. What exactly had Jack told them about me?

"Yes, right," Verity said, lips twitching. "The wench with the watch. Miss Wilde, this is my grandmother."

I recovered enough to curtsy. "Pleased to meet you."

She eyed me over her spectacles. "A fancy miss, are we?" She gave a sniff then returned to her embroidery without another word.

"I am sorry about her," Verity said in a whisper, her eyes crinkled in amusement. "She doesn't get on very well with new people."

"I don't mind," I reassured her. "I know I am imposing."

Before Verity could respond, a female voice came from the doorway. "Oh, a guest! How positively wonderful."

I turned as another woman swept into the room, brilliant red skirts swishing along the floor. Her dark hair was pinned up into an elaborate style, tight curls framing her features—dainty nose, full lips, and expressive brows. Her dress displayed an ample bosom, her frame perfectly soft and willowy. She was stunning, a statue of a Greek goddess come to life.

"Mama," Verity said meaningfully, "this is *Miss Wilde*."

I tried not to stare and I failed. I hadn't at all expected a woman like this to be Jack's mother.

"Miss Wilde?" Mrs. Travers's eyes widened. She and Verity exchanged a glance, the meaning of which I would have paid a hundred pounds to learn.

"Good evening, Mrs. Travers." I managed to curtsy once again. "So pleased to make your acquaintance."

She inspected me as she came nearer, her movements flowing from one to the next with incalculable grace. "My, you are a pretty one," she said. Her voice was like butter, rich and smooth. "I might have guessed."

I hardly knew what to say to that. I cleared my throat instead. "Do forgive my intrusion. I only came to speak with your son. I am told he will return soon?"

"Oh, yes," she said. "Jack always sends word if he will be delayed for dinner. He hates to worry me."

That was interesting. This was certainly a different side of him than what I'd seen, brash and reckless.

"I've invited her to dine with us," Verity said.

"Good, good," Mrs. Travers said airily. "That will give us a chance to know you better, Miss Wilde. I am ever so curious about you."

She seated herself with a grand bustle of skirts and gestured for me to sit on the armchair. Verity sat beside her grandmother, who studiously ignored us all as she held her sewing up to the light.

"I must say," Mrs. Travers said, leaning toward me, smelling strongly of roses, "I am terribly pleased you came. Jack has hardly told us a thing about you, least of all how beautiful you are."

"*Mama*," Verity said with an amused exhale.

"Come, you are as curious as I am," Mrs. Travers said, waving a hand. "Jack has been surly and moping for *days*."

I bit my lip to stop a smile. It was not as though I *knew* Jack acted that way because of me. But if he missed me even a small fraction of how I missed him . . .

"I am sure she simply has business to discuss with him." Verity turned to me. "Have you had more trouble on your estate? Is that why you are looking for Jack?"

"I—well, yes." I could predict nothing about this conversation.

She nodded knowingly. "Jack told me he had Wily Greaves helping with your case."

"Indeed," I said. "He has been quite . . . helpful."

Verity grinned. "A likely story. He is a pest, to be sure."

Mrs. Travers sat forward. "Verity, hush with all that nonsense. I want to hear more about Miss Wilde."

"Where is Jack?" the grandmother said suddenly, her voice grating. "He promised to read me the paper."

I had to stop myself from shaking my head in befuddlement. An enthusiastic sister, a dazzling mother, a crotchety grandmother. This was not at all how I'd pictured this evening going.

But then we heard the front door open, out of view. A spark lit up my spine.

"Speak of the devil and he shall appear," Verity said.

"Pritchett?" It was *his* voice, low and rumbling. Just the sound sent a rush of blood to my head. The maid from before went past the open sitting room door to assist Jack with his things.

Then appear he did, stepping into the open doorway as he raked a hand through his hair. My eyes fixed onto him, the unrelenting pull of a magnet. Was it possible he'd grown more handsome, even with his loosened cravat and messy hair? Or perhaps it was because of his loosened cravat and messy hair. My legs grew shaky, my lungs suddenly grasping for air. It *had* been nearly a week since I'd last seen him, but still my reaction seemed unreasonable.

I knew the second he saw me. His hands froze in midair and he stared, those blue eyes tracing over me in one quick movement.

"Miss Wilde," he said, his voice rough.

I stood abruptly. "Good evening, Mr. Travers." I managed to sound unaffected, as if I'd come for a dinner party.

He stepped forward, his eyes never leaving mine. "What are you . . ." He stopped, blinking and looking around as if he'd just remembered we were surrounded by his family. I swallowed, and any words I'd clung to now fled into the night.

"Miss Wilde came looking for you," his mother offered, since it appeared neither of us would speak. Her eyes danced. "Some business, I gather."

"Yes, business." I collected my wits. "I need to speak to you immediately, if I can."

"What's happened?" He looked me over again as if he might have missed an injury during his first perusal. "Are you well?"

The urgency in his voice made me swallow. "I'm well," I said softly.

"Of course she is," Mrs. Travers said. "Now stop lurking by the door and come sit down, Jack."

Jack did not move any further into the room, still staring at me as if he hadn't heard a word his mother had said. Oh, why had I come? I felt the mad desire to dash behind the window curtains and hide until they all went away. I tore my gaze from his, looking at Verity instead. She must have sensed my embarrassment, my uncertainty, because she quickly stood.

"Let us go, Mama," she said, tugging on her mother's arm. "We'll leave them to talk."

Mrs. Travers shook her head. "I'm sure Miss Wilde won't mind—"

"I'll speak with Miss Wilde alone." Jack's words shivered in the air between us. "Thank you, Mother."

Mrs. Travers gave a dramatic huff. "Oh, all right."

The elderly grandmother protested as Verity helped her to her feet—"Wretched child, taking an old woman from her fire"—but soon enough, the door closed behind the three of them and I was left alone with Jack.

He moved forward to brace his arms on the back of the sofa, watching me where I stood beside the fire. I was more unsure of myself now than I'd been at my first ball at sixteen. Everything had moved so quickly today. Was I truly standing before him now?

"Your family is very welcoming," I blurted to fill the silence.

"Welcoming." His lips twitched. "Is that another word for overwhelming and intrusive?"

The tightness in my lungs eased. He did not seem irritated that I'd ambushed him in his home.

"How did you find me?" he asked, curious.

"It was no easy feat," I said. "Your friend the butcher is to be commended."

He exhaled a laugh. "Ah, Tommy. He is frightening, isn't he? I pay him handsomely to keep undesirables away from my family."

"He did his job well," I admitted. "I nearly gave up. But I had a spot of intuition that turned out to be right."

"Which was?"

"Verity," I said. "I followed her from the shop when she collected your mail."

He gave a rueful smile. "You have found the chink in my armor, Miss Wilde, though I should hardly be surprised."

I missed him calling me Ginny. *Miss Wilde* sounded far too stilted.

"Now that you've found me," he said, coming around the sofa, "perhaps we ought to discuss why. Because charming as I am, I doubt you came all this way because you missed me." He cleared his throat. "Especially as I was less than charming during our last interaction."

He gestured for me to sit again, which gave me a few moments to gather my thoughts. I'd rehearsed it all in the coach, of course, but now, with him not three paces away and the fire warm on my back, it was difficult to remember my lines.

"I have much to tell you," I said, first folding my hands in my lap, then brushing my skirts. His eyes followed my jerky movements, concern touching his brow. I hoped he assigned my nervousness to my news, not to the fact that he made my blood race beneath my skin.

"What's happened?" he asked.

I took a steadying breath and reached into my reticule. "I received a letter," I said, "with the mail this morning."

I handed him the letter and watched as he read. He stilled, staring at the paper. Then he looked up at me, jaw so clenched it sent a bold ridge of muscle across his cheek.

"Tell me everything," he commanded.

I explained about Marchant bringing me the mail, about the footman and the little boy.

"Was there anything else suspicious?" he asked, all business. "Any clues as to the boy's identity?"

"None."

"What did Mr. Northcott think of all this?" Jack's voice was strained, and he stared steadfastly at the fire. For the first time since entering the house, my pulse calmed and resolve wound up my spine.

"I haven't told Mr. Northcott," I said. "I departed for London the same hour I received the letter."

His eyes snapped to mine, sending a bolt of energy through me. "Why?" he asked, and that one word held so many questions.

Instead of answering, I stood and went to the window. "Catherine Davenport visited me two days ago," I said, letting my hands drift over the curtains. "She had ever so much to tell me."

A chair scuffed, and I saw in the window's reflection that he'd also stood.

"I thought if I explained everything to her, she would understand," he said from behind me. "I do not think I succeeded, and I am sorry if I made things worse."

I winced, hearing the same words I'd cast at him the night of the ball. I turned to him, leaning back on the windowsill.

"No," I said simply. "You did not make things worse. In fact, Catherine—well, she and I have called something of a truce between us. She won't tell anyone about our charade."

Jack stared at me, and I decided that I quite liked surprising him. He always seemed to be one step ahead of me—ahead of everyone, really—so it was satisfying to know something he did not.

He let out a long exhale. "I am glad for it. I never intended to make such a muddle of your life. I . . . well, let us simply say this is not the first time I have acted foolishly."

"What do you mean?"

He sent me a long, searching look. "I never told you why I left Bow Street," he said finally.

My heart skipped. I'd wanted to know when we first met, concerned as I'd been with his qualifications. Then I'd grown to know him better, and it hadn't seemed so important. Now I wasn't sure what I wanted. Would what he said change my opinion of him?

"No, you didn't," I said cautiously. If he wished to tell me, I would listen.

He stuffed his hands in his pockets and turned to the fire, sending a wave of golden light across his skin. "A year and a half ago, I was given a case by the chief magistrate," he said. "The murder of a young lady. She was from a prominent family, and the Home Office wanted the case resolved as quickly as possible."

I nodded but did not speak, not wanting to stop him.

He ran a hand through his hair, throwing those already chaotic curls into more disarray and sending twirling flutters throughout my stomach. "I was eager to prove I was up to the task. Too eager. I attacked the case—interviewed all suspects, collected evidence, found what I assumed was proof."

He pulled his brass-tipped stave from his jacket, weighing it in his hands. "I was convinced I knew who the murderer was: the man engaged to this young lady. Everything pointed to him, and he made no secret of the fact that he disliked me intruding in his business. I accused him of the murder publicly and caused quite the scene."

"But it wasn't him," I said softly, already guessing the outcome.

Jack shook his head. "No. New evidence turned up shortly afterward, proving the guilty man was a stable boy in the girl's household, madly in love with her and unable to watch her marry another."

"That is awful." I grimaced. "But why should this have caused you to leave Bow Street?"

He angled toward me, his face all regret, the baton still grasped in one hand. "The innocent man I'd accused was furious, as he had every right to be. I'd dragged his name through the mud in an attempt to find him guilty. He had all the right connections, and in the end, the chief magistrate had no choice but to dismiss me."

My hands tightened around the window ledge behind me. I knew very well the difficult choices a magistrate faced, having watched my father make them again and again. If Jack had truly done what he said, then I could not help but think his punishment just. Still, I ached for him. He had only done his best.

"I know what you are thinking," he said, "and I do not disagree. I deserved to be dismissed. It was painful, leaving my brother officers and a life I loved. But I decided to take what skills I had and make my living another way. I became a thief-taker." He held up the stave, which glimmered in the candlelight. "This was supposed to serve as a reminder of all I'd lost. I would be methodical, careful, not jump to conclusions. I thought I had learned my lesson." He gave a short laugh. "Until I fell into the same trap the night of the ball. I was *so* sure Catherine Davenport was involved. The risks did not matter, because once I had the evidence, there would be nothing she could do."

His eyes fixed on mine. "I was a fool of the highest degree. It was only after I left Wimborne that I realized how much more your opinion meant to me than any reward. And for that I am sorry." He stepped forward, set the stave on the small table beside the sofa. "Miss Wilde, I should gladly return to Wimborne with you, for no other reason than to finish what I began. But I'd like to know if that was your intention in coming here."

His eyes, bold and direct, drew me forward, and my limbs moved without permission. I pushed myself away from the windowsill, coming to stand an arm's length from him.

"When I saw that letter this morning," I said softly, "I admit that it frightened me. But I did not go to Mr. Northcott. I had only one thought." I paused. "I needed *you*."

My words hung between us. The air snapped with awareness, the space that separated us as slight as a summer breeze. I drank in every inch of him—the shadow along his jaw, his dark brows, the taut muscles in his neck as he swallowed. His hand rose, gently brushing one of my red curls that had escaped my coiffure. He bent his head, parting his lips, looking very much as if he might kiss me.

I wanted him to. Heavens, how I wanted him to. The rushing in my chest, the thrill in every limb—I was so powerfully present. Had it only been a fortnight since I'd first met him? How had tolerance turned so quickly to attraction, and then to . . . whatever *this* was? I hardly knew if I could call it love, so subtly had it come. Wasn't I supposed to know if I was in love?

If he kissed me, I had a feeling I might find out.

But something shifted in Jack's eyes. He exhaled and stepped back, clasping his hands firmly behind him. Disappointment flooded me, disappointment that I should not feel, here in a thief-taker's sitting room in a small London townhome so far from home.

But I could not help it. I craved his touch. I'd been denying it for as long as I'd known him, but I ached to learn how it might feel to have his lips brush against mine. He looked so maddeningly attractive at that moment that my mind was quite lost at the thought of what would happen if I simply crossed the chasm between us and pressed a kiss to that crooked corner of his mouth.

But he was right to step back. It wasn't proper. And I'd never hated propriety more.

"I am glad you came," he said quietly, staring at the fire. "I hated thinking I'd ruined so much for you. You can't imagine how many times I've relived our conversation after the ball."

I shook my head. "I am sorry now for the things I said to you."

"They were true," he said. "Much as I disliked hearing them."

"I regret them all the same. You've done so much for Wimborne, for me." I looked down at my hands, twisted before me. "I—well, I haven't felt safe since you left."

Even if I read to him from all my journals, all my girlish secrets and dreams, I did not think I could feel more raw and revealed than I did in that moment. Because my words held so much more than they seemed. More than I had even known I felt until this very moment.

"I need your help, Jack." I looked up at him. It was the first time I'd ever addressed him by his given name aloud, and the significance was not lost on him. His features softened. "And I am glad you are willing to give it, because I've a crook to catch and I know no one better for the job than you."

A grin caught at the corner of his mouth, the spot I'd contemplated kissing a few moments before. "That poor fellow is in for a world of trouble. Between the two of us, he hasn't got a chance."

CHAPTER 18

I accepted Verity's invitation to join them for dinner, and Mrs. Travers insisted that Holloway and I stay the night there instead of at some drafty inn. I hesitated a moment before accepting. It was perfectly proper, of course, what with Mrs. Travers's presence, but it still seemed strange. Did they know that Jack had stayed at Wimborne unchaperoned for so long?

Besides that, this was *Jack's* home, *Jack's* family. I felt every inch the interloper.

Jack's grandmother elected to eat in her room—for which I was guiltily grateful—and so the rest of us changed and went into dinner. As soon as we were seated, Mrs. Travers focused her attention on me. "Miss Wilde, do you enjoy the theater?"

Jack groaned. "Mother, please."

She held a hand to her chest. "It is an innocent question."

"Far from it," Verity said with amused exasperation. "Mama is an actress."

"A tragedienne, my dear," Mrs. Travers corrected.

Verity cast her eyes to the ceiling. "This is simply her way of bringing the conversation round to her."

"Such impolite children I have." Mrs. Travers was unaffected as she sipped her wine. "I only wish to discover what Miss Wilde and I have in common."

"And to see if she has heard of the incomparable Trinity Travers," Jack said, though his eyes twinkled.

But the name clicked inside my head and I sat up. "But I *have* heard of you. My dear friend Beatrice saw you in *Henry VIII* when she was in London last year. At Covent Garden?"

Mrs. Travers brightened. "I knew I liked you." She pointed her fork at Verity and Jack in turn. "These two have no appreciation for the arts."

"I am afraid I am far from a connoisseur," I admitted. "But Beatrice was quite taken with your performance, and I trust her opinion beyond anything."

Verity sighed. "Oh, she will be unbearable now."

Mrs. Travers smiled, her rouged lips an arc of perfect red. "Of course I shall be, if only to remind you that I've been performing on stage since before you were born. Some respect would not go amiss."

It was a fascinating revelation. Mrs. Travers, a famed actress. It was not difficult to see why she might have caught the eye of an earl. She was beautiful, graceful, enchanting. Even I found it difficult to look away from her.

As the meal was cleared away and pudding served, Mrs. Travers dove into a story about performing the trial scene in *Henry VIII*, and I peeked over at Jack. He grinned, holding my gaze until I blushed and looked away. I had the distinct impression that he liked what he saw. Not just me, but me being here in his home, with his mother and sister.

I liked it too.

He leaned my way, and I caught that scent of cedar I hadn't realized I'd missed. "I have something I need to tell you," he said in a low voice so as not to be overheard. "I'd forgotten until now."

"What is it?"

His expression sobered. "You recall that peacher I told you about?"

"The one who said Father had a mole on his staff?" My fork stilled.

He nodded. "I told him to send me any additional information he found. I received a letter from him yesterday. He wrote that not only was he certain there was a mole, but that your father was aware and in fact investigating the matter himself before his death."

My mouth parted. "Father *knew*?"

"So my man says," he said. "Apparently, your father made subtle inquiries around town, collecting evidence in an attempt to discover this informant's identity."

I pressed my lips together. Father had been so different those last few weeks—absent-minded and jumpy. It had to be because of this. An investigation to reveal a traitor would make anyone agitated. But why hadn't he told me?

"If he had evidence," I said, "where is it? Why did he not use it?"

He shook his head. "Likely he didn't have enough proof, and then . . ."

I swallowed. Then he died.

"I hate to ask again," Jack said quietly, "but your father's death. Are you certain there was nothing suspicious in it?"

For a wild moment, I allowed my imagination to take hold. Had Father's investigation had anything to do with his death?

No, I told myself firmly. I knew the truth about this much, at least.

"Father died naturally," I said weakly. "The doctor was certain. But beyond that, I was there. I know the signs of apoplexy well." My voice broke.

Jack watched me, brow furrowed. Glancing at his sister and mother, who were arguing over which theater in London boasted the best stage, he took my hand beneath the table, squeezing it in his.

"Please do not worry," he said. "I doubt this mole is still in place, considering the changes that would have occurred when Northcott became magistrate."

He was right, and the feel of his strong fingers around mine chased away my lingering feelings of doubt and fear. I squeezed his hand back, managing a half smile.

"Jack?"

We both jumped at Verity's voice. She and Mrs. Travers watched us with sly expressions. Jack pulled his hand back and I blushed.

"I was only wondering," Verity said, eyebrow raised, "what you will do with your current case while you are away."

I turned to Jack. "You've another case?" But my surprise was silly. I'd known it was a possibility.

He waved me off. "Nothing that can't wait. Just a merchant whose wife has run off with another man. He wants me to track her down."

I blinked, but Mrs. Travers and Verity did not balk at the mention of such awfulness. Did Jack always discuss cases with his family? But then, Father had always told *me*.

"I could help," Verity said eagerly. "Do some groundwork while you're away."

Mrs. Travers tutted. "Not again, Verity."

"You help with his cases?" I asked, surprised.

"Sometimes," she said, eyes bright. "I scout locations for meets, question women and children, carry messages. It is astonishing how often I am disregarded because I am a woman." She grinned. "But it also allows me more freedom than you might imagine."

"Verity is very helpful," Jack said, eyeing his sister. "But this is a case I'll handle when I return."

"You know I can do it," she said matter-of-factly.

"Not this time," he said, and Mrs. Travers nodded her agreement.

Verity seemed to realize they would not be moved. Her jaw tightened, but she nodded and sat back in her seat.

When I return, Jack had said. Three words should not undo me so. But it was difficult to lie to myself when I'd been wishing he would kiss me only an hour or two ago.

We retired not long after, both Jack and I eager for an early start in the morning. And though the bedroom around me was unfamiliar, the quilted coverlet and narrow windows and brick fireplace not at all like my room at Wimborne, it did not bother me. Holloway helped me undress and I fell asleep as soon as my head touched the soft feather pillow.

We left before dawn, the sky a glimmer of pink above the London rooftops. I traveled in my coach with Holloway while Jack followed on horseback. While I'd enjoyed my brief stay with the Travers family, my heart tugged relentlessly toward home. I needed to return, to ensure all was well.

"I am glad to have Mr. Travers with us this time," Holloway said, peering out the window at him. "Surely he will keep the highwaymen away."

"Surely," I agreed. He was an impressive figure on horseback, all hard lines—his jaw, his shoulders, his back. I found myself sneaking glances out the window, eyeing his masculine profile, the cut of his gaze across the landscape. When Holloway caught me watching, she only gave a knowing smile.

At last Wimborne's brick facade rolled into view, perfectly whole and well, at least as far as I could see. I descended from the coach as Jack dismounted nearby, handing his reins to a groom. But before I could even speak to him, Marchant came down the front steps with a frown. I went to meet him, my heart in my throat

"Is everything all right?" I clenched the skirts of my traveling dress. "Has anything happened?"

Marchant cleared his throat, eyeing Jack beside me. "No one has been harmed. We are all well."

The tightness in my chest eased. It had been a risk, going to London and leaving my home unprotected. Hopefully it would prove to be worth it.

"But?" Jack pressed, moving closer to my side.

"But we did find something," Marchant said. "You need to see it right away."

Jack and I exchanged troubled glances as we followed Marchant west of the house. We crossed the footbridge over the stream and into a thicket of woods.

"What is it, Marchant?" I asked, growing more anxious with every step. "Tell me."

"Mr. Limpton found it early this morning," he said. "While checking his snares."

"Wimborne's gamekeeper," I explained to Jack.

He nodded. "I met him during my rides."

We were deep in the trees now, thick brush tugging at my skirts and hair. It was nearly impossible to get through.

"What is it Mr. Limpton found, Marchant?" I asked. What could be out here in this snarled knot of woods?

"This," he said, pushing aside a leafy branch.

We stepped into a hollow, hardly bigger than Wimborne's scullery. It was completely surrounded by foliage, thick and impenetrable. Or it should have been. But right before us lay evidence to the contrary.

The blackened remains of a fire. A tiny lean-to constructed of spindly branches and brush, a ratty blanket within. The bones of some poultry—pheasant or grouse—scattered through the matted grass.

My blood cooled.

"Someone has been staying here," Jack said, his voice the edge of a knife. "Those ashes are only hours old."

"That was Mr. Limpton's assumption as well," Marchant said. "He normally traps on the other side of the estate, but this morning his dogs caught a scent while he was checking his snares and led him straight here."

I stared at the ashes of the fire, at the grisly bits of meat that still clung to the bird's bones. I swallowed. *Do not sleep too soundly, Miss Wilde. The worst is yet to come.*

Jack peppered Marchant with questions, but I wasn't listening. I fisted one hand against my chest, heart pounding as I spun in a slow circle to take in every detail of the camp. The vandal thought himself safe, tucked into this impossible thicket. If it hadn't been for Mr. Limpton's dogs catching an unfamiliar scent, we never would have discovered him.

"Miss Wilde?" Marchant interrupted my racing thoughts. "I also ought to inform you that Mr. Northcott came to see you this morning. It seems he has something rather pressing to speak to you about."

"Mr. Northcott?" I said absently, still staring at the remains of the fire.

"Yes," Marchant said. "He was utterly perplexed to learn you'd gone to London, and upon hearing you would return today, he elected to wait inside for you."

I blinked. "He is here now?" Mr. Northcott was an exceptionally busy man. What cause could he have to wait all morning for me?

"In the parlor."

My mind clicked. I straightened as an idea leaped fully formed into my head. It couldn't be so simple, could it?

"Ginny?" Jack asked, brow furrowed.

Marchant frowned at Jack's breach in propriety, but I barely noticed.

"We need to speak with Mr. Northcott," I said, meeting Jack's eyes. "Immediately."

"The magistrate?" Jack asked. "Why?"

I turned on my heel and marched back through the brush. "I'll tell you inside," I called over my shoulder.

The men hurried to catch up with me. To my surprise, Jack did not protest my lack of forthcoming. He stayed at my side as we came back out of the thicket and hurried up the lawn. Either he did not want to discuss the matter in front of Marchant, or he had already guessed my intentions.

After climbing the front steps and handing our things to Marchant, Jack and I went directly to the parlor.

"Are you ready?" I asked Jack, pausing at the door.

"As ready as I can be," he said dryly, "without having a single clue as to what I'm walking into."

My mouth quirked up. "I shall try not to enjoy it too much."

I opened the door. Mr. Northcott stood at the window and immediately whirled to face me.

"Miss Wilde," he rasped, his words in a rush. "I heard a carriage and hoped it was you. I am relieved to find you unharmed."

"Unharmed?" I stopped in the doorway. I'd gone to London, not crossed the Atlantic.

He moved toward me, his eyes frantic as they took me in. "I've uncovered some disturbing information about your cousin, and I—"

Jack stepped beside me in the doorway, his arm reaching around me to swing the door wider. The sleeve of his jacket brushed my arm. A pulse of energy shot from where he touched me, spreading like hot oil over my skin.

Mr. Northcott stared at Jack, then shook off his surprise, his expression hardening. He reached out a hand to me, as if rescuing me from a flood. "Miss Wilde, you must come away from that man at once."

"What?" I drew back my chin.

"That man is not your cousin," Mr. Northcott insisted, glaring darkly at Jack.

"Not my—" I blew out a breath. I knew I would have told him the truth eventually, but this seemed like rather pointless drama when we had much more pressing matters at hand. I moved into the room and dropped onto an armchair. "Mr. Northcott, what have you learned?"

Jack followed me into the room, his movements like a lion stalking its prey. Mr. Northcott had barely moved an inch since he'd spotted Jack, and now he watched him as if Jack might spring at him at any second.

"I had my suspicions after the ball," Mr. Northcott said hotly, "though I couldn't say anything without proof. I wrote to an acquaintance in Rothbury asking after your mother's family, and he responded just this morning with the most shocking news that he doesn't know of any family by the name Travers in the area, and certainly not ones related to you. This man is deceiving you."

If I were another girl, I might be flattered that Mr. Northcott felt so protective of me to go to such lengths. But I found myself annoyed.

Instead of speaking to me, he'd gone behind my back and made inquiries that might have further repercussions for my reputation.

"This man is not *deceiving* me," I said, forcing my voice to remain calm. I still needed Mr. Northcott's help, after all. "Mr. Travers is the thief-taker I hired to find my watch, and he has also been maintaining the security of my home. We created the ruse of him being my cousin in order to protect my reputation and to allow him to investigate without suspicion."

Mr. Northcott looked positively thunderstruck. "*He* is the thief-taker? But . . . he has been in your home, *sleeping* here—"

"And the beds are wonderfully comfortable," Jack said from behind me, apparently unable to resist. I shot him a reproachful look, but he pretended not to see as he continued his slow rounding of the room.

I turned back to Mr. Northcott. "I know we took a terrible risk. But I was more than willing if it meant putting an end to Wimborne's troubles."

He shook his head, fidgeting with his watch fob. "We ought to speak privately, Miss Wilde."

"That is not necessary," I said. "I trust Mr. Travers implicitly and he knows the intimate details of my situation better than anyone."

Mr. Northcott twitched at the word *intimate*, and I wished I'd chosen a different word. But I would not give in to his pressure. I would stand on my own two feet, convince him to help me with logic and reason, not by soothing his manly pride.

"Now," I said, "we can argue about whether or not it was the right decision, or how I *should* have done things, but I would much rather put this time to good use and press forward."

"Press forward with what, exactly?" Jack said, finally coming to a stop near the fireplace. He crossed his arms and leaned one shoulder casually on the mantel, looking *very* comfortable. Mr. Northcott turned purple.

"I've had an idea," I said. "I will need both of you to help, and would appreciate a spirit of cooperation."

"Cooperation?" Mr. Northcott sputtered. "You cannot imagine that I would work with such a man."

"I certainly can," I said shortly. "Mr. Travers has proven himself a loyal friend and a valuable asset."

Beyond Mr. Northcott's shoulder, Jack raised an eyebrow. I could not guess if his reaction was to my designation of us as *friends* or of him as valuable.

"He is a thief-taker," Mr. Northcott said, as if that should be enough to convince me.

"Do you always assume the worst about a person before you know them?" I fixed my gaze on him. "That seems a dangerous quality for a magistrate."

Some strange emotion flickered in Mr. Northcott's eyes. Shame? Befuddlement? He turned away, jaw tight. Guilt crept into my stomach. I was asking a great deal of this man, whom I'd just shocked with my revelation about Jack's identity. Hadn't I thought similarly about thief-takers before I'd known Jack? I stood and went to Mr. Northcott's side, laying a hand on the arm of his wool jacket.

"I need your help, Mr. Northcott," I said quietly. "I understand this is not an ideal situation, but it is the hand I have been dealt. Please. Can I count on you?"

He stared out the window, then his eyes met mine before flicking down to my hand on his arm. What was he thinking? I pulled my hand back and desperately hoped he would not assign too much importance to my touch.

"I will need to hear whatever plan you've concocted first," he said finally. "Before I agree."

"A reasonable request," I said, hiding my relief. I returned to my seat and gestured to the settee across from me. He flipped out his coat tails and sat, looking at me expectantly. Jack still stood by the fireplace, his gaze likewise on me. I took a deep breath. It was up to me to convince the both of them of my plan.

"Some time ago, Mr. Travers put forth the idea of setting a trap,"

I said. "Something to lure the criminal in and allow us to apprehend him."

Jack nodded, eyes moving over my face. "But we hadn't thought of what that trap might be."

"I think I have." I nearly went on to say that I was certain my plan was full of holes and misjudgments, but I stopped myself. If I projected doubt, that was what they would see as they evaluated this idea. I had to be confident. "Mr. Northcott, we have just come from the location of a hidden camp, only a few minutes from the house. It is clear the vandal has been using it as a hideout, likely while he goes about causing mischief."

"A hideout?" Mr. Northcott sat back, staring at me.

"Yes," I said. "I would hazard a guess that he comes and goes under the cover of darkness. If we were to surround the campsite, keep watch throughout the night, then we would have a very good chance of catching this miscreant once and for all."

My eyes flicked to Jack. Although I was desperate for Mr. Northcott's help, it was Jack's opinion I cared most about. Would he think my idea had merit? He said nothing, arms crossed as he stared out the window, a furrow deep in his forehead.

"You think to ambush him," Mr. Northcott said. "Catch him by surprise?"

I nodded, trying not to appear too eager. "We must strike first, before he can cause any more harm." I paused. "Truthfully, we cannot do this without you. I know the highwaymen grow bolder still, but we need the aid of your constables."

"I cannot take my men from their responsibilities," Mr. Northcott said. "We cannot know when the man will return to his camp."

"You are right," I said. It was a clear weakness in my plan. "But can we not try at least one night? Surely that is worth the chance to arrest such a criminal."

Jack finally spoke. "And if Mr. Northcott's men are not trustworthy?"

Mr. Northcott bristled. "My men are deputies of the Crown, which is far more than *you* can say."

But I understood Jack's meaning. He was thinking of the mole. If there *was* someone untrustworthy working for Mr. Northcott, then he might warn the vandal about our trap. But I couldn't bring that to Mr. Northcott, not yet. We had no evidence, nothing but hearsay from one of Jack's informants. The magistrate would discount our words, and then perhaps be unwilling to help us.

"I have no doubt your constables are trustworthy," I assured Mr. Northcott. "But it would relieve my mind to keep the specific details of our situation between us three, at least for the time being. Your men can be informed of the larger situation when it becomes necessary."

Mr. Northcott shifted his weight, considering everything I'd said. "Very well," he said finally. "One night." He glanced again at Jack, seeming to bolster himself. "Miss Wilde, I would be remiss if I did not try to convince you to leave this to me entirely. We haven't the need for a thief-taker."

"We do have need," I said firmly. "Though you may not see it yet. Please trust me, Mr. Northcott. Trust that everything I am doing is for the good of my home."

He sighed. "Shall we set this ambush of yours tomorrow night? That should allow me the necessary time to organize my men."

I looked to Jack for confirmation, and he nodded. "Agreed," I said to Mr. Northcott. "Thank you. You cannot know what a relief it is to have your help."

Mr. Northcott stood, towering over me. I stood as well and did not realize he had moved closer until he was right before me, taking my hand in his.

"Do be careful, Miss Wilde," he said quietly, so only I could hear. "I don't like the thought of him here at Wimborne, but I will silence my concerns if you promise me that."

"I promise to be careful." My voice did not waver. It was an easy thing to promise—I had nothing to fear from Jack.

I wasn't sure if Mr. Northcott sensed some deeper meaning in my words, but he hesitated over my hand. Then, turning as if to make his action clearer to Jack, he pressed a lingering kiss to my bare hand. Oh heavens, what was he doing?

"I'll be in contact soon," he said, releasing my hand. "Good day, Miss Wilde." He spared the barest of nods for Jack before he left the room, his cane tapping on the smooth wood floor.

I coughed, rubbing the back of my hand on my skirt. Mr. Northcott's lips had left an unwelcome heat to my skin. Could hands blush?

"He is certainly eager to stake his claim." Jack moved to the open door, looking out into the corridor to ensure we were alone. He closed the door and turned back to me.

"He hasn't claimed me." I raised my chin.

He raised an eyebrow. "Perhaps you ought to tell him that."

"Now is hardly the time to wound his pride once again," I said. "Even if there *is* a mole among his men—of which we cannot be certain—they are still vastly more experienced than any volunteers we might raise from my household staff. We need his help."

"You also need *my* help." Jack's lips turned upwards, slow and wicked, as he moved toward me. "A kiss seems to be the going rate."

If hands could blush, then certainly so could necks, arms, legs, and every other surface of one's body. I had no doubt the heat that rolled over my skin was accompanied by the fiercest red.

"One kiss?" I wasn't at all sure where those words came from, since my mind was still preoccupied with how to *stop blushing*. "Quite the bargain for me, considering the compensation I promised you."

His grin only widened. "I shall leave it to your discretion, then. I would be quite satisfied with either reward."

We were alone in the parlor. I was far too conscious of how close we'd drifted once again, as if an unearthly magnetism drew us together. Two quick steps and I could be in his arms, my lips on his—

I swallowed and looked away. What was it about him that made me lose my senses entirely? I'd never felt this maddening pull toward anyone before, at least not so strongly. How was one supposed to judge what was simple attraction and what was deeper emotion? An ache grew in my chest, not for the first time. A longing for a mother, for someone to explain what it was I felt in my core for this man.

As if sensing my inner conflict, Jack turned the subject. "I am flattered, really, that he considers me a threat. A mere thief-taker."

"He does not like relinquishing control," I said, raising one eyebrow. "A common issue among men."

He laughed. "True enough. But I daresay you surprised him with your thoroughness and ingenuity. He had no choice but to give in."

That only made me want to kiss him more. I focused on keeping my feet right where they were, instead of inching toward him.

"Tell me honestly," I said, more to distract myself than anything. "Do you think my idea will work?"

He sobered. "It is a good plan. I'm not particularly fond of involving the magistrate, but you are right. We need the men. If you trust him, then I will trust you." He looked me straight in the eye, his gaze unyielding. "I am at your service, Genevieve. Whatever you need of me, I am here."

I had the feeling that not kissing Jack Travers would turn out to be the greatest challenge of my life.

CHAPTER 19

Jack set off to patrol the estate and also to revisit the campsite to ensure we had left no tracks earlier. We did not want to alert the vandal that we'd discovered his hiding place. I retired to my study, where I spent a quarter hour debating whether I ought to visit Beatrice. I had so much to tell her and desperately wanted her help to untangle my emotions. But . . . but there was also a part of me that did *not* want her to decipher my heart. If I told her I had begun to have feelings for Jack, she would approve wholeheartedly. Beatrice did not care what Society thought. But I did. This was my life, and Wimborne's future, and I would not risk either without careful consideration.

My eyes drifted to Father's portrait hung across the study, gazing over the familiar brushstrokes and colors, his gentle eyes and serious mouth. I hoped he would have been proud of me and all I'd done. And I thought he would have liked Jack. Well, perhaps not at first. What had Jack said when we'd met? *I tend to make terrible first impressions.* But Father would have liked his determination and his spirit. He would have liked that I had someone looking out for me.

You have Mr. Northcott, a voice inside me said.

But did I? His help seemed to come with very clear strings attached. What would he do when this entire debacle was over and I still did not wish to marry him? Because it was clearer to me now more than ever that I did *not* wish to marry Mr. Northcott.

I closed my eyes. Without any effort at all, a vision came: Jack here at Wimborne, but not as a thief-taker I'd hired. As my husband. His laughing eyes and wide grin, his strong arms about me. His breath warm against my neck as he whispered sweet things in my ear.

My chest filled with such light it was difficult to breathe. I forced open my eyes, staring again at my father's portrait. Was this why he could not wait to marry my mother? I'd always wondered why he'd married her so quickly, but now I was beginning to understand, if my feelings for Jack were anywhere near what my parents had shared.

A surge of envy flowed through me. How lucky Father had been. A man could marry below his class, if he wished, though certainly I knew better than anyone that such actions were not entirely without consequences. But a woman like me, already teetering on the edge of Society? If I loved a man beneath my station, if I dared to marry him, my reputation would never recover.

Only I was not certain it was as important to me as it once was.

Things might be different if I had a family to stand by me. But I could hardly expect *Catherine*, of all people, to do so.

Catherine. I exhaled. After our last conversation, she hadn't seemed inclined to change anything about our relationship. But she'd also been more interested than I would have thought in my problems here at Wimborne. Was it because she was only concerned for Father's legacy? Or did she have the slightest concern for me as well?

I went to my desk and set out a fresh sheet of paper.

Dear Catherine,

Forgive my impertinence in writing to you, since I am well aware you should like to resume our previous pattern of distant tolerance. I simply wished to inform you of the current happenings at Wimborne. On your advice, I have retained the services of Mr. Travers and we are actively involved in a plan that we hope will bring an end to the troubles here on the estate. If we are successful, I will owe much of that to you.

I paused. How to word the next part without sounding too eager?

I also wished to express my gratitude once again for your restraint. I still regret my mistakes, but I have also learned from them. It is my hope that we might mend this divide between us, at least enough to be friendly acquaintances. I have sent a gift, as a token of my goodwill and appreciation.

Yours most sincerely,

Genevieve W.

I hesitated a moment after signing my name. I'd already lost Father's watch. The thought of losing anything else of his made my chest hurt. But I knew it was the right thing to do. Catherine deserved something of Father's; she was his daughter too.

I folded the letter, sealed it with a wafer, and addressed the front. Then I rang for a maid. I would need help to package Father's portrait—I did not want it to arrive at Harpford House damaged.

⊰❉⊱

I busied myself with correspondence and reviewing the household accounts. Tedious work, and yet the sense of normality it gave me was comforting. I continued, lost in a world that was familiar to me, until the sun dropped low in the sky. Finally, I stretched, turning to look out the window and catching my reflection in the sunset-tinted glass. My red hair escaped my coiffure at every pin, limp and lazy curls providing a distinctly unimpressive frame for my face. My ivory muslin dress had more color to it than my pale complexion, and my eyes were tired, clouded. I brushed back my hair with ink-stained hands, sighing. Perhaps when we'd caught the vandal, I would spend less time worrying and more time on my appearance.

A figure on horseback appeared on the horizon, cantering toward the stables. My pulse leapt before I realized it was Jack, returning from his patrol. I let myself inspect him, the steady hand with which he guided his mount, his confident seat and watchful gaze. I couldn't see his features but could picture them well enough—the shadow that crept up his jaw this late in the day, his dark brows and clear eyes.

He disappeared into the stable, depriving me of my view. Wimborne's landscape seemed lacking now. Smaller. I swallowed, realizing I'd thought the same thing when Father had died.

I pushed that thought away, turning to tidy my desk. When I left my study, I noted the late hour as I passed the longcase clock and quickened my pace for the stairs.

"In a hurry to avoid me, are you?" Jack stepped in the front door, pulling off his gloves.

I paused, my stomach twirling. "I would hardly have gone all the way to London to fetch you if I was trying to avoid you."

"An excellent point."

"I am going up to change for dinner," I said. "I'll only be a minute." Well, perhaps a few minutes.

"Do we really need to change?" he mused. "I've always thought it a waste of time when we're already wearing perfectly good clothes."

My eyes wandered over his clothes, which were certainly perfectly good, if a bit windblown from his day outside. But then, I imagined he would look just as handsome drenched by rain or covered in mud. Possibly more so.

I cleared my throat, forcing my eyes to meet his. The corner of his mouth turned upward and I again had the strangest impression that he could read my mind.

"Well, *I* need to change," I said, starting up the stairs in the hopes of hiding my blush. "I look dreadful."

"Dreadful?"

The disbelief in Jack's voice made me turn back. He'd moved to the bottom of the stairs and gazed up at me, eyes narrowed.

"What on earth," he said, "makes you think you look dreadful?"

"Oh," I said, flustered. "Well, everything. My hair is a mess. My dress is wrinkled." I held up my ink-blotched hands. "These will need several washes, I imagine."

His eyes dropped to my hands. He climbed the stairs, stopping just below me, and then my hands were in his. "This," he said gently, tracing a smudged dark spot with his thumb, "is evidence of the work you've done today. Hardly something you need to hide away from anyone, least of all me."

Heavens. My mouth parted, though I slammed it shut again, certain that the only sound to escape me would be unintelligible gibberish.

"In fact," he said, raking his gaze from my hands up to my face, "I find I am quite partial to ink stains. On the right hands, they are irresistible." He raised one hand to his lips, leaving the barest kiss on my fingertips. Heat rushed through my arm and to my chest; my brain fluttered about like a bird trapped indoors.

"Then perhaps—" My voice rasped, and I cleared my throat. "Then perhaps tomorrow I won't be so careful with my ink."

It was a weak flirtation, and by the lift of his lips, he knew precisely how fast my heart was pounding and that my stomach felt like I'd drunk an entire pot of hot tea. He moved closer, our hands trapped between us.

A cough came from below us. "Miss Wilde?"

I jolted, pulling my hands from Jack's. Mrs. Betts stood below us, hands clasped over her stomach as she eyed the two of us. Thank heavens. If it had been any of the servants who still thought Jack was my cousin, we would have had some explaining to do.

"Y-yes, Mrs. Betts?" I managed.

"Dinner is ready," she said, her words clipped with disapproval. "I'll hold it a few minutes and send Holloway to help you change."

I sneaked a glance at Jack, expecting a teasing grin, but he was staring at Mrs. Betts. Not in surprise, like I had been, but as if she'd said something bewildering.

"Jack?" I spoke so only he could hear. "Are you all right?"

His eyes snapped to mine, and he straightened, the motion pulling him away from me.

"Yes, of course," he said, forcing a smile.

I could hardly say anything else with Mrs. Betts there, but I wanted to. Until my stomach let out a rather ferocious growl, protesting its neglect over the last few hours. I clamped a hand to my middle, a laugh bubbling up. He chuckled as well, albeit a second later.

"I shall consider that a vote for dinner immediately," he said, holding out his arm to me. "Come, it's only us."

Only us. How badly I missed having an *us* here at Wimborne. Someone to make plans with, to see every morning at breakfast and every night at dinner. Father and I had been that *us* before his death. Jack was slipping into that void, filling my home as well as my heart.

Blast it all. Why couldn't he have been a perfectly acceptable gentleman's son or naval captain or even a wool merchant? Why did he have to be a thief-taker?

I couldn't think of that now, an uncertain and hazy future. Not with the vandal still at large and the ambush tomorrow night. When my home was once again safe, then I could sort out my heart.

I took his arm, trying to ignore the press of lean muscle through the sleeve of his jacket. "We'll eat now, Mrs. Betts," I called to her.

She nodded and hurried off, thankfully keeping any opinions to herself. Jack looked back at her as we started toward the dining room. I couldn't read his expression—it wasn't one I'd ever seen on his face.

I pushed my unease away. Surely it was nothing, or he would say something. "You mustn't tell anyone we did not change for dinner," I said to turn the subject. "Could you *imagine* the gossip?"

Again, his reaction was a touch too late, as if his thoughts had been miles away. But he smiled, shaking his head. "Oh, you would be torn to shreds for certain," he said. "The audacity of Genevieve Wilde to break propriety's most important rule."

"Never mind that she currently has a thief-taker in residence."

"Special investigator."

"My apologies."

He guided me into the room and to my seat, pushing in my chair behind me as I sat. I sneaked a glance at him as he sat beside me. He looked good there. Too good. Deliciously good.

It was hopeless. I was a ship lost in a storm of my own making. I was in love with Jack Travers and had no idea what to do.

CHAPTER 20

The next morning, I rose early, which was something of a Herculean effort, considering the tossing and turning I'd done all night. Worry had kept sleep at arm's length, and thoughts of Jack banished it further still.

I'd spent long hours lying in bed, staring up at the embellished medallions adorning my ceiling. I was no fool. I knew I was in love with Jack—I'd fallen hard and swift, the rushing current of a waterfall in spring. But my challenges hadn't changed. Little Sowerby's society would never accept him, especially not after this business of him pretending to be my cousin. That in turn would affect everything: my relationships with neighbors, the estate's business ventures, the treatment our children might receive.

I swallowed hard, turning to my side. I was absurd, thinking of children when I hadn't any idea if Jack felt the same way about me. Well, that wasn't true. I had a small idea. I could not discount the way his eyes moved over me, or how his breathing changed whenever I moved near him. But his intentions were a mystery to me, and my useless wonderings brought me no closer to solving anything by the time I finally fell asleep.

After Holloway helped me dress and arranged my hair, I went down to the breakfast room, but it was empty. I ate alone, looking up at every sound in the hopes that Jack would appear in the doorway. Surely, he was sleeping. He'd likely had a long night and was preparing for another one this evening.

I pushed away my barely touched plate as Marchant stepped inside the room.

"A letter for you," he announced.

"Thank you, Marchant." I stood, taking the note from him and recognizing Mr. Northcott's writing. "Has Mr. Travers risen yet today?"

"I believe so," he said. "He requested a tray not half an hour ago."

I furrowed my brow. Why had Jack not come down and eaten with me? He'd acted a bit strange after dinner last night—more quiet than usual, though he'd claimed lack of sleep. I'd hoped he would feel better this morning.

Marchant left with a bow, and I opened the letter, desperate to avoid the deepening confusion that took hold of me whenever I thought of Jack.

> *Miss Wilde,*
>
> *I spent yesterday coordinating between my most trusted men. As you requested, I told them no details, so you have no reason to fear a leak. I have four men ready and willing, and I will bring them to Wimborne tonight at eight o'clock.*
>
> *It is likely the house is being watched, so we will be cautious in our approach. Your speed in allowing us inside will be most appreciated. Upon our arrival, we will discuss the finer points of the plan, about which I imagine Mr. Travers will have much to say.*

I exhaled a dry laugh. He certainly would.

> *Do take care in the meantime, Miss Wilde. I shall not rest easy until I see you tonight.*
>
> *Yours,*
>
> *P. Northcott*

I tapped the note on the table. This was truly happening. While I knew it was necessary, and the best plan possible at the moment, it still felt as if a swarm of bees was taking up residence in my stomach.

I needed to keep busy or I'd go mad. I decided to find Mrs. Betts and make arrangements for tonight—tea and food for the men when they arrived. But as I was coming out of the breakfast room, I spotted Jack coming down the stairs, black hat in his hand. He saw me the same instant.

"Oh," he said. "Good morning."

He slowed as he reached the marble floor of the entryway. My pulse leapt like a hound catching a fox's scent.

"Good morning," I echoed, my hands fumbling to fold Mr. Northcott's letter. Why was it that Jack's proximity made it impossible to perform even the simplest of tasks?

He moved toward me, proving my point yet again as my lungs struggled to breathe. *Breathe!* A life-critical function, and here I was depriving myself of air because a man walked too near.

I scolded myself for my ridiculousness and dropped my hands as he came even with me. Part of me wished to ask him why he hadn't joined me for breakfast. But apparently I was a weak-willed ninny, because instead I dropped my eyes and ran the toe of my slippers along the grain in the marble.

"I received this note from Mr. Northcott," I said. "He has recruited four men for tonight."

He nodded, which I only caught from the corner of my eye, since it was suddenly of great importance that the tassels of my shawl hung straight.

"That is good news," he said. "When will they arrive?"

"Eight o'clock, which should give us adequate time, I imagine."

"Agreed." He shifted his weight. "I'm going to see Wily this morning, tell him I've returned."

"I imagine he won't be assisting tonight." I could not help a smile. "He'll want to keep his distance from Mr. Northcott."

But Jack did not respond with a jesting comment about Mr. Northcott. Instead, his mouth settled into a line. An indifferent expression for most, but for Jack, whose smile rarely left his face, it was extreme. "Yes, I would think so."

My smile faded. Silence followed, made longer by the looming space between us.

"Did you sleep last night?" I spoke lightly, hoping to provoke some reaction, teasing, anything. "You're of no use to me drooping with exhaustion."

He only shook his head. "I slept a few hours. I am perfectly able."

"Good," I managed.

"When I return from town, I will map out the best locations for surveillance tonight." He paused, as if he wanted to say something more but seemed to think better of it. He placed his hat on his head. "I'll return before the meeting." He gave a short bow and strode away, disappearing through the front door.

I stared after him. Something was wrong. And it must be dreadfully wrong to keep Jack Travers from smiling.

⊰✠⊱

The day passed sluggishly. I tried not to think about Jack even as that was all my brain seemed keen to do. The sunshine turned almost too warm, beating through the study windows onto my back. I could only hope the weather would hold for tonight. The last thing we needed was rain.

I gathered my trusted staff in the afternoon—Holloway, Mrs. Betts, and Marchant—to explain my plan. It spoke to the desperation we all felt that none of them balked at the idea of a trap but only nodded in determination.

"Might I offer my help?" Marchant asked, stepping forward to stand before my desk. "I'm not so able as Mr. Travers, but I daresay I can find some way to be useful."

"I do not wish to put you in danger," I said. "We will have the magistrate's help."

"I want to," he insisted. "Please."

My heart softened. Marchant and I had not always seen eye to eye, especially as I struggled to emerge from Father's shadow. But how I appreciated his words now.

"We shall *all* do what we can," Mrs. Betts said, jaw set and eyes hard. "This criminal has roamed free for far too long."

Holloway nodded. "Only tell us what we can do, miss, and we will do it."

I stood, emotion rising inside me. "Thank you all," I said through the lump in my throat. "I cannot tell you what it means to have your support."

They departed soon after, leaving me to pass the hours in increasing anxiety. Would my plan succeed? Or would I simply be putting all these men in danger for nothing? When darkness fell, I saw no sign of Jack, and so I ate alone yet again. *This is foolishness*, I thought as I ate. I should not allow myself to be so overwrought by what Jack may or may not be thinking. I simply needed to ask him straight out what was bothering him.

As the time neared eight o'clock, I took up position near the front door, along with Marchant. He seemed to sense I wished for quiet, and so we did not speak as the minutes ticked onwards. At ten minutes to the hour, the crunch of footsteps came from the gravel drive. I was at Marchant's side as he opened the door. Five men appeared in the dark and my butler waved them inside. They silently filed past us, tipping their hats. I recognized Mr. Crouth and forced myself to smile politely at him even as my stomach turned uneasy. The other constables and watchmen looked familiar, though I could not name them.

Mr. Northcott came last, removing his hat as he stepped inside. When his eyes landed on me, his shoulders relaxed by the merest fraction. He *was* worried for me.

"Thank you for coming," I said to him as Marchant closed the door.

He nodded, and it was difficult to tell what was hidden behind his eyes. No doubt he still thought me a fool for trusting Jack. But I hoped he would not allow his misgivings to cloud his judgment tonight.

I turned to the group. "Thank you *all* for coming. Let us move into the drawing room, where the curtains are drawn. I've ordered tea and it should be ready shortly."

The men perked up at the thought of tea, and I made a note to send them off into the night with their pockets full of sandwiches and sweetmeats.

"Where is Mr. Travers?" Mr. Northcott asked as the men disappeared into the drawing room.

I cleared my throat. "He is patrolling the grounds. He should be here presently."

Mr. Northcott frowned but moved toward the drawing room, looking back at me expectantly.

"I'll be along soon," I assured him. "I need to check on the tea."

He nodded and went inside. Marchant followed, shutting the door behind him.

I, of course, had no intention of checking on the tea. Mrs. Betts was more than capable of preparing a simple tea service. I was waiting for Jack.

I paced the corridor, working my hands nervously before me, glancing at the clock every few seconds. I'd asked the servants to keep the lighting dim, in case someone was watching the house, so only a few candles burned in sconces along the wall. Mrs. Betts and a maid arrived with the tea, both eyeing me as they went into the room and then back down to the kitchen.

Finally, at two minutes to eight o'clock, I heard familiar steps outside. I turned as the door opened. Jack stopped in the doorway when he saw me, lips parting, but then he schooled his features. He closed the door and met me in the middle of the entry.

"You're nearly late," I said, then immediately wished I hadn't. No use starting off such a conversation with an accusation.

"Nearly late is *not* late," Jack countered. He nodded at the drawing room. "Is everyone here?"

"Yes." I shifted my weight. "Mr. Northcott and four men. Marchant has also offered his assistance."

"Good." He moved toward the door.

"Wait." I grabbed his arm. He halted, staring back at me. "Are you not going to tell me why you've been avoiding me?"

He straightened slowly, his eyes indecipherable. A ghost of a smile touched his lips. "What, then, would be the point in avoiding you?"

"So, you *are* avoiding me." I'd expected him to deny it. I wasn't sure if this hurt more or less.

Jack sighed. "Now is not the time for such a conversation." He moved again for the door, but I held tight to his arm.

"I think now is the *only* time for such a conversation," I said. "Since I have to corner you to have it at all."

He worked his jaw, muscles tensing along his neck as he lifted my hand from his arm. He held it a moment, his gloved hands cold on my bare ones, then released me.

"What is wrong?" I whispered, well aware that several men were only a wall away. "What's happened?"

He shook his head. "Nothing has happened."

"But something is wrong," I insisted.

He finally looked me in the eye. "All right." His voice was gravel. "You value the truth, Miss Wilde, so you shall have it."

Miss Wilde?

"I am afraid we have grown too close over the past weeks," he said, taking a step back as if to emphasize his point. "Such things happen when two people spend as much time together as we have. But I think it best if we return to a more professional relationship."

My heart wrenched. It limped along in my chest, each beat more painful than the last.

"A professional relationship." I swallowed hard. Where was this coming from? Last night he'd been kissing my hand on the stairs. Now he was pulling away. No, he was *pushing* me away. I stared up at him, trying to find any hint that this was an ill-timed joke.

He met my gaze with unflinching rigidity—but his fingers tapped restlessly against his leg. I focused on that movement, what it told me beyond the words he spoke.

"We have spent a great deal of time together," I said softly. "Which is how I know you are not telling me the truth."

His shoulders tightened. "I cannot like being called a liar."

"Then perhaps you should not lie."

He gave a laugh, the sound grating and dry in his throat. "We haven't time for this." He marched to the drawing room.

I stared after him, trying to hold together the pieces of my heart. *He hadn't meant it*, I told myself. I knew he cared for me. So why then did he want distance? That unanswered question tugged on the last reserves of my strength. I slipped into the room behind him, resisting the urge to wrap my arms around myself and have a good cry.

The men stood about the table with the tea, enthusiastically eating various tarts and cakes from the tray. Mr. Northcott was not eating, too busy checking his pocket watch and casting Jack a dark look. Jack ignored him, pulling his gloves off and tucking them in his pocket.

The last thing I wished to do at present was address a room full of men, especially Jack. But I had to focus. There was too much at risk tonight to have my head turned by someone so confusing as Jack Travers. I took a steadying breath and tucked away my pain.

"Should we have a round of introductions?" I said, pretending confidence as I swept further into the room.

"This is not a dinner party, Miss Wilde." Mr. Northcott raised an eyebrow.

"No," I said, a bit irritated at his tone. "But if we are all to work together, we ought to know each other's names."

Mr. Northcott sighed, then pointed at each man as he said his name. "Crouth, Rogers, Allanthorpe, Hinton."

"Pleased to meet you." I curtsied then gestured to Jack. "This is Mr. Travers. He is a former Bow Street officer who I've hired to protect Wimborne, and he will be helping tonight."

Jack nodded a greeting as he sat on the sofa in the center of the room. Mr. Crouth did not respond, but the other three men nodded in return, their eyes more curious than guarded. One of them—Mr.

Hinton—glanced at the magistrate. What had Mr. Northcott told them about Jack?

Determined not to let my inner turmoil affect the evening, I strode forward and planted myself on the armchair across from Jack. The men around me shifted uneasily—no doubt unused to a woman in such a situation—then filled in the spaces around us.

"I am sure you all have questions about why you're here," I said, "and I'll not keep you guessing any longer. Wimborne has been the unfortunate target of theft, vandalism, and threats during the last few months. We've recently discovered the location of a small campsite near the house, which we assume the criminal has been using. Our plan is to take up positions around the camp, watch for the man's return, and then surround and arrest him."

The men listened closely, not saying much beyond murmured reactions.

I turned to Jack, who was astutely avoiding my eyes by staring at something over my head. "Mr. Travers has spent the day mapping out the best locations for surveilling the camp," I said, somehow keeping my voice from stuttering on his name. "Mr. Travers?"

Jack took a large folded paper from his pocket and laid it flat on the table before him. The map was rudimentary but functional. At the center was the thicket with the camp, the stream and bridge nearby. Surrounding the thicket were four X's.

"I've marked four locations," Jack said, speaking for the first time. His voice was dull, businesslike. "They all offer views of the hidden camp and much of the surrounding area. Each location will have different sightlines, so it is vital that we keep a watchful eye while in position."

He pointed at the first X, which was the corner of a building I assumed was Wimborne. "The conservatory has a view of the back lawn leading to the thicket. I also chose this location so as to not leave the house undefended in the event our vandal has other plans for tonight." He looked up at Marchant. "You might be best for this position, along with a constable."

My butler squared his shoulders. "Of course."

Mr. Northcott stood stiffly, arms crossed, but when Jack turned to him, he cleared his throat. "Allanthorpe," he ordered, and the man nodded.

Jack reviewed two other locations—a small rise to the south which allowed a broad view and a copse of spruce trees to the west. Mr. Northcott assigned Mr. Rogers and Mr. Hinton to the first, and Mr. Crouth and himself to the second.

"I will take the fourth position," Jack said, pointing to the last X, directly east of the camp. "A broad oak tree with plenty of cover, but with clear sightlines to both the thicket and Wimborne."

My chin jolted up. "You'll be alone?"

"I can manage." He did not look at me, still examining the map. "Now, it should be fairly obvious to all of us if the vandal is spotted. It is not so great an area that shouts and a ruckus would not be heard. That being said—"

Mr. Northcott interrupted. "Perhaps you will allow me to instruct *my* men."

Jack's shoulders tightened. The tension in the air was gunpowder, and it would take only one spark to ignite the entire room.

"Of course," Jack said finally, sitting back. I'd never seen him so aloof, so detached. I did not know this Jack.

Mr. Northcott settled his hands on his walking stick, the action somehow conveying smugness. "If anyone spots the criminal in question, you are to immediately apprehend him. I shall leave the method of doing so to your discretion. If you believe alerting the entire group would aid you, then by all means shout out a warning. If you believe a stealthy approach would be successful, then proceed as you think best."

The men surrounding me nodded, and I had to credit Mr. Northcott for trusting his men to do their jobs.

"Use necessary force," he went on, "but remember that this man needs to answer for his crimes."

Necessary force. I fought a shiver. What would the rest of this night bring?

"Once apprehended, bring the criminal to the house," Mr. Northcott said, "and alert the others. I've no doubt this coward will be little match for us, but take care all the same."

"We've no guarantee he will show tonight," I said, meeting each of the men's eyes. "But I shall pray for your safety all the same."

"I expect that you'll be anxious, Miss Wilde," Mr. Northcott said, "but I assure you, we will keep you safe."

"I *am* anxious," I said, "but not for myself. Please, I wish to be useful. What can I do?"

Mr. Northcott patted my shoulder. "You'll help by staying safely in the house. We will focus more easily knowing you are out of danger."

I should have anticipated this. He had accepted my plan, but clearly he did not think my involvement should extend beyond *talking*.

"This is my home," I insisted. "I want to be involved."

Jack sat forward. "I'm afraid I agree with the magistrate. You ought to stay in the house where it is safe."

I might've laughed—Jack and Mr. Northcott agreeing on something—if I wasn't so irritated. Why should I have no say in this?

"What if I helped keep watch?" I straightened my back, as if that might make me seem older and more capable. "In the conservatory?"

Mr. Northcott exchanged a glance with Mr. Crouth, who hid a smirk.

"What direction does your bedroom face?" Mr. Northcott asked. "West, does it not? It would be most useful to have eyes in that direction, since it will be blocked from our view."

I narrowed my eyes, not at all fooled. He wanted me tucked away in my room, useless and worried.

Mr. Northcott did not wait for a response, taking my irritated silence as agreement. "If there are no questions, I suggest we find our positions."

There was a great bustle as the men hurriedly took a few more bites before they replaced their hats and went out into the entry. I sat in the melee, trying to absorb the last few minutes. But what kept looping through my mind was the fact that Jack was going to be alone. Every other man had someone to watch his back, to keep him awake and help him if trouble arose. And while I was certain Jack could handle himself in a fight, I did not like the thought of him doing so alone.

An idea bloomed in my mind. Could I? Was I brave enough?

"Please do not worry overmuch."

I blinked up at Mr. Northcott, who smiled at me reassuringly. I stood quickly to hide any evidence in my expression of what I'd just been thinking.

"We have the numbers and the advantage of surprise," he said. "Any danger will be minimal."

It occurred to me then that he was not reassuring me so much as he was wishing for a sign of concern for *him*. I supposed I owed him that much. Even if I was currently annoyed with him, I certainly did not want to see him harmed.

"I am grateful for your help," I said. "Do be careful. I should never forgive myself if something were to go wrong."

Jack was speaking to Marchant and Mr. Allanthorpe in the corner, something about securing the locks. That was why I was so surprised when Mr. Northcott stepped closer, his fingers gently tipping my chin upwards. My eyes widened and my stomach plummeted. Was he going to kiss me? Here and now?

But he only looked into my eyes, as if searching for something. Then he dropped his hand and stepped back. "Take care, Miss Wilde. Try to rest."

He swept from the room, his great coat billowing behind him. I caught my breath, hands clenched in my skirts, and my eyes flicked involuntarily to Jack. He was staring at me. When our gazes connected, it sent a jolt through my spine, a burst of energy and desire. He jerked his eyes away, and I was left gasping.

I knew he felt something for me. I *knew* it. I suddenly did not care why he'd avoided me, or why he'd said such hurtful things before.

I only cared that he was safe tonight. And I would do everything in my power to ensure he was.

CHAPTER 21

Leaving Jack still speaking to my butler, I hurried to my room. I quickly buttoned on my forest green pelisse, then threw my cloak over the top, a dark brown wool that would hide me in the night. It was late spring, but the night still turned cold when the sun set. I laced up my half boots, pulled on my thickest gloves, then gave myself a reassuring nod in the mirror. Tonight I could not be the pampered daughter of a country gentleman. I needed to be sharp, alert, and bold.

I darted down the stairs. Jack was likely on his way to his position in the oak tree. I knew precisely which one he'd meant. I had a view of the tree from my study, with its thick, low branches. The front door was thankfully still unlocked and I slipped out into the night.

I crept through the dark, keeping to the shadows of trees and bracken. I had no desire to be shot by a too-eager constable, so I moved carefully and quietly. The night air bit against my face and neck. I pulled the hood of my cloak tighter. The half-moon passed in and out of thick, gray clouds. Would it rain tonight and make everything even more miserable? Wimborne's grounds surrounded me like a void, the blackness watching me, the wind tracking me.

The oak tree soon appeared ahead, its thick branches twisting out and up, like desperate arms reaching for help. I shook my head. The cold and dark and wind were clearly affecting my mental state. But if there was ever a reason to spend an extended period of time out of doors, helping Jack was it.

I picked my way through the dense brush, leaves and twigs pulling at my cloak.

Then I heard a click—the unmistakable sound of a gun being cocked. I froze.

"Do not move," came a deep voice to my left.

I exhaled in one long breath. "Jack, it's me."

A moment of silence. "Blast it, Ginny."

He stepped out of the inky blackness, one hand lowering his pistol. A scowl marred his face, painted in hues of gray. I lowered the hood of my cloak with shaking hands.

"So, it is *Ginny* now," I said, though my heart pounded like a mallet beating down on a nail. "What happened to 'Miss Wilde'?"

Jack's eyes narrowed as he returned his pistol to his bracers. "It hardly matters what I call you. And keep your voice down." His voice lowered to a harsh whisper and he moved closer. "What the devil are you doing here? It was decided that you would remain in the house."

"It was decided *for* me." I also whispered, but I crossed my arms in case my voice did not adequately convey my annoyance. "Since this is my estate, I think my opinion is the only one that matters."

"You are being obstinate," he growled.

"*I* am being obstinate?" I echoed. "Says the man determined to put himself in danger, with no one to help him?"

"I can handle it," he said flatly. "I am accustomed to being in danger."

"Well, *I* am not accustomed to you being in danger." My voice cracked but I only raised my chin. "You are out here for my sake, and I'll not stand by and do nothing."

He opened his mouth to respond, then swallowed hard. We stood facing one another, neither of us moving. His features, so familiar to me after the last few weeks, suddenly seemed foreign and strange in the moonlight.

"Let me help," I pressed. "I'll keep watch. I won't interfere, but I can raise an alarm or run for help or—"

"Go back to the house, Ginny."

There was no room for argument in his voice. Very well. I would have to make room.

"No," I said. "No, I will not. I am staying right here, unless you intend to tie me up and march me back to the house."

"Do not tempt me." His eyes flashed. "I would carry you kicking and screaming if it meant you would be safe."

"But you won't." My voice was calm, collected. "So I am staying."

Jack narrowed his eyes, and the air grew colder. I much preferred his playful grin, but something about the intensity of his gaze made my stomach flip madly. The quiet stretched between us, broken only by the wind and rustling leaves. I stood my ground, shoulders squared.

"Very well," he grumbled. "Stay. But you must promise to do everything I tell you, no matter what happens."

He had to know I would not keep that promise. I could already think of a dozen ways I might break it. But if that is what it took to stay, then I would lie again and again.

Apparently, falling in love with a thief-taker had a negative impact on my morality.

"I promise," I said solemnly.

Jack did not move, as if still debating his decision. Then he strode to the base of the oak tree. With seemingly no effort, he swung himself up onto the lowest branch, as high as my chest and twice as wide. He stood on the branch, bracing himself against the trunk, and then gestured for me to follow him, a challenge in his eyes.

If he thought climbing a tree would frighten me off, he would be deeply disappointed.

I went to the massive tree trunk, and, instead of following his exact route, walked around to the other side and found a crevice perfectly fitted for my foot. There was another farther up for my hand. It took a bit of careful finagling, considering I wore long skirts and a cloak, but a minute later, I was staring defiantly at Jack, our eyes level as I clung to my own branch.

"Get comfortable," he grunted, leaning his back against the main trunk, still standing.

I could see why he'd picked this spot. An opening in the leaves left us with the perfect prospect: the thicket in the distance—a black mass beyond the shimmering stream—and much of the surrounding area. I could see Wimborne to my right, nearly hidden by trees. And even though we could see everything, we were completely tucked away in the tree, with only a quick drop to the ground should the need arise.

I examined my options. The branches we stood upon were thick, wide, and surprisingly level, surrounded by smaller offshoots that I used to steady myself as I moved. I gingerly sat on the V between two branches, just beside where Jack stood, then wrapped my gloved hands around a gnarled knot to keep my balance.

"I would recommend not falling asleep," Jack said, his voice low and tight. "Or you'll have a rude awakening."

I said nothing, not allowing his surliness to take root inside me. He could snap all he wanted, but I was not leaving.

He paused, then sighed. "Tell me if you see or hear anything."

"I will."

Silence descended. The twisted branch was dreadfully uncomfortable beneath me, but I refused to move an inch, keeping my focus on the thicket across the stream. After a few minutes, I sneaked a glance at Jack. The barest gleam of moonlight touched his features as he stared forward. I realized then that I hadn't seen him eat anything in the drawing room, and he'd come straight from patrolling.

"Have you had anything to eat?" I whispered so he could not reprimand me.

He did not look at me. "I'm not hungry."

"That is the first time I've heard those words from you."

Jack said nothing, but his lips spread into a line, as if trying not to laugh.

I leaned forward. "Your mother would be ashamed, you know. You are a terrible actor."

"Actor?"

"Yes," I said. "You wish to appear indifferent toward me, yet your behavior is entirely at odds with our previous interactions. You should have gradually changed your conduct, to cause less suspicion."

He stared at me—startled, I think, by my logic and bluntness.

"Instead," I continued, "you left me to wonder why you changed so suddenly. And when I wonder, I simply cannot let things be."

"We should not be speaking," he said shortly, adjusting his footing where he leaned against the trunk. "We might be heard."

"I sincerely doubt that is your true worry."

"And if I have a very good reason to be withholding?" His voice was carefully nonchalant, but a sliver of pain hid beneath his words.

What reason was that? Why would he pull away from me now, when we were closer than ever, and . . .

The pieces slipped into place and I stared at him. Of course. Of course he would be so selfless.

"Would you like to know what I am thinking right now, Jack?" I asked in a low voice.

He stood too still, as if I might stop talking if he didn't react.

"I think," I went on, "that you've got it into your head that you know what is best for me. You believe that *you* are not what is best for me. And so you are pushing me away."

His eyes flashed to mine, an unbreakable thread binding us.

"You are trying to protect me," I said. "But I do not need protecting, Jack. Not from this. Not when my heart is already lost."

He exhaled. "You cannot say such things."

"Why not?" I challenged. "Is this not what you wanted? To know my secrets and desires?"

"That was before."

Before we'd fallen in too deeply.

His eyes closed. At that, my heart crumpled, a love letter torn to pieces. I'd been right. He was holding himself back, breaking his own heart in an attempt to preserve mine. And suddenly I needed to be near him. I needed him to know what I felt for him.

I released my hold on the gnarled knot—and on any remaining inhibitions. I stood and stepped carefully across the thick branches, so wide I might have laid upon them without fear of falling, though the ground was just below us even if I did. Jack watched me, hand grasping a branch above his head, wariness filling every inch of his face.

I stepped onto his branch, trapping him between me and the tree trunk.

"You don't know what you are doing, Ginny," he said, his voice deliciously low. Despite his words, yearning darkened his eyes.

"Heaven forbid a woman think for herself." I pressed a hand against his chest—warm and unyielding. "I know precisely what I am doing."

I rose onto my toes and I kissed him.

His lips were soft, far softer than I'd expected. Our connection radiated waves of heat, rolling over me like a sultry summer wind. He stood immobile—shocked, for once, by something *I'd* done. Yet I knew I'd affected him by the way he breathed, how his chest moved beneath my hands. He was not indifferent. I slid one hand up to circle his rough jaw, pausing our kiss to catch my own breath.

"Ginny," he whispered against my lips. A warning. A plea.

I took it as an invitation and kissed him again. And then he kissed me back.

I'd never understood the idea of swooning. Any self-respecting woman of sound body and mind ought to be able to stand upright, even when being thoroughly kissed. But now I had more sympathy for the heroines of romantic novels. Jack's lips moved over mine in a way that was utterly possessive, so deep and bold that bright lights danced across my closed eyelids. My insides melted, liquid ore that flowed through my limbs.

His right arm swept me up to him, clasping me around the waist, while his left hand still held fast to the branch above our heads. Thankfully *he* was concerned about keeping us upright, because my knees gave out precisely five seconds after he began kissing me. I sagged against his arm. He pulled back, taking his lips from mine.

"What is it?" His arm circling my waist loosened, allowing me the choice to draw away.

I clutched the front of his jacket, my eyelids heavy, feeling a bit drunk. Clearly kissing was another of his *certain talents.* "You took me by surprise, that's all."

He blinked, and then his wide grin appeared, which lit my heart more than any kiss could. "If you are going to kiss a man, you ought to be prepared for him to kiss you back."

"I shall try to remember that in the future," I said breathlessly. "Do hold tight so we don't fall."

He lowered his head, his nose brushing along my jaw. "It's far too late for me."

My mind was utter mush. It was hot porridge on a cold morning. His kisses moved down my neck, and I shivered, the night air claiming the warmth he left behind on my skin. Then he turned me against the tree trunk, changing places in a smooth motion I thought must be practiced. Except, when did one practice kissing in a tree? He captured me between his arms, and any last remains of reason slipped from my mind. I gave in to oblivion as his lips stole mine again. A blissful sigh escaped me, hardly audible considering how our mouths were currently occupied.

Jack kept one hand on the tree trunk to steady us, but his free hand toyed with my hair, loosening pins and sending curls tumbling down my back. I did not care. I only wanted more of him, of this kiss. It was as if our souls had been yearning for one another, and we hadn't known it until this moment. But now it was clear as a mountain lake. He was made for me, and I for him.

It wasn't the first time I'd experienced a kiss. When I was fourteen, Beatrice's cousin came to visit. Frederick was a worldly two years older than I and we had a lovely summer of flirtation. The day before he left for his home in Hampshire, he kissed me in the rose garden. A sweet and innocent kiss. I'd written pages upon pages in my journal about that kiss, certain it would never be outdone.

After kissing Jack Travers, I knew I could fill a hundred diaries and never capture how it felt.

Which was why I was not at all pleased when he groaned and tried to pull away. "We should not be doing this now."

I caught hold of his cravat and tugged him back. "No, we should have been doing this for the last fortnight."

He gave a short laugh. Making him laugh was the greatest pleasure of my life. Besides kissing him, obviously.

"I meant, because we should be watching the camp," he said, gently prying my hands from his cravat.

Blast. The camp. I peered around his shoulder—the scenery remained unchanged, surrounded by shadow. I mentally shook myself. He was right. I was being foolish and irresponsible. Even if I'd never been kissed like that before—even if my mind was still spinning—I should have better judgment than that.

"You sit over there." He pointed to my original spot. "Far away."

"You needn't banish me," I said, even as I obeyed, settling back onto my horrible excuse for a seat. "I'll behave."

"Yes, well, I cannot speak for myself." He scrubbed a hand over his face and leaned back against the trunk. He looked at me and his grin slowly faded. I did not like that. It meant he was thinking again.

"We should not have done that." He turned his gaze to stare out over the landscape, though I could tell his focus was shattered.

"I disagree," I said. "Talking tends to end in confusion or argument. Best to be clear about our feelings."

"But feelings are not the only thing we have to consider," he said. "You know as well as I do that everything in our lives is more complicated than that."

I pressed my lips together. He was right, of course.

He paused. "I have a chance to return to Bow Street."

I sat upright. "What?"

"When I was in Town," he said, "I spoke to a friend of mine, another principal officer. There are changes coming to Bow Street, including the appointment of a new chief magistrate." He rubbed his neck. "This magistrate was sympathetic to me when I was forced out. I have every reason to believe he will reinstate me once he takes charge."

My fingers curled tighter around the branch I clutched. I hadn't even thought to consider this.

"To join my brother officers again," he said, "to work for the law instead of skirting it—it's what I've wanted for the last eighteen months. It was all I wanted until I met you." He sent me a blistering, aching look. "And I cannot have both."

His words rushed over me, through my head, and out again.

"I cannot leave Wimborne," I whispered.

"I know."

"If it was anything else, I would." Tears pricked my eyes. "Will you not consider—"

"I have," he said. "I have considered it, I swear. But what would I do here? Am I to be a gentleman, live a gentleman's leisurely life?"

No. That much was clear. Jack had too much enthusiasm and energy. A quiet life in the country would be unbearable to him, just as a life in London, without my beloved home, would be heartbreaking to me.

"But this is all irrelevant," he said. "There is perhaps some future where you and I find contentment amidst those issues. But there is no answer for our most obvious problem."

"Which is?"

"The fact that I am not good for you."

"I can decide that for myself, thank you," I said, narrowing my eyes. "Who would you have me marry? Mr. Northcott?"

"No," he said. "You should not marry Mr. Northcott. You should marry someone better than he. Better than *me*."

I began to protest, but he held up a hand. "There is no beating around the bush, Ginny. I know what I am. I am the baseborn son of a peer, a thief-taker by choice."

I leaned forward. "Those are the barest facts of your life, Jack. You are so much more than that. You are loyal and strong, confident and caring."

He stared at me, as if my words were rain in a drought. Then he exhaled and turned back to the thicket again. "It doesn't matter. I know what will happen."

"You are a fortune teller now?"

His jaw tightened. "Your housekeeper."

"Mrs. Betts?" I furrowed my brow.

He gave a mirthless laugh and a shake of his head. "The look on her face when she saw us on the stairs yesterday."

I bit my lip. I remembered. Mrs. Betts's disapproval had been so strong, so immediate. She might see the necessity of Jack's presence at Wimborne, but necessity had grown into something else entirely.

"It was the reminder I needed," he said. "If your *servant* looked at us like that, how would the rest of Society?" His voice wavered. "There is no possible way I can remain at Wimborne, not without ruining you. Not without ruining any children before they are even born."

Children. My stomach flipped even as tears pricked in my eyes, my heart fighting what I knew was true. We'd both been born of scandal, he an illegitimate son, me the result of my father's marriage with a lowly governess. I knew that whatever my challenges had been while growing up, they would be magnified for any children we had. They would be rejected by proper society and maliciously gossiped about.

But there were other things in life that were important. Love. Happiness. Vying for Society's approval had never brought me those. Jack *had*. Nothing had eased the stinging emptiness of Father's death until Jack *had*. I'd spent my whole life clinging to my reputation, and now I discovered it meant nothing to me at all. Father had loved my mother. He had loved her enough to ignore what others said and reach for his future. Could I find the courage to do the same?

"Our children would have parents who love each other," I said, throat raw. "Is that not enough?"

He looked away.

"I am fighting for you." I could not hide the wrenching pain in my words. "Will you not fight for me?"

"I *am*," he insisted. "In the only way I know how. You've a life full of promise. I cannot be the one to ruin it. A magistrate's daughter does not belong with a thief-taker."

I tried to steady my breathing. His words spun in my head.

"You must stop doing that." My voice was the barest whisper.

He swallowed. "Doing what?"

"Trying to convince me that I shouldn't love you."

Jack opened his mouth, but no words escaped. He ran his hand through his dark curls, throwing them in such disarray that all I wanted to do was climb back over and smooth them out. I was already regretting not running my own hands through his hair as we kissed. Now I might never have the opportunity.

Suddenly Jack stiffened, staring over my shoulder. His mouth dropped. "Ginny," he said hoarsely.

I spun. Just beyond the trees, I could see Wimborne's eastern walls. I gasped. A horrid orange glow hovered about the house, like an early sunrise against a coal-black sky. It couldn't be.

It *was*. Wimborne was on fire.

"No!" I did not stop to think. My hands and feet acted of their own volition, carrying me down, down, my skirt ripping on a sharp branch, my hair catching on twigs and leaves. Wimborne was on fire. My life was on fire.

"Stop, Ginny. Stop!"

I dropped to the grass, tripping and catching myself. Jack was right behind me, and as I began stumbling toward the house, he grabbed me by both shoulders.

"You can't," he panted.

"That is my *home*," I shot, the words ripping harshly from my throat.

"Yes, and you running pell-mell toward a disaster is precisely what the vandal wants." He gripped my shoulders tighter.

"I have to help." My hands fisted into his waistcoat. "Do not stop me."

His eyes blazed, reflecting the far-off fire. I thought he would refuse, insist again that I remain hidden. But then he groaned. He grabbed my hand and we ran toward the flames.

CHAPTER 22

I was crying, hot tears splashing down my cheeks. Shouts filled the air as my servants sounded the alarm. I could see tiny figures darting around the fire. They fought the flames, with buckets and bravery. Was anyone still inside? Had my household managed to escape?

We ran, faster than I'd ever run before. After only a minute, my legs burned, but I forced them onwards, Jack's hand pulling me with him. My breaths came heavy and dry.

I was so focused on the disaster ahead that I did not see *him* until it was too late. Movement caught my eye. I turned—an enormous shadow rushed us. It collided with Jack, yanking his hand from mine and slamming him to the ground. A scream tore from my throat.

"Jack!"

They wrestled on the grass, their shapes melding in the darkness. The stranger pinned Jack, slamming his great fists into his face again and again. Jack yelled, throwing his arms up to shield himself.

"Stop!" I ran at the man and pounded my fists against his broad back. I might have been a gnat for all I did. One of his hands lashed out and caught mine, leaving Jack on the ground, moaning and bloody in the moonlight. *Jack.*

The man turned to me, face dark against the light of the fire in the distance. All I saw were two glittering eyes, full of twisted malice. I opened my mouth to scream again. He was on me in an instant, covering my mouth and wrapping a thick arm around my waist.

"Quiet, now," came his raspy voice. "Can't have you alerting the magistrate."

Panic and bile filled my throat as the man dragged me away. I screamed against his hand. I fought, struggling and kicking and thrashing. It did nothing—the man was huge. Shoulders of an elephant, arms as thick as the branches I'd just been climbing.

"Come nicely," he hissed. "No need to fight."

Where was he taking me? My mind scattered like a broken vase. But I could not allow myself to go to pieces. *Focus*, I told myself. *Everyone has a weakness. Find his weakness.*

Fortunately for me, every man had the same one.

I stopped struggling. I did not move one muscle. Such was my abductor's surprise that his arms loosened. I took my chance, turning in his arms and driving my knee upwards as hard as I could.

Right between his legs.

He unleashed an unearthly howl and dropped. I landed hard, my face smashing into the ground. But I had no time for pain. I scrambled to my feet, skirts tangling in my legs, and stumbled away, back toward Jack. Where was he?

A hand caught my ankle and I fell again, catching myself as I hit the ground. Then I was yanked back through the grass, the hand on my ankle twisting, burning against my skin. I kicked at him, grasping handfuls of grass only to be ripped away from them. He was unrelenting. I couldn't escape him, couldn't fight.

"Jack!" I screamed. "Jack!"

Then he was there, a blur in the dark. He tackled my assailant, drove him to the ground. Hot, uncontrollable relief poured through me. He was alive. He was here. I came to my feet, gasping.

Jack got in two quick jabs right to the man's face before he even had a chance to react. The stranger roared and threw out his arms, shoving Jack away. They were both on their feet in an instant. Jack snatched his pistol and raised it, flashing in the moonlight. But the man knocked the weapon aside. It spun into the grass.

The man stalked forward, swinging those massive arms with

unbelievable speed. Jack was even quicker. He dodged and danced, his fists raised before him. He landed a resounding hit to the man's chest that made him wheeze and draw back.

My mouth opened in a soundless scream as the two men circled each other. Jack was hurt, bleeding from a cut over his eye. How could he win this? *My fault, my fault.* I'd made him careless, running to Wimborne. The fire raged beyond—even if I screamed, who would hear me above the shouts and roar of the flames?

My eyes caught a sliver of metal on the ground just beyond the flying limbs and grunts. Jack's pistol.

I snatched the pistol from the grass, the cold metal biting my skin. Was it loaded? Would it even fire if I pulled the trigger?

I did not have time to think. The man landed a fist in Jack's stomach. Jack staggered back, nearly going to the ground again. The stranger closed in.

I raised the pistol with shaking hands and cocked it, but the tip of the barrel dipped and wavered. I was just as likely to hit Jack.

The man drew back his fist to land another bone-shattering hit, and I made a choice. I jerked the barrel up toward the endless nothingness of night and pulled the trigger. The pistol roared, letting loose a blinding flare. My ears rang. I coughed in the smoke.

The man spun toward me, eyes wide. Jack moved—so fast I nearly missed it. The brass-tipped baton flashed in his hands, and before the man could react, Jack drove the baton into the back of his head.

He collapsed, and I swore I felt the ground shudder.

Jack did not hesitate. He scrambled to kneel on the man's back, bringing his hands together as he drew out two pairs of iron fetters.

My lungs heaved, desperate for air, and my legs felt like jelly. Jack was quick. Within half a minute, the man was restrained, his form still.

"He isn't . . . ?" I asked, my voice unsteady.

"He's not dead." Jack was breathing hard. "Unfortunately."

He rose and looked at me. The pistol hung heavy at my side.

"Are you all right?" He took one step toward me.

I was *not* all right. My entire body ached from fighting, my throat was sore from screaming, and I knew a wicked bruise was already forming on my cheek.

But I was alive. I was alive because of Jack.

I dropped the pistol and ran to him. He caught me, his arms reassuring me that he was there. My sobs came wild and unrestrained.

"I thought he would kill you," I cried into his chest. "I cannot—"

But the tears took over and my words were lost. He pulled back and pressed kisses to my lips, my eyes, my cheeks.

"He won't hurt you again," he said in that rough voice of his. "I swear it."

I took a shuddering breath and swiped at my eyes, looking up at him. He cupped my face in his hands, caught me in his eyes. He kissed me again, the action somehow both fierce and gentle. When he drew back, I had to take a few more gulping breaths, my lungs far past their limit.

Then my thoughts swept me up again. "Wimborne," I gasped.

Leaving the assailant unconscious in the grass, we ran together back toward the house. Halfway there, two shapes emerged from the shadows, heading in our direction. Mr. Northcott and Mr. Crouth.

"Miss Wilde?" Mr. Northcott was breathing hard, pistol in hand. I'd never seen him with a weapon before. "What are you—"

He took us in, Jack's bloodied face, my dirty dress and tear-streaked cheeks, and changed his question. "What happened? We heard a shot."

"We caught him," Jack said grimly. "Back there. I restrained him."

Mr. Northcott stared at him in clear disbelief. He shook his head. "Go up to the house," he ordered. "We'll take him from here."

I did not wait for him to change his mind. We ran again through the sweeping blackness until the hellish light of the fire broke before us.

I gaped at the scene. The eastern wall was ablaze. All that remained of the conservatory were the blackened frames of the windows, the remaining shards of glass like glittering teeth. A line of desperate faces stretched to the nearby stream, handing bucket after bucket up to the house. But it made no difference. The fire raged, breaking and smashing the only place I'd ever called home.

I didn't realize I was stumbling forward until Jack grabbed my arm and pulled me to a stop.

"I need to help," I said, my voice echoing in my head. Every event from tonight seemed so absurd—Jack's kiss, the fight, the fire—that surely this could not be reality. But the blasting heat of the flames and the shouts and cries of my staff convinced me otherwise.

"I know," he said. "Come."

He tugged me toward the bucket line, where Marchant stood yelling instructions. I pulled away from Jack and ran to my butler, and his relief at seeing me made me want to throw my arms around him.

"Miss Wilde," he gasped, his face striped with sweat. "You're all right. We couldn't find you."

"Never mind me." I grasped his arms. "Is everyone out? Safe?"

"Yes," he said, pulling me further from the blistering heat. "Now that you're here, everyone is accounted for. I tried to send them away, but they insisted on helping."

My eyes blurred once again. I should never have doubted my household.

"What can we do?" Jack asked.

Marchant waved at the line. "This is all we can do."

I knew he was right. Perhaps in London we might have had a chance with the organized fire brigades and engine pumps. But here in the country?

I would have to watch my home burn.

I stepped backward, overwhelmed, black crowding the edges of my vision. Then Jack was before me, his features blocking out the hungry flames, the heat and noise and smoke.

"We won't give up," he said, taking my hands. "We'll fight."

I stared at him. I was exhausted beyond belief, my emotions frayed. But his words fastened to something deep inside me, a place only he could reach.

I pulled my shoulders back and nodded firmly. "We'll fight."

CHAPTER 23

We joined the bucket brigade, between a stable hand and a kitchen maid. We passed bucket after bucket, the sloshing water soaking my skirts and clinging like ice to my legs.

The fire was unrelenting. We sent runners to every home nearby for help. Dozens came, hastily dressed and bleary eyed, and we formed a second line, then a third. It seemed our efforts did nothing. The fire was hungry, and it consumed both the study and the parlor on the ground floor, and two spare bedrooms above. I could not let myself think about what I'd already lost. I focused on what I could still save, what I could do with my two hands. Jack and I said nothing as we worked. We did not have the energy. But I felt a jolt of determination every time our eyes met. He hadn't given up, and neither would I.

My hands soon wore down, blisters taking the place of the smooth, soft skin beneath my gloves. But I pressed on, not speaking a word of complaint. When I felt the first drop of rain, I thought it was simply sweat dripping down my forehead. But then I heard a shout, and I pulled myself from my focused stupor.

It was raining. I tilted my face up to the clouds, my skin hot and itchy from the fevered pace. The raindrops against my cheeks felt like cooling kisses sent by angels—an answer to the countless prayers we'd all been whispering as we passed our buckets. The small sprinkles quickened until the rain fell in a thick sheet, drenching me within seconds. Cheers sprang up from our ragged group of volunteers.

"Keep going!" Jack shouted, passing me a bucket. I took it without hesitation. "We're not through it yet."

He was right. We continued on, bucket after bucket. A quarter hour passed before the flames choked, drowned by the relentless rain and our unyielding efforts. The light from the fire faded, leaving only the flickering light of the few torches and lanterns my neighbors had brought. Within a half hour, we were tossing buckets onto embers and ashes, a muddy gray mess that soon coated us all.

I reached back to take another bucket from Jack. Instead, I found my hand wrapped in his.

"That's it," he said quietly. "It's over."

I stared up at him. Rain slid down his face, tracing his nose and jaw, dripping from his chin. It had washed away most of the blood, leaving raw skin around his eye. His dark hair was always mussed, but now it was matted, thick with ash. I knew I looked equally disheveled, but I did not care in the least. I threw my arms around his neck. He brought me close, his breath warm on my neck, his fingers curling into my back. My face pressed into the drenched linen of his shirt, the scents of smoke and soap filling my nose. I wanted nothing more than to remain forever in his arms. Safe. Loved.

But forever was impossible.

I pulled back, Jack's arms slower to release me. I'd forgotten for a moment that we were surrounded by my entire household, my neighbors. It was good I hadn't followed my embrace with a kiss, or they'd all have more to talk about besides a fire. Thankfully, everyone was far too busy patting each other on the shoulder and collecting buckets.

Only Mr. Northcott was watching, and as I met his eyes, he turned quickly to shake hands with a neighbor. I sighed. I'd never wanted to hurt him. He'd only ever been kind to me. But I wanted more from marriage than kindness. I wanted love. Unfortunately, I was learning horrible, heartbreaking lessons about love.

I took a deep breath. I could feel the cold now, my soaked clothing clinging to my skin, but it was nothing compared to the ice in my chest. I faced Wimborne, taking in the damage all at once. Nearly a third of my home was gone. Destroyed. The roof collapsed and windows blown out from the heat. The parlor, the conservatory, the kitchen. I clutched my stomach, a hard knot within me. My *home*.

The worst loss of all was the study. I could barely bring myself to look at it. Nothing remained but twisted, charred beams, black and ugly. If I stood in the center of the room and looked up, I would have stared right into the rain-driven sky. It was clear this fire was no accident. Had it been started in the study? Had the arsonist known how deeply it would hurt to lose the place where I felt closest to my father? Everything was lost—his desk, his collection of books, Wimborne's ledgers and records. A small relief came at the remembrance that I'd sent Father's portrait to Catherine. At least that was safe.

"Do you want to look closer?"

Jack moved to stand beside me, hands in his pockets. Did he want to reach for me as badly as my arms ached for him? I was so tired. But this night was far from over.

"No," I said. "No, I want to talk to *him*."

I marched to Mr. Northcott. "Where is he?" I demanded.

Mr. Northcott held up both hands. "Miss Wilde, what are you doing?"

"I have a few questions," I said shortly, "and I am quite certain only one man can answer them. So *where is he?*"

His eyes flicked to a stand of aspen trees where Mr. Crouth stood, one hand on his pistol while the other held a lantern. But my gaze went past him, to the man propped against a tree trunk, hands and feet restrained, as he watched everything with hate-filled eyes. My hands balled into fists. I'd never before wanted to kill a man, but the fiery rage that filled my soul made me realize it was entirely possible.

I tried to move around Mr. Northcott, but he blocked my way.

"I do not think that is particularly wise at the moment," he said. "We are all tired; we don't want our emotions getting away from us."

"My *emotions* are not getting away from me," I snapped. "I want to know who he is and why he has been tormenting me."

"I understand," Mr. Northcott said, and to his credit, he did sound sympathetic rather than condescending. "But I believe it would be best to wait until morning. I have been questioning him for an hour with little progress."

I blinked. "You already questioned him?" I shouldn't have been surprised—Mr. Northcott was not covered in ash like the rest of us.

"Yes," Mr. Northcott said. "He proved resilient."

"There are other means of persuasion." Jack crossed his arms.

Mr. Northcott looked affronted. "I'll not allow torture as means to a confession."

"I won't torture him," Jack said. "Well. Perhaps a bit."

He wasn't helping my case. "I just want to talk to him," I said.

"It does not matter," Mr. Northcott said, his voice a little louder now, "as he refuses to speak to anyone."

"I'll speak to *her*."

The man's raspy voice made my shoulders curl inward—the voice that had hissed in my ears, his filthy hand over my mouth. I turned to the prisoner, and he stared me down without an ounce of fear. That flame inside me leapt again, and my fingers twitched. I'd held a gun for the first time tonight, and now I wished I grasped it again.

"Let me," I said to Mr. Northcott. "Please. I need to know."

He sighed and waved me forward. I approached the bound man. This very night, he had attacked Jack and attempted to drag me off. But I did not care about that now. I just wanted to know *why*.

I could see him better in the light from Mr. Crouth's lantern. Knotted brown hair, features long and gnarled, bruised from where Jack had landed punches. I had long thought I would know the vandal when I saw him, that I would realize who he was and why he hated me. But this man was a stranger to me.

I stopped a few feet away, Mr. Northcott and Jack flanking me. I resisted the urge to take Jack's hand. I would not show this man how much he frightened me.

"What is your name?" I asked, my voice steady.

He gave a dry laugh. "So, you don't know me."

"Why should I know you?"

"I s'pose I shouldn't be surprised," he went on as if I hadn't spoken. "I'm nothin' to you. To your father."

I glanced at Jack. He gave the slightest nod. We'd been right—this *had* been about Father.

"How do you know my father?" I demanded. "Why have you been targeting Wimborne?"

He gave a mad sort of laugh. "Targeting Wimborne?"

I swallowed. "Me, then. You were targeting me. Why?"

He leaned forward with a steely glare, as far as his bindings would allow him. "Because your father took everything from me, and I thought to return the favor."

"What did he take from you?" This man was frustrating to the extreme, answering with riddles and questions.

"My life," he said in a flash of fire. "They caught me poachin', which is no horrible crime. But instead of a fine and a jaunt in prison, your father made an example of me. S'posed to be transported, but they let me join the army instead." He laughed again, a horrible bark. "As if that was any better."

Poaching. My mind raced, trying to make sense of his words. Then I remembered.

"Your name is Garvey," I said. "John Garvey."

"Ah," he said, looking absurdly pleased. "You do know me."

He'd been on my list. The poacher who'd killed that gamekeeper, last summer before Father had died.

"You are supposed to be dead," I said, shaking. Isn't that what Jack had said? That he'd died on the continent?

"Nearly was," Garvey said. "But no one notices one more missing body when there's a fever raging through camp."

"So you came back to England to torment me?"

"It's all you deserve," he spat. "Your father thought he was better than the rest of us. I was only makin' a livin'—"

"A living?" I repeated in disbelief. "You are a thief, no matter what you say. A thief and a *murderer*. You killed that poor gamekeeper. The army was better than you deserved."

Garvey's eyes flashed dangerously. "Better than I deserved?"

Jack stepped forward, one arm in front of me.

"What about what *you* deserve?" Garvey snarled, straining against his ropes. "Livin' in that manor, with servants to wipe your brow and kiss your boots. You know nothin'."

"That's enough," Mr. Northcott said, stepping forward. "You've as good as confessed, and you'll not receive the same leniency as before."

Mr. Northcott began calling orders to his men to transport Garvey to town. My mind spun, too many questions still unanswered. But only one managed to find its way to my mouth.

"My watch," I said desperately. "My father's pocket watch. What did you do with it?"

Garvey blinked. "What watch?"

"You took it from my study. From my desk."

Garvey looked at me as if I was not right in the head. Before he could say another word, Mr. Crouth hauled him up and shoved him forward. I stared after him, lost until Jack touched my arm.

"Genevieve," he said quietly.

"Why did he not know about the watch?" I asked, dazed. I held a hand to my head, pounding and throbbing.

Jack shook his head. "I daresay he would say anything to keep it from you."

Mr. Northcott returned to my side as Jack spoke, and he nodded in agreement. "Don't let that man trouble you, Miss Wilde. We've caught him, and I've no doubt we'll find your watch soon enough."

I could not muster any surprise that Mr. Northcott was agreeing with Jack on this. I only nodded.

"We need to get her out of the rain," Jack said to Mr. Northcott.

"Come to Tamworth Hall," he said. "I'll house as many of your staff as I can, and I'm sure others will offer the same. I'll post a man to watch over Wimborne."

I hadn't given one thought as to where I might rest my head that night. Obviously, it would not be at Wimborne, smothered in smoke and water. The rain still fell, though lighter now, as if nature knew it had already performed the miracle we'd needed.

"A bath and some sleep will do wonders," Jack said softly. "We can face this properly in the light of day."

His steady gaze assured me that he would be there in the morning, that he would stand by me. But for how long? I had difficult realities to face—the burned husk that was my home, the prosecution of the man being loaded into the back of a wagon. But the most frightening reality was that I might soon be facing it all without Jack.

"Very well," I said, my voice hoarse. "Tomorrow."

Mr. Northcott strode away, ordering my coach to be readied. Thankfully, my stables and coach house had suffered no damage.

Jack stepped closer, taking my elbows and turning me to face him. "What can I do?" he whispered. "Please tell me how to help you."

He looked so utterly vulnerable, collar tugged open, shirtsleeves rolled to his elbows—he'd abandoned his jacket hours ago. His face was streaked with dirt and rain, his undaunted smile nowhere to be seen. He intertwined his fingers with mine, not seeming to care if anyone saw us.

I stared up at him, my insides awash in confusion and exhaustion and defeat. He'd told me this very night that we had no future together. It did not matter that he thought he was doing it for me, for my reputation. His words hurt all the same, my heart aching as much as the blisters on my hands. He said he would be there tomorrow, but then what? How long would he stay?

I stepped away, slipping my hand from his.

He followed a step. "Ginny?"

I shook my head. "I'm tired."

I started after Mr. Northcott, wrapping my arms tightly around myself. Jack followed, not speaking.

And I wished as I'd never wished before that I could see my father again.

CHAPTER 24

I woke to sunshine and birdsong.

I rolled to my side, enveloped by thick blankets and soft pillows, and squinted at the window. Soft light slipped from the edges of the curtains. It was late in the morning, perhaps even early afternoon. A few moments passed before I remembered where I was: a bedroom at Tamworth Hall. I was safe. I was alive.

The events of last night poured through my head in a rush of memories. The blinding flash of the fire. Garvey's hand pressed against my mouth. The weight of a bucket in my hands. I closed my eyes again, overcome.

Another memory forced its way forward. The soft press of Jack's lips and the feel of his heart beating beneath my hand.

I sat up, my body protesting. Shoulders, legs, back—they all shouted at me to lie back down. I ignored them, throwing off my covers and limping to ring for Holloway. She'd come with me last night, helped me bathe and change into a maid's borrowed chemise before I fell into bed, utterly spent. She arrived now not a minute later.

"Did you sleep at all?" I asked as she helped me lace my stays, washed and dried during the night. My dress was also cleaned and pressed, the rips mended.

"I slept nearly as long as you did," she said, pulling the laces firmly. "This was all the work of Mr. Northcott's staff."

Yet another thing to thank him for. I had quite the list these days.

"Is anyone else awake?" I asked.

She knew who I meant. "I believe Mr. Travers woke an hour ago."

After she pinned my hair up and buttoned my dress, I hurried downstairs. I'd been to Tamworth Hall many times for dinners and parties, but it was strange to be a guest. Apprehension filled me as I started for the breakfast room. Did I want to see Jack? I hardly knew how to face him after last night—I'd practically thrown myself at him in that tree. My cheeks pricked and I had to remind myself that he had returned the kiss. Returned it and then some.

But his words afterwards had stung just as much as his lips had ignited.

I heard low voices from around the next corner and slowed my steps.

"I imagine you'll be returning to London as soon as possible?" Those were Mr. Northcott's smooth tones.

"I cannot say at the moment." Jack's voice. "Miss Wilde hired me and I will stay until she decides otherwise."

I held my breath. Eavesdropping was wrong. But did I not have the right to know what they said about me?

"Are you sure Miss Wilde is capable of making that decision?" Mr. Northcott asked slowly. "You do not think her unfairly influenced?"

"Unfairly influenced?" Jack's voice was calm but with an undercurrent of tension. "I cannot guess what you mean."

"Come now," Mr. Northcott said. "I am not blind, and neither are you subtle. You've set your aim at her and turned her head."

Jack said nothing, and I tried to picture his face, stone and steel. What was going through his mind right now?

"You must see," Mr. Northcott went on, "how impossible it is. Do you think a woman like Miss Wilde would marry a man like *you*, a near-criminal with no name or fortune?"

My heart withered. It was the very argument Jack had used last night, and yet coming from Mr. Northcott, the words felt more real and harsh. My earlier gratitude to the magistrate vanished like a drop of water on a hot summer's day.

Mr. Northcott's voice remained firm. "I believe you care for the girl. And if you do, then act in her best interest. Leave now before you sink her reputation beyond repair."

I finally allowed myself to peer around the corner. Jack stood with his hands clasped casually behind his back. The only sign of any inner turmoil was his narrowed eyes, fixed on Mr. Northcott.

"I am not the one who decides what is in her best interest," Jack said, his voice unyielding. "Nor are you. It is her decision and hers alone. As for me . . ." He paused, and the silence that followed was so still I could hear my pulse in my ears. "I will not leave her. So long as she wants me, I will be at her side."

I closed my eyes. What did he mean by that? That he cared for me enough to stay, to give up his future at Bow Street? Or was he simply speaking as a thief-taker, completing his job?

"This is absurd." Mr. Northcott drew himself up to his full height. "I am only trying to guide a woman unversed in the ways of the world—"

"She does not *need* guidance," Jack said, each word a bullet. "She is strong and brilliant and perfectly able to manage her own life. If you knew that, we would not be having this conversation."

"You know nothing," Mr. Northcott snapped. "I am acting as her father would wish me to, watching over her and protecting her. And she needs to be protected from *you*."

With that, my anger roared right past any interest in hearing more. I marched around the corner. Jack looked unfairly handsome, even with bruises marring his face. His jaw was smoothly shaved and his eyes bright as he looked at me. But I turned my narrowed gaze to Mr. Northcott. He straightened, lips pressed into a flat line. He knew I'd heard him.

"Good morning," I said, without an ounce of expression.

"Miss Wilde. Good morning." Mr. Northcott cleared his throat. "We were, uh, just discussing you."

"Yes, I gathered." My voice was dry as a week-old biscuit.

From the furrow in Mr. Northcott's brow, I knew he was search-ing for a way to excuse what I'd heard. But I did not care for excuses.

"Mr. Northcott," I said. "I am grateful for all the aid you've given me, both in apprehending Garvey and in housing me and my staff last night. Thank you."

He blinked, glancing at Jack. "Of course. You must know I would do anything for you, Miss Wilde."

Jack raised his eyes to the ceiling, and even amidst my irritation at the magistrate, I had to fight a laugh.

"That being said," I went on, "I do not plan on staying long. I am sure Miss Lacey will take me off your hands, and, owing to the val-iant efforts by my servants and our neighbors, I am determined to see Wimborne rebuilt. In fact, I should like to inspect the house myself as soon as possible."

"Yourself?" Mr. Northcott sputtered. "I cannot allow it. The fire has surely caused grave damage to the structure of the house, and the danger—"

"I appreciate your concern," I interrupted, my words like ice, "but I am afraid I will not be dissuaded."

Mr. Northcott stared, then set his jaw. "As you wish." He stepped closer to me and lowered his voice, though I knew Jack could still hear his words clearly. "But I must tell you, Miss Wilde, that your father would not approve of your actions recently. Not in the least." He cast Jack a scathing look and stalked down the corridor.

Which, of course, left me quite alone with the man who had kissed me senseless just twelve hours previous.

Jack observed me with arms crossed, his waistcoat pulled taut over his chest. He did not speak, only watched me with an intent, almost amused gleam in his eye.

I cleared my throat. "He overstepped entirely," I said. "Though I appreciate your defense of me."

"You hardly needed it," he said. "I quite enjoyed watching you deliver such a dressing down." He leaned forward in an air of secrecy. "Although he *is* right about one thing."

"And that is?"

"Your father would certainly *not* approve of his daughter kissing me the way you did last night."

Heat rushed to my cheeks. "Jack!"

He chuckled and released his arms. "It is my fault, I am sure. Ladies are always trying to kiss me in trees."

I shook my head. "Trying to shove you out of them, more like."

"But you did not shove me last night."

My cheeks burned even more. "No," I said. "I did not."

Why was he acting like this? Last night, he had been so terribly serious, and now he was teasing and flirting again. What had changed? His words rang through my head. *So long as she wants me, I will be at her side.*

His grin slid away and his eyes took me in—every inch of my face open to his inspection. I'd never felt so vulnerable. He knew how I felt about him and I hated that I was so unsure of his intentions. My heart faltered, a painful reminder of all it had endured in the last few days.

He stepped closer, raising one hand to gently trace the ridge of my jaw—swollen and tender from where Garvey had hurt me last night. The brush of his fingers made my brain go fuzzy, as if I'd just woken up from a long nap.

"Does it hurt?" he asked.

"I'm fine," I said, my voice unsteady. "You took the far worse beating."

He smiled wryly. "Remind me never to fight a man twice my size in the dead of night."

"I do recall saying something about you not going alone," I reminded him. "But you are far too bullheaded."

"Ah, well, perfection is overrated." He dropped his hand, sobering. "I haven't thanked you yet. You saved my life when you fired that shot."

Those moments leapt back into my mind—Garvey's grip around my ankle, the sight of Jack charging at us from the shadows. "And you saved mine," I said in a bare whisper. "I knew you would."

His eyes took on a new fierceness, dipping to my lips. I inhaled a sharp breath. He broke our gaze to look up and down the corridor. "Mr. Northcott is not prone to morning games of billiards, is he?"

"What?"

He grabbed my hand and tugged me with him into the nearest room: the darkened—and entirely empty—billiards room. He closed the door behind us and then faced me. My skin tingled.

"Jack," I said, his name a breathless question.

He slowly closed the distance between us, each second burning into my memory. His hands grazed up my arms, leaving raised bumps along my skin, and settled around my face. Gently—oh so gently—he pulled me to him, kissing me. My eyes fluttered closed. His thumbs moved over my jaw, sweetly caressing. This was not his desperate, haunting kiss from last night. This was intimate and exquisite and soft, his lips speaking to me, trying to tell me something I yearned to know.

I kissed him back, his warmth and scent intoxicating. But I was not so lost in his kiss that I had no sense. If this was the last time I would kiss Jack, then I would take full advantage. My hands found their way into his hair, those black, daring curls. I toyed with the curl at the back of his neck and Jack made a sound deep in his chest. My own chest felt so light that if he had not been holding me, I would have floated up and away.

His hands released my face and glided down my neck, shoulders, arms, until they entwined behind my back, bringing me even closer. I tried not to think of how this kiss would soon end, that we would have to face reality once again. I squeezed my eyes shut, my arms clasped tightly around his neck, never wanting to let him go.

We kissed until my lips were sore and swollen, catching breaths between moments of heartbreaking pleasure. My body was made from clouds and sun and wind, unbound from the earth. But even birds have to land. Even the most brilliant sunsets come to an end.

We finally drew away, slowly, our arms still tangled about each other. I looked up at him, afraid to see what was surely coming—a painful realization of what could not be.

But there was no regret in Jack's eyes. Instead, I saw tenderness. I saw *love*.

"There were many reasons I could not sleep last night," he whispered, his breath grazing my skin. "But first and foremost was my desire to kiss you again."

Heavens, was it his life's goal to make me swoon?

"Jack." Swooning would do me no good. I had to know what he was thinking. "I don't understand. Last night—"

"Last night I was an idiot," he said. "Which is not unusual, really, but I can admit to being more featherbrained than normal."

His fingers played with a loose curl beside my ear, the hairs tickling my neck and sending a shiver across my skin. All I wanted was to kiss his fingers, that hard jaw, perhaps explore his mouth a bit more. But I resisted, forcing myself to focus on his words.

"You said this could never be," I reminded him, my hands finding their way to his chest, splaying against the fabric of his waistcoat. "That there were too many obstacles between us."

"I've changed my mind."

My fingers tightened around his lapels. "Why?"

"Because you are impossibly beautiful this morning."

I blew out a breath. "Do be serious."

"What?" he protested. "Is attraction not reason enough? Because it is ridiculous, really, how often I think of kissing you."

As if to emphasize his point, he kissed me again. I was so surprised that my lips half parted, resulting in a kiss far more intimate than before. It took every bit of sense remaining in my head to pull away.

"You must stop kissing me," I scolded him, words I never thought I would say. But my need for answers outweighed my need for his lips on mine, at least for the moment. I stepped away until my back hit the door. "I cannot think when you do that."

"Now you know how I felt last night." His lips still held that hint of a smile.

I took a deep breath, trying to gather my thoughts. "What you said before," I said. "About where we would live. How our children might be treated. None of that has changed."

"No," he conceded. "But the importance I placed on them has."

"What do you mean?"

"None of that matters," he said simply. "All that matters is this. Us. What we feel for each other." He took my hand, pressed a kiss to my knuckles. "Last night, I had a glimpse of my life where you were no longer in it. Where I might lose you. And it terrified me. Because strong as I think I am, I am not strong enough to live without you."

I stared at him. I had never imagined anyone saying such words to me. That someone might love me, Genevieve Wilde, so fiercely and so deeply.

"If you are willing to try," he said, "then so am I. I'll fight for you, Genevieve. I'll do whatever it takes. I'll live here with you, give up Bow Street."

"Jack." My voice was weak, small. Did he mean it? "I cannot ask you to—"

"Ginny!"

I jumped. It was Beatrice's voice, calling from the corridor at a near panic.

"I . . ." I looked up at Jack as I tried to decide what to do. He already wore a half grin in resignation.

"Go on," he said, nodding at the door. "We shouldn't be caught together."

"Or perhaps we should." My mind would never catch up to my mouth.

He laughed. "I think we'll have enough gossip to contend with as it is." He leaned down for one last, sweet kiss. His lips lingered on mine, warm and wonderful.

We. He had said *we.*

"Ginny!"

I forced myself to step back. "I still have much I need to say to you," I whispered.

"Later," he said. "We have time."

It was with those beautiful words in my ears that I stepped back out into the corridor, closing the door behind me as Beatrice rounded the corner.

"Thunder and turf, Ginny," she said in a huff. "Where on earth have you been hiding? No one could find you, and I've been looking everywhere."

"I was just . . ." I looked back at the billiards room. What excuse could I have for being inside at this time of day?

But Beatrice seemed not to care as she threw her arms around me. "Oh, Ginny," she said, her voice tearful. "I am so sorry. I heard about Wimborne."

I did not know if it was because Jack had just kissed me or if the events of the previous evening had finally caught me, but I felt strangely shaky. I let Beatrice embrace me, let her hold me, surrounded by her familiar smell and the sound of her breathing. When she drew away, she held me at arm's length and inspected me. She inhaled sharply as she spotted my cheek, red and bruised.

"What happened?" she whispered. "Who hurt you?"

I sighed and took her hand. "I have a great deal to tell you, Bea."

CHAPTER 25

We retreated to my borrowed room and rang for tea. Over fresh tarts, I told her what had happened in the last few days. She listened in rapt silence, her tea growing cold in her hands.

When I finished, she sat without moving for a long minute. Then she set down her cup, the tea nearly sloshing over the edge.

"I want nothing more than to scold you," she said, "for not telling me all this sooner. You are fortunate indeed that you nearly died last night, as I am inclined to forgive you."

"And if I *had* died?" I asked in amusement.

"Then we would not be having this conversation and the issue of forgiveness would be rather pointless."

Beatrice did not mean any of it, of course. I knew her well enough to hear her worry in every word. She sobered, her eyes serious.

"I am so glad you are all right," she said softly. "How awful it must have been. And to think you might have lost Wimborne entirely if not for the rain."

"It could have been much worse," I said. "As it is, no one was killed or even seriously injured, and I have every hope that the house can be rebuilt."

Beatrice studied me, head tilted to one side.

"What is it?" I asked.

"You only seem a bit too . . ." She paused. "Settled. Too satisfied. After what you've told me, I cannot imagine why."

I knew why, of course. It was Jack. It was entirely Jack. I glanced at the door, ensuring it was closed, then scooted forward on my chair. Beatrice did the same, expression intrigued.

"I have more to tell you," I said, unable to stop my mouth from curling upwards. "About Mr. Travers."

Her eyes widened. "He finally kissed you, didn't he?"

"No," I said, enjoying the moment a bit too much. "I kissed him."

"Genevieve Wilde!" she exclaimed. "You little minx! *You* kissed him?"

I laughed. "I did, and I do not regret it in the least."

"I should say not." She shook her head. "I cannot believe it. And did he . . ." She trailed off, though her question was clear.

"I'll only say that he made it perfectly clear how he feels about me."

"Ha," she said. "Do not think I will not let that go. You will tell me every detail in the end." Her brow furrowed. "But what will happen? Have you spoken of the future?"

I hesitated. Even with Jack's promises, I could not help but feel a twinge of uncertainty. How could I ask him to sacrifice so much for me? "We have," I said. "Just now, actually. Though we have much more to discuss before anything can be decided fully."

"Just now?" she repeated. "Do you mean to say he was with you in the billiards room when I found you?"

I nodded sheepishly, trying to suppress my smile.

She laughed, a sound of pure glee. "I hardly recognize you, Ginny, and I could not be more delighted. If anyone needs to be thoroughly kissed, it is you." She paused. "But you've not been taken by a handsome face, have you? Will he make you happy? Does he deserve you?"

My smile faded and I considered her questions with the utmost seriousness. "I am of the opinion," I said quietly, "that he will make me happier than *I* deserve. He is so much more than he seems, Beatrice. He is full of life, but also good and caring and gentle. He is everything I could have wanted, if only I'd let myself imagine someone so wonderful."

She took my hand, holding it tight. "Then I shall express my absolute joy for you. You have endured more than anyone ought in a lifetime."

"I could not have done it without you." I kissed her on the cheek. "You've been the truest friend. Thank you."

Her eyes glistened. "Oh, do stop making me cry. You'll ruin my complexion."

We both laughed at that. How strange, to be free from the burdens of the past weeks and buoyant at the thought of the future. I was determined never to take such a feeling for granted again.

That buoyancy was put to the test not a half hour later when I arrived at Wimborne and saw the fire's damage for the first time in the light of day. I stared up at my home as Jack helped me down from my coach. The blackened stone along the east wall stood in stark contrast to the white blanket of clouds above us, the lingering smoke harsh in my throat. Entire rooms stood exposed to the elements, their contents reduced to dust, leaving an emptiness behind that nearly choked me.

"Genevieve?" Jack asked, concern clear in his voice.

I faced him and Beatrice, both of them watching me as if I might burst into tears. It was a near thing, to tell the truth. But I took a steadying breath. "Let us go in."

Marchant had come at first light to inspect the house, and he now met us at the front door and led us inside. He pointed out much of the damage as we moved through the house—flame-licked walls and ceilings, the soggy floors—but he also explained how very lucky we had been.

"The fire was almost entirely contained to the east wing," he said. "It is a difficult loss, to be sure, but the library is virtually untouched, as are your private chambers and the entire front of the house."

Beatrice took my arm as we walked, all of us picking through the mess that coated the ground—puddles of ash and rain, fallen beams, and melted, unidentifiable lumps.

"It is awful," she said, looking about the space that had been a wide and airy corridor. "How can you bear it, Ginny?"

I wasn't sure I could. The loss clawed at me, dug deep inside my chest and made it difficult to breathe. This was the home Father had raised me in, the home he had built himself over thirty years ago. Gone was the fireplace where we'd toasted bread during stormy evenings. Gone was the desk Father had worked at every day of his life. Gone were so many of my mother's paintings that Father had carefully framed and hung throughout the house. They had touched my memories so lightly, just one small element of my life, but now that they were gone, I wished I had taken more time to appreciate them.

Jack's hand came to rest on my lower back, his touch warm and reassuring. I looked up at him, and his eyes told me everything I needed.

"Wimborne is all I have left of my father," I said quietly. "It is my home and was my sole focus these last six months." I met Beatrice's eyes, which were hazy with tears. "But in the end, it is just a building. A building can be rebuilt. Even if I'd lost Wimborne entirely, I still have the only thing that matters—the people I love most in this world."

Beatrice squeezed my arm. "Always, dearest. Always."

❧

We spent another two hours inspecting the house, which left me a bit more optimistic. As my butler had said, my rooms were nearly untouched, only saturated by the smell of smoke. The kitchens would need a great deal of work, as would most rooms on the ground floor. Marchant was confident I could return to live at Wimborne during most of the reconstruction, but a few weeks were still required for the staff to return the house to working order. Holloway packed a trunk for me, which we brought with us when we returned to Tamworth Hall, the sun low in the sky.

Beatrice insisted I stay with her and her mother, an invitation I gladly accepted. I was not ungrateful to Mr. Northcott, even after that conversation I'd overheard, but perhaps distance would be best to preserve any last vestiges of friendship between us.

"Tomorrow," I promised Beatrice as we bid her farewell on the front steps. "We'll come tomorrow. I'll take tonight to thank Mr. Northcott and organize my staff." Many of my servants were still staying here at Tamworth while others were scattered around homes in the area. I needed to find more permanent places for all of them until we could return to Wimborne.

Beatrice nodded, then her gaze turned to Jack. "You are also welcome, Mr. Travers. My parents and I would be glad to have you stay with us."

Jack looked taken aback. "I'd thought to stay at the Bull's Head for the time being."

"Don't be silly," Beatrice said, tightening her bonnet's ribbons. "There is no need for you to be traipsing the four miles from Little Sowerby every day to see Ginny. We've plenty of room."

I pressed my lips together, hiding a smile. Beatrice spoke her mind, as always.

Jack did not bother to hide his grin. "Who am I to refuse such an offer? You clearly know my weakness well."

Beatrice waved as she departed, leaving Jack and me on the front steps. We weren't alone, since a footman waited at the open door, but I wished we were. The day had taken its toll on me. The highs and the lows, from Jack's kisses in the billiards room to our difficult excursion to Wimborne. I wanted nothing more than to tuck myself against Jack's side and feel his heartbeat against my cheek.

I sighed. "I imagine Mr. Northcott is expecting us for dinner soon."

Jack grimaced. "I'm afraid you'll have to make my excuses."

"You're leaving?"

"Just for a few hours," he said. "It's been too long since I've seen Wily and he tends to get anxious. Besides, there is something else I need to do."

I bit my lip. "My watch." It seemed small, what with my house in near ruins. But I still wanted my watch back.

Jack rubbed his jaw. "Garvey pretended ignorance, but it must've been a ploy to keep us from locating it. One last thing to cause you pain." He blew out a breath. "I doubt he stayed in the camp every night, so he must have a room somewhere. If I can search it . . ."

"Must it be tonight?" I looked up at him. "I appreciate your determination, I do. Only . . . well, I feel better when you are near. And we still have so much to talk about."

I'd hoped we would find some time together tonight. Even though he'd made it clear that he wanted to be with me—marry me, I assumed—I was not entirely sure what that might look like. Could he be happy in the future, knowing all he'd given up for me?

"We *will* talk," he said, taking my hand and rubbing his thumb across the back. "I promise. But I must do this now, while the iron is hot." His eyes turned teasing. "Besides, I need more time with you than a few stolen moments."

I raised an eyebrow. "Why is that?"

"We are too easily distracted," he said. "It is difficult to speak when one's lips are already occupied."

A smile tugged at my mouth. "I find myself persuaded. Perhaps we might have adequate time tomorrow."

"Nothing would please me more," he said in that low, rough voice that sent a skittering warmth up my spine.

With a kiss to my hand, he left for the stables, where Mr. Northcott had been kind enough to house Jack's mount. I stood on the steps for a long minute, the sunlight fading around me. My mind still tumbled, trying to comprehend all that had happened. How was it that my future could change so much in such a short time?

I sighed, wishing for my journal, now a pile of ashes in Wimborne's study. I needed it now more than ever to organize my thoughts, clarify my emotions. I turned and hurried into the house. Perhaps if I dressed quickly for dinner, I would have time to write on borrowed paper.

Holloway did her best with limited resources, and I was soon outfitted in an ivory evening gown, a string of small pearls at my throat. After she left, I searched my room for pen and paper but found it devoid of both.

I made my way downstairs to Mr. Northcott's study, intent on asking him for the supplies. I knocked and had no response. Upon opening the door, I found the study empty, a low fire still burning in the grate. No doubt he'd just left to dress for dinner. I began to close the door, then paused. Surely, he would not mind if I borrowed a few things from his desk.

Slipping into the darkening room, I went to the desk. I found paper and ink, but no pen. I opened the right-hand drawer, but it held only a few ledgers and letters.

I began to close the drawer, but something scraped inside—the sound of metal on wood. Odd. I pulled the drawer open again, inspecting its contents. Only leather and paper. I felt about the drawer, and as I pressed into the far corner, the wood gave way before my fingertips. The back of the drawer twisted. I leaned forward, peering into the dark hole. A hidden compartment. I would never have expected it of Mr. Northcott, but I supposed everyone had their secrets.

A fact that became all the more apparent when my eyes adjusted and I saw what was tucked within the compartment. A circle of brass and white enamel. Braided red silk. And a ticking so familiar it matched the beat of my heart.

Father's watch. *My* watch.

I snatched it up in disbelief, turning the cold metal over in my hands. *Esse quam videri.* The inscription I'd traced with my fingers countless times.

How . . . *Why* was it here in Mr. Northcott's study? My mind scrambled. Perhaps he'd located it in a pawn shop, or found it on Garvey. But why would he have hidden it away and not told me?

A cold awakened inside me, as if my body had realized something before my head could.

"Well, this is unfortunate," said a cool voice.

I jerked my head up. Mr. Northcott stood framed in the doorway, dark eyes flickering in the bare light.

"You see, that was not something you were supposed to find, Miss Wilde," he said, and closed the door behind him with a click.

CHAPTER 26

Every inch of my body stood tense, a violin string drawn too tight. Mr. Northcott stepped toward me and I backed away, though the desk stood between us. He offered a little smile, as if he found my reticence amusing.

"Might I ask what you are doing here?" he asked mildly, clasping his hands behind his back.

"I—" My hands clenched around the watch. I could not believe I was holding it. "I was looking for paper and ink. To write."

"Writing." He exhaled a short laugh. "So simple a thing with such lasting consequences."

I tried to find my courage, hiding away beneath an overwhelming tide of dread and fear. "What on earth are you talking about, Mr. Northcott?" I forced out. "Why is my watch in your desk?"

"Because my desk is generally a safe place," he said, "when one does not have prying house guests."

"You know that is not what I meant." I held up the watch, the firelight dancing upon the warm brass. "Explain this, sir."

Mr. Northcott inspected me through narrowed eyes, as if weighing the cost of what he might tell me. "I took it," he said simply. "The night of your dinner party."

"*You* took it?" My brain struggled through his words like a carriage through a thick fog. "For what purpose?"

"Oh, I had a very good reason." He strolled casually to the

fireplace. I edged around the opposite side of the desk, determined to keep him as far from me as possible. My mind raced, trying to connect the fragmented clues I had.

"Are you in league with Garvey?" It made no sense whatsoever, but it was the only option I could think of.

He scoffed. "In league. That would denote an equality in partnership."

"But you *are* involved."

"Garvey acted under my direction, yes."

How could it be true? Yet he freely admitted it. I tried to cling to my anger, not knowing what I would find if I released it. "Why did you steal from me? Torment me?"

He raised an eyebrow. "Perhaps some things are better left unsaid. I should hate for you to think unkindly of me, here at the end."

I clutched the back of the leather chair, my knuckles white. Did he mean to threaten me? A sudden possibility flitted into my mind. It couldn't be. And yet I had no other explanation.

I straightened, my stomach roiling. "You are the informant," I whispered. "The mole."

"How do you—" Mr. Northcott stared at me. He recovered quickly, mastering his features. "I suppose I should not be surprised. Everyone keeps insisting you are intelligent."

It was impossible. Mr. Northcott, a traitor? The miscreant who had informed on Father and his constables for money? It could not be him. Not the stiff and serious Mr. Northcott. He was the magistrate, for heaven's sake.

And yet, there he stood, not denying my words—in fact, he almost looked *pleased*.

"Father was investigating an informer before he died," I said. "He was investigating *you*."

Mr. Northcott raised his eyebrows. "Yes. When I inherited the magisterial records, I found traces of his investigation, but it was clear there was so much more. Your father must have hidden his evidence somewhere only he knew, and I was quite keen to find it."

Somewhere only he knew. Somewhere like his study.

"That is why you took the watch," I said in realization. "You thought the evidence was hidden in my study, and you wanted cause to search without suspicion."

My skin felt too hot. Mr. Northcott—honorable, staid, proper Mr. Northcott—had betrayed my father. He'd worked with Garvey and stolen my watch. The more these discoveries settled inside me, the more real and logical they became. Of course it was him. He'd been close to Father, often volunteering to help with patrols and cases and arrests. Why had I not seen it before?

"You were Father's friend." My voice did not belong to me, so shattered it was. "*My* friend."

His eyes did not waver. "I was what I needed to be."

I did not understand, and I was not sure I ever would. But I knew deep inside that it did not matter. All that mattered was that I was in danger, so real and vicious that I could barely see straight. I clutched the watch, the hinge biting into my skin. Jack. I needed Jack. But he would be gone for hours yet, hours I did not have.

I searched the desktop surreptitiously, looking for anything I might use as a weapon. Nothing but books and letters and ink. My eyes flicked to the door behind Mr. Northcott.

"Thinking of running?" he said. Before I could blink, a pistol flashed in his hands, pointing at my chest. "We cannot have that."

The steel barrel shone, the black within promising devastation. I forced my eyes to meet Mr. Northcott's, dark and devoid of emotion.

"This is insanity," I said, my voice shaking.

He sighed. "It was never supposed to be so complicated, I assure you."

I needed to keep him talking. The longer he spoke, the more chance I had of someone finding us. I choked out a laugh. "Oh? How terribly inconvenient for you. And why is that?"

"I only took your watch," he said, "to search your father's study. I planned to return it, perhaps curry some favor with you. Heavens, I even wound it every day to keep it in good condition." He said it as if I ought to be grateful.

"But you didn't find anything." I'd been there the day he'd searched my study. I would have noticed.

"Not with you watching like a hawk," he said, the slightest hint of frustration in his voice. "Then you decided to play the part of a simpleton and hire a thief-taker. Really, Ginny, a thief-taker?"

"Do not use my name," I snapped, which was utterly ridiculous. He had a pistol pointed at my chest.

He went on as if he hadn't heard me. "In any case, my plan was foiled. I could not find the evidence and now you had a man poking into the past, into *my* business."

I opened my mouth, but he held up one hand.

"As much as I'd like to answer all your questions," he said, "we haven't time for a tête-à-tête. We'd best be going before someone comes across us in such a state. Can you imagine?"

He laughed, as if we were in the midst of a romantic tryst. My heart stopped. "I am not going anywhere with you."

"I beg to differ." He tightened his grip on the flintlock. "I think you will go anywhere I tell you."

"You cannot mean to kill me," I said in disbelief. "How on earth will you explain *that*?"

"Easily," he said. "You think I've come this far without plans to fall back on? No, this is simple. Garvey will escape from his cell tonight, with a little help. I hand you over to him and my work is done."

I trembled, remembering those hate-filled eyes. Garvey would not hesitate to finish what he'd started last night.

"I only need to tell the public," Mr. Northcott went on, "that he kidnapped you from your room in the middle of the night. Who will question a heartbroken magistrate?"

He made a forlorn face. I felt sick. It *was* easy. Everyone would believe him. Even Jack. Why would he not?

"I'll scream." Better to die here in his house than somewhere deep in the woods.

"No, you won't." Mr. Northcott smiled. "Not while your thief-taker is at risk. One word from me and Mr. Crouth will see to it that Travers does not see morning."

My throat closed up. Of course Mr. Crouth was involved with this villainy. The blackguard.

"Now come along." He nodded at the door. "We've wasted enough time."

What was I to do? I could never endanger Jack, but neither could I put my life so willingly into this vile man's hands. I wanted to move, to act. I could hardly dive through the window behind me, but I had to think of a way to escape. A way to prolong my life, by a second, a minute, an hour. How?

Mr. Northcott's eyes hardened. "Don't make this difficult, Ginny."

He started toward me. I jolted back against the window, blood surging inside me. But there was nothing I could do. Nothing.

The evidence.

I stopped breathing. It was as if a voice had spoken in my ear. But there was no one here but Mr. Northcott, stalking around the desk.

The evidence, it said again more insistently. I knew that voice. It was Father.

Then I realized.

"The evidence," I blurted. "You cannot kill me until you find the evidence against you."

Mr. Northcott paused, an arm's length away, pistol still raised. "The evidence was destroyed in the fire."

I shook my head. "I knew every inch of my father's study. I would have found it. He must have hidden it elsewhere."

"And you think you know where?"

I hesitated. "I could . . . I could help you look for it."

"Yes, and give Travers enough time to find us."

I bit my lip. That had been my idea precisely.

He narrowed his eyes. "But you knew your father better than even me. If anyone could find it, it is you." He inspected me closely. "Did he really never say anything to you? No word of his investigation?"

I could only shake my head, my voice hiding in my chest.

"No subtle hints? No last words before he died?"

I shook my head again, then stilled. Father's last moments played through my head, his hands pressing the watch into mine. Pointing at the enamel face with clawed fingers. "Here," he'd croaked with all the strength he had left. "Here."

I looked down at the watch in my hands, almost forgotten in the madness of our conversation. It ticked along, uninhibited. Except . . .

Except for that slight delay. The reason I'd meant to bring it into the clockmaker's before it had been stolen. My mind raced. There was no *possible* way. But the possible and impossible now twisted together in unbelievable ways.

"What is it?"

I jerked my head up, dropping my fisted hand to my side. But it was too late. Mr. Northcott stared at the watch.

"It has something to do with the watch, hasn't it?" He strode forward. "Give it here."

"No." I sought for a lie. "It's nothing."

"*Now*." The word was cold as a bitter winter's night. He tightened his finger around the trigger.

I held out the watch, arm trembling. He snatched it from me and his footsteps retreated to the fireplace.

"He left this for you when he died. Why?" He inspected the watch in the light of the fire, turning it this way and that.

"It's an heirloom," I managed. "He wanted me to have it."

"Or is there more to this wretched little watch?" He went to the desk and found a letter opener in a drawer. He shot me a glance. "Be a dear and don't move, Ginny." He set his pistol down on the desk within easy reach, then aligned the letter opener against the rim of the watch. He pried the back casing away.

I winced, a memory leaping to my mind, one I'd often recalled over the last few months. Father and I, standing in the midst of the clockmaker's shop, surrounded by a cacophony of ticking. I was ten, and annoyed that we'd stopped here first instead of the bakery.

"Can't you fix the watch yourself?" I had crossed my arms.

Father quirked a brow. "Heavens, no. The mechanisms involved in keeping time are far too delicate for someone like *me*, all clumsy hands and dull eyes."

My young mouth had twitched at that. He knew just how to make me laugh.

"No," he said. "There are some problems you can solve yourself, and there are some that require the right expertise. A watch is one of the latter. Remember that, Ginny. After all, one day it will be yours."

I'd remembered. It was why I'd never opened the back casing of my watch when the time was off. I'd simply jotted it down on my list—*clockmaker's*. Just another thing to do.

But now.

Mr. Northcott held the watch up again, this time revealing the mechanism inside. "There's something here," he whispered.

In spite of everything, I moved closer. I needed to see. A tiny paper, no taller that my fingernail, was wrapped around one of the pegs supporting the watch face. The edge of the paper had come uncurled and was tugged into the mechanism, slowing its tick by a nearly unnoticeable amount. But *I* had noticed it. And if I had done something about it sooner, perhaps I would not be in this mess.

Mr. Northcott carefully grasped the paper and pulled. It unfurled and came free, springing back into a coil. He held the paper flat on the desk beside the pistol, squinting down at tiny writing.

"What is this nonsense?" he growled.

"What does it say?" My mouth was dry. A note, from *Father*.

He glanced at me, ensuring I was still behaving myself, then read aloud. "'The god that he worships.' That is all it says."

I stared at him and then at the small scrap of paper he held. I could not breathe.

"Does it mean anything to you?" Mr. Northcott eyed me.

It meant *everything* to me. "I . . ."

"Tell me now," he said, picking up his flintlock again. "Our time is running short, as is my patience."

I steadied myself. This was my chance. This was how I could keep myself alive—at least a little while longer.

"I know where the evidence is," I managed. "It's at Wimborne."

"Where, precisely?"

"I am not a fool," I said. "I know this is all that is keeping me alive. I will only tell you once we've arrived at Wimborne."

His eyes flashed dangerously. "If you think this a game, you are sorely mistaken, my dear. You will not win."

"You can take me to Wimborne," I said, grit in my voice. "Or you can shoot me now."

He considered for ten endless seconds. "Let's get on with it, then."

After reassembling the watch and slipping it into his pocket, Mr. Northcott hurried me from the house, his hand gripping my elbow so tightly I knew it would bruise. He hid the pistol beneath his jacket, though I could still feel the press of it against my back. We saw no one, the servants occupied with preparing for dinner.

When we emerged into the dying sunset, Mr. Crouth met us, his lips set in a horrible grin. I had no energy to divert toward him—I focused inward. I needed a plan. I needed to escape.

Mr. Northcott exchanged quiet words with Mr. Crouth, then the constable departed, placing his hat on his head as he looked back at me with mocking eyes. If I died tonight, at least I'd never again have to pretend to like that man.

A bit of black humor, as Father used to call it.

Mr. Northcott led me down to the coach house in the near dark. He kept me outside, sending a groom to ready his coach while we watched from the shadows. When it emerged, Mr. Northcott bundled me inside quickly. No one saw me but the driver, and he looked so unaffected by the entire affair that I wondered if this was not the first time Mr. Northcott had spirited away a young woman dressed in scant evening wear.

He sat on the forward-facing bench, pistol resting on his thigh, while I pressed myself into the farthest corner. I folded my arms across my chest, bumps covering every inch of my exposed skin. I hadn't so much as a shawl to fight the evening chill.

"Here." Mr. Northcott held out a carriage blanket. "Let it not be said that I wasn't a gentleman."

"You think offering a blanket to a woman you abducted is the mark of a gentleman?"

Mr. Northcott laughed, but it was a mean laugh. Cutting. "The mark of a gentleman. No, that would be *wealth*, of course. Something too many take for granted."

Wealth. That word caught my attention. There was still so much I did not understand. Perhaps if I could learn his motivations, his intentions, then I could somehow extricate myself from this disaster. I needed him to talk.

I leaned forward. "Is that why, then? You did it for the money? I thought Tamworth was doing well."

"It is *now*," he said. "When my father had the decency to die, I took charge. But his debts were worse than anything I'd imagined."

Though a respectable family, the Northcotts had never been fabulously wealthy. The late Mr. Northcott in particular had been terrible with money. He'd often asked Father for loans, which Father always gave, too generous by half.

"I was going to lose Tamworth," he said. "I was going to lose everything. I fell into a stupor, drinking and gambling with abandon. What was a little more debt, after all? But then I tangled with a bad character, one who did not take it well when I could not pay. But he knew my connection to your father. So we struck up a deal. I would provide information about the magistrate and the constables—their plans and patrols—and he would forgive my debt." He shrugged. "After I'd earned out my debt, well. . . . It was something of a lucrative business. My contacts expanded exponentially. These days, much of the criminal underground in the area depends upon me, though most haven't any idea who they are dealing with."

I shook my head, bitterness rising inside me. "All those years. All those years you spent with Father. He loved you like a son."

He leaned back. "It was necessary to cultivate a relationship with him. You know what they say about keeping your enemies close."

I tried not to picture it, all those evenings with Mr. Northcott at our table, or with Father in his study. All that time, he'd been a traitor. But he'd played his role perfectly, helping Father, courting me.

A new realization slapped me in the face. "Is that why you wished to marry me? To get to Father?"

His lips curled upward. "That, and the fact that a man can avoid a great deal of scrutiny if he marries the daughter of the beloved magistrate. Who would ever suspect *me* of criminal connections? You were the perfect cover. Then, after your father's death, it became more. I *needed* to marry you to find the evidence."

"Except I would not marry you," I said. "I refused you."

A muscle in his forehead twitched. "You cannot imagine how it has hung over me these last months. I could only wait, hoping you would not stumble across anything damning. But after you rejected me the second time, I had to take more drastic action."

"Garvey," I said, thoughts racing. "That was his role in this. The rock through my window, the threatening note. All to frighten me into marrying you." It made sense now why the vandal had seemed to know so much about me. He hadn't—Mr. Northcott had.

"He arrived in town a few months ago," Mr. Northcott said, "blind with rage and craving revenge. He was disappointed your father was already dead, to be sure, but perfectly happy to focus on a new target once I planted the idea in his head. Rather an obedient fellow. No qualms about arson, thankfully."

The fire. Mr. Northcott had surely told Garvey about the trap and ordered him to start the fire to destroy the evidence.

"I was supposed to be the one to catch him," Mr. Northcott said, irritated. "A last effort to secure your affections. But it was all for naught. Once he spotted you, he went racing off and ruined my plans."

I was shaking, from the cold and dread and unending realizations of just how dangerous this man was.

"If you've been helping Garvey," I said, "then he knows your face. You think he will not give you up? Turn king's evidence?"

He laughed. "What sort of fool do you take me for? He never knew who slipped instructions beneath his door. Didn't care either, so long as my information was good."

I shook my head. How could I ever have imagined marrying this man? If Jack had not come into my life, would the increasing danger at Wimborne have driven me to Mr. Northcott?

But certainty took hold inside me. No. Even at my most frightened, my most desperate, I would not have given in.

"It wouldn't have worked," I said. "I'd never have married you."

His jaw twitched. "Not once you fell in love with the thief-taker."

I stared out into the black night. He was right. After Jack, there was no chance I would have settled for anything less.

My determination grew. Mr. Northcott had threatened Jack if I misbehaved, but I had to be realistic. He would not let either of us live. If I could escape and find Jack, then perhaps we stood a chance. I only had any power until Mr. Northcott had the evidence. After that, I would be at his mercy. If an opportunity presented itself, I had to take it.

"You won't escape."

I jerked my head up. How had he known I was thinking that? Did he know me so well after all? *No*, I told myself. It was simply what anyone in my situation would be thinking.

"I'm not trying to escape," I said shakily. "You hold all the cards, you'll recall."

"Still," he said, "I should tell you I've a man on horseback following us. Even if you leap from the coach, you cannot outrun him. So do not waste your energy on *hope*."

He said it as if the word was abhorrent. But I clung to it. Hope. It was all I had.

Jack. My fingers curled tightly into my arms as I tried to steady my breathing. Where was he? And would I ever see him again?

CHAPTER 27

Wimborne loomed in the darkness as the coach stopped before the front door. The broken windows gaped like open mouths, not a light or living being to be seen.

"You said you posted a man to watch the house," I accused. Why this of all things irritated me in the midst of my own kidnapping, I could not say.

Mr. Northcott only laughed. "I said many things, Ginny. You mustn't condemn every vice of mine, or you'll drive yourself mad."

He opened the door and gestured for me to precede him out, perhaps imagining I might assault him from behind if he went first. It was tempting, to be sure, but I stepped down onto the drive, Mr. Northcott directly behind me, pistol at my back.

"We'll return shortly," he said to the coachman. He took a lantern from the coach, then urged me up the stairs and through the front door. There was no point in locking it. The Bramah locks were useless now, with entire walls open to all and sundry.

"All right." Mr. Northcott halted in the entryway. "Where are we going?"

I hesitated. How to delay this as much as possible?

"No games," he reminded me in a hard voice.

"The library," I stammered. "It's in the library."

He pushed me forward with the pistol, the light of his lantern stretching my shadow before me. This part of the house was mostly untouched, though the scent of smoke still stung my nose. I tried to relish every second as I walked. Would I ever again see my home in the light of day?

When we reached the library, I paused, looking back at Mr. Northcott.

"Go on," he said.

I slowly—very slowly—opened the door. I would prolong my life by every second possible. He followed me inside and set the lantern on the table in the middle of the room. The walls were lined in bookshelves, each one full to bursting. I hadn't spent much time in this room since Father's death, far too busy *keeping* myself busy. But the two of us had spent many happy hours here before that, content in the company of books and each other.

"Where is it?" Mr. Northcott demanded, shattering my memory. "What did that clue mean?"

I exhaled and went to the bookshelf beside the tall bank of windows. My eyes skipped over the titles until I found what I searched for. I pulled the volume free, letting my hand rest on the paneled calf cover.

"Bring it here," Mr. Northcott said. "Let me see it."

My jaw tightened, but I had no choice. I returned to the table, book in my hands. "The people of Lilliput had never seen a watch before Gulliver arrived," I said quietly. "But they supposed that it was 'the god that he worships,' seeing as he 'seldom did anything without consulting it.'"

I set the book on the table, the morocco leather spine with its gilt lettering shining in the lantern light.

"*Travels into Several Remote Nations of the World*," Mr. Northcott read aloud, picking up the volume. "I don't know it."

"Perhaps by its other name," I said. "*Gulliver's Travels*. Father's favorite book."

Interest flamed in Mr. Northcott's eyes. He set down the pistol and flipped the book open. I winced at how roughly he handled the book, bending pages as he skimmed through. At first, it seemed he would be disappointed. Nothing but printed words, the blur of the red-speckled edges. Then—

"Here we are," he breathed.

In the second half of the book, loose pages appeared, tucked safely into the binding. Mr. Northcott pulled them loose, stacking them beside the book as he worked. I recognized Father's writing, though the light made it difficult to read. The stack of papers grew with every second—an impressive investigation. What would those words reveal? Witnesses? Rumors? What had Father collected?

At the end of the volume, between the last page and the back cover, Mr. Northcott pulled out one last paper, this one folded and sealed. He gazed at it a moment, then flashed it my way. *Genevieve* was written across the front. My heart leapt.

"For you, I think." He held it out to me. I reached for it in disbelief, but he snatched it back, laughing. "No, no, I shall keep that for myself. Can't have any of my secrets floating about."

I clutched my stomach. Out of everything that had happened tonight, this hurt the worst. A letter from my father. His words from beyond the grave. How often had I wished for one more bit of wisdom from him? My wish had been granted, however cruelly. I would never read that letter.

Mr. Northcott folded the papers neatly, then tucked them—along with the letter—into his jacket. My eyes darted to the pistol on the table. Could I reach it before he did?

But my courage failed me. In this moment, I wasn't brave or bold or brilliant. I was terrified. I did not move.

Mr. Northcott picked up the pistol. "I'm glad we were able to sort that out. Now, shall we?"

I forced myself not to glance back at the shelf where I'd retrieved the book. It was part of Father's treasured first edition of the book, which actually split the story between *two* separate volumes. I'd left the matching second book still on the shelf. If there was even the slightest possibility that there was more evidence tucked within its pages, I could not draw attention to it. One day, someone would find it. Catherine, perhaps. She would inherit Wimborne upon my death, after all. How very fitting.

I could not speak as Mr. Northcott hurried me back through the house and into the coach. I was numb. So numb I did not even look back to bid my home a last farewell. I curled into myself.

"Where will you take me?" I stared out the window at the cloaked man who followed us on horseback. Mr. Northcott was right. I could not escape.

"We've an appointment to keep," he said. "Garvey will be so pleased to see you."

I did not react. I had nothing left.

We traveled the outskirts of town. Night descended in full, swallowing us as the coach rumbled on. Mr. Northcott seemed content to ride in silence, though his hand never left his pistol and his eyes stayed fixed on me.

How he stayed so alert, I did not know. My head ached and my limbs felt like jelly. I tried to stay sharp—I had to be ready if an opportunity presented itself. But if I was unsuccessful, then these would be my last moments. I was determined to spend them as best I could.

I thought of Jack. I thought of our first meeting, when I'd threatened him with a vase. I thought of his then-irritating grin, his constant goading and flirting, his impulsivity and unwavering confidence.

Then softer memories came. His comforting words when he'd found me crying while reading my journals. His gentle touch as he washed the perfume from my wrists the night of the ball. His sweet kisses and whispered promises that morning in the billiards room.

But most of all, I remembered how I felt when I was with him, when he looked at me with those brilliant blue eyes. As if I were something to be loved and adored. As if there was nothing more important to him in all the world.

Father's words came back to me. *If you care for the things you love,* he'd said, *if you protect them and cherish them, then they will shine.* I gave a wistful smile. He'd been right, as usual. Because it was perfectly clear that Jack cherished me. He made me shine.

I'd found love. I'd found Jack. And now I would lose it all.

"Happy thoughts?"

Mr. Northcott's voice broke into my reverie, a bucket of chill water on the soft glow of my memories. My smile faded. "You would not understand."

He opened his mouth to respond, but a bone-jolting *crack* split the air. The horses shrieked and the coach veered. I pitched forward, catching myself against the opposite seat.

"What the devil?" Mr. Northcott hissed.

The driver shouted commands, trying to regain control of the horses. The coach began to slow. Had a wheel broken?

My heart hammered inside me. No matter the cause, this was my chance.

I righted myself on my seat, my hand against the door as if I was bracing myself. Mr. Northcott still held the pistol, but he peered out the opposite window.

This was it. I tried to gauge how fast we were moving. If I jumped too soon, I would break both my legs. Too late and Mr. Northcott would catch me. But it was impossible to tell in the dark. I'd have to risk it.

Another *crack* whipped through my ears. I froze. That was no broken wheel. It was a gunshot.

"Stand and deliver!" called a male voice from outside.

Highwaymen.

Mr. Northcott's mouth dropped and he turned to look at me, my hand on the door. His eyes flashed. "Away from there," he ordered, raising his pistol again.

For the briefest of moments, I considered ignoring him, flinging open the door and jumping, no matter that it might earn me a bullet. But again, I couldn't do it. I pulled away, breathing hard.

"If you want to live another minute," he threatened, "*do not move.*"

"Shall I stop breathing to please you?" I snapped.

Mr. Northcott looked as if he wished to smash me alongside the head. But then the coach jerked to a halt, and he had bigger problems to contend with.

"Your money or your life," came another voice, this time from behind the coach. Mr. Northcott did not miss the significance of its location—his jaw tightened. We were surrounded.

"Rogers!" Mr. Northcott shouted to our cloaked escort. "How many are there?"

Scattered laughter came from all sides. "Your man abandoned you at the gunshot," said the first voice again, a scratchy tenor. The leader, I assumed. "There's five of us, and your driver looks none too determined to put up a fight."

Mr. Northcott worked over those words, teeth grinding.

"You said you worked with the highwaymen," I whispered.

He glared at me. "The ones I work with know better than to waylay my coach."

"Come out, the lot of you," the leader said. "If we see a weapon, we shoot. A dead body is easier to rob than a live one, after all."

I hesitated. Death was a surety if I stayed with Mr. Northcott. But were my chances any better with a band of highwaymen? These were not the romanticized bandits from the stories—gentleman thieves who only stole from the wealthy, who let their victims go free if a lady agreed to dance with him. No, I knew well enough that *these* men were baseless criminals, desperate and cruel. I would find no harbor with them. But it spoke to how much I hated the man beside me that I would rather face these brutes than let Mr. Northcott take my life. I moved to the door.

"Stop!" Mr. Northcott hissed.

I ignored him. I opened the door and stepped down, stumbling as my slippered feet met the uneven ruts of the road. The carriage lantern sent skittering shadows in every direction, but I could make out the shapes of horses and riders.

Someone whistled. "A real piece, ain't she?"

I raised my chin, glaring into the dark.

"Now the gentleman," the leader said. He was directly before me, the silver glint of a pistol pointed at the coach door. He was nothing more than a slim, black silhouette against an even blacker sky. I could just make out a mask over the top of his face, though it was hardly necessary in this dark.

"I think not," Mr. Northcott said coolly from inside the coach. "In fact, it would be best for all if you simply let us pass."

I glanced over my shoulder at his dim outline, cloaked by the lantern light that kept our eyes from peering inside.

"Now why would we do that?" The leader sounded amused. "We've a livin' to make."

Mr. Northcott's voice hardened. "Yes, but you won't *live* much longer if you lay so much as one finger on me."

The men laughed. Their leader leaned forward. "Is that right?"

A pistol cocked inside the coach.

"I do not bluff," Mr. Northcott said. "I am armed and I daresay I can kill at least two of you before you get to me. Or we can make a deal."

The leader sat back in his saddle. "I'm listenin'."

"I've some money," Mr. Northcott said. "And a ruby ring. The lady will give you her jewelry as well. You let us leave and we shall go on our way without reporting you to the local magistrate."

The leaders snorted. "You must think me mutton-headed. We've got you at the end of a rope and that's your offer?"

"What then?" Mr. Northcott demanded.

One of the shadows peeled away from the blackness. Another highwayman, this one with a larger frame and a confident seat. He was also masked, with a cap to cover his head. He directed his horse beside the leader, whispering in his ear.

The leader listened, then addressed Mr. Northcott again. "You've more than money and jewelry to bargain with." He jerked a nod at me.

I shivered. I was suddenly very aware of my silk evening gown, whipping in the wind against my figure.

"Her?" Mr. Northcott asked in disbelief.

"It's a cold night," the leader said. "I could use some warming up and she seems feisty."

His voice. There was something in his voice—a jaunty cadence.

Mr. Northcott laughed. "She is worth far more to me than—"

"Than your life?" the leader growled. "I am making a more than generous offer. Leave the rum doxy with us, along with your money and goods, and you'll go free."

I sucked in a breath. *Rum doxy*? My pulse ticked faster, so that I could hardly hear over the rush in my ears. I stared at the leader, then at the larger man beside him. I could see nothing of his features, hidden in the night. But his horse was russet brown, with a patch of white on its chest. Just like. . . . I mentally shook myself. Was I so desperate that I was imagining things? But if there was even the smallest chance that I was right, then I had to take it.

Mr. Northcott was considering the leader's words. His dilemma was so clear, I could nearly see his thoughts. If he demanded I come with him, there was a very real chance he would lose his life. If he left me, he left a loose end.

"You cannot leave me here," I said with unfeigned shakiness. "They'll kill me." I needed him to hear those words, cement them in his mind.

He stared at me a long moment before his eyes flicked up to the leader. "I agree to your terms," he said. "I only ask that you . . . take care of her when you're finished."

"Such heartlessness," the leader said, and I swore I could see his clever eyes, the sharp angles of his face. "Who is she to you?"

Mr. Northcott gritted his teeth. "No one. Now, have we a deal?"

"You needn't worry," the leader said. "We'll take care of her. You have my word."

Mr. Northcott hesitated another moment, then gave a frustrated exhale. He tossed his coin purse out the open door, a ring right after, the ruby sparkling in the lantern light.

"I won't forget this," he growled. "One day I'll see you on the gallows."

The leader gave a cheeky salute. "I look forward to it."

His large comrade stayed silent. I could feel his eyes on me even as I tried my hardest to discern any detail of his face or form. Was I making an enormous mistake?

Mr. Northcott turned back to me. I thought he might say something. But he only closed the coach door and shouted at his driver. The coach jolted forward and disappeared into the night. He'd really left me, as if I was simply a spare trunk he no longer needed.

I whirled back to the leader. Was he . . . grinning? The broader man beside him had already dismounted, throwing his reins to one of his compatriots. I stood stock-still, desperately—wildly—hoping I was right. Or had I allowed wishful thinking to blind me?

But then he strode toward me and there was no mistaking that loping stride, the determined set of his jaw, and that burning in his eyes as he ripped off his mask.

"Jack," I whispered.

He whisked me into his arms, burying his face in my shoulder. I gasped and threw my arms around his neck. He was real—solid and whole and here.

"You beautiful, brilliant girl," he whispered into my ear. "You played along perfectly."

My heart would give out, I was sure of it. It beat so fiercely in my chest, as if calling to the man who had claimed it. I clung to him, squeezing my eyes closed.

"I wasn't even certain it was you." I could barely speak with how tightly he held me. "You played your part a bit too well."

He pulled back to press his lips to my forehead, holding my face between his hands. "I am sorry," he said. "We had to make it believable."

I took a deep breath, my mind beginning to catch up with everything that had happened. "Why the ruse?"

"I would not risk you," he said, his voice deadly quiet. "I refused to entertain any plan that involved Northcott holding you hostage and bargaining with us for your life. It was Wily who came up with the idea to play highwaymen and steal you away. We had to ride hard to get ahead of you, but we made it."

I glanced over Jack's shoulder at the highwaymen's "leader," who winked at me.

"Miss Wilde," he greeted me cheerfully. "Lovely night, innit?"

I could not help a smile. "I thought I heard your dulcet tones earlier, Wily. How glad I am to see you." I glanced around at the three other men surrounding us. "Who else have I to thank?"

"There will be time enough for gratitude later." Jack shrugged off his great coat and tucked it around my shoulders. His warmth and scent encircled me, nearly as good as having his arms around me. Nearly. "Right now, we've a crooked magistrate to catch."

"Mr. Northcott? But he's gotten away."

"Good," Wily said. "If she thinks that, then so does he."

"You'll have to ride astride with me," Jack said apologetically. "We don't have an extra mount."

"I've room on my horse," Wily said with a wink. "If you'd prefer."

His unexpected levity made me smile. "Perhaps next time, Wily."

"Certainly not next time." Jack shot a glare at his friend as he led me to his mount, the russet horse I'd recognized before.

"Can't blame a man for asking," Wily said, shrugging.

Jack lifted me about the waist and I settled astride onto the saddle. I tugged down my skirts, but my hemline was still nearly to my knees.

"I suppose you did not bring my riding habit," I said, blushing as his eyes raked over my stockinged leg, white in the moonlight. He grinned and mounted behind me.

"No," he whispered in my ear, wrapping his arms around me to take the reins. "But I cannot bring myself to feel badly for it."

We started off, down the rutted road and through the night. We could not gallop, not with the two of us, but we managed a quick pace. Our escorts surrounded us, two ahead and two behind, so that I soon felt as safe as if I were home at Wimborne. Or perhaps that was simply a result of being tucked against Jack's chest, his breath warm against my neck.

"Tell me," I insisted after we settled into our pace. "How did you know where I was?"

"That blasted Crouth," he said. "He set an ambush for me outside of town."

"He tried to kill you?" I blurted.

"Yes. *Tried*," he said darkly. "Unfortunately for him, Wily was with me, and he is a crack shot."

"He shot Mr. Crouth?"

"Just in the leg," he said. "Just enough to make him willing to talk. He told us everything—that Northcott was the mole, that he was taking you to Wimborne and then to meet Garvey."

"I found it," I said. "The evidence against Northcott. Father hid it in a book. But Northcott has it now."

"We'll get it back." His arm tightened around my waist. "I cannot imagine your fear, Ginny. I am sorry Northcott had me fooled. I am sorry for not being there."

I shook my head. "Don't be sorry. You came." My throat closed over. "I needed you and you came."

"Never doubt that," he said, barely audible. "Never doubt that I will come for you."

I leaned back against his chest, so solid that my breathing slowed and steadied. I glanced at our escorts. "But who are these men? Friends of yours?"

"Not quite," he said. "I only knew one person we could trust, and whose manor happened to be directly along our route."

I sat up. "Catherine? These are Catherine's men?"

"And her husband."

"Mr. Davenport is here?" I turned on my saddle to get a better look at the riders.

"Not presently. He is setting a trap for Northcott ahead with his other men."

I shook my head, marveling. "That is brilliant. You had Mr. Northcott completely fooled. And me, for a short while."

"I *am* the son of a famous actress, you know." I could hear the grin in his voice and I laughed, a sound I would have thought impossible only an hour ago.

We rounded a bend in the road. Ahead of us stood Mr. Northcott's coach, surrounded by men with pistols and rifles. As we watched, Mr. Davenport—pistol in hand—approached the door and opened it. Two other men reached in and pulled Mr. Northcott out, relieving him of his pistol.

"What is the meaning of this?" Mr. Northcott shouted. "Why have you stopped me, Davenport?"

We arrived in a thunder of hooves, Jack pulling us to a stop just a few feet from the coach. Mr. Northcott's face when he saw me was unforgettable. His eyes widened, his skin so pale he looked like a ghost haunting the woods.

"Miss Wilde," he stammered. "You've—you've escaped the highwaymen. I was going for help."

"Escaped?" I repeated. "Yes, I have. But not from the men who stopped us. From you."

"Me?" Mr. Northcott managed a nervous laugh. "She's delirious. From fear, I imagine."

"I am not delirious," I said, managing a strange calm. It helped seeing the man so ill at ease. "I am perfectly sane and sensible. Though even if I was mad, it wouldn't save you now, Mr. Northcott."

Mr. Davenport glared at the magistrate. "You are past the point of making excuses, sir. We all know the truth. You are a traitor to the Crown, and when Miss Wilde discovered you, you abducted her."

"Fortunately," Jack said as he dismounted behind me, "Mr. Crouth was kind enough to inform us of your plans."

Mr. Northcott stared at Jack, seeing him for the first time. He seemed to put together what had happened—that the highwaymen had not, in fact, been highwaymen. His eyes hardened.

Jack helped me down from his horse and I stepped forward, Jack at my side.

"It is over, Mr. Northcott," I said. "You've dealt in darkness and secrets long enough. When you inevitably go before a grand jury, I will ensure that everyone knows what you've done."

Mr. Northcott stood so still he did not seem to breathe. Then he shook his head, his lips curling upward into a disturbing smile.

"It doesn't matter," he said, and the new calm in his voice set the hairs along my arm standing straight up. "You've lost too, *Ginny*. I've taken your reputation from you. Go on and marry the thief-taker. You'll never be received by anyone. Your children will be outcasts. No one will want to be associated with a woman who—"

"That is *enough*." Mr. Davenport's voice echoed in the dark. "I'll hear nothing more from you, Northcott. You've no defense, so far as I can see, and I will see justice served."

"Likely at the end of a rope," Jack said. "I find the irony amusing, don't you?"

Mr. Northcott had no response, his eyes burning coals. I glared back at him. His stinging words meant nothing to me. He was only a bitter, selfish man who had finally, finally lost.

"Check his jacket," I said. "You'll find the evidence my father collected against him."

Jack strode forward and pulled open the flaps of Mr. Northcott's jacket. The magistrate glowered but could do nothing as Jack pulled out the papers.

"Here it is," Jack said. "And this."

My pocket watch gleamed almost cheerfully in the lantern light. Jack started back toward me, reaching for my hand. "Come. Let us get you home."

It happened too fast.

When Jack's back was turned, Mr. Northcott wrenched his arms free from the man holding him, knocking him away. He snatched a tiny Queen Anne pistol from his boot and swung it wildly to aim at Jack.

Jack, who stood facing me, unknowing.

Jack, my Jack.

I threw my arms around him and spun so I was between him and Mr. Northcott. Between him and the pistol.

A roar and a flash. A thud in my back. I stared at Jack, and he looked down at me in horror.

Fire leapt through my body, vicious, angry. It twisted, a hot knife in my very soul.

I cried out and Jack caught me in his arms as I collapsed. "Ginny!"

Shouts all around me, blurred motion as Mr. Northcott was tackled and restrained. But I could not turn my head to see it. I could not move. The pain tore through me. It ripped me open and cackled at my weakness.

"Ginny!"

I felt myself being lowered to the ground, each movement bringing new agony. I whimpered. Mr. Davenport called for bandages and a lantern, but his voice was distorted. Echoing.

"Look at me, Ginny." Jack's command jolted me and I forced my eyes open. His face loomed in the dark, pale edges and shadowed angles. But his eyes glittered, like so many of the stars above him.

"Jack," I whispered. "I think I've done something terribly stupid."

He shook his head, those two stars disappearing as he closed his eyes in anguish. I tried to touch his face, but I choked as the pain crashed over me again, an unstoppable wave.

"Stay still," he said, grasping my hand in his. There was blood on his hands. My blood. "We'll take care of you, I promise. Everything will be—"

But his voice broke off and he bent to press his forehead against mine. Every inch of my skin was alive—alive and in agony. I felt the drop of his tear as it fell to my cheek, pressed close to his.

"Don't leave." His voice rasped in my ear. "Don't leave."

My vision spun. The black beckoned. Why was he making me stay? I wanted to leave—the pain was too much. Emptying.

Oblivion pulled at me.

The stars flickered out.

CHAPTER 28

Heaven was a confusing place.

Sometimes I drifted in clouds of white, no pain or discomfort. A gentle breeze wrapped around me, carrying me through the blessed calm.

Then I would drop back into blurred chaos. Shouts, the rumbling of a carriage. A hand clutched tight around mine. That blinding agony in my back.

"—need a doctor," a voice said.

"We're close," said another. "We'll—"

I slipped away again. Back to the clouds. Safety.

But if this was heaven, where was Father? Where was my mother? I was alone here. I did not want to be alone. I wanted . . . what did I want?

A smile as wide as the sun. Eyes as blue as the sea. And a love as wild as his heart.

Jack.

Jack.

❧

The first thing I noticed was the quiet. It filled my ears, whispering, rustling. Peaceful.

I lay perfectly still as awareness slowly sunk into me, my eyelids pale pink and heavy. I did not try to open them. I simply breathed

and listened to the sound of my heartbeat. My mind moved sluggishly, reaching for every small detail to make sense of my surroundings. The softness beneath my head. The wisp of a breeze across my
cheek. The smell of jasmine.

Jasmine?

Someone coughed. I turned my head and pried one eye open,
though I immediately winced as sunlight blasted my vision.

"Ginny?"

That was not the voice I wanted to hear. I tried again, peering
through the narrowest slit in my eyelids. Catherine's face appeared
beside me, brow furrowed.

"She's awake," she called to someone. A maid? "Send for Dr.
Minton."

Doctor? Why should I need a doctor? I was reminded in the next
second when I tried to sit up and my back screamed.

"Oh," I gasped, falling against my pillow.

"You must be careful," Catherine ordered. "You're injured."

Injured. Memories rushed back into my head, swirling and tumbling like the muddy waters of a swollen spring river. I remembered
Father's watch, heavy in my hand. I remembered the black and hopeless carriage ride. The highwaymen. Jack. Mr. Northcott's pistol.

I looked around the room, my head feeling as if it was stuffed
with straw. I did not recognize anything—not the floral wallpaper or
the wide windows that overlooked a wooded hill.

"Where—" My voice was dusty as an attic. "Where am I?"

"Harpford, of course." Catherine went to a nearby table and
poured a glass of water. "They could hardly take you to Wimborne."

"Where is Jack?"

Catherine raised one eyebrow, no doubt at my calling him by his
given name, but she said nothing of it. "He is speaking with my husband. He will be furious you dared to wake the only time he left your
side since last night."

Catherine helped me sit against a mound of pillows. My back

twinged, but not so badly that I could not breathe through it. She handed me the glass and I drank deeply, my throat aching.

The sun was setting outside my window. I'd been asleep nearly a whole day. How did I have no memory of it? Last I remembered, Jack had me in his arms, everything around us a foggy haze.

When I lowered the glass, Catherine watched me, seated primly on the edge of her chair.

"Dr. Minton said the laudanum would leave your mind a bit fuzzy," she said. "But you were in such pain, he kept you heavily dosed."

That explained my lack of memory—I'd been unconscious.

"The doctor thinks the bullet glanced off your ribs," she went on matter-of-factly. "You've broken one or two for certain. It kept the bullet from your lungs, but you still lost a great deal of blood."

"Oh." I twisted the fabric of my blanket in my hands. "I suppose I was lucky."

"So he said."

I let myself feel everything fully for the first time. The fear and pain that had smothered me in those moments after Mr. Northcott fired. Jack's face—the utter helplessness in his eyes. I looked away, not wanting Catherine to see my emotions as I struggled to breathe.

"Ah, well," I said. "A bit disappointing for you, then. You would have had Wimborne."

I spoke lightly, attempting a joke. But it failed, leaving instead a silence so deep I thought we both might drown in it.

"I do not want Wimborne," she said suddenly, staring at her hands in her lap.

"Then why . . ." I did not know how to phrase it. Why had she acted so horribly to me when I had inherited our family home?

She crossed her arms. "I do not want it. But neither did I want *you* to have it." She gave a dry laugh. "Not very sporting of me."

I pressed my lips together, sensing that something was happening behind that impossible-to-read veneer.

"When I heard about the fire," she said, "I was distraught, truly.

And then when Mr. Travers appeared and told us Mr. Northcott had taken you . . ." She shook her head. "You must know that despite my—my feelings toward you, I never wished you or your home any harm."

I swallowed. "I know that, Catherine. I do."

She hesitated again, her eyes filled with so many conflicting emotions I could not begin to read them all. She tore her gaze from mine.

"I wanted to thank you for Father's portrait," she said, her voice thick. "I . . . well, it cannot have been easy to give up, and I want you to know I will treasure it."

She'd said *Father*. Before today, she'd only ever referred to him as *her* father. I took a deep breath, trying not to make too much of a simple slip of the tongue.

"It was only right that you have it," I managed. "You are the eldest sister."

She shook her head. "What an elder sister I have been." Her eyes flicked to mine, vulnerable, broken. I realized then that she was as afraid of me as I was of her. There was so much pain between us, our pasts and presents colliding.

I had a choice to make. I could cling to resentment. Or I could choose hope.

"Thank you for sending Mr. Davenport after me," I said softly. "I dare not think what might have happened if not for your help."

Her mouth parted and she blinked rapidly. "Of course," she said. "Of course." She turned, and I thought I saw her swipe a tear from her cheek. "You must stay at Harpford for as long as you like. Until you are ready to return to Wimborne."

Beatrice would never believe it. Me, staying with Catty Davenport. Yet I also knew she would understand when I did not hesitate to answer. "I would be most grateful."

This was our chance—for Catherine and me to be more than what life had given us. I could not say if we would ever be truly close as sisters, but all we could do was try. And it seemed we were both finally willing.

We sat up when we heard footsteps pounding in the hallway. I knew those steps. The door burst open and Jack tumbled into the room, barely catching his balance. His eyes latched onto mine, so blue and bold that I caught my breath. His clothing was rumpled, his dark curls tousled as if he'd been running his hands through them constantly.

Of course, disheveled Jack was my favorite Jack, so it did nothing to relieve the swarm of butterflies that now took flight inside my chest.

"Ginny," he said, his voice hoarse.

"Really, Mr. Travers." Catherine found her feet, hands planted on her hips. "You simply cannot barge into a woman's bedchamber unannounced."

"Jack Travers to see Miss Genevieve Wilde," he said, not even looking at her as his eyes took me in. "There, I've been announced."

Incredulity spread across Catherine's face. Jack had that effect on most people. But seeing as she'd been kind enough to take me into her home, I managed to refrain from laughing.

"Catherine," I said, drawing her glare to me before Jack could say anything worse. "Might we have a few minutes?"

She frowned. "This is not at all proper."

"Please?"

She gave a sigh of long-suffering. "Fine," she said, shooting a warning glance at Jack. "But I will be right outside the door."

She swept from the room, leaving Jack and me alone. We looked at each other in silence for a long moment. His eyes devoured me, setting every inch of my skin aflame in the best possible way.

"How are you?" he asked.

"Well enough," I said. "A bit sore, but I imagine that is to be expected."

"A bit sore." He rubbed a hand over his face. "Blast it, Ginny. What the devil were you thinking, jumping in front of me like that?"

I straightened, though it sent a stinging pain through my back. "Was I supposed to let Mr. Northcott shoot you?"

"Yes," he said. "That is precisely what you should have done."

"I am sorry, but that was simply not an option."

"You nearly got yourself killed."

I raised my chin. "I would do it again without hesitation."

"So, you decide the best time to be impulsive is while staring down the barrel of a pistol?"

His words pounded away at my head, and my temple throbbed. The fight drained from me. I closed my eyes and dropped my head back to the pile of pillows.

A still silence, then soft footsteps. The bed dipped as Jack sat beside me, taking one of my hands. "I'm sorry," he said. "I'm sorry."

I opened my eyes. I saw regret in his features—along with pain, exhaustion, and something much deeper. Something that made my heart constrict.

"Try to imagine," he said, his voice ragged. "Try to think how I felt, holding the one person I love above all others in my arms. Your blood coating my hands, dripping into the dirt. Your life escaping. All because you took a bullet meant for me. Imagine that, Ginny, and tell me my anger is misplaced."

I bit my lip. His words painted an awful portrait, yet I had made the right choice. The only choice. "Would you have done it for me?" I whispered.

He shifted on the bed, facing me more directly, eyes narrowed. "Yes."

"Then you have no argument." My words broke with emotion. "Because I *did* imagine all of that. And I made the only decision I could."

He released my hand and turned away, but not before I saw the shimmer in his eyes. "I am not worth your life."

I stared at his broad back, his head low. I wanted nothing more than to reach out and embrace him. But then, why shouldn't I? I'd risked my life for him. I thought that earned me a few privileges.

Slowly, because the muted pain in my back had begun to lap away at my reserves of strength, I eased myself forward. I wrapped one hand around his firm upper arm and he stiffened, but did not pull away. I tucked my head against him, my face fitting perfectly in the crook of his neck.

"I want you to listen closely, Jack Travers," I said softly. My breath wafted against his neck and he swallowed hard. "I love you. I love your goodness and your courage. I love your compassion, your strength, your endless energy and drive. And if you think that I was going to let Mr. Northcott rob the world of someone so wonderful, then you do not know me at all."

I could feel his breathing, shallow and uneven. Then he faced me, his eyes endless, his lips parted. He ran his intent gaze over me, from my messy hair to my determined mouth.

"You are a dream, Genevieve Wilde," he whispered. "A dream."

His fingertips found my chin and tipped my face upward. He kissed me, his lips brushing over mine so tenderly, so lovingly, that I trembled.

"I want to marry you," he said. "Let me be the one to love you and care for you and protect you." His voice caught. "I want nothing in life but to be yours."

I smiled, my heart glowing with such brightness that I was surprised not to see sunbeams bursting from my chest. And yet, I hesitated.

He noticed, of course. He pulled away to see my face. "What is it?"

I tried to find the right words. "All I want is to say yes. But are you sure this is what *you* want? A quiet country life? Will you not regret your choice in five years? In ten?"

"I am choosing *you*," he said. "We can make our life however we wish it."

I shook my head. "But I want you to be happy."

"Then let me relieve your fears." He took my hand. "The reason I was not at your side when you awoke was because I was speaking to Mr. Davenport. He received word this evening—he has been appointed as interim magistrate."

"Mr. Davenport?" My mouth dropped. "But that is wonderful."

"Indeed. Especially since he believes the appointment will be made permanent, and he finds himself in need of trustworthy constables." He raised his eyebrows meaningfully.

"You?" I blinked. "A constable?"

"Yes," he said. "While a few weeks ago I might have claimed that crime in the country was laughable compared to London, it has become clear that is certainly not the case. I daresay I'll find a bit of excitement. Enough to keep my heart pumping and my mind sharp."

"A constable," I said again, marveling at the simplicity of the idea. The job suited Jack perfectly, and there was no doubt in my mind he would excel at it. My heart beat faster. This was real. The future that had seemed so impossible now fluttered within reach, beautiful and glimmering. With Mr. Davenport and Jack in charge, Little Sowerby would be safe once again. Mr. Northcott's corruption would be a ghost in the past.

Mr. Northcott. I looked up at Jack. "What has happened to Mr. Northcott?"

"Locked away and awaiting trial," he said. "Mr. Davenport has already reviewed the evidence you found. From what I read, your father knew that Mr. Northcott was the mole, but he also knew he needed to prove it. He was well on his way. Witness statements, records of suspicious activity, false alibis. He'd even begun following Mr. Northcott. It would have only been a matter of time, if . . ."

"If my father had lived," I said quietly.

He reached into his jacket pocket. "Mr. Davenport wanted you to have this."

It was the letter from Father, the one Mr. Northcott had so cruelly teased me with. I took it from Jack, hands shaking, and broke the seal. Father's handwriting spread over the page like a caress.

Dearest Genevieve,

It is my greatest hope that you'll never read this letter. I am only writing it as a last resort, in case I cannot conclude my investigation. I feel myself growing weaker, and I am afraid. I have left so much undone and I haven't enough time. I worry constantly over what will happen if I leave you too soon, and so I am giving you the watch with its message, one only you will understand. You will see it eventually, whether it takes one month or ten. You will find this evidence I've collected, evidence that points to Northcott as a traitor, and you will know what to do with it.

I hope you'll understand why I haven't told you. It is far too dangerous. If Northcott catches wind of my actions, I do not know what he will do, to you or me. I do not know who to trust. It is better to continue on my path and hope for the best. But I am planning for the worst.

I am truly sorry, Ginny, if I am not there with you now. I know you are strong, but I wish you did not have to be. Know that I love you and Catherine with all of my heart. Please tell her that, if I cannot. I have always been so proud of my beautiful daughters. No man is luckier than I.

Your loving father

I blinked the tears away, handing the letter to Jack. He read it, his hand in mine. When he finished, he folded the letter carefully. "His work was not in vain," he said, voice gruff. "Mr. Northcott will pay the price of his crime."

We sat in silence as I absorbed his words, my mind sluggish.

"I have one more thing for you," he said, reaching again into his pocket. "I've been keeping it safe."

He placed Father's pocket watch in my hands. The last time I'd held it, I hadn't known if I would live or not. I ran my fingers over the etching, almost reverently, the red silk watch chain vivid against the white of my bed linens.

"I cleaned it for you," he said, "and wound it. We might take it to a clockmaker to be sure it's all right, but—"

I held it close to my chest with a little laugh. "Yes," I said. "It will certainly need a visit to the clockmaker. A bill worth paying."

"Speaking of bills," he drawled, raising an eyebrow, "there is the matter of my payment."

"Payment?"

"My reward. For finding the watch." His lips twitched. "You promised me ten pounds, if you'll recall."

I narrowed my eyes. "I do believe we amended that agreement. A reward or a kiss, was it not?"

"True enough," he said. "I daresay I owe *you* now, after that business in the tree."

Laughter bubbled through me, causing a jolt of pain. I winced and pressed a hand to my back. "Drat you."

His brow bent in concern. "Is your back paining you?"

"No, it is your terrible jokes."

He exhaled a laugh. "Good. I would hate for you to enter this marriage blindly."

"No." I sobered. "I am entering it with my eyes wide open."

Jack carefully cradled my face between his hands. "I'm not hurting you?"

"I might be injured, but my lips work perfectly well."

"A fact I shall take full advantage of."

But he paused, his eyes softening as they traveled over my face.

"I knew when I first saw you," he said, thumbs tracing my jaw, "that you were extraordinary. Using that vase to defend yourself against a thief." He chuckled at the memory. "I was so immediately taken with you. It was rather ridiculous."

"You were?" I breathed. To hear him speak of our first memories together—it was a sweetness I could not describe.

"Indeed," he said. "You were clever, willful, and entirely too beautiful. My heart did not stand a chance."

There it was. That beautiful, toe-curling warmth that lit me up inside like my soul was on fire. Why had I fought against this for so long? "If only I had not tried so hard to protect my own heart."

"Oh, but I was determined." His lips moved closer, hovering over mine, teasing me. "Because yours, my love, is a heart worth stealing."

He kissed me once again and I sighed against him, perfectly content to lose myself in the unparalleled pleasure of kissing him.

A sharp knock came at the door. "Ginny!"

I groaned as we pulled apart. "Catherine."

"She is determined to ensure nothing tawdry occurs under her roof," Jack said with a grin.

"Then I shall have to ensure Wimborne's repairs go as quickly as possible, so as to be back under *my* roof."

"Yes, then the tawdriness can abound."

I tried to hide my laugh, which only resulted in a rather unseemly snort.

"Ginny!" Catherine was growing impatient.

I sighed. "I suppose we ought to tell her the good news."

"Excellent," Jack said. "I have been looking forward to seeing her face."

"You are wicked."

"I've never claimed otherwise."

And he kissed me once more, just like the perfectly wicked thief-taker he was.

$\mathcal{E}$PILOGUE

Four Months Later

It was late in the evening. Too late.

Holloway tried her best to distract me. She took extra care with my curling papers and fussed with my sleeping jacket and poked at the fire. But eventually she left, and I paced my bedroom alone as the clock ticked along with excessive cheerfulness.

At ten o'clock, I settled into bed with my journal and a small writing desk, though I knew it was hopeless. My mind wandered regularly off the page. I jumped at every sound, though it was just the normal music of Wimborne settling in for the night. What could be taking him so long? Had there been an unexpected obstacle? *Be calm,* I told myself. *Everything will be all right.*

Finally, I heard him, footsteps coming up the corridor. I set my desk on the bed beside me and came to my knees as the door opened. Jack stepped inside, face weary, and my heart rose inside me.

"And?" I asked breathlessly.

He closed the door behind him and looked me straight in the eye. "Guilty," he said, his voice both worn and victorious. "Guilty on all counts. Assault, kidnapping, conspiracy."

I sank back onto my heels. I should not have doubted. Justice had prevailed tonight, as I knew it must.

"The jury looked as angry as any I've seen," he said, sitting on the chair near the fire, pulling off his boots and letting them clomp to the floor. "No one was surprised. Well, save for Northcott."

I made a noise of disbelief. "The arrogance of that man. Even with all the evidence brought against him, he still thought he would go free."

"But he did not," he said, fixing me with his gaze, "and your testimony was the key. No one could deny the truth after they heard your story."

I'd been called to testify two days before. It had been awful—long, hot hours of answering questions about the night Northcott had taken me and the events leading up to it. The worst part was facing Northcott. He'd watched me, eyes gleaming, lips curved up into a smirk. Afterwards, I'd been shaking and agitated. Jack was needed during the trial, and so Beatrice had taken me home and held my hand for hours. I couldn't face another minute in that courtroom, which was why I'd waited at home tonight for the verdict.

"What kept you?" I moved to the edge of the bed and wrapped one hand around the bedpost. "I thought you would've been home hours ago."

"Davenport wanted it done with." He tugged at his cravat, pulling it free. "The barrister had dragged everything out long enough. So we stayed until it was decided, then there was the usual madness of paperwork and clearing the court."

I pressed my hands to my stomach, leaning my head on the bedpost. "It is over. Finally."

Jack shrugged out of his jacket, tossing it to the chair behind him. Then he came to sit beside me and wrapped one arm around my waist, pulling me tight against his side. "It *is* over. You will never have to see him again."

"*Any* of them."

Jack had made it his personal mission in the last few months to find and prosecute every individual connected to Northcott's corruption. Crouth and Garvey had both been tried weeks ago and transported. Without Northcott supplying them information, the highwaymen hadn't stood a chance—Jack caught them in the act. One turned king's evidence in the end, and that was enough to convict them all.

My emotions had run ragged through it all: the ongoing reconstruction of Wimborne, recovering from my wound, building a new relationship with Catherine. Jack was there to put me back together, to hold me until all my pieces melded together and healed.

It is over. The words rang in my head. My chest lightened, the last bit of shadow flitting away.

"Wily asked after you." Jack's lips lifted as he released me and began unbuttoning his waistcoat.

"Wily?" I raised an eyebrow. "What on earth was he doing there?"

He laughed. "Oh, he was nowhere near the courtroom. I met him on my way home. Apparently he has a job in London, but I daresay he'll be back. He's grown as fond of this little town as I have."

"Not much work for a fence, though."

"No," Jack conceded. "But one never knows. Perhaps we might convince him to become a pawnbroker."

I grinned. "The day Wily gives up his lifestyle is the day I voluntarily go on a picnic."

"What is so wrong with a picnic?"

"Do you know me at all?" I asked. "I cannot see what is pleasant about eating on the ground. Ants might crawl into my sandwich or a bird might drop something foul in my lemonade."

"You mustn't forget the weather," he said, straight-faced. "Heaven forbid it rain."

"Hush, you." I tossed a pillow at his face. He caught it, laughing.

"I'd wager," he said, moving closer, an impish gleam in his eye, "that if you picnicked with *me*, I could bring you around to the idea."

It was a lovely, silly conversation to be having, on this of all nights. But I needed it. I craved Jack's teasing and lightheartedness, even as I loved him for his determination and goodness.

"Why would that be?" I asked, unable to stop my own lips from twitching.

"Because *I* will be there, of course," he said, as if that were obvious. "Picnicking with one's husband is ideal. No one to impress or worry over. And if we get terribly bored, we will simply send the servants away and have our own bit of fun."

"Jack!" I pushed him away with a laugh. He always managed it, making me laugh.

"What?" he said in confusion. "I only meant wading in the stream. What were you thinking, my devilish dear?"

I shook my head, smiling like a fool. After Father had died, I could never have imagined a future with so much joy and hope. Yet here I was, living a life that felt like a dream most days. These last months of marriage had been a gift. Jack was a gift. And I would never take him for granted.

"Very well," I said. "If you plan a picnic, I will come. But only if you promise to protect me from all the aforementioned dangers and mishaps."

"I promise," he said, a note of sincerity finding its way into his voice. "I always will."

He leaned in and kissed me softly. My heart blossomed.

Esse quam videri. To be, rather than to seem.

To all the world, I seemed happy. And the world was perfectly right.

$\mathcal{A}$CKNOWLEDGMENTS

There were definitely moments in writing this book when I did not think it would ever reach publication. So many times, I wanted to throw it out the window and never look at it again. This book would not exist without the help of so many of my friends and family, and I am incredibly thankful they pushed me to finish.

To my long-suffering husband, who shoos me away to write while he handles bedtime—thank you for always making my dreams a priority.

To Heidi Kimball, Arlem Hawks, and Megan Walker—you three are my rocks! Your infuriatingly accurate critiques of this book made me work harder than I ever have before, and now that I've forgiven you for it, I love you all again. Thank you for your constant encouragement and for fighting traffic across London with me so I could visit the Bow Street Museum. It was a dream!

To my amazing beta readers: Jessica Christian, Cassy Watson, Jan Lance, Jillian Christensen, Deborah Hathaway, Martha Keyes, Esther Hatch, and Tiffany Odekirk. Thank you for every single one of your comments, questions, and typo catches! I would be lost without you all!

To my wonderful publisher, Shadow Mountain, for their amazing work in making this book a reality. A *huge* thank you to Heidi Gordon, who was the first to believe in Ginny and Jack and champion their story throughout the publishing process; to Janna DeVore, for her insightful edits; to Heather Ward, for creating the most beautiful cover I've ever seen (seriously, I'm going to frame it); and to the wonderful marketing team for all their efforts to get my book into readers' hands. I am truly blessed to work with the best!

Lastly, to my readers, thank you again and forever. I wish I could tell each one of you how much I appreciate your support, your kindness, and your excitement. I hope you read this and know how grateful I am to you!

JOANNA BARKER firmly believes that romance makes every-thing better, which is why she has fallen in love with writing Regency romances. When she's not typing away on her next book, she's listening to podcasts, eating her secret stash of chocolate, or adding things to her Amazon cart. Joanna's books have received praise from *Publishers Weekly*, the Historical Novel Society, Readers' Favorite, and more. She thinks being an author is the second-best job in the world—right after being a mom. She is just a little crazy about her husband and three wild-but-loveable kids.